INKED

ARMOR

ALSO BY HELENA HUNTING

Clipped Wings

Cupcakes and Ink

INKED ARMOR

HELENA HUNTING

GALLERY BOOKS

New York   London   Toronto   Sydney   New Delhi

G

Gallery Books
A Division of Simon & Schuster, Inc.
1230 Avenue of the Americas
New York, NY 10020

First Gallery Books trade paperback edition May 2014

GALLERY BOOKS and colophon are
registered trademarks of Simon & Schuster, Inc.

For information about special discounts for bulk purchases,
please contact Simon & Schuster Special Sales at
1-866-506-1949 or business@simonandschuster.com.

The Simon & Schuster Speakers Bureau can bring authors to
your live event. For more information or to book an event contact
the Simon & Schuster Speakers Bureau at 1-866-248-3049
or visit our website at www.simonspeakers.com.

Interior design by Ruth Lee-Mui

Manufactured in the United States of America

1 3 5 7 9 10 8 6 4 2

Library of Congress Cataloging-in-Publication Data is available.

ISBN 978-1-4767-6430-6
ISBN 978-1-4767-6432-0 (ebook)

Kato, this one's for you.

ACKNOWLEDGMENTS

Brooks, you really are solidly solid.

Micki, Tatiana, and the rest of my S&S team, it's been a whirlwind, but an awesome one. Thank you!

Alex, Anne, and Kris, big hugs for helping me tame the beast. I'm so fortunate to know all of you.

Filets, you make me proud to be one of you.

Enn, you're the woman and you're made of awesome.

Deb, you are the most amazing person. If not for you, I never would have started on this crazy journey in the first place.

Thank you to my friends and family who have been such staunch supporters through this entire process, from inception to publication and all the steps in between.

To those of you who have been on this journey with me from the very beginning until now, I am indebted to you. Thank you for believing in my words.

INKED
ARMOR

1

TENLEY

At 6:23 in the morning, the front door opened downstairs and the security system let out a chirp, signaling Trey's arrival. I held my breath as I listened for the sound of the code being punched in, then a warning beep, followed by Trey's irate curse.

Last night I'd changed the security code for the seventh time in as many days. I started doing it after I woke up to him standing over my bed, screaming bloody murder about the tattoo on my back. Verbal abuse from my almost brother-in-law was not a good way to wake up. Since he'd thwarted my attempts to have the lock changed, I made the alarm system the bane of his existence.

Trey strung together creative new phrases describing exactly what he thought of me; he knew the alarm would start shrieking at any moment. I reached for my iPhone, jammed in the earbuds, and scrolled to the playlist I'd created for this freak show. Hard rock filled my ears as the alarm went into full panic mode.

Before long he started pounding on my door. Nabbing the

remote from my night table, I turned on the surround sound hooked up to the flat-screen and blasted techno beats, then went into my bathroom to shower. Trey hated techno.

The pounding had ended by the time I'd showered and dressed. With practiced stealth, I silently turned the dead bolt on my bedroom door. Opening it a crack, I peeked out. No Trey, but that didn't mean he was gone. He'd waited for hours before; his persistence knew no bounds.

Just outside the door was a pile of papers and a pen for me to sign over the property. He'd shown up each morning without fail, but in the past week his tactics had changed slightly. Occasionally he left the papers and ambushed me later in the day or the evening. The past couple of days, he'd gone back to waiting me out.

My response never changed. I always tore up the papers and watched them scatter like fat snowflakes on the floor. Their destruction had become a ritual I enjoyed.

I was about to shred the ones left for me this morning when I noticed they weren't the usual documents. The stack was thinner. I leafed through the pages, frowning as I absorbed the content. The back page held my sloppy signature. Based on what I was reading, I'd signed over power of attorney to Trey.

I had absolutely no recollection of reading this document, never mind signing it. According to the date, it was drafted and made legal two months after the accident. I'd been released from the hospital at that point, but I hadn't been in any state to care for myself, and Trey had put himself in charge of my medication. Now I understood why.

"Trey!" I crushed the documents in my fist and rushed down the stairs.

He was sitting at the kitchen island, typing away on his laptop with a coffee at his side. As if it were his house and not mine. I slammed the laptop shut on his hands.

"What the hell is wrong with you?" He stood, his chair toppling backward. The metallic clatter echoed in the open space.

"What's wrong with *me*?" I shoved the papers into his chest. "What's wrong with *you*? Do you think you can bully me into signing the house over?"

He seized my wrists to stop me from attacking him. His lip curled. "I have power of attorney. I can take *everything* if I want to."

"Have you lost your mind? Do you honestly think this is going to hold? I wasn't even lucid when I signed this." I struggled against him, the bones in my wrists grinding painfully as his grip tightened.

"Sign over the house and it won't be a problem."

"Not to you, and especially not now!" I spat.

"Sign over the fucking house, goddamnit!" he roared.

"Why are you so intent on making me do this?" I screamed back.

"Because the estate is useless to me until I have possession of this house!"

He released my wrists and turned away to lurch around the kitchen, his wiry body jerking as he tried to get a handle on himself. Trey had never before lost control. I rubbed my wrists, red marks marring the skin where he'd held me too hard. His nostrils flared, eyes burning with hatred. He took a deep breath and adjusted his tie.

"There are five houses on the property; why do you need this one?" I asked, his motivation lost on me. Although, with him, logic need not apply.

"Are you really that stupid? I can't sell the estate unless I own *all* the houses."

"But in your parents' will—"

"The will doesn't matter anymore! My parents are dead, no

thanks to your brilliant wedding plans, so what they wanted is irrelevant."

The shot of guilt hit me like a bullet to the heart. "That's not fair."

"You don't like the truth? Is it too much for you to handle? Should I get you a pill?"

"Enough." I held up my hand.

I could never live in this house—not when it symbolized everything that might have been, but would never be. I couldn't stand the thought of it leaving his family. Especially when he had so many close relatives who would jump at the opportunity to call the estate home if they could afford it. The property had been in his family for generations.

"Even if I signed over this house, your uncles still own the summer home, don't they?" I asked.

"My uncles will sell."

"How can you be sure?"

"Because everyone has a price. I'm just not sure what yours is. I mean, you stayed with Connor even after he fucked his way through half the female population of Cornell while you were on your little break, or whatever you called it," Trey sneered. "And then you jumped all over that fucking proposal. So maybe the money is more important than you're letting on. You've been more than willing to relinquish your self-respect these days, from what I witnessed in Chicago. What if I doubled the offer? Would you take it then?"

Any shred of empathy I may have had for Trey dissolved. Connor hadn't been perfect, and neither had our relationship, but Trey's allegation sounded like another of his ploys to hurt me. True or not, I didn't need that stain on Connor's memory.

"Why do you have to be so cruel?"

Trey's smile was malicious. "You are the only thing standing in my way, and I will do anything in my power to get what I need. If you don't sign it over, I will take it. The request was a courtesy, but I see you're too self-absorbed to understand that. As usual."

I held up the crumpled papers, my resolve hardening. "This will never hold."

"We'll see about that."

He righted the toppled chair and picked up his suit jacket. He tucked the laptop into his briefcase, but before he closed the case he withdrew yet another set of papers. These I recognized.

"I'll just leave these for you, shall I? In case you change that little mind of yours." With that, he turned and walked out the door.

As soon as Trey's car disappeared around the bend in the drive, I sank down in one of the chairs. His words were like slivers working deep into my skin.

My relationship with Connor had always been tricky. He was older by several years, and he'd had some unrealistic expectations, mostly old-fashioned notions of propriety. In hindsight, it had been all about keeping up appearances. If we'd gotten married, I would have had to balance that my entire life. All my "little quirks," as Connor called them, would have been shelved or channeled into more acceptable things. Or hidden under clothing or hair, as my tiny tattoo and ear piercings had been.

Connor had been halfway across the country for years, only coming back to Minnesota during the summer months and holidays. When we started dating, he flew back more often. But the distance strained the relationship, and in my final semester of college it became too much to juggle. I needed to focus on school, not pine for a boyfriend so far away. So I gave him a reprieve. It lasted eight weeks. I'd never asked him about that span of time. It hadn't seemed necessary to know, because shortly thereafter he proposed.

Unfortunately, that little barb from Trey brought up other concerns that had nothing to do with Connor. An image of Hayden with Sienna all over him popped into my head. The thought made my stomach turn. I couldn't stand the idea of him with anyone but me. Which wasn't fair because I left him, not the other way around.

If he went back to her in my absence, I had no one to blame but myself. Two weeks was long enough for her to find a way to sink her claws back into him, especially with how I'd left things. It made the urgency of tying up loose ends even more pressing. I missed him so much it was a constant, painful distraction.

I smoothed the power-of-attorney papers out on the counter. Unlike sorting through Connor's effects or managing the financial aspects of the settlement, this wasn't something I could handle on my own. I snatched up my purse and the documents and headed for the garage.

The familiar drive to Minneapolis didn't take long, and I soon reached Williams and Williams Attorneys at Law. I should have called ahead, but Frank Williams was a longtime friend of my father's. I was certain he would see me, even without an appointment.

The elevator ride to the twelfth floor took forever. The confined space made me anxious; I hadn't been to Frank's office since I signed the paperwork regarding the settlement from the airline and my parents' will.

The receptionist looked surprised as I entered. "Tenley!"

"Hi, Catherine. I'm afraid I don't have an appointment, but I'm happy to wait if Frank is available."

"Is everything okay? Is there a problem with the settlement?"

"It's about Connor's estate. I have . . . some questions."

"I'll be right back." She went down the hall to Frank's office, and less than a minute later he appeared, Catherine following behind.

"Tenley! It's so good to see you." Though he smiled, I saw his concern as he folded me in a fatherly embrace. I hugged him back. "How is Chicago treating you?"

"I'm taking a short break. There are some things that need my attention here."

"Why don't you come to my office and we can talk." He looked to Catherine. "Can you reschedule that lunch meeting?"

"Of course."

"I'll let you know if we need to rearrange anything else this afternoon," Frank said, and led me to his office.

Once the doors were closed, I filled him in, handing over the documents. Frank lifted the bifocals hanging around his neck, his frown deepening as he scanned the pages.

"Why haven't I seen this before?" he asked.

"I just found out about it this morning. I came directly to you. Is Trey right? Can he take everything?" The property and the value attached to it didn't concern me. It was having control stripped away, the potential for more loss too much to handle.

"This is your signature?" He flipped to the back page and turned it toward me.

"Yes, but I had just been released from the hospital and was on a lot of medications. I don't remember signing that."

"That son of a——" Frank shook his head. "He can be disbarred for this."

"Is there anything we can do?"

"I'll need a few days, but I'm sure I can have this rescinded. He should be taken to task over this——but I have a feeling you won't be interested in going that route."

"I don't have the energy to take him to court. I just want to make sure he doesn't have any power over me, and that he doesn't get the house. I want this behind me so I can move on."

"If that's what you prefer. Now, Catherine said something about Connor's estate. Is there more we need to deal with?"

"Yes." I pulled out a copy of Trey's transfer-of-ownership papers and the proposed remuneration.

So much had changed since I'd signed the papers for the settlement. I'd been drowning in guilt over accepting financial compensation for such overwhelming emotional losses. For the past year I'd believed the loss was a direct result of my selfishness. Trey had played on that, but I'd finally seen that what had happened was far beyond anyone's control. I wouldn't allow him to hold that over me anymore.

Four days later I was back in Frank's office with Connor's cousin Weston.

Frank had been able to overturn the power of attorney. He'd also uncovered some information about a recent proposal for the Hoffman estate, which sprawled over ten acres with five houses. Trey had applied to the city council for commercial zoning and demolition.

My house and its two-acre parcel of land was a gift from Connor's parents, meant for us once we were married. We were supposed to move in when we returned from Hawaii—except that hadn't happened.

I'd been shocked when I found out the property had been left to me. Trey had been livid, particularly since Connor, who'd specialized in real estate law, had left him with no loopholes to take it from me.

While his plans for the property were unknown, some of the houses, if not all of them, were at risk of being torn down. That was not acceptable.

In drawing up the new transfer-of-ownership agreement, Frank included a clause that stipulated the house and two acres would remain under the residential zoning bylaws. And since the house was smack in the middle of the estate, that kiboshed Trey's plans.

Pen in hand, Weston looked up at me. "You're sure about this?"

"Absolutely. Connor would have wanted to keep the estate in the family." Weston's family also held half the deed to the summer home. Once my house was signed over, Trey was effectively screwed.

Weston and Connor had been close growing up. Weston had almost come to the wedding, but it hadn't worked with his schedule. He'd been gravely disappointed, but now I was glad for that small mercy.

With a respectful nod, he bent over the papers, signing at each of the yellow tabs. When his signature was scrawled on the last page, he set the pen down.

"Is that it?" I asked Frank. "The house is Weston's?"

"That's it. The keys will be passed over tomorrow evening at five."

That would give me enough time to get the rest of Connor's effects boxed and sent off to charity and to pack my bags. The tension of the past few weeks drained out of me. The power of attorney had been reversed. The house wasn't my responsibility anymore; it belonged to someone who deserved it. I hadn't wanted any money for it, but Weston insisted. Frank had assured me we could set up a trust fund. My parents' house was the only thing left now. I still wasn't ready to part with that.

Weston pulled me into a hug. "Thank you for doing this for Connor. I know it must be hard for you to give this up."

It was more of a relief, especially knowing the house was safe now. "I'm sorry you'll have to deal with Trey."

He laughed. "Don't worry yourself about that. I've been dealing with him my entire life. It's about time someone put him in his place."

After I left Frank's office, I went to my parents' house. Despite my daily visits, I hadn't accomplished much in the way of cleaning out my childhood home. Sadness overshadowed the warmth of the familiar surroundings. Being in the house without my family hurt; it had become a mausoleum instead of a home.

I wandered through the house, lingering over familiar treasures, boxing up things I felt compelled to take with me. I could almost see my parents in the living room, cuddled up on the couch watching TV. I missed my father's dry sense of humor and my mother's warmth. I missed summer dinners in the backyard, Friday movie nights, camping trips in the rain. I missed the life I had before it fell apart.

Yet I realized that even if I could have it all back, it would never be the same. I was a different person now. I could no longer live in the protective cocoon of my previous existence; I had seen too much. The trauma had triggered my metamorphosis.

I stopped in the doorway to my bedroom. The black comforter went perfectly with the band posters and the framed prints of Escher and Dalí. My parents had always allowed me creative freedom. Maybe they'd believed it would be enough of an outlet for my rebellious tendencies, but it hadn't been. My mom had argued with me over the piercings as they traveled up the shell of my ear. When I brought up the possibility of a tattoo, I got a lecture on the type of image I should want to project.

When Connor echoed their sentiments, I went out and got one anyway. When he got upset, I retaliated further by dying my hair poppy red right before a huge family event. I wasn't allowed in the pictures, but I snuck in the back anyway.

I had always straddled the line; many of my interests were unacceptable in my social sphere. So I fostered them through the subjects I chose to study.

Until Hayden.

I crossed the room and ran my fingers over the bedspread. What would Hayden have thought of my teenage bedroom? What would my parents have thought of him? Would they have been able to see past the unconventional exterior? I wanted to believe they could.

They might have seen him as a passing phase, something to try out and eventually move on from. Maybe before the crash I would have regarded Hayden as an experiment in deviance, but I doubted it. I would still have been drawn to him. But I wouldn't have had the courage to act on that attraction. His allure would have been overshadowed by my desire to fit into an impossible mold. My loss had made him accessible in a way he wouldn't otherwise have been. Hayden understood my impulse for difference.

His quiet, unassuming intelligence and his unique perception of the world kept me intrigued. Beyond that, our physical connection far surpassed mere need. From the very first time, sex with Hayden had been transcendental. I'd never experienced anything like it before him.

I missed our physical connection. I missed the way he tasted, the feel of his skin, the endless lines of ink covering his body. I wanted him back—but I needed to be worthy of him first.

Moving around my old bedroom, I peeled the posters off the wall and rolled them up, threw some knickknacks I couldn't leave behind in a box, then went downstairs to lock up. The next time I came to Arden Hills, it would be after I'd decided what to do with the house. With every additional piece of my past I released, I felt more capable of embracing my future.

Driving away, I resolved to do the one thing I'd avoided since my return. I stopped at a greenhouse and picked up poinsettias. They wouldn't last long in this weather, but I wanted to leave something beautiful behind. As I pulled into Hillside Cemetery, I felt a pang of guilt for not having done this sooner. The memorial service had been horrible, not healing, which contributed to my avoiding the cemetery.

Trying to understand why the crash had taken so much from me was pointless. I'd internalized that pain, allowing it to take over my life, but I couldn't anymore. Not if I wanted to go back to Chicago, to Hayden. It had taken returning to Arden Hills for me to finally realize that the tragedy wasn't a punishment for my transgressions.

At the cemetery, I visited everyone: the friends I'd lost, Connor's parents, my own. I spent a long time at my mother's grave, telling her about Chicago. I told her how much I hated my adviser and how I wasn't sure if I could manage his unrealistic expectations, his ever-changing demands and his unwanted interest in me. I told her about my job at Serendipity and the friends I'd made; how much she would have liked them even though they were different. And I told her about the tattoo and the artist who'd changed my world, and that I wanted to be with him, despite being afraid.

Connor I saved for last. Soft flakes began to swirl around me as I set the white poinsettia beside his gravestone. I sank down on the grass, heedless of the cold damp.

He'd been stolen from life so early. I traced his name on the stone, followed by his dates of birth and death. He was a constant in my life; I'd grown up with him. The summer before I started college, things had changed between us. He looked at me differently. Treated me differently.

Dating had been a natural progression. In the beginning we kept it quiet. The secrecy of it had been part of the draw: the sneaking around, the frantic make-out sessions when we found ourselves alone. I liked the rebellion of it all, that he was older, that his attraction to me made him reckless, and that I wielded such power over him.

In the cold, quiet of the cemetery I mourned my old life, finally allowing myself to grieve Connor, our families, and our friends in a way I hadn't before. The guilt and pain flowed out of me in streams of tears, yet there was a peace I'd never before felt. I would always love Connor, but he was gone. It was time to let go.

2

HAYDEN

A few days, a week, just a little longer. Everyone told me she needed time. Her silence told me she needed time.

Fuck time.

Time went on and on. An endless cycle of sleep, wake, bear the agony, and repeat. I fucking hated time.

Tenley had been gone for three weeks. Every day without her was sensory deprivation, drawn out and torturous from beginning to end. The first week, I called her every day. Her phone always went to voice mail. She never called back. I stopped calling because it sucked to know I'd been discarded so easily.

Memories of her were everywhere: home, work, Serendipity. I couldn't escape. So at least I understood why she came to Chicago in the first place: to get away from the ceaseless reminders. I couldn't figure out what had compelled her to go back, though. She could run from me all she wanted, but returning to the place she'd fled from didn't make much sense. Unless she was looking to shackle herself to the guilt again. It was easy to deny the possibility of a future when she let the past drag her down. I knew. I'd done that for years until Tenley came along.

There was a soft knock on the door to the tattoo room. Lisa was checking up on me again.

Inked Armor was closed, but for the past three weeks I'd spent most of my free time at the shop or Tenley's empty apartment. Being alone in my condo was unbearable. At least in the shop I could pretend things weren't so shitty. Hints of her presence still lurked like shadows, but not in the same way as at her apartment or my condo. It was depressing as hell. Regardless, I went to her apartment every day, if only to briefly check on her things. On the worst days, I stayed for hours and steeped myself in the pain of being there without her.

Lisa poked her head in the door. "Hey, I tried to call you."

"Sorry, my phone must be off."

I picked up a deep red pen and filled in some color on my sketch. It wasn't the right shade. The design ruined, I filed it in the folder along with the others and grabbed another sheet of paper.

"Cassie's expecting us in an hour. Why don't you put that away and catch a ride with me and Jamie?"

"Yeah, about that. I don't think I'm going to go."

After I'd bailed on Thanksgiving, Cassie had taken to inviting the Inked Armor crew over on Sundays. Initially I refused because someone had to be at the shop. Then Lisa changed the hours so we weren't open on Sundays. No one consulted me. Since Chris and Jamie were partners, and they both agreed, majority rule made it so. Lisa cited the slower pace of winter as a rationale when I fought her on the decision. I wasn't stupid. Forced social interaction wasn't going to work. Tenley was the only thing that would make things better, and she wasn't talking to me—so I was fucked.

Lisa snagged the wheelie chair and sat down, rolling over to the opposite side of the desk. TK gave a groggy little mew at the disturbance. She got lonely being in my condo by herself, so when I came to the shop during off hours to get away from the nothing-ness, I brought her along. She came with me to check on Tenley's apartment, too.

"You can't miss dinner this time," Lisa said.

"I want to finish this."

I laid the new sheet of paper over the outline and began tracing the design again. Once I perfected the color scheme, I planned to persuade Chris to put it on my skin. I would have preferred Jamie to take on the piece because it was portrait, not tribal, but he'd al-ready said no. So had Chris, but I could get him to change his mind. I didn't have room left on my arms for it, unless I covered over an old tattoo. I was seriously considering doing that because I wanted the piece on display. The prospect of new ink made me feel better.

Lisa put her hand over mine. I pulled away, the physical contact unmanageable.

"Why don't you take a break? The art will be here when you get back."

"I'd rather not." I could feel her eyes on me, assessing. I prob-ably needed a shower and I definitely needed to shave, but that took effort.

"How long have you been here? Did you go home last night?"

"Yeah." It was trueish.

"Did you sleep?"

"For a few hours."

Ever since Tenley had left, sleep had been elusive. I clocked in three, maybe four hours before the nightmares began. Sometimes they were about my parents, but mostly they were about Tenley. In the most frequent one she was dressed in cream-colored satin, a small red spot marring the fabric between her breasts. The mark spread, turning the cream a brilliant shade of red. In the dream,

I could never get to her. Stuck in a doorway, I watched helplessly as the life drained out of her. Eventually her skin turned the color the satin had been.

I could never go back to sleep. The nightmares were too vivid. After the first one I'd called Tenley's cell in the middle of the night. I hadn't left a message, but like a loser I called back several times just to hear her recorded voice.

"I think you should come," Lisa pressed.

"I'm not very good company right now, and I don't want to leave TK alone." My foot bounced on the floor as I waited for Lisa to leave me alone.

"I know you miss her, but shutting everyone out isn't going to help."

I set the pencil down and closed my eyes. Lisa wasn't going to let up. "I don't feel up to going, so can you back off?"

Startled, TK dug her nails into my leg.

"Fine. If that's the way you want it." Lisa shot out of her chair and reached over the desk. She scooped TK out of my lap and started for the door.

"What the fuck are you doing?" I stood too fast and got an instant head rush, forcing me to sit back down.

"Going to Cassie's. See you later."

I tried again. This time I managed to stay on my feet despite the dizzy spell. "Give me TK."

"No."

"Give me my fucking kitten!" I shouted. It was completely irrational for me to be so upset. Lisa wasn't going to run off with her, but rational and I hadn't seen much of each other lately.

Lisa cradled TK gently against her chest, stroking her puffed-up fur. "Not until you agree to come to Cassie's."

"You're going to blackmail me into going to dinner?"

"I get that it's hard, Hayden, but what you're doing right now isn't going to bring her home. Cassie is worried sick about you. I'm worried about you. We're all worried about you. You're not coping."

"I'm coping just fine."

"Really? Because last time I checked, isolation and lack of personal hygiene are two pretty good indicators that someone isn't."

"Can we not do this right now? It's too hard. I just don't know . . ." The anger seeped out of me, replaced with the consuming emptiness I'd felt since Tenley took off.

Lisa stepped away from the door. "Let's go up to your place so you can shower; maybe even get rid of the hipster beard you've got going on. Then we'll head to Cassie's."

I sighed, too tired to fight. "Fine."

TK jumped out of Lisa's arms and bounded over to me, weaving between my legs. When I lifted her up, she stretched and put her paws on my chest. Then she nudged my chin with the top of her head, as if she approved of the plan.

We left the shop and I locked up. Jamie was parked out front, waiting in the car. He got out and the two of them trailed behind me as we entered the lobby of my building. It was both advantageous and problematic to live above where I worked, especially now when I didn't want to be in my condo. They followed me up the stairs to the second floor. It took me a while to find my keys, and my hand shook as I slid it into the lock. I couldn't remember if I'd eaten today. Or the day before—which accounted for the lightheadedness in the shop.

I stepped inside and toed off my shoes, putting them in the closet. "Uh, give me a second. I wasn't expecting anyone to come over; I need to put a few things away."

That was a lie. My place was immaculate, as always. That I'd been able to endure Tenley's constant disarray was evidence of her importance in my life, because that shit usually drove me nuts. Though things such as shaving had become optional since Tenley went away, my OCD tendencies had kicked up a notch in other areas. My compulsion for organization and perfection became more extreme the longer she was gone.

I walked down the hall, flipped on the light, and went right. I checked every room, saving my bedroom for last. The tightrope of anxiety unknotted as I hit the switch and light bathed the room in a warm glow. I surveyed the smooth lines of my slate-gray comforter and the pillows propped against the headboard. The red and black one in the center was the only thing that disrupted the flow of the lines. I'd taken it from Tenley's apartment because it was the one she slept on.

I returned to Lisa and Jamie, who were patiently waiting at the door. They were well aware of what I needed to do before they could come in. They'd already taken off their shoes and put them in the closet.

"We're good?" Jamie asked.

"Yeah. Make yourselves comfortable." I waved them down the hall into the living room.

"Wow, Hayden, it's a real mess in here," Jamie joked, and almost ran into Lisa, who had stopped in the middle of the room.

"Oh, wow," she breathed.

She was reacting to the new art on the wall. Lisa and Jamie hadn't been over in a while. Not since things had become interesting with Tenley. They used to come by after work for pre-bar drinks because of the convenience. The last time I'd been out, other than that one time to The Dollhouse, was the night I'd watched Tenley throat-punch that handsy fucker way back in September.

I hadn't known that night was the beginning of the end for me. Without her I was in a worse place than I was before her arrival in my life, and now I had no vices.

"You've been busy," Jamie observed in his quiet, nonjudgmental way.

"Helps pass the time when I can't sleep."

Lisa moved closer, staring at the framed drawings. It made me feel exposed to have her inspect them. Mine were the only eyes they were meant for.

"Did Tenley see these?"

Even hearing her name hurt. "Only the one in the middle."

I wanted to rewind my life three weeks. I would have kept her naked in my bed instead of retrieving TK from her apartment; the cat would've survived a night without food. Then maybe her not-quite brother-in-law wouldn't have taken her away.

But it hadn't panned out that way. Tenley had left me. When she returned, there was no certainty I would still factor in as part of her equation. Based on her lack of communication, I assumed we were through.

I was a head case. She'd been gone almost half as long as we'd been together, but I didn't seem to be getting over her well. "I'm gonna get cleaned up. Help yourself to a drink if you want one. You know where everything is."

That drained feeling took over again as I crossed through my bedroom to the bathroom. I turned on the water and returned to the bedroom, where I stripped out of my clothes, then separated them into the color-coded laundry hampers before I returned to the bathroom. I checked to make sure it was hot and got under the spray.

Twenty minutes later I was clean, shaved, and dressed. Normally I would do the tie-and-collared-shirt thing for events at Cassie's, but jeans and a button-down was all I could manage.

I found TK in her usual spot: on my bed, curled up against Tenley's pillow. "I'll be back later," I said, scratching under her chin.

Before we left, I changed her water and put some food in her dish. When we reached the street, Chris and Sarah were standing by the car door. Talk about feeling like a fifth wheel. I almost did an about-face back into my building.

"You take the front seat, Hayden, there's more legroom," Lisa said, climbing into the back after Sarah.

I folded myself into the passenger seat, appreciating the way Chris had to pretzel himself in behind me, even when I pulled my seat forward.

As we made the short trip to the outskirts of the city where Cassie and Nate lived, Lisa and Sarah talked about some spa bullshit they'd organized. If Tenley were still here, they would have hijacked her for the expedition.

Cassie and Nate lived in a Century home at the north end of Chicago, close to the water. We parked in their driveway and everyone filed out, except for Chris. He grunted an expletive as he held on to the door and heaved. It was like watching someone extricate himself from a clown car. I smiled.

"You"—he pointed at me—"get to sit in the back on the way home."

"It's not my fault you don't have the common sense to buy a vehicle with doors, since it snows five months out of the year."

"I don't need a steel box—my girl's got one." He wrapped an arm around Sarah and pulled her to his side.

The low thwack and the chastising whisper that followed irked me and I looked away. I hated that I was too fucking sensitive to deal with their happiness. Crossing the stone drive to the front steps, I rang the doorbell.

I'd stopped going over to Serendipity after Tenley left. Cassie had to hire another part-time employee in her place, at least it wasn't a girl this time. Cassie said it was just for the holiday season, but I couldn't deal with seeing someone else sitting behind the cashier's desk. So Lisa and Jamie made all the coffee runs now. Cassie didn't send her new employee by with deliveries for me, either, which was a relief. That might have pushed me over the edge.

Instead Cassie brought the books over herself, one at a time,

ensuring biweekly visits. I accepted them, aware she was checking up on me. I didn't allow her to corner me in private, though,
because I knew what the conversation would consist of, and I
couldn't go there.

Cassie answered the door as though she'd been waiting by the
window for us to show up. "Hayden! I'm so glad you came." She
threw her arms around me, hugging me fiercely.

"Lisa didn't give me much of a choice." I patted Cassie back.
The contact felt foreign and uncomfortable.

"You've lost weight. Are you eating? Can I get you something?"

This was why I'd refused to come. I didn't want pity or concern.

"I'm good for now, thanks."

She pulled me inside, allowing the others to enter the vesti-
bule. The attention shifted away from me as she greeted everyone,
giving hugs, making chitchat. Nate came out of the sitting room, a
glass of scotch in his hand. I shed my shoes and coat and headed for
him. We did the handshake/back-pat thing.

"How are you?" he asked, looking at me the same way everyone else did these days.

"Fine. I need a drink, though."

I skirted around him and went to the bar, pouring myself a
healthy dose of scotch. Nate always had the good stuff. I didn't
bother with ice because I didn't want to water it down. I took a
seat and sipped my drink, working on keeping my hands steady.

Beers were opened, wine was poured, appetizers set out;
everyone got comfortable, couples cuddling up on various pieces
of furniture. Conversation went on around me as I watched my
scotch disappear—talk of Christmas plans, New Year's celebrations, organizing last-minute shopping trips. On and on. Around
and around. And none of it mattered. It was nothing I wanted to
be part of.

I wondered what Tenley was doing, whether she had plans for the holidays. She probably had friends back in Arden Hills who wanted to spend time with her; people she'd left behind. Or maybe she'd be back here by then. I'd get her a present just in case, even if she didn't want to be with me anymore.

I set my glass down and headed for the stairs, too fidgety to stay still any longer. The railing was smooth beneath my palm as I climbed the spiraling case. Sometimes stairs made me uneasy.

Beyond the smells, the climb to the second floor was the thing I remembered most vividly from the night of my parents' murders. The slow ascent as I tried to stealthily get to my bedroom before I woke them up. Mischief's warning meows as I reached the landing. The endless hallway. The unusual slice of light coming from under their bedroom door. And the rank odor of death followed by the horrifying visual when I pushed it open, knowing something was wrong.

When I reached the top, I exhaled the breath I'd been holding. I peeked in every room and stopped at the one that had been mine during my brief stay with Cassie and Nate. I sat down on the edge of the bed, exhaustion sweeping over me. The last three weeks had been a constant roller coaster of anxiety, and the stress had worn me down. I wasn't sure how long I sat there, but eventually someone knocked.

Nate pushed the door open. "I thought you might be up here."

"I needed a breather."

"You mind some company?" He handed me the glass I'd left downstairs, refilled.

When I shrugged, he sat next to me. He leaned forward, his elbows rested on his thighs as he swirled his drink, ice cubes clinking against the crystal.

I waited for him to say something. Nate was the kind of guy who laid it all out there. It had been a problem for me when I'd stayed with them before. He wanted me to talk about what I went through. When I told him about the nightmares back then, he insisted I see a shrink—someone other than him, who could have an impartial view. I refused. Not long after I turned eighteen, I moved out, and things had gone downhill fast from there. With no one to enforce any boundaries, I went off the rails. It had taken a good two years before my head came out of my ass.

"No offense, Hayden, but you don't look very good."

"You should have seen me before I shaved." When he didn't say anything, I sighed. "I'm not sleeping well."

"Are you having the nightmares again?"

"It's not a big deal. They happen when I'm stressed."

For the past couple of years they'd been manageable. Every once in a while I went through a period when they resurfaced, but after a few weeks they let up again. Until Tenley had left. Now they came nightly.

"What are they about?"

"The usual." That wasn't quite accurate.

"Are they like the ones you had after your parents were killed?"

"Kind of."

While the dreams about my parents unnerved me, the ones about Tenley scared the crap out of me. Usually they were more like snapshots of memories and flashes of events, such as the interrogation with Cross. Some of the nightmares were about previous women, who always morphed into Tenley. That my subconscious allowed such a thing freaked me out. But as much as they sucked, they were just dreams fused with memories. Nothing Nate needed to know about.

"Do you want me to prescribe you something to help with the sleep?"

"Nah, it'll pass." Meds were in my cabinet already, and except for one time a couple months back, I refused to take them. I might not be handling things well, but I knew what drug dependency looked like. Prescription or not, I had no desire to fall into that pit of self-destruction. We sat there for a while and I expected him to throw something else at me, but he didn't. Eventually the words just came out, even though I'd vowed not to talk about it with him.

"I keep going back to the night she left, wondering if I could have done something differently. And there's this one thing her brother-in-law said that I can't get out of my head."

"What's that?"

"He said I was her punishment."

"Punishment?" A crease formed between Nate's eyes. "For what?"

"I don't know. Surviving?" I rubbed the back of my neck.

"That seems a little extreme, considering what Tenley's been through."

"She didn't deny it, though. So it has to be true."

"I'm not sure I agree with that. It depends on the context, doesn't it? And that brother-in-law of hers sounds like quite the bastard from what I've been told. I think the better question is, do you feel that way about yourself?"

I hesitated. "Maybe? Tenley could have been slumming it, like he said."

"Slumming it? You don't live in the projects."

"I'm not exactly aspiring to be in the upper class, though, am I? My high school diploma was granted out of pity, not merit. I have no postsecondary education and I definitely don't conform to societal expectations."

Generally, the only people who wanted to be around me were the ones who wanted my art on them. It didn't say much about me as a person.

"First of all, the upper class is primarily made up of narcissistic assholes, so it's better not to aim for that status. Secondly, your problem in high school wasn't ability. Your diploma was granted because you are competent. You were leagues above your peers and you were bored to tears. Which is partly why you behaved the way you did."

"I would have been a pain in the ass even if boredom hadn't been an issue."

"Maybe. But let's be honest, Hayden—as much as I loved your parents, they didn't exactly keep close tabs on you."

He was right, though it felt like a betrayal to think of them as anything less than perfect. Not until I started coming home drunk and high did they try to put a leash on me. By that time it was too late.

When I stayed silent, he continued, "Nonconformity has been your mantra since you developed independent thought. Plus, you were their only child and they couldn't say no to you. When you lost them, you lost yourself, too. But that doesn't make you some-one else's punishment."

I held up a hand. He was spewing too much affirmation crap. "Enough with the headshrinking."

Nate smiled, amused. "It's a natural impulse, I'm afraid. And there's nothing wrong with therapy."

"I'm not crazy."

"I didn't say you were."

"I don't need to talk about my shit."

"Everyone needs to talk about their shit."

"I knew I shouldn't have said anything," I said, irritated that I'd opened my mouth in the first place.

"You've spent the last seven years owning the death of your parents. That's you punishing yourself. So it would make sense for you to internalize Tenley's leaving as if it's a reflection of something you've done, rather than an external force."

It was hard to fight the truth. That was the reason I never al-lowed myself to get close to Nate. I talked too much when I was around him.

"I keep everyone on the periphery on purpose." I shook my

head at the irony. "And the second I let Tenley in, she leaves me. It fucking hurts. It's like there's this huge hole in my chest, and if she just came back, it would go away and I would be fine. Except that's not true—because there will always be this thing between us now."

"You're referring to her deceased fiancé?"

Nate waited silently.

It embarrassed the shit out of me that he knew my business.

"Here's the thing I can't figure out: If I hurt this much over someone who is still alive and I've known for a few months, then how did she manage to move on after losing nine people? That's why I think I'm her punishment. Like she picked me because I can never be right for her."

"Love doesn't always have convenient timing."

"Tenley doesn't love me." I wished people would stop saying that. At first I believed it, but after weeks of silence, I didn't anymore. I'd gone all the way to Arden Hills to get her back, only to end up being thwarted by that fucknut Trey. If I ever saw him again, he wouldn't be walking away with teeth.

"Did she tell you that?"

"She left me. I think that says it all."

"Have you considered that maybe she left because she doesn't know how to handle how she feels about you?"

"She left because she had to deal with her estate."

"I'm sure that's part of the reason."

"Whatever. The reasons don't change the fact that she's gone." I downed the rest of my scotch and pushed up off the edge of the bed. "I need a refill."

Dinner was more of the same. I zoned out, thinking about Tenley. Christmas was barely more than two weeks away and I worried how Tenley would handle the holidays. In the past I'd drowned them in booze and drugs. Now I limited it to scotch; sophisticated drunkenness and all that.

After dinner I made everyone leave the kitchen so I could clean up; creating order out of chaos helped ease the anxiety. I wanted to get home because I hadn't checked Tenley's apartment yet today and the deviation from my routine exacerbated the OCD, making me a slave to compulsion.

When I finished putting away the last of the dishes, I went back out to the living room. The girls were huddled around Cassie's phone. I leaned over to check out what had them so riveted and heard Lisa whisper something about Tenley. They rarely mentioned her in front of me on the chance I might lose my shit. Or the not-so-off chance. Lisa moved her head and the screen came into view; it contained an e-mail from Tenley.

"What the fuck?"

I snatched the phone out of Cassie's hand and did a quick scan before she grabbed it back. It was a money transfer for Tenley's rent. She'd sent it early. She usually paid on the fifteenth of every month, and the message along with it said she was fine, but she wasn't sure when she would be back. At the end she asked how I was doing; if I was managing all right. As if she felt sorry for me. It was such a fucking kick in the balls.

"She's been e-mailing you? For how long?" I asked. Unable to mask the goddamn hurt, I channeled it into anger.

They all shrank back, surprised by the outburst. Sarah and Lisa exchanged a look.

"Has she been in contact with you, too?" I looked from one to the other. Their guilty expressions were enough of an answer. I pinned Lisa with an accusatory glare. "Are you shitting me? *You*, of all people, kept this from me? You're supposed to be my friend. Where's your fucking loyalty?"

"We didn't want to upset you," Lisa explained.

Upset didn't begin to cover it. I couldn't believe Tenley had been in touch with everyone but me. "Fuck all of you."

3

HAYDEN

I shoved my feet in my shoes and grabbed my jacket from the closet.

"Hayden, wait!" Lisa called.

I spun around. "Don't talk to me right now."

"You need to check yourself, man," Jamie said, coming up behind Lisa.

My eyes swung over to him as he moved in closer, probably worried about her safety. "Go fuck yourself."

I wrenched the door open and stepped outside, slamming it behind me, but the release of aggression brought no satisfaction. It felt as if someone had dumped acid on my emotions. I passed Lisa's Beetle and headed down the driveway. It was freezing out and I wasn't dressed for the weather, but I didn't care. I needed to get my ass far enough away to catch a bus or cab it home. I couldn't be around any of them right now; I was too raw.

The door opened behind me and the thud of boots against the asphalt grew louder, so I picked up the pace.

"H! Hey, bro, hold up!" Chris called out.

Just what I needed. When his hand came down on my shoulder, I pushed it off and kept going. "I don't want to hear it."

"Come on, man. I know you're upset but you can't walk all the way home."

I wheeled around. "I sure as hell can. There's no way I'm getting in that car with those two."

"Tee only got in touch with Sarah last week. And it wasn't to chat. She had some assignment that needed to be handed directly to her adviser, so she called in a favor."

"What about Cassie and Lisa?"

"I don't know. Why don't you come back in and you can ask them."

I shook my head. "I need space."

Chris didn't follow me any farther. He knew when to leave me alone. I was too volatile, and it was best for everyone if I had time to cool off. A few minutes later, Nate's black Mercedes pulled over ahead of me. The passenger-side window whirred as it descended, and he leaned across the seat and opened the door. "Why don't you let me drive you home."

He'd drive five miles an hour all the way to Inked Armor if I refused to get in. I dropped into the passenger seat and plugged in the seat belt.

"It's okay if you're angry," he said as he pulled back onto the road.

"We're not talking about this," I snapped.

"That's fine, too."

I fiddled around with his radio, unable to tolerate the strained silence. All the stations were preset to '70s rock.

"Can I just say one thing?"

"You're going to anyway, so you might as well." I stared out the window. I could see my reflection in the tinted glass every time we passed a streetlamp, and I looked as destroyed as I felt.

"This is only the second time Tenley contacted Cassie since she left. The first time was to let Cassie know she had to leave for a while, and to provide a list of potential employees while she was gone. Both times, she asked about you."

I didn't reply. I had nothing to say. So what if she asked about me? Her worry seemed less about how I was doing and more about the remorse she carried around with her. It was like a cinder block tied around her neck.

When we reached Inked Armor, I grabbed on to the door handle, but Nate hit the lock button and held it down. "Hold on."

I sighed. "I'm not in the mood for this shit."

"Too bad, because I have something you need to hear. Bad things happen to people, Hayden. All the time. You have firsthand experience with this. It's not something we can control, but we do choose how to handle it. You need to start dealing with what happened to your parents. It's not going to go away just because you want it to.

"Cassie is terrified you're going to self-destruct all over again. When she lost her sister, it was tragic, and watching you almost go down along with Eleanor nearly destroyed her. Don't put her through that again."

"You're seriously pulling a guilt trip on me over this?" I asked, irate.

"You need to get some help. If that's the only way I can get through to you, then so be it. I won't see my wife in that much pain again."

The click of the door's unlocking was my signal to get out.

He peeled away from the curb, tires squealing. The guilt hit its mark. Of course Cassie suffered after she lost her sister—but I hadn't taken into account how my actions affected her. She and Nate had taken me in despite the problems I posed. I hadn't been able to tolerate their care or concern and I'd gotten away as soon as I could.

Nate was right. I was walking a fine line toward imploding again. Not much about me had changed in the last seven years.

Feeding TK was the first order of business when I got home.

After she scarfed down the contents of her bowl, I tucked her under my arm and went to Tenley's apartment. After opening the door, I took off my shoes and placed them on the mat beside Tenley's ratty, purple Chucks. I did a walk-through, checking all the rooms before I returned to the kitchen.

The fridge was almost empty: a package of processed-cheese slices, condiments, the beer I'd brought over, a pitcher of water, and the lemons I used to keep her fridge smelling fresh were all that remained.

I grabbed a beer and popped it open, then went through the fridge and tossed anything that had gone off. Next, I went to the cupboard under the sink and retrieved a new box of baking soda. Punching the perforated edge, I set it on the bottom shelf and chucked the old one. Then I threw out the lemon half from yesterday and replaced it as well.

Her bathroom was next. Though it was unused, I cleaned it out of habit. The bedroom was always my last stop. Unprepared to go there yet, I went back to the living room. A copy of Tenley's thesis paper was on the coffee table, which I read whenever I stayed for a while. Tenley was smart, and her paper made me question what the fuck her adviser's problem was. He had her running in circles for no reason.

All the curtains were pulled shut. I swept them aside, looking down at the Inked Armor sign across the street. Tenley would have been able to see right inside the shop from this vantage point, just as I'd been able to see inside her apartment from the window in my bedroom. God, it felt like a lifetime ago that I'd creeped on her while she was in her kitchen, making a drink. Even then I'd wondered if she was hiding any ink. I'd gotten the answer to that question, but the cost seemed pretty fucking high now.

I dropped the curtain and turned to face the empty living room. I scanned her bookshelves, pausing at the photo albums at the top. The albums became newer as they progressed across the shelf. Everything I was looking for and all the missing pieces would be in there. I tipped one of the spines and pulled it down.

The faded leather binding was well worn; it looked to be as old as Tenley. Inside were faded Polaroids with names and dates written across the bottoms in neat cursive. Tenley's parents smiled out from the page, oblivious of what would become of them so many years in the future.

Tenley was almost the spitting image of her mother, from the arch in her eyebrows to the pout of her lips. But her gray-green eyes were from her father, along with the impish glint. I followed her parents' story from college and dating to holidays on the beach and finally their wedding. A couple who'd appeared in many of the college photos stood beside Tenley's parents as the best man and the maid of honor.

In the second album babies appeared for the maid of honor and the best man, and the carefree faces of youth showed the harder angles of adulthood. Tenley's mom held those little bundles of poop with the fascinated awe reserved for infants. First there was a dark-haired boy, and a few years later a fair-haired one appeared. The names Trey and Connor were written elegantly at the bottom. Tenley had known the guy she was supposed to marry her entire life. I put the album back and withdrew the next one.

On the first page, Tenley's mother stood on the back porch of a clapboard house, a pink streak of cloud hovering along the horizon. A small smile played on her lips, and her hand rested low on her stomach, a soft swell barely hidden under her dress.

Then Tenley arrived. The pictures of her as a baby, a toddler, a little girl, were endless. Every so often, the other family would appear in the albums. As the kids aged, it became obvious which one was that dick Trey. He had the same hard look about him, as if the world were a pain in the ass and he couldn't stand dealing with the people in it. His smiles were forced, his stare disengaged. Connor, the blond one, was his antithesis. His smile was bright and open, his fascination with the world and Tenley clear from an early age.

I pulled the rest of the albums off the shelf and pieced together a more comprehensive picture of Tenley's life. She grew up in a middle-class family, passing through her teen years with no gawky phase. She clearly spent a lot of time with her family, or at least they captured those moments as often as they could.

Photos showed her with her father sitting in the front seat of a fire truck, his pride and her excitement obvious. In others, Tenley and her mother stood side by side in the kitchen baking cupcakes, or planting flowers in the garden. One even showed Tenley working on homework at the kitchen table, her finger pressed against her lip in fabricated concentration as she flipped off the camera. I had to look for the subversion to catch it. A glimmer of mischief was always present in her eyes. It gave the impression she was waiting for the camera to leave so she could get up to no good.

I leafed through pictures of her graduation from high school and her transition to adulthood. At prom she wore beat-up running shoes and a hideous dress while her date wore a tux. Those photo albums were vinyl instead of leather, covered in band stickers and filled with pictures of Tenley and her friends. Her outfits were grew more outrageous once she hit college. Nothing ever matched. She often paired vintage with frilly. Self-portraits showed her with each addition of steel up the shell of her ear, and in others she was with Connor. So many of her with Connor.

He was broad-shouldered and blond, a pretty boy who played sports and wore polos emblazoned with a Cornell Law School logo. When she was with him, her style changed completely. Apart from her shoes. She was forever wearing ratty sneakers. She was always smiling in those pictures, eyes on the camera as she stood within his protective embrace. His expression bordered on a smirk, coveting a trophy no one else could have.

Near the end of one album Connor disappeared for a while, and some of the girlfriends I'd seen interspersed throughout figured more prominently. Connor reappeared in the last album, around the time Tenley graduated from college. The genuine happiness I'd seen on her face before was gone; she smiled but seemed distant, preoccupied.

The engagement photos made me feel betrayed. The ones of her trying on wedding dresses and laughing with girlfriends made me livid. Nine memorial photos at the end turned me inside out. No way in hell would she have ended up with someone like me if she hadn't been in that plane crash. The knowledge was caustic on so many levels.

I reshelved the albums one by one, sliding the last one into place. Then I noticed the one on the shelf below.

Bound in black leather, it was brand new. I picked it up hesitantly. The first pages contained pictures of Northwestern's campus, and the storefronts of Serendipity and Inked Armor. Shots of her life in Chicago followed. Cassie, Lisa, Sarah, Jamie, and Chris all appeared in various photos. Others were of her peers at school, even that douche bag Ian. But those were few and far between.

There were lots of shots of TK—and even more of me. Pages and pages dedicated to me. Me in her kitchen, washing dishes. Me glaring at the pile of books on her coffee table; another of me arranging them. My arms appeared in several close-ups, with even more of my profile, particularly the side with the viper bites. She'd even taken pictures of me in Inked Armor. She took such care to label them all with dates and explanations. I didn't know what to think.

The album was only half-full. The last page had been titled "Date Night," but there were no pictures.

I shelved the album and headed down the hall to her bedroom. TK was in her favorite place; snoozing between the pillows. I lay down beside her, more drained than I remembered being in my life.

Unable to stop my eyes from closing, I let the memories of being here with her wash over me. When my parents died, I missed the little things, those small reminders that they were gone and never coming back. With Tenley I missed everything, all the time. Right now I missed the feel of her body beside mine. I missed waking up sweaty because we'd been spooning for hours. I missed rolling over and pulling her into me, the tickle of her hair on my face, the smell of her skin. As I was sucked into the void of sleep, I wondered if I'd ever get any of that back.

Death had a distinct odor. I didn't recognize it when I snuck in through the front door, but the heavy, metallic tang in the air made me pause. With a frown, I stepped inside the foyer, moving right to avoid the creaky floorboard. The smell was all wrong. My drug-hazed mind couldn't process the sensory information as it zipped through my neural receptors, heading straight to the black abyss of narcotic numbness and into mass confusion.

The door closed with a quiet click; in my paranoid state it sounded like a bomb detonating. I cringed and waited to be blinded by the living room light. Nothing happened, though. The house stayed silent. Mom occasionally waited up in the rocking chair, the most uncomfortable piece of furniture in the house. It ensured she wouldn't fall asleep.

I shed one sneaker and then the other, arranging them neatly beside Dad's polished black dress shoes. They weren't supposed to be there. My parents weren't due home for another hour, and I wasn't supposed to be out since I was grounded. The decoy I'd set up in my bed must have worked.

I treaded stealthily down the hall, taking great care not to make any noise. Something was off, though. The nauseating odor grew more pervasive as I moved deeper into the house, and a sense of dread settled in the pit of my stomach. It had to be the pot. And the booze.

I hit the staircase slowly, just lucid enough to know my balance was shoddy. A shadow moved across the landing, scaring the piss out of me. Mischief, the ancient family cat, padded down the hallway, meowing loudly.

"Shh, shut up, Mis," I hissed. I leaned down and stroked her back in hopes of quieting her, but the wailing continued. "Shut it!"

Worried she would wake my parents, I scooped her up. She burrowed into my arms, her little body trembling, nails digging into my skin. I should have known then. Mischief never came to me, not even when her food bowl was empty.

No muted glow came from the bathroom, where a tiny night-light usually shone the way. The metallic odor saturated the air now, cloying.

Pale light seeped out from under my parents' bedroom door. Through the pot-induced haze of denial, the unwelcome truth surfaced. The smell was disturbingly familiar. Copper. Iron. Salt.

I pushed the door open a crack and peeked inside. The first thing I saw was the painting of the red angel, lying on the floor. I opened the door a little more. Mischief screeched and clawed out of my arms in an attempt to escape what I couldn't. But I didn't even feel her nails.

Dad lay on his side in bed, his eyes wide and glassy. A brownish-red trail trickled down his forehead from the small hole there. Blood darkening to maroon marred the sheets surrounding his head. The pillow behind him was a deep red Rorschach of brain matter.

Even though I wanted to look away, my gaze shifted right. A single bullet wound marked my mother's chest. Black-red stained her peach-colored shift, darkest in the center and brightening as it fanned out. Her eyes were open, sightless and horrified. I wondered who'd suffered the fate of watching the other die first, knowing what was coming next.

Then the scene morphed and I was no longer seventeen. The bedroom was my own. There was only one body, dressed in creamy satin, the small hole in her chest turning the pale fabric red. No matter how hard I tried, I couldn't cross the threshold of the doorway to save her.

I woke with a shout. Bolting upright, I glanced around the darkened room. I was in Tenley's bed. Heart pounding, covered in sweat, I fanned my hand out over the space beside me, hoping to find her warm, whole body. There was nothing but emptiness. Panic set in, until I remembered she had left. Yet the clarity of the nightmare didn't fade as lucidity returned.

I couldn't get the image of Tenley's bleeding out to stop flashing behind my eyes like a horror movie. Bile rose in my throat. I stumbled to the bathroom, blinded myself with the light, and barely made it to the toilet as I threw up. The nightmares weren't getting better. As the scene replayed in my head, my stomach gave another violent squeeze, and the remnants of dinner splashed into the bowl until there were only dry heaves.

I stayed draped over the seat with my forehead resting on my arm, unable to move, afraid I was in for another round. I finally pulled myself up on shaky arms, supporting my weight on even shakier legs so I could rinse with water and a mouthwash chaser.

My lack of control disgusted me. After so many years, it should have been easier to deal with this shit. I turned away from the sink and glanced across the hall to Tenley's bedroom. The comforter was bunched up and the pillows were scattered on the floor. No dead Tenley. No blood staining the sheets.

I left the bathroom light on as I made my way back to the bed. The clock on the nightstand flashed 4:47 A.M. I wasn't about to fall back asleep, where I'd be pulled into that fucked-up nightmare again. I palmed my phone and sat down on the floor, my back against the edge of the bed. The wood frame dug in just below my shoulders; the padding of the mattress cushioned the back of my head. Tenley's mattress was softer than mine. I liked it better.

I keyed in the password. Went to contacts. Stared at the Tenley and TK thumbnail attached to her information. I hadn't called in two weeks, afraid she would answer, afraid she wouldn't. But right now I needed to hear her voice, even if only the recording. I hit call and watched the screen light up, the faint ring coming through. Two rings, three . . . one more and voice mail would kick in.

But the fourth ring was cut short. I stopped breathing. I never actually expected her to answer.

4

TENLEY

The sound of my cell pulled me out of a dream. I resisted, Hayden's beautiful face fading as I blinked in the darkness. I grabbed the phone before the call went to voice mail. The clock on the nightstand read close to five in the morning.

"Hello?" I said, my voice gravelly with sleep.

There was a soft exhale. "You answered," he said in disbelief. "I didn't think you would. I called before and you never did. But this time . . . why didn't you answer before?"

At his distress, I curled around the phone wishing I could hug him through the device. "I wanted to."

"Then you should have."

Over the past three weeks I almost had, a number of times. The ache in my chest, which grew worse every day, had become a stab of agony. If I'd answered his calls, I would have gone back to Chicago, instead of taking care of things in Arden Hills, regardless of whether I deserved Hayden.

"I know. I wish I had. Are you all right? Did something happen?"

"I had a bad dream." He sounded so small, as though it shamed him to call for such a reason.

"Oh, Hayden. I'm so sorry." My eyes welled with tears. "What was it about?"

Another soft noise came through the receiver. Some rustling. A low thud repeated twice, a third time, a fourth. A choking noise, followed by a loud slam. The distance made me powerless. I wanted to reach through the phone and take away the pain, as he'd done for me so many times.

"Hayden?"

"Sorry." He coughed. "I dropped something."

I wasn't fooled. "Was it a nightmare?"

"I thought it was real. When I woke up I thought—" There was another low thud.

"Was it about your parents?"

"No."

"Was it about me?"

"Yes." His voice cracked. "You were, you were, you were— Fuck!" Hayden stumbled over the words.

"It's okay, now. I'm right here. I'm right here and I'm fine. Nothing bad happened to me." I hoped if I kept talking, I could calm him. "It was just a dream."

"I couldn't get to you. You were dying and I couldn't—the bleeding, there was so much blood and you were, and you were—" He started to hyperventilate. "I was so fucking empty without you. I'm so empty." He broke then. His words bled together, becoming nonsense. "I didn't know it was going to feel like this. I didn't know. I wouldn't have let you—I want, I want—"

I clapped a palm over my mouth to stop my sob, horrified that I'd done this to him. I thought when I left, he would see what a bad choice I was. Instead he was falling apart.

"Shh, it's okay, Hayden. I'm so sorry. I wish I was there with you," I said softly.

"Then come home," he pleaded.

"I will. Leaving you was so hard. I know I should have called and explained. But I only have a few more things to take care of."

"And then you'll come home?"

"Yes. As soon as I can." I wiped away tears with the back of my hand.

"Promise?"

"I promise."

During a long stretch of silence, I listened to him breathe.

"Tenley?"

"I'm still here."

"I—nothing is the same without you." His breath left him in a rush. "Come home soon, okay?"

"I'm trying. It's been really complicated."

"How much longer are you going to be?" His voice rose with panic.

"I don't know. I'd leave right now if I could—I swear it, Hayden."

"But I need you here. I miss you. I can't—" There was a pause, and when he spoke again, his tone was flat. "I'm sorry. I shouldn't have called."

"I'm glad you—" There was a click. "Hayden?"

The line was dead. I looked at the screen, confused as to what had happened. I pulled him up in my list of contacts. The first picture I ever took of him in my apartment appeared on the screen, the one of his feeding icing to TK. I smoothed my thumb over it. I missed her almost as much as I missed him. I hit call. It rang and went to voice mail. I tried again. This time it dumped me straight into voice mail.

"No, no, no!"

I should have told him I missed him when I had the chance. I tried again; got voice mail again. He'd given up on me. The realization made me sick as I hit redial over and over, hoping I could undo some of the harm. But it was more of the same. He didn't pick up.

"Damnit!"

I hurled my phone across the room in frustration. The second it left my fingertips, I dove after it, but it was too late. It hit the wall and clattered to the floor. I snatched it up, praying I hadn't damaged it in my moment of stupidity. The screen had spider-webbed on impact.

"Shit! No!" I punched the button violently, keying in my password, but it was no use. I couldn't get past the first screen. I threw open the door and ran down the hall to the office. I fumbled with the landline, punching in Hayden's number.

"Please, please, please, please . . . ," I begged, crossing my fingers he would pick up. He didn't.

Tears blurred my vision as I tried to call my own phone. It let out a weak ring, then died.

I needed to get to Hayden. I should have tried to explain long before now, even if it didn't make any sense. He could be mad at me for having a poor excuse. Anything was better than this. His refusal to talk to me made me hyperaware of what my silence had done to him. I'd been so caught up in what I thought I needed to resolve here, I hadn't realized the impact it would have on him.

I ran from him because I was in love with him. That, and I feared I'd never be enough. Right now, I wasn't—but staying here wasn't going to fix that. I had to get home to Hayden so I could make things right.

I ran back to my room. This house was just a holding cell of loss now; I couldn't stay here anymore. I'd have to force myself to accept that I suffered enough.

I needed to accomplish so much before I went back to

Chicago, but my departure would be nothing like my arrival. I would leave on my own terms.

I jumped into the shower before the water had a chance to warm. I shivered my way through washing my hair and was in such a rush to get on with things that I almost forgot to rinse it. Once dressed, I pulled my hair into a wet ponytail and crammed my belongings into my suitcase. I had to sit on it to get it to close. Then I lugged it down the stairs and out to the garage.

Connor's car was full. The backseat and trunk were packed with the boxes of his belongings I intended to donate to various charities. The few things I couldn't bear to part with were in a tote box on the front passenger seat. I'd planned to drop it off at my parents' place last night, but I'd been exhausted after my visit to the cemetery.

I took a deep breath, willing myself not to break down, and took my suitcase back inside. I left it in the kitchen and grabbed my purse.

On my way out of the garage, I almost took off the passenger-side mirror. At least I'd managed to leave before Trey showed up. If I was lucky, I'd be able to avoid another confrontation.

I made it to my parents' house in record time and carted the tote inside. My plan was to dump it in my old bedroom closet and deal with it later, whenever I felt capable of returning. The house was as cool inside as it was outside, so I dropped the tote in the hall and went down to the basement. The pilot light in the furnace had gone out. That wasn't the real problem, though; it was the burst pipe and the slick of ice pooled on the floor. I'd have to call in a plumber. It was barely seven in the morning, though, and I didn't have a phone. Nothing would be open until nine and I didn't have that kind of time.

I pressed my palms against my eyes, weighing my options. Arden Hills was a small town. I knew lots of people whose doors I could knock on, even at this early hour. I left the house and drove to Lake Johanna. One of my dad's old friends lived out there; he'd be able to help me. The farmhouse was as I remembered it, except the paint was faded by the sun and the porch worn down by time. The inhabitants were the same.

They invited me in, made me breakfast, and talked about the farm and their eight grandchildren as we ate. I sat there, smiling and nodding, because he'd agreed to drive out to my parents' house and fix the pipes.

My next stop was the Apple store at the Rosedale Center just outside town. Everything was going fine until I tried to pay. My Visa was declined. So was my MasterCard. I had to use the phone in the store to call the bank. My accounts had been frozen first thing this morning. Trey had to be involved; it was the only explanation.

I called my lawyer, Frank, then spent the next two hours at the bank, sorting things out. Trey had given himself signing authority over my account after he'd illegally forced me into signing the power-of-attorney papers. I was fortunate he hadn't drained the account, and that this wasn't the one with the bulk of my money. Eventually Frank worked things out, but no one could find Trey, which meant he had to know about the house sale by now.

I lost it when I got back in the car. It took me another twenty minutes to get myself under control before I could return to the Apple store to get my new phone.

Once I had it, the first thing I did was call Hayden. He still wasn't answering. I retried at every stoplight.

It was four in the afternoon by the time I finished dropping off Connor's effects at the Salvation Army. Snow had started falling earlier, and the daylight had faded to dark gray by the time I returned to what would soon become Weston's house. My tires squeaked over the blanket of white as I pulled up to the front door.

Before I went inside, I called Frank to make sure the keys were ready to be passed over. He assured me everything was in order and promised to let me know when the key drop was official. They still hadn't found Trey, which was worrisome, but at least his car wasn't in the driveway. He'd left several messages on my phone but I hadn't checked them, knowing it wouldn't be anything I'd want to hear. I kept the car idling in the driveway since I only needed to leave my key on the kitchen table and grab my suitcase. I couldn't wait to go home.

I turned the key in the lock and pushed the door open. The waning sun left the main floor in gray, looming shadows. I flicked on the light and stopped short. Trey sat at the kitchen table, hands clasped on top of a stack of papers, as still as a lake at dawn.

"I didn't see your car."

His face was like stone, betraying no emotion. He didn't look at me when he replied, "I parked in the garage."

He wore a suit, but he was utterly disheveled, his tie loose, the top buttons of his shirt undone, the collar askew. Stubble covered his chin and cheeks; his hair stuck straight up at the front; and the circles under his eyes were rimmed in red.

My suitcase sat where I had left it, halfway between him and me. He swept a hand toward the bag. "Going somewhere?"

"I'm heading home," I said, my voice amazingly steady.

"To your parents' house?" His hand returned to the tabletop, smoothing over the glass surface.

"No."

"No?" He cocked his head to the side. "You've decided to stay at the main house, then?" Trey had moved there after the death of his family and had tried to make me stay there with him when I first returned. It lasted three days before I got out from under his thumb and the constant stream of antianxiety medication he snuck into my food.

"No, Trey. I'm going home. To Chicago."

"Back to the degenerate. How lovely." He smiled with malice.

I took a step closer to my bag. The fifteen feet of tile floor between me and it seemed like miles. I didn't want to get any closer to Trey than I already was. A seething undercurrent of fury lurked beneath his veneer of calm.

"I should give you some credit—you're smarter than I thought." With a sweep of his hand, he spread the stack of papers out like a card dealer. "I see you managed to have the power of attorney reversed."

My heart kicked in my chest. I'd hoped to be gone long before the papers for the house reached him. "I did what I had to do."

"I'm sure. But did you think I wouldn't find out before you left?" His voice rose, gaining momentum and volume until it was a yell. "That you could go behind my back and give the fucking house away and then run again?"

In one swift move, his chair screeched across the tile floor and he upended the table. The papers flew into the air and rained down, red ink and yellow highlighter flashing amid the white. The table landed on its side, the tempered-glass top shattering into a wave of sparkles. Trey stepped through the debris, glass crunching under his soles, hands cranked into fists as he stalked toward me. "I was still able to have your accounts frozen. I'm sure that made your escape a bit more of a challenge."

"The problem is fixed now." I stood my ground, though all I wanted to do was bolt.

He stopped right in front of me, his expression still flat. "I will undo this."

"You can't, Trey. It's out of your control. I won't give you the house so that you can destroy it. Your father wouldn't have wanted that."

"My father is dead. What he wanted doesn't matter."

"To me it does. I'm done here, Trey. I won't allow you to tear me down anymore."

I turned away; nothing good would come of this conversation. When he grabbed me, I wrenched my arm away. He came at me again and I pulled my sleeve up to my forearm, exposing the bruises he'd created during our last altercation.

"I'd advise you to keep your hands to yourself, Trey. I've already documented these with my lawyer."

"I-I didn't—"

"Weston will have the keys to the house shortly. I'm guessing you won't try to bully him the way you've bullied me. But if you feel physical coercion is necessary, at least he's on a more level playing field. Good-bye." I stepped around Trey, grabbed my bag with a trembling hand, and wheeled it to the door.

Trey recovered from the shock of seeing the damage his temper had done, his response scathing. "You don't think I'll permit you to take Connor's car, do you?"

"I don't need your permission. Connor's car is mine now."

There was nothing else he could take from me. The thing he wanted had been signed over to his cousin; Frank had made sure the agreement was airtight. Trey's hands were tied and if he'd been through the documentation, he knew it.

I opened the door, ready to leave this all behind me.

"I never should have let you leave in the first place," he said.

As if the choice had been his to make? I turned, the icy wind prickling the back of my neck. "What did you say?"

"You should have been mine," he said bitterly.

Trey had always been callous, unrepentant for the hurt he inflicted on others. But in that moment the façade dropped and I saw someone crippled by narcissism.

"Is that what you thought would happen when you brought me back here?"

"I took care of you, and now you're leaving me with nothing. You owe me."

As though I were a possession to be passed along.

I left without another word. There was nothing to say.

5

TENLEY

About ten minutes later, Weston called and I pulled over. The keys had changed hands. Only then did I realize I still had my set, and Trey still had his.

"Don't worry about it," Weston said. "I'm having the locks changed this evening. With Trey you always have to stay one step ahead."

"I was never very good at that."

"Oh, I think you were better at it than you know. And you're always welcome to visit. All you have to do is call."

"Thanks, Weston."

"Take care of yourself, okay?"

"I will. You, too."

I stopped at a gas station about three hours into the drive. I was halfway to Chicago and utterly famished. For the first time in weeks, I actually had an appetite. I bought a huge bag of chips, a monster chocolate bar, and a Coke.

I called Sarah after I gassed up to let her know I was on my way back, but she didn't pick up, so I left a voice mail and sent a text as backup. I'd given her my apartment key so she could feed TK.

I considered my options as I continued home. Hayden had a key, but he wasn't answering my calls, so that ruled him out. Besides, a conversation was waiting to happen when I saw him, and showing up in the middle of the night wouldn't make that discussion any easier. The possibility that I might not be able to right my wrongs terrified me.

Three hours later I stood outside my apartment building, buzzed Sarah, and prayed she was home, even though her car wasn't parked in her spot. There was no response to my buzz. Maybe she was at work. I went back to Connor's car and resignedly punched The Dollhouse into the GPS. I wanted to be home, and I wanted to see TK. If I couldn't have Hayden tonight, at least I could have her.

Fifteen minutes later, I pulled into the parking lot of the strip club. I called Sarah again but still got no answer, which made sense if she was waitressing. Parking in a well-lit area, I grabbed my purse and locked the car. The building was painted black, garish lights flashed out the name of the club, and a neon light showed a half-naked woman bending, standing, bending, standing, as she flickered on and off, her bare ass on display with each flip of her skirt.

I couldn't believe Sarah worked here. But if it paid for her MBA and left her debt free after college, I could see the logic.

I headed for the entrance, a bit nervous. I scanned the lot, searching for Sarah's car, but couldn't locate it. The staff might have separate parking, though; safer for the girls who worked there. A huge man with arms the size of my waist guarded the front door. He looked me over in a way that made me feel naked even with my hoodie. I wished I had my jacket on.

"ID." He held out a meaty palm.

I rooted around in my bag for my wallet and pulled out my driver's license. He scanned it, looked at my face, then handed it back to me. "Where's your escort?"

"Pardon?"

"Your escort," he said, annoyed. "You need a male escort to come in here."

"Oh, I——" I chewed my lip, unsure how to proceed. "I have a friend who works here, her name is Sarah."

"Sarah, huh? So you're looking for a job?" He smiled wryly. "You're a little skinny, but that porcelain-doll thing might work for you."

He opened the door and grabbed the arm of a scantily clad woman who passed by. "This one's looking for a job. Take her to the boss lady."

The woman looked at me, laughed, and turned back to him. "Are you serious?"

"Says she knows Sarah."

I thought to correct him, but if it got me in, I'd take it. All I needed was to get my key and I'd be on my way.

She gave me a doubtful look and turned back to the bouncer. "You're wasting everyone's time. She wouldn't last a shift." With a look of exasperation, she motioned for me to follow her.

I trailed behind her as we skirted the perimeter of the club, taking in all the men in business suits, seated close to the main stage. Toward the back of the club were two smaller stages, cordoned off with red-velvet rope. On either side were plush couches where men in suits lounged while dancers writhed in their laps.

I didn't want to think about Hayden with his hands all over any of these women, or vice versa. I wondered if money had ever been exchanged on his part. The thought sickened me.

"So you know Sarah?" she asked, eyeing me suspiciously.

"Yeah."

"You tell that bitch she needs to stay away from my clients." She flipped her bleached hair over her shoulder. "Otherwise I'm going to mess up that pretty face of hers. Wait here," she ordered.

"Is she work—"

She slipped through a door guarded by another heavily muscled man before I could finish the sentence.

"Hey," I shouted to him over the pounding music, my uneasy feeling growing. "I'm looking for my friend Sarah. She works here."

He tapped his ear and mouthed, "I can't hear you." Then he went back to staring menacingly at the crowd.

Frustrated, I turned to look for her. The interior of the club was painted midnight black, casting shadows over the clientele. I searched for Sarah's almost-white blond hair, but couldn't locate her through the flicker of strobe lights. Tables full of men watched a naked woman gyrating on a pole, their eyes straying only when a mostly undressed waitress passed by. I hated that my friend waitressed here, and that Hayden had once been immersed in this lifestyle.

The door beside the bouncer slammed opened and Sienna appeared in all her red-patent-leather glory. The dress she wore was suctioned to her body. Her fake breasts were pushed up so high they looked like flesh-colored grapes ready to burst. Marks were on her arms, as if someone had been holding on to her hard, and one of her cheeks was bright red. A man dressed just like the one guarding the door came out behind her, adjusting his belt.

She snapped at the security guard, clearly put out. He motioned to the front; I saw Sarah's name form on his lips; then he gestured to me. Sienna glanced at me and hatred flashed across her face, before she recovered her composure and a grin distorted her mouth.

I was confused. Hayden had said Sienna used to dance here.

But as I saw the way everyone deferred to her, I realized he'd failed to fill in the rest of the blanks. Despite what her state of undress suggested, Sienna wasn't a stripper anymore; she was in charge of this club. And I was in a bad spot.

"Well, isn't this a surprise," she purred. She sauntered over to the bar and leaned on the brass rail, eyes fixed on me. "What are you doing here?"

"I'm looking for—"

Her fake smile dropped and she cut me off. "Oh, I know exactly who you're looking for. I told Hayden he'd get bored. I *told* him you wouldn't be able to handle him, and he didn't listen." She towered over me in her absurd heels. "He's so fucking pathetic. Always thinking he can be better than he is, but we both know that isn't true—don't we?"

"I-I don't—" I was stunned. He'd told me that his life was different, that *he* was different, prior to me, but I hadn't imagined anything like this.

"I-I don't. I-I," she mocked. "You're a waste of his time. Did you come here thinking I might give you some pointers on how to keep him interested?" She sounded bitter. "I can save you the trouble, sweetheart. There's nothing you can do. Hayden likes to keep his options open. He'll never be satisfied with you; it's just a matter of time before he comes running back to me."

It had been a long, difficult day and my nerves were already frayed. This was not what I needed. If I let my emotions get the better of me in front of her, I was liable to lose it.

"I shouldn't have come here," I said, backing up. "I'll go."

Sienna stepped to the side, trapping me between the bar and the wall. "You sure you don't want to have a look around? See what it's going to take to keep him for a while longer?"

"I should just leave." I swallowed hard as she came closer, penning me in.

She tilted her head to the side. "I don't get it. What does he see in you? Look at you." She picked up my ponytail and wrinkled her nose, then dragged a fake nail down my cheek.

I jerked my head away. "Don't touch me."

She caught me by the chin, holding on hard. We were in the shadows, covered by her entourage of security. She leaned in close, her mouth beside my ear. "You think you know Hayden, but you don't. When I discovered him, he was busy fucking his way through the girls in this club. Everybody wanted him and I was the only one he came back to, over and over again. I gave him what he needed, *any way* he needed it. You know what's going to happen when you can't keep up? He's going to come back to me. He always does."

"Let go of me." I pulled at her hand.

Her grip tightened, nails digging into my skin. "I'm feeling generous, so I'll give you a little tip. If Hayden starts to wander, there's one sure way to get his attention. Do you want to know what it is?"

When I didn't react, she said, "Just fuck Chris. That's what I did when I found Hayden fucking three other girls at the same time." Sienna let go of my face and stepped back. "Oh, you look shocked. You poor little thing. Didn't he tell you about that?"

"You manipulative whore," I whispered, stepping away from her.

"*What* did you just call me?"

I should have expected the backhand. I was a second too late when I raised my arm to deflect it, although I prevented the full force of the hit. As her nails raked across my cheek, my elbow connected with her nose. There was a satisfying crunch; she screeched an expletive and shoved me; and I went down. Unable to brace for the impact, I landed on my tailbone and my head smacked the black tile, starbursts obscuring my vision and sharp pain shooting through my hip. Her security detail intervened as she came after me again; a massive arm wrapped around her waist and hoisted her in the air as she kicked and screamed obscenities.

"Put me down! I'm going to fuck that bitch up!" Blood ran down her mouth and chin, dripping on her plastic dress. She was hauled back through the door she'd come out of, the security guy struggling to keep a solid grip on her.

I pushed up on weak arms. My hip was screaming; my head didn't feel much better. I gathered the scattered items on the floor and shoved them back in my purse, checking for my keys and wallet. Both were there. I could sense eyes on me even though the music was blaring and the girl on the stage was still gyrating away. If I weren't so focused on the pain in my body I would have been mortified.

I had to use the brass rail along the bar to pull myself up. It hurt so much, I tasted bile in the back of my throat. I looked around, searching for the exit.

When I finally found it, the bouncer who'd let me in was heading my way, eyes narrowed, hands clenched into fists. I looked around for another way out, but the emergency exit sign was all the way across the club.

I'd never make it.

6

HAYDEN

In was one in the morning. The TV was on but I wasn't watching it. I was staring at the series of pictures on my wall. All Tenley. All the time. My phone rang. "What?" I grunted, aggravated by the interruption.

"You need to get your ass over to The Dollhouse and clean up your mess."

"The fuck? Who is this?" I held out the phone and checked the screen. The number came up as unknown.

"It's Jay, dipshit. Your girl broke Sienna's nose."

"What the hell are you talking about?" Jay was head of security. We'd known each other for years and we didn't have any problems.

"Jesus. Don't you keep tabs on the bitches you're fucking?"

"Wait. What?"

"For the love of Christ, I thought you quit the blow. Your little china doll came here looking for you and got into it with Sienna.

Get your ass in gear and come get your girl before Sienna puts her in a ditch."

"You mean *Tenley?*"

"How the fuck should I know?" There was an irritated sigh. "Long black hair, tiny thing. Knows one of Sienna's girls, Sarah. Ring any bells?"

"That's not possible. She's not even in Chicago."

"I don't know where she *told* you she was, but right now she's in the damn club, and Sienna's on lockdown. You have ten minutes to get here."

The line went dead. I grabbed my keys and bolted down the stairs to the parking garage.

There was no way Tenley was back. I would know if she was. *Or maybe not.* She'd called twenty times today and I hadn't answered. She didn't leave a voice mail, and I was too pissed off for calling her early this morning to trust myself to talk to her again. Still, I assumed she would have texted if she was coming back. Even if she didn't, the news would pass through someone else.

I called Chris as I pulled out of the underground parking. It went straight to voice mail so I tried Sarah and got the same damn thing. It took me less than ten minutes to get to The Dollhouse. I drove right up to the front entrance and parked in the tow zone. I got out and locked the door.

Max said, "Stryker, man, you can't do that—"

"Jay called and asked me to pick something up. I'll only be a second."

"That little spitfire belongs to you?"

I stopped. "Shit. He wasn't fucking with me? Tenley's here?"

"Little, dark-haired thing? Sweet face with an ass to match?"

I wanted to grind his face into the side of the building for that comment, but he was twice my size. "I won't be long."

The smell of sweat and sex hit me when I walked through the

door. What sounded like heavy bass when I was outside became a crap dance beat inside. I surveyed the club, searching for Tenley among the suits and dirtbags. In the back corner, I saw a well-dressed businessman put his hands on a dancer.

Security stepped out of the shadows, prepared to shut the guy down. A wordless conversation took place between the guy on security detail and the dancer, then she stepped down off the couch and reached for the suit's hand. He followed her into the shadows. While security and the suit exchanged words, the dancer picked at her fingernails, looking bored. When the men were finished dealing, the suit and the dancer disappeared through a hidden door. Business as usual. The possibility that Tenley could have witnessed any of this made me ill.

I headed to the back of the club, where security guarded the hallway leading to Sienna's office. Jay had been working here longer than I'd frequented the establishment. He'd seen a lot of dancers come and go, and a lot of management, too.

"You called."

"Sienna's a little worked up over what your girl did to her face. It took a lot of persuading to keep her from dragging this one out back and tossing her in a Dumpster."

"Hayden?" Tenley said.

I closed my eyes briefly at the sound of her voice, then turned.

She looked terrified. She was tucked into the corner, sitting on a barstool with her hands in her lap. I didn't want her exposed to this place, seeing what went on here, coming to obvious conclusions about what I did when I was a regular patron.

"What the hell are you doing here?" I asked, anger replacing my relief at seeing her.

"I needed to find Sarah."

That Sarah would be the first person she sought out was just another kick in the balls. I bit back a bitter retort when the strobe lights hit her face, illuminating a trio of vicious red lines. I moved closer, lifted her chin, and tilted her head. Scratch marks ran from her temple to her mouth. Even still, the contact was as electric as it had always been.

"What happened?" I asked with more bite than I meant to.

"I had a chat with Sienna."

"She did this to you?" When Tenley nodded, I looked to Jay. "I want to talk to her."

"I don't think that's in your best interest."

"Tough shit. I want to know why the fuck I'm picking Tenley up with marks on her face."

"Well, Tenley's right here. I'm sure she can tell you."

"I want to hear it from Sienna. Tell her I'm here—I guarantee she'll want to see me." I was banking on her anger and her bitch tactics. She'd jump at the chance to try to fuck with my head because that was what she was good at.

"Maybe we should just go," Tenley said softly, sliding off the barstool.

"Not a chance," I snapped.

Tenley ignored me and shifted forward, wincing as her left foot hit the floor and then her right. When she took an unsteady step toward me, her knee buckled, and she latched onto the bar.

I grabbed her by the waist. "What the hell?" I shot Jay an irate glare.

Fights happened all the time at The Dollhouse. The girls got territorial over clients, drugs, whatever. But security never let it get far. After a couple of slaps they were hauled off each other. Messed-up faces and ripped-out extensions didn't make money.

Whatever had gone on between Tenley and Sienna, Jay had let it happen on purpose. Probably until Tenley defended herself. It pissed me off.

"I'm fine," Tenley said thinly, her fingers digging into my shoulders.

"Bullshit," I spat, annoyed she was lying.

She could hardly bear her own weight. I drew her closer until her entire body was pressed tight against mine. As angry as I was, I was too fucking needy to give a shit that she was only holding on to me because she'd drop like a stone otherwise. That ratcheted up my frustration even more.

I kept my arm fixed around her waist, feeling her gasps against my stomach as Tenley found her balance. She kept a hand on my forearm as she took a step back and struggled to put weight on her right leg.

"Sit down and don't move," I ordered, lifting her back onto the stool. She complied, which was pretty fucking atypical. She looked to be seconds away from tears. Rightfully so. Sienna was not a person Tenley should be messing with, nor were any of the other people who worked at or frequented The Dollhouse. At least here, in the shadows, she was safe from the lecherous stares of the douche bags in the club.

The standoff with Jay ended when Sienna burst through the door, which almost hit the side of his head. "Time's up, bitch—" Then she saw me.

Of the two women, Sienna was definitely the worse for wear. Her eyes already had shadows underneath and her nose was swollen. Her hands went to her hips and she pushed her chest out. She wore some horrific red pleather getup that was so short it barely covered her ass, and the front was so low her nipples were almost showing.

"Came here to collect your trash?" Sienna asked. It came out all garbled.

I stepped in front of Tenley, blocking her from Sienna's sight.

Sienna said, "You know, after that bitch fit you threw at Lisa's, I did what you asked. I backed off because you needed to do that stupid girl for whatever reason. But I sure as hell don't appreciate your toy coming to my club, talking smack to my face."

Tenley huffed from behind me but I ignored the commentary on my relationship with her. Sienna wanted to rile me up and it wasn't going to work. "What kind of smack?"

She gestured to Tenley. "That slut broke my fucking nose!"

I bristled at the pejorative. "Watch your fucking mouth."

"Your little plaything called me a whore!"

I kept my tone flat to avoid feeding into her dramatics. "So you thought you'd fight her?"

"She came in here and acted like she had you all figured out. She got what she deserved. I should have her arrested for assault." Sienna swiped under her swollen nose, where a thin trail of blood was making its way down to her lip. I was sure her coke habit didn't help the problem.

"So you're telling me Tenley hit you first?"

"You need to muzzle your bitch," Sienna hissed.

I leaned in and Jay shook his head in warning. I put up a hand in a show of submission. I wasn't stupid; he'd lay me out with one shot. "Answer the damn question. Did Tenley hit you first?"

"She came into my club!"

I'd heard enough. "You really are a piece of work." I started to turn away.

Sienna grabbed my arm, her nails digging into the skin as she pressed herself up against me. "Get your head out of your ass, honey," she said in my ear. "Her purity isn't going to rub off on you. Once the novelty wears off, you'll do what you always do. And then what will you have? Nothing."

"I'm not looking to purify myself. I'll own the shit I've done, but I don't have to end up like you. You keep falling into the same hole, wondering why, when you're the one holding the shovel. I hope you enjoy burying yourself."

"Fuck you!" Sienna shoved my chest. "Get out and take your skank with you!"

"Glass house, Sienna. Watch yourself."

"You asshole!" she screeched, grabbing for an empty glass on the bar, but Jay snagged her around the waist before she could reach it.

Tenley's eyes were wide as I hauled her out of the way. When Sienna went on a rampage, it meant lots of broken things, and sometimes that included people. Security swarmed her, keeping her from getting her hands on anything she could throw at me. She lived a sad life, and I was glad not to be part of it anymore.

I half carried Tenley across the club. When I burst through the front door, my car was being towed out of the parking lot.

"Fuck."

Max just gave me a look that said I should have known better.

"Where's your car?" I barked at Tenley.

"Over there." She pointed across the lot.

I headed in that direction, my arm around her waist. She was still having trouble walking without support. Her Prius was no-where in sight. "Where's—"

Tenley lifted a remote, a red BMW beeped, and the engine turned over.

"Whose douche mobile is this?"

"It was Connor's. It was my only way back home," she replied, looking up at me with sad eyes.

Well, wasn't I an asshole.

"Thanks for getting me out of there."

There was an awkward moment when I wanted to kiss her, but I realized she was waiting for me to let her go so she could get in the car. When I did, she dropped her head and started to hobble toward the driver's side.

I grabbed her hand with the keys in it. "Uh, yeah, you're not driving."

She passed the keys over without an argument, which told me

how much pain she was in. I helped her around to the passenger side. She had to lift her leg at the knee to get it into the car. I got in the driver's side, where I practically ate the steering wheel, the seat was pulled up so far.

The air in the car was thick with tension, and Tenley was quiet as I pulled out of the parking lot onto the street. I glanced at her every so often. I had too many questions I wanted answers to—about tonight, about the last three weeks, about the night she left.

Finally, the silence too much, I asked, "What the hell would make you think it was a good idea to come to The Dollhouse?"

"Sarah has the key to my apartment and she wasn't answering her phone. I figured she was working."

"I have a key to your apartment. I would have let you in. Then we could have avoided this shit."

"You weren't answering my calls. I wasn't sure you wanted to see me."

We were right back to the very beginning, when she was all skittish around me. What damage had Trey done while she was in Arden Hills? I had a feeling her time there had been pretty fucking horrific. Which meant I needed to stow the anger brigade and stop snapping at her.

"No matter what's happened between us, Tenley, you still could have come to me. I wouldn't have turned you away."

For whatever reason it was the wrong thing to say because her shoulders sagged and started shaking.

"Kitten?"

That made it worse. She pressed her hand over her mouth, but a sob slipped out. Thankfully, we were almost home. I pulled into the underground parking and cut the engine, flicking on the interior light so I could see her.

She was caved in on herself, the way she'd been after the first tattoo session. I smoothed my hand down her back. Like me, she'd lost weight. I could feel the prominent ridges of her spine through the layers of clothing. It scared me that she was more fragile than when she'd left.

She sucked in a couple of deep breaths, shuddering on the exhale. When she lifted her head, her emotions were under control again, but just barely. "I'm sorry. I didn't mean to get so upset."

"It's okay—dealing with Sienna would make anyone crack. Why don't you come up to my place? You'll never be able to handle the stairs to your apartment." I hoped the excuse would be enough to get her to agree. I had no idea where we stood, but I didn't want her to go.

"I want to see TK," she whispered.

"She's up there. She'll be happy you're home."

"TK's at your place?"

"I've been taking care of her while you were away."

"Oh." She sniffed, then swiped at her eyes with the back of her hand. "That's good. Thank you for doing that."

I shrugged. "I wanted to."

I got out of the car and came around to Tenley's side, where she was already hoisting herself out. If she was still having this much trouble tomorrow, I was taking her to the doctor for X-rays or something. Her lips were set in a thin line, which I took to mean she was in pain and wanted to hide it.

"You need anything from the trunk?" I asked.

She shook her head, so I locked up the douche mobile and we headed for the elevator. She kept looking over at the staircase. No way could she hike three flights to my condo with the way she was limping. I told her so.

"I don't like elevators," she said as the doors opened.

I wasn't partial either, but carrying her wasn't an option. "It's a quick ride."

She hesitated, but when I put my foot over the sensor to

prevent the doors from closing, she went inside. Tenley tucked herself into the corner, gripping the handrails that circled the mirrored steel box. I hit the button for the second floor, then put my arm around her. When we started to move, she latched onto me, burying her face in my chest with an apology. She had no reason to be sorry; the motion of the elevator probably mimicked the sensations of the plane when it dropped. And the windowless, confined space would worsen the vertigo.

I held on to her, stroking her hair, watching our entwined reflection in the mirrors surrounding us. When the elevator stopped and the doors slid open, Tenley practically pitched herself into the hall.

She'd only been to my place once, but she remembered where it was and started down the hall. I wouldn't make her wait until I'd checked all the rooms tonight, as I normally would; she needed to sit down immediately.

Inside, Tenley braced herself on the wall as she gingerly removed her shoes. I put them in the closet beside mine.

TK bounded down the hall and came to me, winding around my legs, peeking out at Tenley.

"Come here, baby girl," Tenley cooed as she melted into the floor.

TK cocked her little head to the side uncertainly and stayed close to me.

Tenley clicked her tongue against the roof of her mouth and snapped her fingers. The expression on her face was heartbreaking, as if she expected the snub.

I crouched down and scratched TK's head. "It's okay, little buddy, that's your mom. She went on a trip, but she's back now." TK mewed and peeked out from between my ankles. "That's right, go say hi. She missed you, just like we missed her."

TK trotted over and sniffed at Tenley's outstretched hand. It took TK a minute, but eventually she got close enough for Tenley to pick her up. The real crying started then. Silent sobs shook Tenley's body as she folded around the kitten.

I tried not to be jealous of a stupid cat, but it was difficult to not feel slighted that she got a more heartfelt greeting than I did. The only reason Tenley had touched me so far was because she needed my help, and the elevator freaked her out.

"I missed you so much. I'm sorry I was gone so long. I won't do it again, I promise." Her eyes lifted to meet mine, teary and bleak.

Maybe her words weren't just for TK, maybe they were meant for me, too. I wanted to believe that, but her disappearance and refusal to call made it impossible to trust her. Actions spoke louder than words. As glad as I was to have her home, I was still angry with her for leaving in the first place. *Conflicted* didn't begin to describe it.

I was also exhausted. It was almost three in the morning, and I hadn't slept much the past week, let alone the last three.

"Why don't you come to the living room? My couch is more comfortable than the floor. Besides, I want to take a look at the scratches on your face."

"You don't have to do that."

"Yes. I do. Now come." I put my hands under her arms and helped her to her feet while she cuddled TK to her chest.

She took in the surroundings as though she were seeing them for the first time. When we reached the living room, she sucked in a breath, her eyes on the new art adorning the walls.

I ran a hand through my hair, frustrated that my feelings for her were so apparent in the designs. "You want something to drink?"

"Please." She sank down into the corner of the couch and pulled her legs up, turning so she could see the pictures hanging above it.

"You want beer or wine? Or something stronger?"

"Stronger might be good."

I poured two glasses of scotch, resisting the urge to shoot mine and refill it immediately. I was pretty wound up and I had a lot of questions, but overwhelming her two minutes after she walked in the door—particularly after a showdown with Sienna—wouldn't be in either of our best interests.

I handed her a glass and Tenley took a tentative sip. Her nose scrunched up in disgust.

"You don't like it?" I asked, holding back a grin.

"It's fine." She took another sip, but her lips puckered as she swallowed.

"Don't be a martyr. I'd rather you not force it down to be polite."

"Sorry." She passed me the drink, and I poured the contents into my glass.

"It's an acquired taste. I'll get you something else." I stood up. "And I want to take care of those scratches."

"Okay."

She was so timid sitting there on my couch, curled up in a little ball, all the fire stolen out of her. I wanted the old Tenley back, the one who was frisky and snide. I poured her a glass of red and left her with TK sprawled over her lap.

I retrieved the first-aid kit from my bathroom, then wetted a facecloth with scalding water and wrung it out. By the time I got back to the living room, it would be cool enough to wipe her scratches.

"Let's check the damage." I sat beside her, getting in close so I could have a good look at what was done to her face.

"It doesn't feel bad," Tenley said softly, setting her wine on the coffee table.

The sleeve of her hoodie shifted with the movement, exposing part of her forearm. There were marks there, too. I took her hand and pushed the sleeve back. She flinched, even with the gentle contact. The bruises were old, faded to greenish yellow, wrapping all the way around her wrist. Like a manacle.

"Where did these come from?"

"They're nothing." She kept her eyes down as she pulled her sleeve over her wrist.

"Don't bullshit me."

She recoiled, and when she looked up, I could see her trepidation. She swallowed and clasped her hands. "Trey got a little aggressive."

"Aggressive how?" My imagination threw out all sorts of scenarios, and all of them made me want to run him over with my car. Repeatedly.

"He grabbed my wrist harder than he should have. It wasn't intentional, and I bruise easily."

"Are you making excuses for that cocksucker?" I asked, incredulous.

"No. You asked what happened, and I'm telling you."

She was still too timid. I didn't like it, and her explanation had a lot of holes. "Did he leave any more marks?"

She shook her head. "Just the ones on my wrist. Do you want to look at my cheek now?"

I let it go. For now. While I inspected the scratches, she sat perfectly still, the model patient. It reminded of when I put that little cupcake tattoo on her, an inch to the left of her kitty.

I tilted her chin up and angled her head. She shifted closer, and her shin pressed against the outside of my thigh. Her hand came to rest on my knee. I jerked at the contact, and she pulled away. I wanted to reach over and put her hand back, but didn't.

"Sienna has sharp nails," I said. She'd raked them over my skin more than once.

In a couple of places, blood had welled and dried. The paranoid side of me wanted a doctor to check for tetanus and worse, but no bodily fluids had been passed—so Tenley was probably safe.

I hated that my past was the cause of this; Tenley had already dealt with enough. We both had. This wasn't how I'd envisioned her return. I ran my fingers gently along her cheek, and she jumped.

"Does that hurt?" I asked, worried.

"No." It came out a little breathless.

I dabbed at the scratches with the facecloth, wiping the blood away. Then I sprayed them with disinfectant and used a Q-tip to apply antibiotic ointment.

When I was done, Tenley shifted to the side, hissing at the movement.

"You need to get your hip checked out—it's a mess."

"It's just achy."

"Don't lie to me. It pisses me the fuck off."

She shied away, which was understandable. I was irritated and taking it out on her. So much for sidelining the anger.

I slid my arms around her, pulling her against me. Her back hit my chest and I dropped my forehead on her shoulder. "You don't have to front if you're in pain. It doesn't help either of us. Just let me take care of you."

The stiffness in her body eased, and I closed my eyes as her fingers drifted along the back of my hand to my forearm. God, I missed the way it felt to be close to her; to touch her, to be touched by her. Up, up, up her hand went; over my biceps, my shoulder, my neck, until it reached my hair, sliding through the strands. I lifted my head, my nose skimming her collarbone. I barely resisted the urge to follow with my mouth. We had too much to talk about to go there yet.

She turned into me. "I missed you."

Her palm rested against my cheek and she urged my head up higher. Her mouth was right there.

She was the one who leaned in.

She was the one who drew me closer.

Her lips pressed against mine. She tasted just as I remembered . . . but it wasn't the same.

7

TENLEY

What I was doing to Hayden wasn't fair. I owed him a conversation in which I allowed him his anger. One where I accepted responsibility for leaving without an explanation. But it had been weeks since I'd felt anything good at all. His arms around me gave me the first true grounding since my return to Arden Hills.

So I kissed him. With a noise somewhere between despondency and acute need he dragged me closer, crushing me against him. TK's little claws dug into my thighs as she jumped off my lap; she mewed at being displaced onto the floor. The ache in my hip flared as I moved to achieve more bodily contact, but I ignored it.

I might have started the kiss, but Hayden took control of it. I quickly found myself laid out on the couch, Hayden hovering over me, one leg working its way between mine. His mouth was hard, those steel rings biting into my lip. One hand went to my hair, gripping it so he could control the angle.

I needed the connection, physical and otherwise. The glorious weight of his body settled over me; his erection pressed against my hip and I moaned. With one hand firmly on the back of his neck to keep him close, the other traveled down to the dip in his spine.

I slid my palm beneath the waistband of his jeans and met bare skin. No boxers barred the contact. I dug my fingernails in the soft skin over hard muscle and pushed down. Familiar warmth rushed through my limbs and funneled straight between my thighs. He tensed and I held on tighter, terrified of what was coming. I was desperate for him, and he was going to stop this. I could tell in the way he slowed the kiss.

"Fuck." Hayden scrambled away from me. "We can't be doing that."

"It's okay." I sat up and reached out for him.

Hayden shot off the couch and grabbed his scotch. "No, it's not okay. We have shit we need to work out, and that kind of business isn't going to help a damn thing."

He was right, of course. Not that I would say it outright.

"I know you're angry with me." I touched my lips. They were still wet.

"Angry? You have no idea what the past three weeks have been like for me." He headed for the kitchen, putting distance between us.

"Yes, I do." At least I could imagine.

We'd been in a similar situation before, I realized. After the engagement party at Lisa and Jamie's, when I found him in the bathroom with Sienna and that other woman. One of us putting up walls for protection; the other looking for a way in. This time I was the one seeking forgiveness, while Hayden donned his armor.

His hand came down on the counter with a heavy thud. "No. You don't. You left me—not the other way around. So don't tell me you know, because you don't. It fucking ruined me."

"Do you think it didn't hurt to leave?"

"Oh, yeah, it must have torn you right up. So much that you didn't even bother to call. Not *me*, anyway. Not once."

This was what I had been expecting; the anger, the hurt. "I couldn't call you."

"Why not? Trey wouldn't have approved? Did he chain you up in a cell and refuse to give you access to a phone? Or were you only allowed to have contact with your girlfriends? That must have been it: only the degenerate was off-limits."

"That wasn't it. If I'd talked to you, I never would have stayed."

"And would it have been so bad, to come back here and be with me? How stupid do think I felt after I went to Arden Hills to bring you home, only to have you shut me out completely?"

"What? You came to Arden Hills? When?" I asked, stunned.

"The night you took off, I came after you. Trey wouldn't even come to the door. Just threatened me through the goddamn intercom and called the fucking police."

"Oh my God. I didn't know, Hayden. He never told me." The first two days had been the worst. I'd locked myself in Connor's old bedroom and cried until I didn't have any tears left.

"*I* would have told you—if you'd bothered to return one of my fucking phone calls. But you didn't. Not even once. I don't get it. I don't even understand why you wanted to be there in the first place. Especially with that asshole lording over you. I would have helped you find a lawyer to deal with things here, if you'd let me."

"It wasn't that simple. There were things I had to take care of."

"Everyone is gone; you could have dealt with it from here!" Hayden yelled.

At this verbal slap in the face, I closed my eyes against the pain. When I opened them again, I could see his regret, but the words were out and he couldn't take them back.

"I know they're gone, Hayden. I live with it every day." I got up. He left the kitchen, barricading me between the couch and coffee table. "I'm sorry, that was a dickhead thing to say. I didn't mean it. I'm just trying to understand. The last time we were together, we were closer than we've ever been. When Trey showed up, you let him shit all over what we had. Then you pretty much backed him up when you told me to leave and disappeared for three weeks. I'm confused. I want you here, but I'm just so—"

He stopped, unable to get the rest out. I could see his conflict; fear overriding everything. As though what he wanted to say would make me disappear again.

I hadn't given him any reason to think otherwise. As far as he knew, I was only here to pick up TK. I'd thought the kiss would show him what I wanted, but of course it hadn't. Because last time, I'd told him how I felt about him and then left.

"You have every right to be upset with me for what I've done," I said. He looked so wary. "I didn't think there was any other way than to leave with Trey. The anniversary of the crash was less than two weeks ago, and there was a memorial service. I lost my whole family; I needed to go. But you're right—I should have called to explain. I wish I had." I took a step toward him and he took one back.

"*I* called *you*. All you had to do was answer."

"Like I said, if I had I would have come right home. Going back to Arden Hills wasn't just about settling the estate. Trey's showing up made all the wounds fresh again. He's always been good at capitalizing on my weaknesses, particularly my guilt over what happened." I summoned the courage to confess the most difficult part. "I felt responsible for all of it. I had such cold feet about the wedding. I thought it was normal to have reservations, but then . . ." My voice cracked, and I had to take a deep breath before I could go on. "All those deaths—they sat on my shoulders. I had to make peace with that, Hayden. Otherwise I would have come back here with the same ghosts haunting me. And then where would we be?"

"I wish I had known some of this before you left me."

There it was again—the phrase that made my heart ache, as though my departure had been about his abandonment. For him, that was exactly what had happened. "And I wish I'd been strong enough to tell you. But I wasn't—and I'm so sorry for that."

"Yeah. Me, too." He exhaled heavily. "Look, this is a lot to process and I'm . . . a little overwhelmed and tired. You must be wiped from the drive and that shit with Sienna, and this." He motioned between us. "So maybe it's best if we get some sleep. I don't want to say anything else I might regret."

"Okay." I swallowed the lump in my throat. I didn't have the right to be disappointed. "If I can borrow the key to my place . . ."

"What? Why?"

"Because you want to go to bed."

"Yeah, but I don't want you to leave." He cleared his throat. "Besides, you're limping and you're not getting back in that elevator, so you might as well stay here."

My heart leapt. "I'll sleep out here on the couch." It was comfortable enough. Although not nearly as comfortable as Hayden's bed and Hayden's warm body.

He frowned. Ran a hand through his hair. "Uh—that's not necessary. I've got a spare room."

My spark of hope was doused with disappointment. The last time I was here, he'd said that no one had ever seen his bedroom, let alone slept in it. He wouldn't ask for intimacy with me now. Too much had changed. I followed him down the hall and he stopped at a door I hadn't noticed during my previous visit.

He flipped on the lights. A desk was in one corner with a filing cabinet beside it, and a double bed was against the far wall. Just like every other room in his house, it was immaculate. The covers were pulled up tight. If I checked, I was sure the sheets would be tucked in hospital style. Beside the bed was a nightstand with a small lamp.

The clock read 4:14 A.M. I'd been awake for almost twenty-four hours. My body and my mind were spent; I was functioning on pure adrenaline. When it ran out, I would crash hard.

"I'll get you a toothbrush and something to sleep in." Hayden went down the hall and disappeared into his bedroom.

I sat on the edge of the bed and ran my hand over the red comforter. The sheets were dark gray, the walls were paper white.

He came back with an armload of clothes and a toothbrush still in its package. "I wasn't sure what you'd want, so I brought options." He set the clothes on the edge of the bed. "There's a bathroom down the hall to the left. If you need anything, you know where to find me."

"Thanks for letting me stay."

"I'm just glad you're home. I'll see you in the morning." He leaned over, kissed the top of my head, and ran his fingers through my ponytail.

After he left, I sorted through the clothes. The drawstring pants might have fit him but would be enormous on me. There were two shirts, one short sleeved and one long, as well as a pair of boxer briefs. I shed my clothes, glad to be out of them. Part of me wanted to jump in the shower, but it was approaching dawn. It would have to wait until later, after sleep.

The long-sleeved shirt fell below my butt. The boxer briefs, while too large at the waist, were manageable as long as I rolled them over a couple of times to keep them up.

My hip still ached, partially from being manhandled by Sienna, but also because of the long drive. It didn't hurt nearly as much as when Hayden first picked me up from The Dollhouse, but it was still uncomfortable enough to make me limp. I rooted around in the pocket of my discarded jeans and found the travel Tylenol I carried at all times.

My teeth felt fuzzy, as if they were wearing sweaters, so I

headed to the bathroom. I found the toothpaste in the medicine cabinet, brushed my teeth, and rinsed with mouthwash even though I wasn't going to need fresh breath tonight.

Hand towels and washcloths were in the top drawer of the vanity. I ran a washcloth under hot water and washed my face, careful to avoid the scratches Hayden had cleaned. Since a shower wasn't an option, I leaned against the edge of the sink and dragged the washcloth down my legs, the damp warmth pleasant.

There was a knock on the door and I called for Hayden to open it. He stood at the threshold with a pile of towels in one hand, a glass of water in the other. He wore pajama pants and nothing else. Usually he slept naked, so the pants were for my benefit and his discretion.

His eyes moved from my face down my body and back up. Then down. And back up.

"I thought you might want these in case you're up before me. Unless you decide you'd rather shower at your own place, but I'll leave them here so you have the choice." He passed the towels over. "And I figured you might want a glass of water in case you got thirsty." He passed that over, too.

"Thanks." Hayden was obviously flustered. Seeing him like that made me want to laugh or cry, maybe both.

He rubbed the back of his neck, blinked a few times. "You picked the shorts."

"The pants were too long. These are a little big, too. I'll probably ditch them when I go to bed," I said, not considering the implications.

His body was beautiful. The black lines of the phoenix came to an abrupt end just beyond the center of his broad chest. Then after a blank expanse of skin, a burst of color began at his shoulder and traveled down his right arm. The two halves of a whole. Although Hayden wasn't so simple as to have a light and a dark side. Both sides espoused the dichotomy that he embodied; the bleeding heart on his forearm was wrapped in flowering vines, cracked on one side, blooming on the other. The koi traveling along his arm fought its way upstream. The lilies floating on the water changed from white and pink to dark purple, half-wilted by the time they reached his shoulder. Hayden's dark and light sides merged, flowing into each other.

Tonight was the first time I truly saw how divided he was, and how much he battled to embrace the light. I had a feeling the tattoos on his back were a reflection of how dark he could get. One in particular was rather eerie, but whenever I'd asked to see it up close, he'd distracted me with other activities.

He'd lost weight while I was gone. Probably a good ten pounds, or more. The six-pack he sported was more pronounced, and a hint of bone was at his hips instead of layers of defined muscle covered with ink. His waist was narrower; his pants hung low to the point of obscenity. I gawked shamelessly.

He lowered a hand from the doorjamb to cover the problem that was rising below the waist. "I, ah—I'm gonna go now. To bed."

"If that's what you think is best."

I yearned to reach out and trace the lines of the phoenix. Particularly where it circled the glint of metallic black piercing his nipple. And lower, where it disappeared under the waistband of his pants. He'd already shut me down once, though; I wasn't about to try again. His hesitation was understandable.

"Yeah." Hayden took a step back. "Bed is good."

"I'll see you in the morning, then." I rolled up the waistband of my shorts once more for good measure.

"Uh-huh." He nodded, eyes on my legs. "Unless you need me." He gave his head a shake. "Something. Unless you need something. I'm just a few steps away."

He turned and headed down the hall. I got a glimpse of the tattoo on his right shoulder, the one I hadn't seen up close before. It looked like a child swaddled in a blanket, but its eyes were terrifying—ancient, evil, full of despair.

He looked over his shoulder when he reached his bedroom door. "Night, Tenley."

"Night." I smiled weakly. I wanted an invitation into his bed, even if it was just for sleeping. I craved the feel of his body close to mine. It was hard to be in his space and not next to him, yet it was just, considering what I'd put him through.

He went into his room, leaving the door ajar. TK came scampering down the hall and paused at my feet, rubbed herself against my leg, then trotted to Hayden's bedroom. All of the things that had been mine weren't anymore.

I heard him talking to her and considered the possibility that I might not have the right to take TK back. I'd been so neglectful of both of them. A few seconds later the light went out, and I was alone.

I left the towels on the vanity and took the glass of water with me to the spare room. Turning the covers down, I slipped between the cold sheets. I didn't think I'd be able to sleep with Hayden so close and unreachable, but fatigue settled in, dragging me under.

A shout startled me awake. Disorientation incited panic, until I remembered I was in Hayden's condo, sleeping in his spare bedroom. It was 7:00 A.M., which would have been a reasonable time to get up if I hadn't gone to bed just two hours earlier. Another sound came from down the hall, the pitch low and masculine.

I slipped out of bed, testing my right leg before I put too much weight on it. It was still sore, but the Tylenol made it more manageable. I stole down the hall, the dim light from the bathroom the only illumination.

I silently pushed open the door. Hayden's sheets were twisted around him, pillows scattered on the floor. His body was covered in a sheen of sweat despite the chilled air. TK was sitting on the floor, her fur standing on end. Hayden flailed and moaned plaintively. Words tumbled out of his mouth as he thrashed in the sheets, the grip of the nightmare too tight to escape from.

I hurried to the bed and climbed up beside him. I called his name quietly at first, then louder, until I had to yell. But he remained stuck inside his head. Out of options, I put a hand on his shoulder and gave him a tentative shake, and another, and another.

He sat up with a start. His eyes darted aimlessly, scanning the room but not truly tracking. His gaze came to rest on me; wild and panicked. "Tenley?"

"It's okay. I'm right here. It was just a dream." I pushed his hair off his forehead.

Hayden caught my hands in his and brought them to his mouth, lips moving over my knuckles. He made a deep sound in the back of his throat, a hybrid of despair and relief. Then he started checking me over, patting me down. His hand smoothed over my chest and he looked at his palms, then he repeated the action, rambling about blood.

He found the hem of my shirt and his hand went underneath. His palm slid over my stomach and between my breasts, searching for something. Unsatisfied with what he found, he tugged my shirt over my head. His palm flattened against the center of my chest.

"It's not there." He looked over my shoulder, smoothing his hand down my back.

"What's not there?"

"The bullet. There's no bullet."

"I'm fine, Hayden." I put my hand over his and moved it higher. "See? I'm fine, there's nothing there. It was a dream."

"Nothing. There's nothing. There's no blood." His breath left him in harsh pants.

Hayden enveloped me in a grip that made it hard to breathe. I rubbed slow circles on his back to comfort him, resting my chin on his shoulder. Lowering my face, I kissed his overheated skin. It was damp and salty with sweat.

"Please don't leave me. Not again. Please. It hurts too much to be without you. I don't know how. I don't—" He murmured pleas until he was too frantic to speak. His vulnerability was a shock.

"I'm here. I'm not going anywhere," I said, seeking to reassure him.

Cassie had been right; he was more fragile than I would ever have thought.

When his breathing finally slowed and his grip loosened, I urged him back under the covers. He went willingly. I drew them up over both of us and he curled himself around me. He pushed his forehead against my neck and got as close as he could, almost blanketing my body with his. His hand kept up a slow stroking. He returned to the center of my chest each time, making sure I was whole.

"It's always the same dream. I can't get to you in time and then you're gone, and there's nothing I can do to stop the emptiness."

Like mine, his nightmare seemed like facets of his past twined with the present. His parents had been murdered. If his subconscious had replaced them with me, my abandoning him was the catalyst for these dreams.

"I'm right here with you, Hayden. Everything's okay now." I held him close.

Eventually his hand came to rest on my sternum, his nose pressed right into my throat. His breathing evened out and the tension left his body, but he kept his arm locked around me, as if I'd disappear if he let go.

8

HAYDEN

My face was warm, damp. A rhythmic thump-whooshing lulled me into tranquillity. My cheek was resting on a chest, which explained the sweaty face. The thump-whoosh was the heart beating in the body I was wrapped around.

I opened my eyes. Tenley was in my bed. For the briefest moment I wondered if the last three weeks had been an incredibly shitty dream. But the scratches on her cheek told me the hell I'd lived was real.

She'd come back. Finally. Unfortunately, we didn't have one of those reunions filled with sunshine and rainbows. Instead it was former strippers and catfights.

I still didn't understand how she'd ended up in my bed, acting as my pillow. Going by the feel of things, she was completely naked. Not a good thing for her to be when I was sporting a hardcore case of morning wood and we needed to have a serious talk. The impulse to whack off had deserted me the night Tenley left

Chicago, but seeing her in my shirt and boxers last night had re-
suscitated my comatose dick. I hadn't been in any frame of mind to
manage myself, so I'd bolted. Plus her hip was obviously sore. Sex
would have made it worse.

Tenley made a little chuffing sound, which meant she was
waking. Then she stretched, her limbs vibrating. I'd missed this,
more than I wanted to admit. My emotions made me weak, and
my anger flared. Being pissed didn't deflate my hard-on, though.
It had the opposite effect. I rolled onto my back to get a little
space, and maybe some perspective, because I had no idea how
to proceed. My brain and my body wanted two very different
things.

Tenley didn't make it any easier when she threw her leg over
mine, her naked body coming up against me. She hadn't been joking about losing the shorts. I could feel every part of her, including
that sweet, hot place pressed firmly against my thigh. She snuggled
in closer, unaware, and her hand moved down my chest. I caught it
before it reached my navel.

She lifted her head, blinking sleepily. "Hi." Her voice was all
sultry rasp.

My dick reacted by jumping, stupid appendage that it was,
excited for something it had no business wanting. She shifted, her
bare breasts brushing my arm, and I tensed at the overload of sensation. I fought the desire to roll over, wedge myself between her
thighs, and take what I wanted; to just get inside her so I could feel
that connection again.

"How'd you end up in here?" I asked.

She took in her surroundings, confused. Our compromising
position must have registered, because she was suddenly alert. I let
go of her hand and she sat up. The covers dropped. The first thing
I noticed was the too-prominent jut of her collarbones. The slight
bounce of her perfectly luscious breasts distracted me, though.

The temperature change became evident as her skin pebbled, her nipples tightening. Those little, jeweled barbells winked, spotlit and waiting for my mouth or hands. I looked away.

Tenley quickly gathered the covers and pulled them up to her neck. "You had a nightmare. You don't remember?"

I shook my head.

"I'm not sure you were very lucid. You, ah, took off my shirt. You were checking for something. A wound, I think?" The sheets rustled, with a whisper of fabric moving against skin.

I glanced at her. She had covered her nakedness with the black shirt from last night. "Did we—"

"No. It wasn't anything like that. You were upset from the nightmare. I stayed until you calmed down and then we both fell asleep. Nothing else happened."

I couldn't imagine not remembering sex with Tenley. "Good, that's good—"

Like the snap of an elastic band, the nightmare returned in a slide show of horrific images. It was the one that troubled me most these days, where she bled out from a bullet wound to the chest. Except last night the satin sheath had been black instead of white, so I couldn't see the blood leaking out of her.

The memory of the dream must have registered in my expression because her head dropped. Her hair swept forward, shielding her face. She twisted her fingers in her lap, and tears fell onto the gray comforter. They sat on the surface for a few prolonged seconds before they soaked in, turning the fabric almost black. "I'm so sorry I hurt you," she whispered.

"I believe you."

Unable to stop myself, I lifted her chin so I could see her face. Her fears matched mine. I wanted to go back to the way things were before she left, but so much had happened. We had to establish a new balance, and that would take time.

I rolled onto my side to face her. "Want to tell me what happened last night with Sienna?"

"I left Arden Hills in a rush. I called Sarah when I was on the road to let her know I was on my way. I just wanted to be home. Anyway, she didn't pick up, so I left a voice mail. I stopped at the apartment, but her car wasn't there—"

"You were right across the street and you didn't shoot me a message?"

"I wanted to, but you hadn't answered my calls and I wasn't ready—"

"You've been gone for three fucking weeks. How much more ready do you need to be?"

"I know how it sounds—but I'd been up since you called yesterday morning, and it was late when I got here. I wanted to see you, but I was tired and emotional. I thought it would be better for both of us if I didn't show up in the middle of the night."

I could see her point, but it still hurt. "So that's how you ended up at The Dollhouse."

"My plan was to get the key and leave. When I mentioned I knew Sarah, the bouncer took that to mean I wanted a job and let me inside. If I'd known Sienna was the manager, though, I wouldn't have gone in. They took me to see her, and obviously she recognized me. She said some things I didn't like, and I did the same. When she got aggressive, I defended myself."

I was proud of Tenley for taking on someone like Sienna. It was reckless, but ballsy. "What exactly did she say?"

Her eyes shifted away. "That I couldn't handle you. That you'd get bored and go back to her."

Typical Sienna. "That's bullshit. I'd rather fuck a cactus. So I'm guessing whatever your reply was, she didn't like it."

"Not so much."

"What did you say to piss her off?"

Tenley's cheeks flushed. "It's not important."

I arched a brow and stared her down. "Oh, no? I'm going to disagree with you on that, considering the state of your face."

She relented with a heavy sigh. "I called her a whore. That's when she got aggressive."

Tenley was leaving something out. I could tell by her lack of eye contact and how fidgety she was. "What else did she say to you?"

"Nothing much. She just wanted a reaction. You said yourself that she likes to lie."

I shifted closer so Tenley couldn't hide her face and slid my hand along the side of her neck. Her pulse was hammering against my palm. I skimmed her jaw with my thumb, back and forth. She leaned into the contact. "What else, Tenley?"

"She told me why she slept with Chris."

My stomach sank. I covered my panic with sarcasm. "Oh? And what was her convoluted logic?"

"She said she did it to get your attention."

"Well, wasn't that clever of her," I replied derisively. Sienna's version of the events was undoubtedly highly modified, with all the important parts left out. The situation that had led to Sienna's getting into Chris's pants had been an epic clusterfuck. I should have known I'd have to deal with this shit sooner or later; there were too many lingering connections with the people from my past. But to have a discussion like this on the first day Tenley came home? My black cloud of doom just kept expanding, submerging me in toxic emotional waste.

"She said you—" Tenley chewed on her lip. Shook her head. "Never mind. It doesn't matter."

"It sure as fuck *does* matter. What did she say about me?" Sienna had clearly told Tenley more than I would have.

"Can't we just let this go for now? I know you're upset I went to The Dollhouse, but it's done. What Sienna said is irrelevant."

I scrubbed my hand over my face, annoyed. Frustrated. "Don't do that. I want to know what she said so I can either defend myself or explain." I sighed. "I won't downplay events, Tenley. I'll tell you whatever you want to know. I think we're past pretending our omissions don't have an impact on either of us." When she remained silent, I needled her, "Did she tell you about the four-way?"

"I-I . . . It—it d-doesn't—"

"I'll take that as a yes. Are you going to lie and tell me you're cool with that? It doesn't look like you are. In fact, you look a little nauseous. Are you *sure* it doesn't matter?"

She fiddled with the edge of the comforter. "Of course I'm not cool with it. But there's nothing I can do to change it, and neither can you. Why are you pushing me like this?"

"Because I'm still *pissed*, Tenley!" My anger at Sienna, at Tenley, and myself suddenly combined into one big need for a fight. "You up and *ran*, with no explanation, for almost a fucking *month*! How could you do that to me?"

She was silent for a minute. Then she said, "You're right. I ran. I admit it." She took a deep breath. "I was terrified of what I had with you, Hayden—and not just because of how much I'd already lost."

That got my attention. "Why, then?" I asked more quietly.

"Because it made my relationship with Connor feel like a fucking farce. The way I feel about you? I never felt *anything* like that for him. Maybe I could have been happy with him, but I'll never know, because he's dead.

"And that's my fault. I'm the one who wanted the destination wedding. Do you have any idea how difficult it is to reconcile the reality that I never would have met you if my whole family wasn't dead? I'm not justifying my running. I'm just telling you why I did."

Well, that showered me with a monsoon of perspective. Trey's appearance would have brought all her guilt to the forefront. And the memorial service and the estate gave her the perfect escape. It would have been extremely difficult to handle.

I sighed. "I can understand why you went. But I still wish we could have talked it out before. The last three weeks were shitty."

"And I'm sorry for that. It was the same for me. I'd change it if I could."

"How do I know you won't do it again? How am I supposed to trust you after this?"

Her gaze dropped; when she looked up, her eyes were shiny with unshed tears. "The only way is time, I guess. Will you give me that? I'm sure you have more questions, and I'll answer them all if it will help. I'll do whatever you need me to—even if it means giving you space."

This was way more difficult than I expected it to be. "No thanks on the space. I've had enough of that—but I don't think we can just pick things up where we left off."

"I'm inclined to agree. So where does that leave us?"

"I have no idea. This isn't something I've done before."

"Me either. Not really, anyway." She ducked her head.

"Is there a story behind that?"

"Yes. But the ending isn't very nice."

So it had to do with Connor. "You planning to tell it anyway?"

"Do you want me to?"

I wasn't so sure now was the best time. "Maybe later."

Her shoulders sagged with relief. "Okay. What now, then?"

I glanced at the clock. It was almost noon. "I've got to go to work in an hour, but we could go somewhere and get breakfast first."

"You'd want that?" She gave me that shy, little smile I liked so much.

"Yeah. I'm gonna shower first, though."

"I should probably do the same."

It was on the tip of my tongue to ask her to join me, but then I figured it might not be the best idea. Showering included nudity, which would inevitably lead to sex. While I wanted that with a desperation that bordered on pathetic, it wasn't smart. It would feel good, fantastic even, but my head was already too mixed up.

Getting to the shower without Tenley's noticing my massive hard-on was going to be an epic feat, though.

"Wait." Tenley grabbed my arm as I threw one leg over the side of the bed.

"Yeah?"

"Maybe I could—"

"I don't think—"

Her intentions were obvious. "I just want—"

"—it's a good idea—"

"—to kiss you."

She didn't give me a chance to argue. Her hands smoothed over my shoulders and up the sides of my neck. Her touch was exactly the balm I craved, and I loathed my weakness for her. When she leaned in, I gave her my cheek.

She dropped her hands and sat back on her heels, looking at me with sad longing. "You don't want to kiss me?"

"I didn't say that."

"It's just a kiss. I'm not expecting more."

She made it sound so innocent, but I knew better. Last night when she'd kissed me, I ended up dry-humping her. And we both had more clothing on then. "We're in my bed and you're only wearing a shirt. You may not have expectations, but I don't have much in the way of restraint right now."

"You don't need to restrain yourself for my benefit."

"I'm still mad at you." There was no point in denying it.

"I know." Her fingers drifted along my jaw. "And I understand if you can't forgive me yet."

"It's probably going to take a while."

"I expect so." She leaned in again, slowly, until she was only an inch away from my mouth.

I regarded her with wary anticipation. "Making out isn't going to fix things."

"No, but it might help alleviate some of the tension."

Her lips touched mine. She met no resistance so she did it again, going to the left side, to the viper bites.

"I missed your mouth," she said, nipping her way along.

I groaned in response and she tilted her head to the side, her tongue flicking across the seam of my mouth, a tentative request for access. One hand left my neck and glided down my arm. She stroked along my fingers until they unfurled from the fist I was making.

"It's okay to touch me," she said.

"It's really not a good idea," I muttered.

She ignored me, though, and moved my not-so-reluctant palm to her hip. I gripped the shirt and it bunched tight, conforming to the dip in her waist and the swell of her breasts. It didn't at all help my conviction to postpone sexual gratification. Until maybe tonight. After I had the day to process all the shit we'd talked about in the past twelve hours.

"I missed the way you taste." Her tongue pressed forward, all soft exploration and warm, languid sweeps.

Conflicted though I might be, my body was all for getting close to her. And the closer the better, as far as my dick was concerned. My brain appeared to have migrated south and didn't see any problem with where we were headed.

Tenley's hands were on the move again. The one against my neck slid higher into my hair. Her fingers curled and tugged, angling my head to the side. The other one went on a tour over my forearm, up my biceps to my shoulder, then down my chest. She paused at the barbell, her index finger drawing circles before she continued her downward trajectory. The descent stopped at the waistband, where she started tracing the perimeter, back and forth, over and over.

I tensed when her fingers dipped past the elastic barrier, so fucking close to the head of my cock. Contact from the waist up was manageable; anything below and I was liable to drop the pretense of civility. "I thought you didn't expect more."

Her fingers stilled. "Do you want me to stop touching you?"

"I don't know." Which was a stupid thing to say because I sure as hell didn't want her to stop. Not one little fucking bit.

She retracted her fingers and settled her palm on my chest, pushing me down on the bed. Her hair fanned out over my chest, tickling the skin as she kept up with the kissing, teasing soft nips interspersed with mind-bending strokes of tongue. Eventually I snaked my hand around the back of her neck and drew her closer.

She shifted around, bracing her weight on one arm, then she started up with the touching again. And stupid fucking me soaked it up. I'd been deprived for too long. The slow progression from my arm to my shoulder, over my chest down to the waistband, and then back up was infuriating. My hips shifted of their own accord, seeking what I was denying us both. She brushed my erection through the fabric.

And I snapped.

In a smooth surge, I wound an arm around her waist and rolled on top of her, settling between her thighs. Even through the thin cotton I could feel the heat and wetness, welcoming me home. I fumbled with the hem of her shirt and yanked it up. She started to pull it over her head, but I swatted her hands out of the way. She might have started this, but I was going to finish it.

Fuck waiting. Fuck necessary conversations. Fuck getting the answers. I ran my palms heavily along her ribs, to the soft swell of her breasts. The barbells were fully healed now, so there was no need to be gentle. I dropped my head and sucked the taut skin into my mouth. Her hands went to my hair, pulling me closer as she arched under me. I bit down, probably harder than I should have, and she gasped.

"I told you it wasn't a good idea, but you didn't listen, did you?" I was rerouting the anger into sexual aggression. I shifted in the cradle of her hips; my erection nestled right where I wanted it.

"I'm sorry. I missed you." Her hands moved down my back and under the waistband, nails digging into my ass.

"Then you should have come back sooner."

"I wanted to."

"I don't want lip service. You shouldn't have left me here without any fucking clue as to why you were gone. You should have done something about it."

"Then let me show you." Tenley tried to slip a hand between us and get to my cock.

"Oh, no, you don't." I threaded my fingers through hers and brought her arm up over her head, pinning it to the bed, and did the same with the other one, clasping them together with one hand so I had the other one free. "I'll give it to you when I'm damn good and ready."

With a quick shove I pushed my pants down to free my aching erection. Then I shifted my hips back, my cock sliding along her slick skin. I kept it up for a long time, until she was panting and moaning. Every time she got close to an orgasm, I stopped. Then I resumed the slow glide until I was on the verge of coming myself. I slid lower, the head nudging past her entrance. I stopped.

"Please, Hayden." Her eyes were glassy, her cheeks flushed. She struggled against the hold I had on her hands.

"Please what?" I asked tightly.

"I *need* you. Please." Some of the heat in her gaze evaporated.

"I never stopped wanting you while I was gone. I just didn't think I deserved you."

Relief replaced the near-violent fear that had settled under my skin. Her admission made me powerless against the covetousness to reclaim what was mine. I pushed forward and Tenley lifted her hips as my piercing eased past the threshold. I closed my eyes as the sensation of being connected to her like this again consumed every rational thought. I wanted it to erase all the hurt and the pain, but instead it reminded me of how alone I'd been without her, and how I never wanted to go through that again.

I released her hands and they immediately smoothed down my back and up again, clinging to my shoulders. Then I started a heavy fill and retreat. As I picked up momentum, Tenley's legs tightened around my waist. I was far from gentle, slamming into her relentlessly. With grim satisfaction I watched her come apart underneath me, over and over again, her eyes never leaving mine. When the lick of fire shot down my spine, I buried my face in her neck even as she pleaded with me to look at her. I couldn't handle being that transparent, so I denied her. I came so hard, I nearly blacked out.

9

TENLEY

We never made it out for breakfast. And Hayden was late for work.

"You're going to come in and say hi to everyone, right?" he asked as we passed through the lobby of his building.

"Maybe I should wait until later," I replied hesitantly. The sex left me feeling awkward and did nothing to assuage the strain lingering between us as we walked side by side, not touching.

"They've all missed you, too. It wasn't just me you left behind."

The reminder of the pain I'd caused brought on a fresh wave of remorse. I'd exchanged one guilt for another, but at least I had some control over this situation. This I could fix. Hopefully.

"Okay. I'll come with you."

His shoulders relaxed and he took my hand. I imagined the pendulum swing of his moods would continue as we sorted through the emotional turmoil I'd created.

We stepped out into the cold afternoon and headed right, passing the storefronts at street level. Hayden had the shortest commute in the world. I glanced at Serendipity, across the street. I'd need to go there next and face Cassie.

The door tinkled as we entered Inked Armor, and silence fell over the shop.

"Hi," I said meekly as Lisa and Jamie stared. Surprisingly, neither looked all that shocked to see me.

Lisa shot up and came barreling toward me from behind the cash register. "I'm so glad you're home! When did you get back?" She threw her arms around me, squeezing the breath out of my lungs.

"Late last night." I returned the embrace.

"You should have sent me a message," she whispered, too low for anyone else to hear. Lisa was the only one I'd kept in constant contact with. And only because she'd sent me persistent messages the whole time. She was a difficult one to ignore. I squeezed her arm, so she knew I heard her.

"He knows we were all in touch with you," she murmured, then stepped back. "You've lost weight," she said with disapproval. "And what happened to your face?"

"It's not a big deal." I glanced toward the back of the shop, where her office and the private rooms were. I needed to get her alone so I could ask how Hayden found out. It would explain his comment last night and why my silence was so upsetting, beyond the obvious reasons.

Lisa's eyes moved surreptitiously to Hayden. He crossed his arms over his chest and dropped his head, eyes on the floor. I was sure as soon I left she would ask him all the questions she couldn't ask me.

Jamie saved me from further interrogation by drawing me in for a hug of his own. "You've been sorely missed."

Chris came out of the supply room when he heard all the commotion, laden down with an armful of supplies. "Tee! You're back!" He dropped the supplies on the closest surface and lifted me right off my feet. "It's good to see you, girl." He set me down. "Sarah tried to call you last night, after she listened to your messages. It's my fault she missed them in the first place." He gave me a sheepish smile.

I laughed, even though tears slid down my cheeks. Lisa grabbed me a tissue and Hayden put a protective arm around my shoulder, pressing his nose into my damp hair. "Too much, too soon?" he asked.

"A little overwhelmed is all," I replied, embarrassed.

"You're not alone there," he whispered.

While it was good to see them, conversation was a bit strained; they obviously had questions they didn't feel comfortable asking yet.

When Chris's first client arrived, I took the opportunity to make an exit. "I've got some things to take care of today." But Hayden and I had been in such a rush to get out the door, we hadn't discussed when we'd get together again.

Hayden shoved his hands in his pockets, rocking back on his heels. "I've got a break between clients around five. Why don't you come back then? Unless you're busy with whatever." He kicked the toe of my shoe with his.

"No, I'm not busy. Maybe we could get something to eat."

Hayden nodded. "Yeah. Okay. Food would be good. And I'll need to pick up my car at some point."

"I'll take you," I offered.

"Sure."

"I'm going to stop in and see Cassie. Can I bring you something back from the café?" The conversation was terribly uncomfortable, especially with Lisa and Chris and Jamie all pretending they weren't listening. Chris was the only one who was actually occupied with something legitimate, but even he kept glancing in our direction.

"I'm good. My client will be here any minute."

"Okay. I'll see you a little later, then."

"Yup."

I waited for some parting gesture of affection—even just a peck on the cheek—but none came. I turned toward the door, disappointed by his dismissal.

"Tenley?"

I looked over my shoulder. "Yes?"

"Aren't you forgetting something?" The keys for my apartment dangled from his finger.

"Right. Of course."

He placed them in my palm and closed my fist around them. There was a pause, and then he yanked me forward. His hand slipped around the back of my neck and his mouth came down, hard and insistent. His tongue shot between my lips, an echo of the aggression in his bed less than an hour ago. When he was done, he released me. I stumbled back; light-headed and off-balance.

"Don't go far," he said darkly.

"I won't. I promise."

But I could tell he didn't believe me.

My next stop was Serendipity. I was nervous about seeing Cassie. Her concern about my abrupt departure was clear in our brief e-mails. She never mentioned how Hayden was doing, even though I asked both times. At first I assumed it was because of her loyalty to him, but after seeing him fall apart last night and this morning, I was no longer convinced that was the case. I'd broken him, and I was sure she wanted me to realize that on my own.

The bell above the door chimed and her head lifted. Disbelief flickered across her face, as well as the same wary uncertainty I'd seen on Hayden's. "You're back."

It was the new greeting.

"I got in last night."

"Does Hayden know?"

"He's the first person I saw." Well, that was mostly true.

"How is he?"

"Confused. Hurt. Angry. Relieved, maybe? We had a long talk last night, and again this morning."

"He hasn't managed this well." Accusation was in her tone.

"I know. Neither have I." Her disapproval hurt. She had given me fair warning early on about Hayden. She would hold me accountable for what I'd put him through.

She slipped off the chair and came out from behind the counter. "Come here."

Her embrace was exactly what I needed; it held her forgiveness. I wanted to apologize, but I didn't know where to start.

"I didn't mean to hurt him. Or anyone."

"I'm certain that's true." Her hands rested on my shoulders. "And now that you've seen what it's done to him, I'm also very sure you won't ever do it again."

A silent *or else* was tacked on at the end, but I took no offense. I expected nothing less from her.

After I left Serendipity I went to my apartment. Sarah's car wasn't in the driveway, but exams were this week, so she could well be in the middle of one. I hadn't thought to ask Chris while I was at Inked Armor.

The key turned smoothly when I slipped it in the lock, which was unusual. Most of the time I had to fiddle with it to get it to open. I braced myself for the mess I'd left behind, but my apartment had been cleaned. The books I typically left strewn on the floor were stacked neatly on the coffee table. The blankets were folded and placed over the arm of the couch, the pillows in the corners. Hayden was the only person who would take that time and care with my things.

I took off my shoes and hung up my coat, moving through the space like a voyeur. Everything felt so foreign, as if it were someone else's home instead of my own. My bedroom was as tidy as the rest of the apartment, not a thing out of place. Or rather, everything had been put in a better, more reasonable spot. The pillows on my bed were artfully arranged against the headboard. I lifted the edge of the comforter and checked the sheets. They had been changed and had hospital corners.

In the kitchen, the fridge had been cleaned out; a fresh-cut lemon sat on the top shelf. My water jug was full, slices of lemon floating on the surface. Hayden must have stopped by recently, and more than once. He'd been waiting for me to come home.

In need of a distraction, I opened my laptop and printed out the most recent version of my thesis. I'd made little progress in my time away, too consumed with everything else. While Trey's forged legal paperwork had bought me some time and pity from the dean of the program, I was behind the timeline for the complete rough draft. I'd have to work doubly hard to make up not only the missed time, but also the class I TA'd.

At least my scholarship hadn't been revoked. Yet. Professor Calder had expressed his concern over the possibility that my funding might not continue, and I was sure I'd hear more about that, and his other issues, when I met with him. I planned to drop off a current draft in case he had a chance to look at it before second semester began. If there was one thing I hadn't missed while I was in Arden Hills, it was my adviser meetings.

The temperature had done a nosedive in the last week and my car windows were covered with frost. I got in the car and blasted the heat, shivering as I waited for the windshield to clear because I didn't have a scraper. While my teeth chattered and the car warmed, I sent Hayden a message to let him know I was heading out to pick up groceries but would be at Inked Armor by five. I didn't even get the phone back in my pocket before Hayden fired a message back. He requested I pick up beer and food for TK, specifying the brand for both.

Northwestern was my first stop. It was quiet on campus. Most students were shut away in the library or coffee shops, cramming for exams. Classes wouldn't resume until after the New Year. The buildings would be open during the day until the end of next week, when marks were due. I had twenty-seven essays to mark and submit by next Friday, which wouldn't be a problem since I didn't have a job anymore. Cassie and I had yet to discuss if I would resume shifts at Serendipity.

I took the stairs to the third floor. My hip was stiff but not overly sore. After the fight with Sienna and the sex with Hayden, I expected it to feel much worse. Maybe the workout helped. With a smile, I pushed through the door beside the bank of elevators. As I rounded the corner, a familiar-looking girl with long, sandy-blond hair stepped out of my adviser's office with a giggle. All the way down at the other end of the hall, she didn't notice me.

A hand shot out and dragged her back through the doorway by her waist. I stepped out of view and flattened myself against the wall. The giggling stopped abruptly, followed by a whisper of voices. I held my breath and waited. Another titter filtered down the hall, cut off by the soft click of a door's closing.

I stayed where I was for several minutes before I peeked out again; then I crept down the hall to Professor Calder's office. A muffled moan came from the other side of the door. It was followed by the sounds of furniture dragging across wood, and then a rhythmic slapping started. The rumors were true.

I slipped my phone out of my back pocket, went to the video-camera feature, and hit the record button as the woman began moaning in earnest. I held the phone up to Professor Calder's nameplate. There was a loud smack, like a palm hitting skin, and low tones of admonishment. Then the banging started, loud and hard. I hoped my phone picked up the muffled sound of the woman calling out his name. When I was at risk of gagging, I pocketed my phone. Quietly, I slipped the title page free from my draft and scrawled a message. Returning it to the folder, I dropped the package into the box beside his door.

Even though it let me out on the wrong side of the building, I left through the stairwell beside his office. The door closed with an echoing slam, which was the point. I wanted to incite paranoia. As I stepped out into the frosty December afternoon, I decided I'd learned one good thing from Trey: blackmail could be an effective tool for self-preservation.

10

HAYDEN

People were annoying the hell out of me today. Lisa and Chris, to be precise. They kept looking at me, obviously waiting for something. Maybe they thought I was going to flip my shit or sit down and have a little love-in to share my feelings about Tenley's being back, which wasn't going to happen. And not just because I hated the sharing bullshit. My feelings were all over the place, and I was still sorting them out.

It was just past two in the afternoon. Tenley had gone to run some errands and all I could think about was when she'd be back. I pulled the folder for my client this afternoon, as well as Nate's designs. He was supposed to stop by later in the evening to take a look at them. I figured his impromptu drop-in had more to do with what had happened at dinner on Sunday than the actual tattoo, but I didn't mind either way. Nate's intentions were good, even if he was looking to get all up in my head.

I left his design at my workstation and took the other one to the private room. The tattoo would span from midrib to upper thigh, down the right side of my client's body. It was a cool design and Amy was a cool chick. I'd done a few smaller pieces for her in the past, but this was her first foray into a multisession tattoo. I was pretty damn excited to be working on another substantial piece.

I left the door open and started setting up. We were only going for a two-hour session because ribs hurt like an SOB and I didn't want to push it. That should be enough to tackle the outline, provided we didn't take too many breaks. Amy was realistic about her pain tolerance, which was a nice change from some of the douche nozzles who scheduled four hours of my time, then pussied out halfway through.

"Hey." Lisa was in the doorway, leaning against the jamb.

"Is Amy here already?" I checked the time. It was only ten past. While she was prompt, she didn't usually show up this early for a session.

"Not yet." Lisa came inside and shut the door.

"What's up?" I knew damn well why she was barricading me in here. Lisa had been waiting for the chance to grill me ever since I'd walked through the door with Tenley.

"How are you?"

"I'm fine."

"Just fine?"

I smoothed out the stencil. "You don't need to pussyfoot around the issue. Ask what you want to ask."

"What's going on with you and Tenley?"

I would have thought the way I'd kissed her before I sent her off answered the question. Apparently not. "We're working things out."

"Which means what, exactly?"

I frowned. "It means what it means. Or are you looking for a play-by-play of our conversation so you can give me your unbiased opinion on what you think I should do?"

"Sarah called me this morning. Apparently she had an interesting conversation with Candy late last night."

Shit. Bad news traveled fast. I hadn't even seen Candy at The Dollhouse, but my focus had been elsewhere. I got real busy checking to make sure I had the right ink. "Yeah? What'd she have to say?"

"That Sienna got into it with someone whose description fits Tenley's, and Sienna's nose ended up broken. Candy also might have mentioned to Sarah that you stopped by The Dollhouse. She said Sienna was all in a rage after you left. Do you want to fill in the missing details?"

"Tenley left her keys with Sarah when she went back to Arden Hills. She stopped at The Dollhouse thinking Sarah would be there and had a run-in with Sienna instead. Things got heated. I picked her up."

"Tenley called you?"

About twenty times. I'd ignored them all. "No. Jay did."

I could tell there was a lot Lisa wanted to ask, but she chose her questions carefully. She started with the most telling one. "Did Tenley stay at your place last night?"

"Yeah. She was pretty shaken up after The Dollhouse bullshit. Sienna pushed her around a bit before Tenley fought back. She couldn't manage the stairs to her apartment because of her hip. Besides, TK was at my place and Tenley wanted to see her."

I was rationalizing the hell out of my actions, but I didn't need Lisa's judgment. I'd spent enough time without Tenley. Now that she was back, I wasn't inclined to play it cool and take all sorts of space. Even if the smarter course of action was to dip a toe in and check the temperature before diving headlong into a boiling pot of water. I was a diver, not a dipper.

"Did you have sex with her?"

"Seriously? I don't get all up in your personal business and ask if you're putting out for Jamie on the regular," I snapped.

"Jamie and I have sex daily. Usually in the morning, because that's when Jamie has the best longevity and it puts me in a good mood. There. Now I've shared. Your turn."

I cringed at the mental image. "*Why*, Lisa? Why would you tell me that? I don't need those details."

"Oh? And here I thought that's what this was about. The only time you've been reticent about your previous sexual escapades is when you were with Sienna, and when you broke your own stupid rule with Tenley. Based on how dodgy you're being, I'm pretty sure I know the answer to the question anyway."

"And your point is?"

Lisa arched a brow. "I'm just checking to see where you're at. She's been gone for weeks and you've been a mess. She comes back, and the first thing you do is fall into bed with her? After everything that's happened, do you think that's a good decision?"

"We talked first."

"And everything's better? After one conversation?"

"There were two conversations. One last night and one this morning."

"And when did you get it on, in between the two?"

"After the one this morning." Because that made it so much better.

"Oh. Well, then. Two heartfelt chats later and you're over her leaving with no explanation?" Lisa asked snidely.

"No, but it's not like I can pull a do-over, can I?"

"I believe you've tried that before, with little success."

I glared at her. "I don't understand why you're being like this. I figured you'd be glad we were sorting shit out." Although, if I was honest, the sex with Tenley complicated the situation. All my anger, frustration, and fear had funneled right into the hard, fast, mind-blowing, multiple-orgasm bliss. While it had been a good form of stress relief, it unearthed a barrage of other crap I wasn't ready to deal with. I kept that shit to myself.

"I'm happy she's back, but you need to be careful, and not just for your sake. You two have a lot to sort through."

"Like I said, we're working it out. She gets that I'm angry with her for leaving, and I'm not telling her everything is fine now that she's back."

"That's great. But there's more to this than Tenley leaving, and the things you learned about her. You've got your own skeletons you're not dealing with. You can't keep them buried forever."

There was a knock on the door and Jamie poked his head in. He looked from me to Lisa and back again. "Sorry to interrupt," he said slowly. "Amy's here."

His timing couldn't have been better. "Perfect. I'll be right out."

"Do you want a minute?" he asked.

"Nope. We're good here."

"I'll let her know." Jamie's head disappeared and he left the door open.

When I tried to get around Lisa, she put a hand on my arm, a gentle request to hear her out.

"Remember that talk we had about things not always being black and white, back before you started the outline on Tenley?"

"What about it?"

"Maybe you need to find a middle ground, so this thing with Tenley isn't all or nothing. She obviously wants to be with you, like you want to be with her. All I'm suggesting is this time you might want to slow down and get all the important stuff out of the way first."

Lisa had a valid point. I wasn't good at taking things slow and Tenley was no exception. I'd practically lived in her apartment as soon as I got into her pants. But it wasn't just about the sex back then, and it wasn't now. It made the whole issue difficult to navigate. I wanted her, and I wanted to be with her; separating the two needs was a challenge. They were entwined; one begot the other. But then, I'd never felt about anyone else the way I felt about Tenley.

"Have you been talking to Nate?"

Lisa's nose crinkled. "What? Why?"

"Because you sound like him with your life metaphors and therapizing."

"'Therapizing'?"

"I'm pretty sure it's a word. If not, I'm petitioning to have it added to *Webster's*."

Lisa rolled her eyes, then grew serious once more. "Therapy wouldn't be the worst thing in the world for you."

"I already know what's wrong with me."

She gave me a look. "Just think about what I said. I'm on your side. Tenley was good for you before she left. I hope she still is. I would hate to see it all fall apart again because you're still protecting each other from your pasts. Relationships are no easy thing. Anyone who tells you otherwise is full of crap."

Lisa left me standing there, somewhat stupefied. She and Jamie didn't fight, not that I ever saw. Occasionally Lisa was snippy or Jamie was in one of his moods, but they were always respectful of one another and affectionate to the point of making those around them gag. I often teased Jamie for being pussy whipped and he didn't deny it. It never occurred to me that they had issues—but then, I guess I wouldn't have that insight, considering how guarded I was. No one had ever gotten close enough for me to contend with real problems. Not until Tenley. So far, I seemed to be sucking at it.

I was still a little dazed when I came out of the room to greet Amy. Since Chris didn't have a client, they were chatting it up. Amy had her hand on his forearm, her head thrown back in laughter.

"Hey, gorgeous!" she exclaimed when she saw me.

"How's it going?" I accepted the brief hug.

"Awesome! I'm superpsyched." She tilted her head to the side. "You look different."

"I haven't had a haircut in a while." I scratched the side of my head. My hair was getting long and I'd been in too much of funk to ask Lisa to take care of it.

"No, I noticed that last week. I meant to tell you that you look almost civilized with all that hair. But don't worry, the piercings keep you badass."

"That's a relief. I wouldn't want to go mainstream or anything."

"How tragic would that be? Still, there's something . . . I don't know. I'll tell you when I figure it out." She looked me over in a clinical, assessing way, which wasn't unusual for her since she worked as an EMT. When she couldn't come up with anything, she dropped it and clapped her hands together. "Should we get started?"

I smiled. "Let's do it."

Like Lisa and Tenley, she was feisty, but less subdued. In two-hour blocks, Amy was an awesome dose of energy. I always finished a session with her wanting to run a marathon or something.

I led her to the private room and gave her specific directions on what clothing she needed to remove. Because the tattoo spanned from ribs to thigh, she'd have to lose everything from the waist down. We could work around her shirt, but she couldn't wear her bra. We had smocks to cover the important parts, but I'd still be looking at most of her ass the entire time. It was unavoidable.

I left the room to let her undress and checked my phone for messages from Tenley. There weren't any, so like the sucker I was, I sent her one. Her reply came immediately. She was at the pet store and wanted to buy TK something new to play with. I suggested kitty weed. She questioned my parenting skills. I considered briefly what it would be like to have a real kid and abruptly shut down that train of thought. No way would I ever want that responsibility, or the mess or worry that came along with it. TK was more than enough.

Amy poked her head out into the hall. "I'm all set."

"Cool." I pocketed my phone and we got down to business.

As expected, Amy needed frequent breaks. Even with a stress ball, the area over her ribs was extrasensitive. Where Tenley was slender but curvy, Amy was rail thin. She was a runner, so there wasn't much body fat as cushioning. She held her own, but she was ready to call it quits after two hours. In that time I managed to complete the outline, so we'd be ready for color next time she came in.

After the ink was dressed, she changed back into her clothes and met me in the main studio. Lisa wanted to see Amy's new body art. Neither one thought to head to one of the empty rooms in the back for privacy. Instead, Amy, who wasn't shy, lifted her shirt to display the tattoo traveling from beneath her nonexistent breasts to her nearly curveless hips. Lisa got right in there and checked it out, while two frat boys gawked at them from chairs across the room. They were waiting for Lisa to hook them up with some new piercings. At least, that's what they'd told her. I was putting money on one of them chickening out, since their proposed piercings were of the below-the-belt variety.

As Lisa and Amy nattered away about the color scheme for the design, the bell above the door tinkled and Tenley walked into the shop. Her face was flushed from the cold. The collar of her black winter coat was flipped up to shield her face. She wore a hot-pink hat with a black skull and crossbones on it. The skull had a bow on the top of its head. She looked cute. Her eyes met mine as she removed the hat and shook out her hair.

Tenley's smile dropped and her expression went flat as Amy's arms came around me in a sideways hug. "I'm a devout client. I will never let anyone work on me but you."

Chris coughed from his station.

"If I was into tribal, I'd defect, darling, and you know it," Amy called out.

Chris raised a hand in acknowledgment and went back to filling in black lines on an intricate Celtic design.

"There's someone I want to introduce you to," I said, and extended a hand to Tenley. I waited until she was right in front of me. "Tenley, this is Amy. Amy, this is Tenley."

"Hi!" Amy shook her hand enthusiastically. "Are you one of Hayden's clients, too?"

Tenley glanced at me before she answered. "Hayden's been working on a back piece for me, but it's been a while since I've been in his chair."

"Oh? So it's a multisession? Let me tell you, once you get started, it's hard to stop, especially with this talent." Amy rubbed my arm.

Tenley's eyes were homed in on Amy's hand as it smoothed down my biceps, and Tenley's lips turned up in a coy smile as she traced a line of ink on my forearm. "Yes. Hayden is incredibly talented. I'm very fortunate to have his art on my body."

Amy blinked. Lisa coughed to hide a snicker. The innuendo was hard to ignore, and an annoying part of my body reacted accordingly. I'd said something to the same effect a long time ago, before we were together. It had come out sounding just as explicitly inappropriate. Tenley was staking a claim, and it was both amusing and hot. How Lisa figured I could manage a sex hiatus was beyond me. Pretty much everything Tenley said or did made me want her.

"Actually, Tenley's my girlfriend." I put an arm around Tenley's shoulder and pulled her into my side. She burrowed right in, her thumb hooking into a belt loop.

"Oh. Of course." Amy nodded. "I told Hayden there was something different, and here you are."

"Here I am," Tenley said quietly.

I leaned down with the intention of kissing her cheek. She turned her head at the last second and I connected with her mouth, instead. Her tongue flicked out, all subtle like, skimming my bottom lip. I liked the jealous side of her. It made me feel better about my own territorial impulses.

Once Amy settled up, Tenley and I went to get the douche mobile since it still had all her stuff in it. As soon as we were in the car, she was all over me. The front seat had plenty of room for her to maneuver. She was half straddling me, her lips on mine with one hand rubbing over my crotch through my jeans. My dick was throwing a party.

"Whoa. Take it easy, kitten."

She took advantage of my mouth's being open and shoved her tongue in it. Her hand snaked under the waistband of my pants. She couldn't manage the coordination or the patience necessary to kiss me and get her hand down far enough to find what she was looking for. Which, incidentally, was bent at an awkward angle. She pulled my fly down. Part of me wanted to help her out, but the other part—the one that considered the merits of taking things slowly—decided now would be a good time to act on that advice.

I put my hand over hers. "Tenley, I think—"

She kept fumbling with my belt. I went limp and stopped kissing her. She made an impatient noise and pushed her tongue past my lips again. Although the urge to react was strong, I remained unresponsive.

"Kiss me," she ordered, and nipped at my bottom lip.

"No."

"Fine." She went to work on my belt with both hands.

"Tenley, stop." I ran my hands down her arms and circled her wrists. She flinched and jerked them away. I'd forgotten about the bruises from that fuckhead Trey.

"You don't want me to touch you?" The panic and fear in her eyes was echoed in her voice.

I definitely wanted her hands on me, but the location was all wrong. Besides, her motivation was questionable. "How about you tell me what's got you so worked up."

"We only have an hour before your next appointment. I want to make the most of it."

"By getting it on in your deceased fiancé's car?"

She blinked, stunned, and dropped heavily into her seat.

Well, that soured the mood. "I'm sorry. That was a dick thing to say."

"You're right, though. I wasn't thinking. I just wanted to be close to you."

"There's more to it than that," I challenged.

"I didn't like the way she was touching you."

"Amy's a client and a friend. She's touchy with everyone."

"Her hands were only on you," Tenley pointed out acidly.

"She's just a client," I reiterated, unsure where Tenley was going with this and why she was so agitated over it. She'd never been like this before, but then, a lot had changed in a short time.

"So you've never been with her?"

My eyebrows shot up. "Uh, no. The only client I've had sex with was Sienna."

"Aside from me, you mean."

"Yeah. But you're different, and so are the circumstances. Where is this coming from?"

"You were with Sienna for years." Tenley traced the divots on the inside of the steering wheel.

I rubbed my forehead. "We've talked about this before. Sienna and I fucked. And, yes, we did it on and off for a long time, but it wasn't a relationship."

"I'm not sure I agree with that."

"Just because I put my dick in whatever hole she offered doesn't mean we had a relationship." Tenley grimaced, probably because I was being unnecessarily crass, but I needed her to understand the distinct differences between her and Sienna. "We didn't go out on dates. I never spent time with her if I wasn't high or getting laid. For fuck's sake, she was the one who orchestrated all the third- and fourth-party participation."

Tenley's eyes widened. "*All?* As in more than once?"

"Why do you look so surprised? You've been inside The Dollhouse. You've met Sienna. You hang out with Sarah and you know what she does to pay her tuition. You've seen the people I used to spend my time with. None of this should come as a shock. I can't keep apologizing for shit I did before I knew you." My stomach churned as the words spilled out. I was so damn tired of looking at my past and justifying why I did the things I did.

"I'm not asking you to apologize."

"Then what *are* you asking for?"

"I just want . . ."

"What, Tenley? What do you want? Do you want to take this down to base needs? Do you want me to be the person you fuck and nothing else? Am I too complicated for you? If so, I'm not sure I can be that accommodating, because my stupid fucking feelings will get in the way. I'm sorry if that's an inconvenience for you."

Tenley looked horrified. "That's ludicrous. What would make you think that's what I want?"

I rubbed my temple. "I don't know. Maybe it has something to do with the way you tried to get me to fuck you as soon as we stopped fighting last night. Or the way you ended up naked in my bed this morning, looking for more of the same." Even as I said it, I knew it wasn't fair.

"You can't be serious! I ended up in your bed because you were having a nightmare, not so you would fuck me. I missed you. I wanted to be with you because of how I feel about you, not because I wanted an orgasm."

"Yeah, well, it's hard to know with you," I snapped. "This shit is all I know, Tenley. The fighting and the fucking, it's what Sienna used to do. She'd push my goddamn buttons until I went off, and then she'd let me fuck all the anger out. This whole scenario is too damn familiar."

What Tenley and I had was about more than sex, but I couldn't seem to get a handle on my emotions. Or my fears.

This wasn't how I'd thought things would go this evening. We were supposed to get my car, have a quick bite, and I'd head back to work. Then I'd invite her over at the end of the night to hang out. I hadn't expected a fight in her dead fiancé's car, incited by a make-out session.

"I'm sorry Sienna did that to you, but I'm not her. Sometimes people have sex after they argue to connect, not just to get off. That's what I wanted—not control, or payback, or anything sinister." Tenley reached out, but when I shifted away, she retracted her hand. "I was terrified you'd go back to Sienna while I was gone. Or find someone else to replace me. I worried about that all the time."

"First of all, you're not replaceable. And you think I didn't worry about the same thing? I kept going over what I could have done differently to keep you with me."

"I never wanted anyone but you."

"How the hell was I supposed to know that? You told me to leave, for fuck sake! Maybe if you'd made some attempt to contact me, I wouldn't have been in hell for the past few weeks. One phone call would have been enough."

"I told you why I didn't—"

I raised a hand and cut her off. "I know you had your reasons, except you aren't the only one who was affected by your decisions. We both have fucked-up pasts. There's nothing simple about what's going on between us. I'm trying to let this shit go, but you've been back less than twenty-four hours. Beyond that, if you can't get over the things I've done, then maybe this isn't going to work."

"What are you saying?" I could feel her anxiety. It rivaled mine and I felt awful for the spike of satisfaction. Tenley hadn't asked for her past, any more than I'd asked for mine.

"I don't know. I think maybe we need to slow things down. Start over, or whatever."

"Are you asking for space?"

"No. I think maybe we need to back things up a bit. My head's all messed up over this, and as much as I want to be with you, I'm not sure it's a good thing for me right now."

"Be with me?" Her fingers tightened around the steering wheel and her eyes flared with panic. "As in . . . ?"

"As in sex. We need to put that on hold."

Her grip loosened, but the frown of worry remained. "Indefinitely?"

Based on previous experience, I doubted I'd last more than a couple of weeks, at best. I wasn't telling her that, though. "For a while. We need to sort through our shit before I can go there again. It makes me feel too much, and I can't handle it."

"Okay. If that's what you think is best."

I pinned her with a glare. "I've heard that before. Don't make this hard for me. It won't help either of us, and it'll just make me more pissed at you."

"I won't. I promise."

*   *   *

We had just enough time to retrieve my car from the impound lot
and book it back to Inked Armor. Tenley paid the fee because she
felt responsible for my car's being towed in the first place. Afterward, I gave her the keys to my place because she wanted to check
on TK. She hadn't asked to take her home yet and I wasn't going to
bring it up. I wasn't all that keen on parting with her, but I would
if that was what Tenley wanted. Which made me a huge sucker and
irritated the fuck out of me.

Nate showed up at six on the dot, and at his request we went
over the sketches in one of the private rooms. It meant he wanted
to interrogate me, much like everyone else.

"Cassie tells me Tenley came home," he said as he sifted
through the photos in his file and the drawings I'd done based on
our design discussion.

"Yeah."

"How's that going?"

"All right."

He looked up from the paper in his hand.

"Things are a little tense."

"I'm sure they are. You want to talk about it?"

"Nah, I'm all talked out today."

Nate let it go. He narrowed it down to two sketches and
pointed out the things he liked about both of them. It would be
easy enough to merge them into one drawing. I asked him for a
week to work on it and we scheduled a follow-up appointment.

"Have the nightmares let up at all?" Nate asked as I returned
the sketches to his folder with the notes we made.

"Not so much."

"So they're getting worse?"

I frowned. "How would you know that?"

"Lots of stress in your life. Tenley's leaving would echo the loss
of your parents, and the loss of control."

"Yeah, well, maybe now that she's back it'll get better."

I didn't think that would be true, though. The nightmares had worsened over the past few weeks and were increasingly vivid. I had new dreams beyond the one where I found my parents' bodies, and the ones where Tenley replaced them. Some were definitely memories. Others were less clear. The newest ones creeped me right out.

"Did you ever see the crime scene photos?" I asked before I lost my nerve.

"No. But I know you did," he replied cautiously.

I nodded slowly, mulling over what I'd seen and what I remembered. It was so long ago, and I'd been so fucked up. "All the art from my parents' house, is it in the storage unit?"

"I haven't gotten rid of anything, so I assume so. What's this about? Was there a piece you wanted? I could come with you."

"I don't know. Do you remember if they ever took one for evidence?" It was such a hazy time for me. Nothing about those months after my parents' deaths was clear, apart from haunting images of their dead bodies and parts of the interrogation afterward.

"I don't believe so. Is it something you'd like to look into?"

"Do you remember the angel?"

"Pardon?" Nate's confusion was obvious.

"I could have sworn it was on the floor, but it wasn't in any of the crime scene photos." Even as I said it, I started to second-guess myself. Memories weren't always reliable.

"I'm sorry, I'm not following." Nate leaned forward, elbows resting on his knees.

The intensity in the way he regarded me made me uneasy and I shut down. I was probably misremembering, and I sounded like a mental case. "It's nothing, just part of a stupid dream. Never mind."

"Are you recalling things you didn't before? It's not uncommon for that to happen years after a trauma occurs. I could set you up with someone to talk to about it, if you don't feel comfortable with me—"

"Don't start, Nate—"

"Hear me out before you say no. I know this woman. She's easy to talk to." When I interrupted, he talked over me. "All I'm suggesting is that you give it a shot. It's just one hour. There's no obligation beyond that. If you don't like her, or it's not for you, then I'll drop it."

"I'll think about it," I said, mostly to shut him up.

"You do that." He clapped me on the shoulder. "If you decide you want to go to the storage unit for whatever reason, or you feel like taking me up on my offer, just call. Otherwise, I'll see you next week."

"Later, Nate." I shuffled the sketches to avoid further eye contact as he left.

I still wasn't sold on the idea. All that talking would resurrect my shitty past. I didn't see the benefit in sifting through the sludge just so someone with a PhD in head-fucking could tell me I had PTSD. Labeling it wouldn't make it go away.

11

TENLEY

TK was curled up on Hayden's bed, sleeping on a pillow from my apartment. She lifted her head, gave me a groggy mew, and settled her chin on her paws. I climbed up beside her and scratched between her ears. With a graceful roll, she stretched out, eating up the attention. She had grown since I'd left, but not much. I liked that she still looked more like a kitten than a cat.

"I missed you," I said, stroking her striped belly with its white patch in the center.

She purred in response and scampered into my lap. Her paws came up on my shoulders and she nudged my cheek with her nose. I lay back on Hayden's pillows; they smelled like him. It was something else I missed. I'd been wearing one of his shirts when I left Chicago. I slept with it until it lost its scent.

He'd changed the sheets before we left this morning. While the undeniable chemistry was still present, the connection we shared had been absent. I hoped it wasn't gone permanently. The last time we were together, right before I'd left, had been so much sweeter. I'd wanted to tell him how I felt about him. I still did. But he wasn't ready to hear it, and I was still working up the nerve to say the words. They carried no weight if I couldn't persuade him I wasn't going anywhere again.

I stayed with TK longer than I meant to, caught up in memories and worries. At nine, I headed back to Inked Armor. The shop didn't close for another hour, but if I made myself available, Hayden might decide he wanted to spend more time with me.

He was in the middle of a consultation when I entered the shop. At least this one was male, a repeat customer based on the amount of ink on his arms. Jamie and Chris were busy with clients; both of them glanced up and gave me a nod. Hayden paused in his conversation with his client and gave me a half smile.

"Hey, kitten," he said, "I'll be a while yet. Lisa's in the office working on the books."

I bit the inside of my lip to keep my grin from becoming too wide. That he was still calling me by that nickname had to be a good thing. "Okay. I'll see if she wants some company."

Hayden's client regarded me with speculative interest as I passed, but Hayden didn't offer introductions, so I continued to the rear of the shop. The door to Lisa's office was open, but I knocked anyway. Before, I might have barged in, but I didn't know where the boundaries were now and I didn't want to take anything for granted.

Lisa glanced at me from behind the computer screen as her fingers flew over the keyboard. "Hey! Come on in."

"I don't want to interrupt." I remained in the doorway.

"Interruptions are always welcome, and we have catching up to do." She stopped typing and turned her full attention to me. "How's your first day back been?"

"Okay."

She stood up and rounded the desk, pulling me in for a hug. It was exactly what I needed.

"I'm sorry I put you in a difficult position," I mumbled into her lavender hair. She'd dyed it while I was away. It used to be the pink of cotton candy.

"What are you talking about?" she asked, releasing me.

"All the texts and the e-mails while I was gone."

"Oh, that. I'm the one who harassed you, not the other way around, so you have nothing to apologize for."

"Still, you're Hayden's friend. I didn't want to jeopardize your relationship with him; it's why I didn't respond at first." It took five days of nonstop messages before I messaged her back. If Hayden had done the same thing, I would have folded much sooner.

"Hayden's like my brother. We're pretty solid. Besides, someone needed to keep tabs on you."

"Is that what you were doing?"

"You bet. You came back right on time. I already had my road trip planned if you hadn't shown up by the end of this week." While a hint of teasing was in her tone, I had a feeling she was serious about coming to retrieve me.

"How did he find out about the messages?"

"Sunday night we were checking your e-mail to Cassie, and he saw it. He wasn't happy. He told us all to fuck ourselves and tried to walk home from her house."

"Oh my God." It put our recent conversations into perspective; the sense of betrayal would have been fresh.

"He'll get over it."

"I hope so."

"You're okay, though? Everything in Arden Hills is settled now?"

"I still have to deal with my parents' house, but there's no hurry and I'm not ready yet. But for the most part, things are taken care of."

Frank had been in touch to assure me the business end of the house deal went smoothly. Trey hadn't tried to contact me since I'd walked out. The bruises on my wrists had faded, and in a couple of days they'd be just a memory.

"I'm glad. If you want to talk about it, I'm here. In the meantime, I've got some stuff to show you."

I appreciated that while Lisa had been persistent in keeping in touch, she hadn't pushed for information or explanations. She only wanted to ensure I was okay. She led me out of the office and into the private piercing room. She locked the door before she pulled out a tray of jewelry.

"I just got back and you want to coerce me into more steel?"

"Coercion is hardly necessary with you." She uncovered a wide selection of curved barbells.

I shook my head. "Oh, no. No way. Hood piercings take weeks to heal."

"Four to six to heal completely—"

"Like that's a selling point? That's *so* not an option—"

Lisa held up a finger. "But healing time doesn't dictate usability. As long as you take good care of it, you can start rolling your marble safely after a week."

"A week?"

"Mm-hm." Her smile and the gleam in her eyes were mischievous.

I glanced down at the tray of pretty silver barbells of varying styles and sizes. Hayden's reasons for putting sex on hold were understandable. A piercing would put me out of commission and relieve me of the temptation to push him. That would be better for both of us. And this would be better for me when it healed, from what Lisa had told me. Not that I needed to worry about my ability to orgasm with Hayden around.

"When should we do it?" I asked.

"How about right now?"

"Now? But——" I glanced over at the closed door. Hayden was still with his client.

"It takes two minutes. All you need is to strip from the waist down."

I released a puff of air. Connor would have blown a gasket if I suggested a genital piercing. Hayden, on the other hand, would lose his mind in a good way.

"Let's do it. But we don't tell Hayden."

"My lips are sealed."

I waited while she set up the chair. The stirrups reminded me of a gynecologist's office. I expected this would be an equally unpleasant experience, with a more pleasurable result. When everything was set up, I dropped my pants and underwear and took a seat in the chair. Even though she was my friend, it was no more uncomfortable to have Lisa peering at my girl parts than it was an obstetrician, likely because she made it seem like no big deal. She walked me through each step of the process.

"This will be the most uncomfortable part." She held up the clamp. "Take a deep breath."

I did as I was told. The stinging pinch muted the quick stab of pain when she pushed the needle through sensitive skin. She followed with the barbell. Once it was secured in place, she released the clamp and blood came rushing back.

"And we're done. In about six weeks you can start changing it up, see what gauge of ball you like best."

I closed my legs for the sake of modesty. "Good to know."

Aside from the dull throb, it wasn't that bad. I dressed while she cleaned up. I had just buttoned my jeans when the doorknob rattled.

"Tenley? Lisa? Are you in there?"

"Just a second!" Lisa called out.

She tossed her gloves in the garbage and I opened the door. Hayden stood on the other side.

"Are you done with your client already?" My pitch was too high.

"Yeah." Hayden looked from me to Lisa. "What are you two up to? Why was the door locked?"

We both spoke at the same time.

"Lisa was checking to see how my industrial was healing—"

"Tenley wanted me to look at one of her nipple rings—"

Hayden crossed his arms over his chest. His tongue poked at his viper bites and his eyes narrowed into slits. "Which one was it?"

"Both. I wanted Lisa to have a look at both," I replied quickly.

"Your nipples looked fine to me this morning."

I mimicked his stance. "That wasn't your area of focus, though, was it?"

"I think I would have noticed if there was a problem. I'm pretty fucking familiar with your nipples," Hayden shot back.

"I'm going to check and see if Jamie or Chris needs me for anything." Lisa tried to squeeze by, but Hayden blocked the door.

"Oh, no, you don't. I want to know what the hell is going on. I smell bullshit."

Lisa rolled her eyes. "Oh, for God's sake, Hayden. Back off. Girl nipples are different from your tiny little man nipples. Ours take twice as long to heal, and with all the friction Tenley's got this morning hers are a little tender. She wanted to make sure they weren't at risk of infection. Now look at what you've done." Lisa flailed her hands in my direction. "You're embarrassing her. Thanks for being a jerk." Lisa shoved his shoulder and stalked off.

Hayden turned back to me, chagrined. I was beet red. Not because I was embarrassed, but more because I couldn't believe Lisa had managed to pull off the lie.

He ran his hand through his hair and then down over his pecs, where his metallic barbells were. His gaze lowered to my chest. "Shit. I'm sorry. I didn't think about that at all. . . ."

"It's okay. I asked Lisa to look because of our talk earlier." I was pushing the lie now, and I felt bad about it. But this wasn't like my other omissions. This wouldn't cause any harm.

"Right. Of course." He nodded like a bobblehead. "I'm done for the night. Do you want to come up to my place and hang out?"

I tried not to get too excited. "Are you sure?"

"Yeah."

I doubted he meant hanging out in the way he used to, but I smiled, feeling suddenly shy. "I'd like that."

On Sunday evening, Hayden asked me to come to dinner at Cassie's. Everyone was going and he wanted me there.

Sarah and I had seen each other several times by that point. Her forgiveness came easily, which was a relief. She understood why I left better than anyone else, maybe because she'd been exposed to the nightmares that plagued me. Whatever the reason, her support was a blessing. While Lisa seemed to be another easy alliance, she would always have Hayden's back over mine. Hayden pulled into the driveway, behind Sarah's Tercel. I was glad she was here already.

As I gaped at the stately home, Hayden put his hand on the back of my neck. "You okay?"

"This house is beautiful."

"Nate bought it a number of years back, when the market was slow. It needed a lot of work and he's good with real estate. It's how he managed to snap up Serendipity before they turned it into another condo or a high-rise. I bought Inked Armor off of him. It used to be a barbershop."

"I thought he was a clinical psychiatrist."

"He is. Real estate is his hobby."

"Aren't hobbies usually a little more relaxing?"

"I guess for him it is. We're going to renovate a property together in the spring."

"I didn't know you were into that kind of thing."

Hayden shrugged. "He asked me while you were gone. I thought it would a good way to pass the time." Hayden cut the engine. "We should go in; they're probably waiting for us."

Dinner at Cassie's was full of holiday talk. She enlisted me to make cupcakes. Last year I'd been in the hospital, pumped full of drugs, so it wasn't a day I remembered. This year I'd be lucid enough to miss the family traditions. My ornaments, the ones my parents gave me every year, were in a box in my closet. I'd have to get a tree so they'd have a place to hang.

"You're off tomorrow?" I asked Hayden as we drove back toward Inked Armor after dinner.

"Yeah. What's up? You want to do something?"

"I'm supposed to go shopping with Sarah and Lisa in the afternoon, but I want to buy a tree, too. Christmas is barely a week away."

"I'll take you to get one in the morning. We can strap it to the top of the douche mobile."

"We can take my car."

"And risk ruining the paint job on the roof? Not a chance."

Hayden hated Connor's car and that it was still parked behind Serendipity. He made a passing comment about pretentious douches driving BMWs. Connor hadn't been a douche, but he had had moments of pretension.

"Do you want to set it up at your place or mine?" I asked.

"Mine. Definitely mine," Hayden said. "TK will love that shit."

He drove past his building and rounded the corner leading to the lot behind Serendipity, which meant I wasn't being invited up. Since the first night I'd returned, there had been no sleepovers. It was part of Hayden's plan to keep us from making bad decisions. I would've preferred bad decision-making to sleeping alone, but we were together almost every evening after he finished work. It wasn't enough, but it was better than nothing.

Hayden said a thorough good night which resulted in fogged-up windows and an inordinate level of sexual frustration on my part. I hoped his cautiousness waned by the time Christmas arrived. I headed upstairs to my apartment. Being without Hayden would have been easier if TK was waiting for me, but she was still at his place. Sarah wasn't home either, so I was without a distraction for the rest of the night.

Once inside I kicked off my shoes, tossed my jacket on the hook, and rushed to my bedroom. I stripped out of my clothes and rooted around in my dresser for bedwear. Upon my return, I discovered my apartment had two temperatures in the winter; "hot" and "sauna." There was no in-between. Intent on dishing out some payback for the makeout session in the car, I ditched my bra and changed into a camisole and a pair of shorts. Then I went back out to the kitchen to pour myself a drink. Crossing to the window, I drew back the curtains, sat down on the sill, and waited.

I used to do this every night when I first moved in, before I'd gone into Inked Armor and everything changed. I'd taken up the habit again. Especially now that I knew where Hayden's condo was located on the wall of windows across the street. Hayden and I had developed a new bedtime ritual. It made the lack of sleepovers a little less difficult to take.

My gaze shifted to the Inked Armor sign. It remained lit, lending a soft glow to the sidewalk below. Bundled up in scarves and hats and heavy coats, people hurried along the streets. I looked up at the condos above the shop and smiled when a slice of light appeared in the window almost directly above Inked Armor. The curtains were pushed aside and a figure eclipsed the light.

Hayden's profile came into view, shadows cutting across his body. He'd taken off his dress shirt. A thin undershirt covered the majority of his ink, but it was tight enough to provide an adequate view of his heavyset shoulders and broad chest. I liked it best when he appeared in nothing but his ink, but I would take what I could get. TK was in her favorite place; draped across his shoulders.

My phone rang.

"Hi." I lifted my hand in a wave and he mirrored the movement.

Hayden's deep voice came through the line. "You changed."

"I'm ready for bed."

"You look a little underdressed to me, considering the weather."

"It's hot in here." I fingered the strap of my camisole, gazing up at his shadowy profile in the window above me.

"You don't think you'll get cold?"

"I wouldn't be if you came over," I whispered hopefully.

His heavy exhale told me I was pushing it. "I thought you said you weren't going to make this difficult for me."

"I'm not trying to."

"Are you sure about that?" His posture matched his tone; stiff. I didn't want him mad at me. Not with me still sleeping in my own apartment.

"I just miss you." I brought my fingers to my lips and touched the window.

There was a long pause. When he spoke again, his voice was soft, the edge gone. "I'm not far. Good night, kitten, I'll see you in the morning."

"G'night, Hayden."

He ended the call and lifted his hand in a parting wave before he dropped the curtain. A few minutes later the light in his bedroom went out. I stayed at the window for a long time. It took me ages to fall asleep after I finally went to bed, knowing Hayden was still out of reach.

My phone woke me in the middle of the night.

"Tenley?" Hayden's voice wavered.

"I'm here. Is everything okay?" I sat up, blinking away the bleariness. It was three in the morning.

"I had another—" He coughed. "You weren't here. You weren't beside me, and I just needed to make sure you were okay. I'm sorry."

"It's all right. Everything's all right." I listened to his panicked breathing as I got out of bed and went to the window with the view of his condo. He was standing at his window as he'd been a few hours earlier. "Do you want me to come over?"

His fingers drifted over the glass. "Please?"

"Give me five minutes." I kept him on the line while I pulled on clothes, talking him down, reassuring him I was on my way.

Hayden met me at the front door of his condo building, even though I had keys. He didn't end the call until I was standing right in front of him. His hair was a riotous mess, the sides sticking out, the top standing on end in some places and lying flat it others. His eyes were bloodshot and his jaw was tight.

"Was it the same dream?" I asked as he pulled me tight against him, burying his face in my hair. From what I understood, his nightmares had become a nightly occurrence.

"Sort of. It starts out the same every time but it keeps changing."

He led me to the elevator, punching the button until the doors slid open. I couched my anxiety as I stepped inside; Hayden required my strength more than I needed his. When we were closed inside, he made quick work of the buttons on my coat. His cold hand went under my hoodie to my sternum and then slid around my back. As on the night I first returned, it wasn't sexual.

He kept his hand pressed against my skin as the elevator chimed and the doors opened. He was too unnerved to get his key in the lock, so I let us into his condo. TK met us at the door, weaving between our legs. Hayden didn't even bother to put his shoes away once we were locked inside, which spoke to his state. I put them in the closet, along with my own.

"Do you want to tell me about it?" I asked when we were sitting on his couch, him with a glass of scotch and me with water.

He might need the alcohol to chase away the shakes, but I wanted to have my faculties about me. My legs were draped over his and his arm was around my back, holding me as close as he could without climbing on top of me.

"It used to be that I couldn't get to you. Now I can, but when I get close enough to touch you, you disappear. Then there are other dreams that are more memories than anything. I can't get them out of my head; not when I'm sleeping, not when I'm awake. I feel like I can't get away from it anymore."

I stroked his cheek with the back of my hand. It was awful to see his subconscious playing on his fears.

He was silent for a moment before he said softly, "What if something happens to you? What if there's nothing I can do to stop it? What if someone takes you away from me again?"

I snuggled deeper into his arms, trying to comfort him with closeness. "No one's going to take me away from you."

"But you can't know that. Even if you promise you're going to stay, even if I believe that, something could happen to you, and then where would I be? Alone again. I'll be alone and all I'll have left are these fucking nightmares. My head is too full. I can't—I can't—" His panic took over.

During the initial months after the plane crash, panic plagued me like a ghost. That helpless, out-of-control feeling that at any moment the thing I needed most would disappear. Back then, it had been the medication. Now it was him.

I peeled his fingers from the glass in his hand before he shattered it with the force of his grip. Then I straddled his lap to wrap myself around him. He clung to me as I whispered reassuring words. We were so similar in our pain. If only we could cancel each other's out.

12

HAYDEN

Five days. That was how long the sleepover boycott lasted. Yet even with Tenley in my bed, I couldn't shake the nightmares. They were worse than ever, but at least with her next to me the content of the dreams didn't include her.

Something in me had snapped. The wall I'd erected had come crumbling down, and I couldn't get it back up. All the things I never wanted to remember about my parents' deaths were resurfacing with a clarity that woke me in the night, leaving me sweaty and shaking.

It was six in the morning. Tenley was asleep in my bed. I should have been there, too, but it was pointless when all I did was toss and turn. Instead, I sat on my couch in the living room. The Christmas tree Tenley and I had put up earlier in the week blinked cheerily from across the room. We'd decorated it together with the ornaments she brought over, and the predawn glow of the flashing white lights was a bitter counterpoint to my somber mood. My laptop was open on the coffee table. I'd been scanning the same articles over and over, looking for some seed of information. Anything to help make sense of the memories I couldn't reshelve in the Do Not Enter section of my brain.

I couldn't ignore them anymore; the memories had holes I wanted to fill. So much about that time was vague, except for the week prior to my parents' murder. My actions then set the wheels in motion.

My mom knocked on the door to my bedroom. I shoved the porn mag under my covers and touched the mouse on my laptop. The banal essay I'd finished three days earlier for my Man and Society class popped up on the screen.

"You can come in."

She poked her head in the door. "We're on our way out."

"Okay, cool. You look nice." I said it not just to suck up, but because she did. She was wearing a red dress. Her dark hair was pulled up, away from the delicate features of her face.

"You don't think it's too much?"

"Did Dad say something?" Leave it to him to make her second-guess her choice minutes before they had to leave.

"No, no. I just wondered if I should have gone with black."

"Red is better. Makes more of a statement."

I grinned, and a genuine smile lit up her face as she smoothed her hands over the skirt. She was soft around the edges, the way a mom should be. Not like those over-liposuctioned Stepford types she'd be with tonight. Guaranteed they would all be in black, or some animal-print monstrosity. Thank Christ I was too old to be dragged out to those boring events.

"Are you guys gonna be late?"

"We'll be back around midnight. No friends in the house while we're gone."

"Sure thing, Mom."

"I'm serious, Hayden. No friends. Your father will sell that car, and you'll be taking the bus until you can afford to buy your own."

"Okay. No friends in the house. Promise," I said to fend off the coming lecture.

"If you're going out, lock the doors and be home by ten thirty. No later."

"Sure. Have fun." I hit a couple of keys on my laptop to make it look as if I needed to get back to work.

She glanced around my room. "I'd tell you to clean your room, but that would be pointless."

Dad called for her from the bottom of the stairs, and her heels clipped on the hardwood floor as she turned to leave.

"Hayden?"

I looked up.

"I love you. You know that, don't you?"

"Yeah. Of course. I love you, too, Mom."

My father called for her again, impatient this time.

I waited until the car pulled out of the driveway before I called Damen to pick me up. I'd lost the keys to my car two weeks ago when some chick I picked up puked all over the backseat. The keys would be mine again when I coughed up the cash for the detail job. While I waited for Damen to arrive, I downed half the mickey of vodka a girl from my part-time job had bought for me.

My dad had long ago locked up his liquor cabinet due to the number of times I'd raided it. I checked my wallet. I'd already burned through my paycheck and was down to my last ten bucks. I headed to my parents' room and lifted the painting from the wall to access the safe hidden behind it.

I punched in the code and smiled as the release latch gave way. My mom's best jewelry and my dad's rainy-day money were stashed inside, along with some bank shit. I lifted a couple of twenties, shoved them in my wallet, and locked the safe. I only felt a little bad about taking the money. I'd put it back when I got paid at the end of the week.

"Look at you, Mission: Impossible," Damen said from the doorway.

I dropped the painting on the floor. The corner of the frame dented the hardwood. "You scared the shit out of me! How the fuck did you get in here?"

"The front door. I knocked first."

I frowned. My parents usually locked up when they went out. I hung the painting on the wall, tapping the edge until it was perfectly aligned. A scuff mark marred the edge of the frame that hit the floor. I rubbed at it, but the mark remained. Hopefully my dad wouldn't notice.

"What the hell is that supposed to be, an angel of death?" Damen asked, eyeing the painting. It was an angel rendered in shades of red.

"Shut it. My mom painted it."

"It's pretty fucking weird." He picked up a diamond earring my mom had left on the dresser, rolling it between his fingers.

I grabbed it out of his hand and put it back. "Don't touch anything. My dad will notice if something's been moved."

"You need to chill out. Come on, the bitches are in the car."

"Oh, yeah?" I scanned the room to make sure nothing else was out of place. "Who'd you bring this time?"

"Some randoms. Don't worry, there's one for you."

I grinned. "Let's roll."

Damen grabbed the mickey from my hand and polished it off as we booked it down the stairs. I locked the door and checked the planter for the spare key before I followed him to the SUV parked down the street.

Damen was a few years older than me. He ran a tattoo shop call Art Addicts downtown where I got my eyebrow pierced. I'd gone back a few times with friends and discovered he had a side business of the less-than-legal persuasion. He had hookups and seemed to know a lot of skanky girls. Those traits made him an appealing acquaintance.

Some loser I didn't know was sitting in the front seat, staring out the windshield. I opened the back door and a cloud of smoke poured out. Two guys who looked vaguely familiar were in the middle with a chick I'd seen at the tattoo shop squeezed between them. She looked at me and then over her shoulder at the two girls in the very back. I didn't recognize either one. They both had on too much eye makeup. The fake blonde was busy hauling on a joint. The real blonde was putting on lip gloss. I climbed back between them.

"One of those is for me," Damen said as he pulled away from the curb.

"Is that right?" I put an arm around both of them. "Which one is mine?"

"Me," they said at the same time.

"I'll just keep them entertained until you're ready then, yeah?" I called up to the front.

"Not too entertained. I'm not into sloppy seconds."

Music blared through the speaker system, making further conversation impossible. Not that talk was necessary.

It was twelve thirty by the time I got home. I was wasted. And high as a kite. My parents' car wasn't in the driveway so I assumed they weren't home. I was wrong. They'd parked in the garage. My dad was sitting on the stairs when I came in, his tie loose around his neck, his shirt untucked, the top two buttons undone. He was calm. Which meant he was really fucking mad.

I heard the soft tread of feet coming down the hall from upstairs. "Is he home?"

My mom came into view at the top of the landing, her eyes red-rimmed. She'd been crying. She pulled her pale blue satin robe tight around her and came down the stairs, skirting my father, who still hadn't moved.

"Oh, thank God! You have no idea how worried I was. I told you ten thirty. I was very explicit about that." Her voice cracked.

It made me feel like shit, which was precisely the point. "I'm sorry, Mom. I lost track of time."

"It's after midnight! You have school in the morning! Where have you been? What happened to your neck?"

She was much shorter than me, especially without her heels, and she had to lift her head to meet my eyes. I couldn't focus well; the combination of weed and booze made me logy and uncoordinated. She grabbed me by the chin and forced my head to the side. "Are those hickeys? What kind of girl are you spending your time with? You smell like a bar! I have had it, Hayden. What's it going to take?" Her anger gave way to more tears and I just stood there, feeling like the asshole teenager I was.

"All right, Eleanor, I'll take it from here." Dad rose from the stairs and gently settled his hand on her shoulder.

She spun around and pointed a finger in his face."Don't! Don't treat me like I'm too fragile to handle this. I birthed him."She turned back to me. "I can deal with the holes in your face Hayden, but this"—she gestured to my neck—"I have a real problem with you spending time with girls who think this is appropriate. What if you get her pregnant? Then what are we going to do? I'm too young to be a grandmother! Not to mention the drinking and the drugs. And don't try and deny it, Hayden. I'm not stupid. I know what that smell is!"

I shoved my hands in my pockets, weaving on my feet, and slurred,"I don't think you're stupid, Mom."

My father shot me a look that should have made paint peel off the walls."Eleanor, I agree.You have every right to be upset with him. However, this conversation would be better served in the morning, when he's coherent."

She seemed to realize he was right.With a graceful flourish, she lifted the hem of her robe and went back upstairs. Mischief, our black-and-white cat, who loathed me, wailed in my direction and followed her.

When the door to my parents' bedroom slammed shut, my dad turned around. His arms hung loosely at his sides, but his fingers flexed and clenched repeatedly; his disappointment and exhaustion were obvious. I was wearing him out. He didn't yell. He didn't swear. He didn't kick me out of the house. Any of that would have been preferable to what he said next.

"You better take a good long look at what you're doing with your life, Son. The decisions you make now will have a direct impact on your future. If you're not careful, you're going to put your mother in an early grave. And if it's just you and me?Well, I'm not sure either one of us will survive that."

Less than a week later, they were dead.

"Hayden?What are you doing up so early?"

Tenley stood in the middle of the living room. Her hair was a tousled mess. She wore one of my long-sleeved, black shirts with shorts underneath. We still hadn't had sex since she first came home. In the past eight days, the only thing we'd done was kiss. It was driving me fucking insane. And times like this, when I needed a distraction from the shit going on in my head, I wanted to say screw it and, well, screw her.

"I was just checking out some articles."

"At seven in the morning? How long have you been up?"

"An hour maybe?"

Tenley crossed the room and dropped down beside me. She glanced at my open laptop on the coffee table. "Do you mind if I read it?"

"Go ahead." I wanted her closer, so I moved her into my lap while she scanned the article. I wondered what the content looked like from her point of view. She clicked on the links I'd book-marked. The related articles petered out when the case went cold.

"You've been looking at these a lot lately."

"Yeah. But it doesn't go anywhere, as you can see. I keep looking for something because there are things that just don't fit, you know? There were problems with the evidence, but the articles don't say anything about it."

She tucked my hair behind my ear. I needed to get it cut.

"The lack of closure must be so horrible."

I took her hands in mine and kissed her knuckles. "I want answers. I want it to make sense. There are images . . ." I shook my head against the memories. "And the smell—I think that was the worst part. For a long time I kept thinking it would fade, but it hasn't. There's so much I can't remember very well. The night it happened is mostly a haze, up until I came home. Then it's so fucking clear, it's in hi def."

Tenley's smile was sad. "I know what you mean about the smells. Some parts of the crash are black holes, but others . . ." Goose bumps rose along her arms. "Scents trigger the worst memories."

That was it exactly. Violent death had a distinctive odor. The residue was like a black smear on my life I couldn't clear away, no matter how much time passed.

After a minute of silence when we were both wrapped up in shitty memories, Tenley kissed my temple. "I know talking about it is hard, but have you ever considered—"

"If you're going to say therapy, you can stop right there. Nate's been up my ass about it for years."

She looked utterly taken aback. "You've never talked to anyone about this?"

"I'm talking to you."

"I mean a professional."

"What's the point? I already know why I'm fucked up. I don't need someone to tell me that for a hundred bucks an hour."

"You're not fucked up, Hayden." I raised an eyebrow and she sighed. "It's not about the why. It's about finding ways to deal with what you went through, so it doesn't rule your life. That's the reason I've decided to attend a grief-counseling group."

"What? When are you doing that?"

"There's a group starting in January on campus. It's been a year—it's time."

I smoothed my hands down her arms. "But you already dealt with things. Isn't that what going back to Arden Hills was about?"

"It was the first step of many. The memorial service, while awful at the time, helped in some ways, and the estate has been taken care of. But the rest of it . . . I still harbor a lot of guilt. It's going to take time for me to let go of that."

The guilt I understood. That lecture from my dad played out in a constant loop some nights. If I'd made different choices, they might still be alive. If my parents hadn't been so concerned about my sneaking out, they would have stayed at their function longer the night they died. Instead they came home early and were shot to death in their bed. While I was out getting wasted with Damen.

I regarded Tenley with skepticism. "Won't talking about it just bring up all the crap?"

"Probably, yes. But I can't just keep it all inside and let it fester."

I didn't comment. Seven years later I was still angry; still shut down in a lot of ways; still pushing boundaries.

"Anyway, that wasn't where I was going with this. I'm not sure how cases like your parents' work, but shouldn't there be a file or something you can access? Maybe there are public records?"

"There might be. I've never looked into it."

"Wouldn't the local police have information?"

I scoffed. "Yeah, and they were superhelpful when all that shit went down. You've met that dick Cross. He's the reason everything got fucked up in the first place."

"There must have been other officers working the case, though. Maybe it's worth looking into. It might give you some peace."

Her argument made sense. Doing something proactive would be better than reading the same damn articles over and over, getting nowhere but deeper into my own head.

"Can we drop the subject?" I asked.

"Of course—I didn't mean to push you. Do you want to talk about something else?"

She had one arm draped around my shoulder, her fingers gliding up and down the back of my neck, into my hairline. It felt good. Better than good, actually.

"I don't feel like talking anymore."

"Oh. Okay. Do you want some space? I can go back to my place—"

"No. I don't want that, either."

I pulled her closer and she shifted a little, her ass settling in the dip between my legs. My cock swelled, sensing the proximity of the Promised Land. If she noticed, she didn't say anything. Instead, the fingers of her free hand began tracing the ink on my arm.

Starting at my wrist, she followed the vines to the bleeding heart into the bend of my elbow, where the flowers exploded into life.

She made no attempt to go beyond where the short-sleeve shirt ended. After our conversation in the car—where I pretty much threw a shit fit over her leaving and laid all my cards on the table—she hadn't pushed for anything. She was more than happy to sit around my place without so much as a make-out session.

Even in bed she was all PG, wearing lots of clothing, avoiding positions that might encourage important-body-part contact. In the morning when I spooned with her and my stupid ass hard-on jabbed into her low back, or on the really great days when it nestled against the cleft of her ass, she didn't press against it. It was driving me up the fucking wall. I had no idea where to draw the line, and the longer I waited, the more I wanted to tromp all over it. If she'd just start something, then I'd have the excuse I needed to keep going. That way I could have the connection I was desperate for, in the only way I knew how to get it.

I pulled her in tighter, my hand moving down to her bare upper thigh. Then I shifted my hips up, a furtive attempt at a little friction. Tenley's fingers stilled and her head lifted from my chest. I met her questioning gaze with a forlorn one of my own. I should have asked Lisa what the fucking time frame was supposed to be. I had no clue.

Tenley's fingers were on the move again. They drifted up my arm over my shoulder to my neck, skimming my jaw until they were no longer tracing tattoos, but the curve of my lip. I parted them and she took the invitation. Her thumb slipped inside my mouth. I bit down and sucked, feeling the smooth ridge of her nail and the warmth of her skin. Pulling free, she replaced her thumb with her lips, the softest brush of skin against skin. She kept coming back, kisses drawing out, becoming deeper.

When she slowly shifted around, giving me ample opportunity

to stop her, I didn't. Instead I urged her to part her legs and straddle me. That wet heat was only an inch away from where I needed
it to be now, though fabric impeded direct contact. Tenley's ass was
like a magnet for my hands and they went there immediately, gripping the soft, pliant flesh.

My dick was so fucking ecstatic. If it had hands, it would have
torn right through my scrubs, moved those pathetic shorts of hers
aside, and dived right in. Instead it punched helplessly at the fabric,
and I made a pained sound because my balls were so tight, they
were on the verge of exploding.

When her hands glided down my chest to the hem of my shirt,
I caught her wrists by reflex.

"This doesn't have to lead to sex," she said. "I could just make
you feel good. Would you let me do that?"

My mouth worked independently of my brain, probably because
all the blood in my body was currently pooled in the appendage all
snug and cozy between Tenley's legs. "I don't know if—I want—"

"We're adults, Hayden. We don't have to stay stalled out in
first gear forever. We can go as far as you're comfortable with. You
tell me what you want, and I'll give it to you."

As if it were that easy.

Our palms connected. Then she pressed her lips against the
back of my hand. When I didn't stop her, Tenley bit down on a
knuckle and gave it a wet kiss. A promise of what was to come
should I relent on my own inane restrictions.

She guided my hands to rest on her upper thighs, right below
the hem of her shorts. Her mouth moved across my jaw until she
reached my lips. Her tongue met mine in a leisurely sweep, over
and over, until I was lulled into a sense of false security that we
weren't going to take this any further. Her fingers traveled up and
down my forearms at the same languid pace, then went lower and
dipped under the hem of my shirt. I stiffened.

"I just want to see you. I miss looking at you." When she put it that way, it seemed like a reasonable request.

I raised my arms and she drew my shirt over my head. Tenley folded it neatly and set it on the arm of the couch. She started at my shoulders, smoothing her hands down my chest, over my stomach, and back up again. After that, her fingers went to work tracing my ink. Her exploration was slow to the point of painful, but I didn't complain. Her touch was exactly what I needed; the thing I'd been denied for so long. I couldn't remember why I thought it made sense to prolong the misery.

And then she went lower.

My grip tightened on her thighs.

She peeked up at me through her lashes. "You don't want me to touch you? But you're so hard."

Talking about how hard I was did not help my resolve.

"Please? You're like this all the time. It must be torture. I could make it better."

I couldn't deny the truth in what she said. I was *always* hard around her. It sucked to have perpetual blue balls.

She shifted forward, her hot, cotton-covered pussy settled right over my erection. She ground her hips in a slow circle. Her lips moved from my shoulder, up my neck to my ear, and she whispered, "I just want to *touch*."

She brushed over the outline of my straining cock and I had no will to stop her. All I could think about was how *good* it would feel when it wasn't my own shitty hand doing the work.

Her nails were longer than I'd ever seen them, the white tips filed in a gentle curve. As she released the tie on my scrubs, I watched with mind-numbing anticipation. I'd never before been this excited about a goddamn hand job. Once the tie was undone, Tenley's hand slipped inside the waistband.

She grazed the head and I groaned, looking down at her wrist as it peeked out from the dark fabric. She hummed in approval as she followed the ridge and circled the steel ball. Her warm hand wrapped around the shaft and she freed my dick from my pants. I was so fucking ready to blow, the head was almost purple. Her thumb slid back and forth along the slit, which felt unfucking real.

"Look at you," she murmured. "You need some relief, don't you?"

An animalistic grunt was all I could manage.

Her free hand, which had been resting on my chest, joined the other one. She laced her fingers together, circling the shaft, her thumbs stacked on top of each other. The slow stroking started. My hips arched and I felt the abrasive brush of cotton against the head. Her oversize shirt was getting in the way, particularly of my view.

"Let go for a second," I ground out.

"What?" She squeezed harder instead.

I tugged on the hem of her shirt and leaned in to kiss her neck. "I want this off."

"Oh."

She did as I asked, and I let out a strangled sound because she wasn't touching me anymore. Then she shifted her hips and my erection was right between the cotton of her shorts and the bare flesh of her inner thigh, and, *God*, it was warm.

As soon as the shirt was off, her hands returned to their rightful place, and satin-smooth strands of her hair tickled my chest. I moved it out of the way and cupped her breasts, my thumbs sweeping over the tight nipples. I was rewarded with a soft sigh.

With one hand on my shoulder, she rose up on her knees and used the head of my cock to push her shorts to the side. Underneath were smooth satin panties, with a much more appealing texture than cotton. Her face was flushed as she looked down to watch her body move against me, the smooth steel ball of my piercing sliding right over where her clit was.

She maintained a steady rhythm, her body stiffening as she breathed out an expletive with the next aggressive shift of her hips. Having her grind herself all over me was enthralling, her breasts bouncing. I was at eye level with them so I leaned in and covered a pierced nipple with my mouth, flicking my tongue against the barbell. She gasped and bucked, gripping me tighter, moving faster. I held on to her hips as her movements became more frantic.

Her eyes flipped to mine, an emotion close to shock crossing her face, replaced with a bliss that verged on agony. *"Oh, God."*

The sound that followed was the sexiest thing I ever heard. Her body shook as she arched forward; then she sagged against me, panting into my neck. Watching her come like a freight train left me hanging on the edge.

She mumbled something into my neck and her lips swept over to my mouth. Despite her release, her kiss was full of pent-up need and longing. She shimmied back off my lap, momentarily confusing me until she sank down on her knees between my legs.

A small part of my subconscious pointed out the lack of fairness. She only got a dry hump and I was going to get to watch my cock disappear between those pretty, full lips of hers. But I didn't complain when she pulled my pants down my legs.

She wrapped one hand around the shaft, and her eyes never left mine as she leaned forward and swirled her soft, wet tongue around the head, then took it in her mouth. The last time she'd done this had been in a dimly lit parking garage.

I had replayed the hazy image in my head a million times, but *nothing* could have prepared me for the vision of a half-naked Tenley, in skimpy shorts, with my dick in her mouth. She hummed around me and my eyes rolled up. Tenley moved to work me from a different angle, the piercing clicking along her teeth. Her head moved down with her hand as she took as much of me in as she could.

That sight should go down in the annals of cocksucking history.

I wanted to snap a picture of her and use it as my screen saver, especially when she sucked her way back up. Then her cheeks hollowed and she popped off. She pressed her tongue right over the steel ball on the underside of the head and licked up, as if it were an ice cream cone.

"Do you have any idea how hot you look?" I asked, my voice rough.

Her smile was full of smug satisfaction as her lips closed around me once again. She sank down until I could feel the back of her throat. I wrapped her hair around my wrist and cupped the back of her head, guiding her mouth. Her palm twisted on the upstroke, lips reaching the ridge, tongue swirling around the tip and pressing into the slit.

"Christ." I gritted my teeth.

As I got closer, my fingers involuntarily tightened in her hair. She looked up at me through thick lashes and hummed as I moved her faster over me, sending the vibrations straight through my shaft. This time on her way up she left a gap between her hand and her mouth, exposing an inch of slick, wet cock. I felt the click of steel against her teeth as she grazed the sensitive skin and tugged up on the barbell. I closed my eyes because the sight, with the sensation, would end this far sooner than I wanted. But it didn't help. All my muscles tightened in response to the impending orgasm.

"I'm gonna come," I warned.

I expected her to speed up, which I would have done, but she slowed down, fighting against my hand on the back of her head. I was so close, just teetering on the brink, but not going over. It was the best torture I ever had.

She slowly slid back up, her hand following close behind. Even though watching made it more difficult to hold back, it would have been a crime against the blow-job gods *not* to, and I kept my eyes trained on Tenley's mouth. This time she came off completely.

Her fingers tightened in a viselike grip around the base of my shaft, and the palm of her other hand smoothed over the head. She pressed her thumb down over the tip, blocking the barrel of the gun. The pressure built as the sensation spiraled and spread.

"Hayden," she said in a moany-breathy-sex voice I wanted more of. Her lips brushed back and forth over the piercing as she waited for a response.

"Yeah," I groaned, my body shaking with impatience. I just wanted to come.

"Would you like to finish in my mouth?" she asked, all polite innocence.

"Fuck. Yes. *Please.*"

Her mouth closed around the head as her thumb slipped away and her grip on my shaft loosened.

"Jesus!" My head slammed back into the couch as I exploded; hot and violent and pulsing as she sucked and swallowed. When I finally stopped coming, she gently laid my used cock on my stomach. Then she leaned over and gave it an affectionate kiss and a pat, as if it were her pet. Which it kind of was.

"Don't you feel better now?" Tenley asked as she rested her head on the inside of my thigh, her smile in no way masking her pride.

I ran my thumb tenderly over her swollen bottom lip. "That would be the understatement of a lifetime. Was that thing you did at the end something you picked up from that magazine you read?" One of those chick mags was always on her coffee table boasting of articles like "Endless Orgasms!" Maybe they weren't so useless after all.

"No."

I froze. "Where did you learn how to do that?" I should have been grateful my girlfriend went down on me and was awesome at it, but, no, I had to be a jealous ass and get all pissy with her.

Tenley just gave me a look. "From watching porn."

13

TENLEY

Okay, so that wasn't completely true. I didn't learn that special little trick from watching the usual Internet crap with women being gagged by giant penises. While googling *apadravya and oral sex*, I found a series of instructional videos that were both hot and helpful. No way did I want to risk cracking my teeth on his barbell.

"What kind of porn?" Hayden's voice was deep, and his tongue slid between his lips.

"Wouldn't you like to know."

I sat back, away from the erection lying across Hayden's belly. It had yet to deflate, making it too much of an enticement. My orgasm had been unbelievably intense, but I still wanted more. More closeness, more touching, more release. I wasn't sure I could handle it, though. Not yet with my only partially healed piercing, and the sexual heat between us. I stood up, using his thighs to brace myself as I rose.

"Where do you think you're going? You can't say something like that and walk away."

"Oh, I'm pretty sure I can," I teased.

His hands smoothed up the back of my thighs and went under the hem of my shorts. With a playful squeeze, he pulled me forward. He looked up at me, cocky grin on his face, chin resting just above my pelvis. The position was achingly reminiscent of the first time I'd seduced him into my bed. He'd tried so hard to resist.

He pressed a wet kiss right above the waistband of my shorts. The weeks since his mouth had been on me felt like an eternity, but I was already hypersensitive from all the over-the-clothes action. Additional attention below the belt could set back my healing time, and that wouldn't do.

He lowered his head and the tip of his nose swept over the crest of my pelvis.

"I might be persuaded to put my mouth to good use if you tell me a little about your porn-watching habits."

The shorts and my underwear were the only things preventing Hayden from doing just that. He was still mostly hard. It wouldn't take much for both of us to be naked and sprawled out on the couch, or the floor.

I twirled his hair around my finger. "That's a generous offer, but I'm supposed to go Christmas shopping with the girls later this morning. And if you start with that mouth of yours, I'll be late for sure."

"You went shopping two days ago. Why do you need to go again?"

"I still need to pick up a few things." I'd bought most of the presents, but hadn't gotten anything substantial for Hayden yet. I had a viable idea, but I needed Lisa's help to execute it.

"What kinds of things?"

"Top-secret things."

"What time are you supposed to meet them?" Hayden shoved his hands farther under my shorts, kneading the skin.

I had to clear my throat before I answered. "Eleven."

He looked across to the kitchen clock. "It's barely after eight. I have more than enough time to make you feel good before you go."

"That might be true. But do you think if you put that talented tongue on me, it'll end there? Once we get started, there isn't going to be any stopping—and I'm not interested in being bound by time constraints."

If Hayden went down on me and found what I'd been hiding, I was 100 percent sure that magnificent erection of his would follow. Sensitive or not, there was no way I could say no to him.

Hayden sighed. "You seem awfully intent on denying me the opportunity."

"Not denying, postponing. I'm more than happy to take a rain check. We should go for breakfast," I said, changing the subject.

"I prefer eating here."

I ignored the comment. "I'm going to get dressed."

He slouched down on the couch and pouted. He reminded me of someone who'd had his hand smacked for reaching into the cookie jar. I quashed the pang of guilt and headed for his room. Putting it off was for the greater good—mine more than his, but still, he'd be happy about it later.

I put on a warm sweater dress and tights. He stomped down the hall and appeared in the doorway as I smoothed the dress over my hips. He looked frustrated. And suspicious. Although his pants were back on, they did nothing to hide the problem resurfacing within. I focused on the mirror and dragged a brush through my hair, feigning oblivion.

He sauntered across the room, stopped a few feet behind me, and pulled the drawstring at his waist. The pants slid down his thighs. My eyes moved over his chest, down to his hips. Hayden picked up the discarded pants and strolled over to his closet, that massive erection bobbing. It would have been comical if he hadn't looked so predatory.

As he turned his back, I watched his reflection in the mirror, taking in the gorgeous lines of his body and the artwork. The muscles in his back flexed when he dropped the pants into a hamper. The evil eyes of the shrouded-child tattoo followed me as he searched his closet for something to wear. He came out a few minutes later with clothes slung over his arm. I unzipped my cosmetics bag, making of show of applying concealer.

"You're looking a little too hot for a shopping trip."

He laid his clothes on the dresser and nudged me out of the way to get some boxer briefs. His underwear was folded in neat little squares, lined up according to color and type. He snatched a pair of black ones and closed the drawer roughly.

"Would you prefer I wear a pair of sweats?"

"Yes." He reached across me to the other side of the dresser and I felt his erection at the small of my back. "I need socks." He put his arm around me and dragged me back into him so he could open the drawer. I stayed perfectly still as that hard length pressed against my spine.

"If I was any more covered up, I'd be in a snowsuit."

He skimmed my sides. "It's the way this hugs all your curves that's the problem."

He moved away. Jabbed his legs into his boxers and yanked them up. The waistband snapped against the head of his erection, and he grimaced. He rearranged himself and went about getting dressed, having given up on coercing me. When he finished buttoning his jeans, he went into the bathroom and shut the door. Hard. The water came on.

A few seconds later the door flew open and slammed into the wall. Hayden's expression was fierce as he stalked across the room and stopped in front of me.

"Why won't you let me lick your kitty?"

I was almost positive my underwear incinerated on comment. I swallowed hard. "I don't want to be late."

"Bullshit. We have more than two hours. You can put your mouth on my cock, but I can't repay the favor? You're hiding something."

Behind the accusation was hurt. Hayden was likely spinning scenarios born of paranoia. We were still working on rebuilding trust, and jeopardizing that with something as inconsequential as a secret piercing seemed silly.

I sighed. "It was supposed to be a surprise."

"What was?"

"I got some new steel."

"What? When?"

"That first day I came back. Lisa did it for me. It's still sensitive."

"What kind of piercing?" It came out sounding guttural.

"Vertical hood," I breathed.

Hayden's mouth dropped open. He blinked. And blinked again. "I wanna see it."

"I don't think that's a good idea." I backed up and hit the dresser.

Hayden planted one hand on either side of me. "Why not?"

"Because if you see it, you'll want to touch it, and we're in your bedroom and the bed is so close and then we'll be naked and I'll want you in me and it's not healed so we shouldn't do that yet," I rushed out.

"Just a peek." His hips pressed against mine.

I put my hands on his chest. "Later."

"Now." He nipped at my jaw.

"Please, Hayden. It's so sensitive—I don't want it to take longer to heal. I'll show you tonight."

His forehead dropped against my shoulder. "This is like torture. You know that, right?"

"It's torture for me, too." But I needed to stay firm or I'd regret it later.

"I knew you two were bullshitting me about the nipple ring being infected." His hand drifted over my hip and down to the hem of my dress, sliding under and up.

"What are you doing?" I asked, panicked. "Nothing." His hand went into my tights from behind.

"It doesn't feel like nothing."

He kissed me softly.

I gasped when his fingers glided lightly over the smooth skin. "Hayden," I pleaded.

"You said I could see it tonight. You didn't say anything about touching." His tongue slipped past my lips, penetrating and retreating at the same time as one of his fingers slipped inside me.

I whimpered and he retracted immediately, moving higher until they reached the tiny steel ball.

"Fuuuuck," he muttered, circling the piercing.

The barbell shifted, sending an electric jolt ricocheting through me. His mouth was going to feel incredible. His hand disappeared and he stepped back.

"Maybe I should call and delay the shopping trip," I said hopefully.

"Nah. I think you're right; you can show me later. And while you're out today"—he lifted his fingers to his mouth and tasted them—"you can think about what I'm going to do to you tonight."

"Which would be what?" I asked, ridiculously breathless.

"I'm going to make you come so hard, so many times; the only thing you'll be able to think about is what it will be like when I'm finally inside you again."

14

TENLEY

The tension didn't dissipate as we headed to the diner, but at least when he was driving, his attention was on something besides me. I was achy and irritable after his teasing. Was this what guys felt like when they were left hanging? Hayden was distracted while we had breakfast, but I didn't think it had to do with sexual frustration.

When we got back in the car, he tapped the steering wheel nervously. "Do we have time to go somewhere?"

"Sure. Lisa isn't picking me up for an hour."

"Okay. Good." He kissed me on the cheek before he put the car in gear.

Hayden drove down back streets until we reached Hyde Park. As we went deeper into the maze of streets, the houses grew progressively larger and the front gardens more elaborate. He stopped in front of a two-and-a-half-story Victorian complete with turret and a circular front porch. Huge planters were on either side of the front steps. The windows were leaded glass and the shutters were painted a sharp black, a lovely contrast to the brick. The house was beautiful.

"This is where I grew up," he said, shifting the car into park.

"It's incredible."

"It was. I guess it still is. I didn't appreciate it as much as I should have when I was a kid." He took my hand, rubbing my knuckles with his thumb. "It took a long time to sell after my parents died. Nate took care of it because I was too young to do it on my own. It's been up for sale a few times since then."

"Is it because of what happened?"

Sometimes events left a shadow. When Connor and his family died, the house still retained an echo of their presence. I wondered if with Hayden's parents' death, the echo was more like a scream.

"Legally you have to disclose a murder to potential buyers, so it was a deterrent. Last year it went up for sale in early fall. It was a good time of year to sell. Everything looked Norman Rockwell perfect. The leaves had turned yellow and orange and the gardens were fantastic. My mom was all about her gardens." He paused, caught up in a memory.

I waited for him to continue, aware Hayden didn't share this information with just anyone.

"I came to an open house because I was curious, you know? The family living there had turned my parents' bedroom into an office. It didn't look the same, but it still made me panicky to be in there."

"I can only imagine." I squeezed his hand.

"There was a safe built into the wall. My mom hung one of her paintings over it to keep it hidden. Whoever bought the house did the same thing, which was the point, I guess. But it freaked me out because the art on the wall was one of those medieval angel prints. It threw me because the one my mom had up was an angel, too, except modern. And the color scheme was way different, but it still freaked me out. . . ."

He lapsed into silence, chewing on his viper bites as he looked out the window at the house. "I have this fucked-up memory from the night my parents were murdered."

I shifted to face him. Hayden rarely spoke about his parents, or the events surrounding their deaths.

"I've never talked about this with anyone. And I don't know if I'm remembering things wrong since I was so fucked up." He played with my fingers as he gathered his thoughts. "The moment I opened the door to their room, everything became hyperclear, but at the same time I sort of . . . stepped outside of my body. You know when you're in a dream, and it's like you're watching the events from outside yourself?"

I nodded. "I know exactly what you mean."

"That's what it was like. That painting that hid the safe was the same one my entire life. It wasn't valuable or anything. It was a piece she'd done when she was in art school. Most of them were landscape paintings, except this one. It was an angel, but it was done in shades of red. It was . . . dark."

"Dark how?"

He contemplated the question. "It was just different. Usually the things she painted were beautiful. This one wasn't like that. Not conventionally, anyway."

"Like the tattoo on your shoulder?"

"That was the first big piece I got after my parents died. Damen put it on me. It wasn't meant to be beautiful at all, but the things my mom painted were. This one was beautiful and disturbing at the same time.

"When I was a kid, like five or six, and my dad was away on business, I'd come into their room in the middle of the night. I'd make my mom sleep on his side of the bed. I told her it was so I could have her pillow 'cause I liked it better.

"But it was really so I didn't have to see that painting, 'cause it scared the shit out of me." He looked away. "Anyway. The first thing I saw when I cracked opened the door was the painting. It was lying on the floor. I didn't understand what had happened, at first. Then I saw my parents. There was so much blood." He shuddered. "Even after I realized they were dead, I kept fixating on that stupid painting."

"You were in shock."

"I guess. There was spatter all over the wall and the floor. I worried that the blood was on that painting, but it blended in and I couldn't see it. I knew when the police came they'd take everything that wasn't nailed down as evidence, and I couldn't stand the thought of losing it. Not because I liked it, but because of what it meant to my mom. I couldn't force myself to go into that room and do anything about it, though."

His eyes shifted from the house to me, his expression one of guilt and shame. I understood them both so well.

"It was like if I could just put the painting back where it belonged, it would undo what happened, and I would be okay. Except I couldn't go into the room. I went downstairs and called the police and destroyed the living room because I was too scared to go back upstairs. I just wanted it all to be an awful trip. I kept hoping my mom would come down and tear me a new asshole because of the living room."

"It must have been terrifying," I said hoarsely, imagining his pain.

"I don't know why all this shit is coming back now, after all these years." He stared out the windshield, his gaze unfocused.

I could guess as to the reason.

"You know what the most fucked-up part is, though? In the crime scene photos, the red angel painting wasn't there. I swore up and down it had been on the floor. I remembered it so clearly, but crime scene photos don't lie—right?" He looked at me for confirmation. It was awful to realize he didn't trust his own memory.

I didn't know what to say. "Do you know what happened to the painting?"

"If it's anywhere, it would be in a storage unit across town. That's where Nate put everything that wasn't auctioned off after we sold the house."

"We could look for it, if you want. I'd be happy to go with you."

"Maybe after the holidays or something."

The front door of the house opened, and a woman stepped out with five teens. They headed down the front steps to the black minivan in the driveway.

"The house was bought by some foundation and converted into a group home," Hayden said.

"Was that hard for you?"

"No. I was glad, because I don't think a family should live there. It's like the house is tainted by what happened." Even though it was hot in the car, Hayden shivered. "I can sit here and look at the outside and it's mostly manageable. But being inside wasn't good for me. After I went to that open house, I flipped my shit."

He twirled a lock of my hair around his finger and watched it unfurl like a ribbon. "I hadn't been with Sienna in months, but that night . . . I went to her. It was so fucking dumb. I was angry at myself for what happened to my parents, and I wanted to stop feeling . . . anything. It was the worst thing I could have done, and the last time I was with her."

He put the car in gear. "I don't know why I'm telling you this."

I waited until we were a few streets away from the house. "I'm glad you shared that with me."

"All it does is show you how fucked up I am."

"We both have issues, Hayden. At least now I understand better what happened to you."

We drove in silence until Hayden stopped at a red light. To the right was a police station. "That's where Cross and his partner interrogated me."

"That must have been horrible."

"Yeah. It was shitty. I was pretty out of it, though."

He flicked on the turning signal and checked over his shoulder before he turned into the station's parking lot. He slid into an empty space and put the car in park, but didn't let go of the wheel.

I rested my hand on the back of his neck. "Are you okay?"

His head dropped forward. "I don't know why I stopped here."

"Do you want to go in?"

I fingered the hair at his nape, dragging my nails back down repeatedly, hoping to calm him. He let go of the steering wheel and flattened his palms on his thighs.

"I don't know. We don't have time. You're going out with the girls in half an hour."

"Sarah's always late. There's no way we'll leave on time. I'll send a message and let them know I'm running behind."

This was incredible progress. I didn't want something as inconsequential as shopping to interfere. It took another minute or two before he turned off the engine.

"Will you come with me?" he asked in a small voice.

"Of course." I leaned over and kissed his cheek.

"Thanks." He opened the door and came around the car to help me, gripping my hand as we crossed the parking lot. He pushed through the first set of doors and stopped abruptly. "God, nothing has changed."

I peered through the second set of glass doors, wondering where Hayden had gone in his head. He squeezed my hand and tugged me forward.

People in suits and uniforms crossed with purpose through the main foyer and down hallways. Every officer who passed us gave me a brief, curious glance, but their eyes quickly moved to Hayden and stayed there. I could feel their judgment as they took in the heavy-soled boots and the worn jeans. His black winter coat was nondescript, drawing attention up to his face.

His hair was a mess. What once had verged on a Mohawk was now grown in on the sides. The length should have toned down the severity of his appearance, but the wind and the lack of a haircut made it wild and out of control. The piercings in his face and his hostile expression only added to the problem.

Hayden's tongue ring appeared and made a circuit between his lips. He ignored the stares and headed for the information desk, pulling me along beside him. The receptionist was busy answering phone calls. She glanced up at Hayden and then at me, holding up a finger. Hayden was antsy, eyes darting around the room as he leaned against the counter. His knuckles rapped restlessly on the desk, his foot joining in as the receptionist continued to field phone calls.

A passing officer stopped, regarding us both with curious speculation. Her hands went to her hips. It seemed to be a standard pose for police, putting them in reach of their gun. She looked from Hayden to me. "I'm Officer Miller. Is there anything I can do to help you?" Her tone was soft and mild concern was in her eyes.

I forced a smile and put a hand on Hayden's arm. "He's looking to speak to someone about a closed case."

Officer Miller asked me if we had a case number for reference.

"I didn't know I needed one," Hayden said, his voice as hard as his face.

Her eyes settled on Hayden. "It simplifies things if we have a case number. What was the offense?"

"Murder," Hayden replied flatly.

I cut in to explain. "His parents were murdered several years ago. The case was never solved—"

"I'm looking for information beyond what was in the newspapers. I thought—I don't know what I thought." Hayden grabbed for my hand again. "Maybe I should do this another time."

"Whatever you want, Hayden. We can come back if that's what you need," I reassured him. I'd seen him distraught a few times, but this was beyond what I'd witnessed before.

Officer Miller's stance relaxed as she realized his abrasiveness was a result of nerves. "Do you think you might have new information?"

"I don't know. Maybe? There are some memories—" He stopped midsentence, looking over Officer Miller's shoulder.

Officer Cross passed through the lobby, spoiling any progress we'd made. As soon as he saw Hayden, a flashing red beacon of mutiny amid the regimented, he altered his course and headed for us like a missile aimed at a target. Ready for destruction.

"Miss Page, how are you?" His smile was calculated as he extended a hand. I shook it out of obligation.

Hayden bristled beside me, his eyes narrowing. Officer Miller picked up on it immediately, and her demeanor changed, the easygoing nature replaced by suspicion.

"Officer Cross. It's nice to see you, again," I lied.

"I heard you went back to Arden Hills to take care of some family things. I hope everything's all right."

My smile faltered. "Um, yes. Everything's been dealt with."

"Well, that's certainly good to hear."

"How would you know that?" Hayden asked the question I'd been wondering, his tone icy.

Officer Cross turned to Hayden and smiled arrogantly. "I stopped in at that little antique store. What's it called? Serenity?"

Officer Miller's focus was on Hayden as his eyes drilled holes into Officer Cross.

"What brings you here, Stryker? Another parking infraction?

Maybe an indecent-exposure charge?" Although Cross was smiling, no humor was in it.

Officer Miller gave him a dubious look. "He'd like some intel on a case."

"Oh? What case is that?"

"My parents' murder."

Cross's arrogant smile dropped. "The case is closed."

I jumped in, worried he might push Hayden's buttons and set him off. "Hayden was hoping to access public records. I'm not sure how to go about having a case reopened, but if he could just see whatever files are available—"

Cross caressed the butt of his gun. "That would require new evidence."

Officer Miller frowned at Cross. "To reopen the case, that is. Typically it's best to start with the investigating officer."

Hayden exploded, just as I feared. "Fuck that! I'm not talking to the dick who screwed up the investigation in the first place." Hayden's voice rose as his anger gathered steam and railroaded ahead, oblivious of the damage he was doing. "This fucker had me in a room for three hours, showing me close-ups of my father's gray matter splattered all over the goddamn wall, while the person who put the bullet in him got away with it."

I put a hand on his arm. "Hayden, I know you're upset, but this isn't helping."

He shook me off, fists clenched. "I knew this would happen," he spat.

"You need to take a step back," Cross said, chest puffing up, his satisfaction obvious.

Hayden's head snapped toward him. "Pardon me?"

"You need to step away from Miss Page."

"What? Why?"

People were staring; hands moved unnecessarily toward hips

where Tasers and guns were located. Hayden was many things, but he wasn't violent. Although where Cross was concerned, he might make an exception.

"It's okay." I moved closer to Hayden, latching on to his arm.

Officer Miller frowned, watching the interaction with professional detachment.

"Miss Page, I advise you to step back," Officer Cross said.

"Are you *serious*? You think I'm going to hit her?" Hayden asked, incredulous.

"I think you're forgetting that I've seen you worked up before, Mr. Stryker. You're very agitated right now," Officer Cross replied, calm and rational.

Officer Miller looked at me, her expression both questioning and concerned.

"Agitated? Of course I'm agitated! We're talking about my dead parents and how *you* messed up the investigation. How do you jump to the conclusion that I would abuse my girlfriend because I'm pissed at your incompetence?"

Cross's face darkened with anger. "I'm going to have to ask you to leave the premises, unless you're looking to spend the evening in a cell."

I said, "He didn't mean that. I'm so sorry—"

"Don't apologize to him!" Hayden snapped at me and leveled Cross with a hateful glare. "You're a fucking joke. I would never hurt Tenley—she's my goddamn world."

He stormed out of the building.

Officer Miller deferred to Cross. "Do you want me out there?"

"He's not a violent person. He won't damage anything," I said, even though they'd obviously made up their minds as to the type of person Hayden was.

I turned to Officer Cross. "It was very hard for him to come here. It brings up terrible, painful memories. All he wanted was some information."

"He pulled the attitude."

"Is that how you want to see it? Do you think your judgment goes unnoticed? Just because he doesn't ascribe to your set of norms doesn't mean he's a felon or a murderer. You should know that better than anyone else. The most dangerous criminals are the ones who appear the least threatening."

I could feel the stares as I turned and headed for the door. When Officer Cross called after me, I ignored him. For the first time in my life, I didn't care about anyone's perception of me. It was liberating.

I pushed through the door and stepped out into the sunshine to find the man who mattered most.

15

HAYDEN

I stormed across the lot, my head a mess. I wanted to go back in there and punch Cross in his smug face. But that wasn't an option because then I'd be arrested for assaulting an officer. I'd acted like a complete asshole in there. Tenley was probably mortified.

When I got to the car, I leaned against the side and crossed my arms over my chest, working to get a handle on my emotions. I was way too aggravated. Cross had that effect on me. Most of the time I could keep a lid on my temper, but he and Sienna made me crazy.

A minute or two later, Tenley came out of the building. I met her halfway and put an arm around her as soon as she was close enough to touch.

"I'm sorry I lost it in there."

Tenley returned the embrace, burrowing into my chest. "It's okay. Cross was antagonistic, as usual."

I helped her into the car, then went around to the driver's seat. "I wish I'd handled that better."

"Next time we go, you'll be better prepared. It's been an intense morning, and I'm sure you didn't expect to run into Officer Cross. It definitely didn't help, and neither did his judgment." Tenley fingered the sleeve of her coat, picking at a loose thread.

"The judgment I'm used to. Sometimes it gets a little tedious, though." I let my head drop back against the seat. "You know I would never raise a hand to you, right?"

Tenley's eyes went wide. "Are you seriously asking me that?"

"I'm just making sure."

"Cross said that to wind you up." She took my hand. "Do you want me to cancel my plans with the girls?"

"Why would you do that?"

"It's been a difficult morning."

I wasn't sure if I should be embarrassed or grateful that my girlfriend was so concerned about me. "That's cool of you to offer, but I have clients lined up this afternoon."

Besides, as enticing as the thought was, if I stayed home with Tenley, I was liable to do a lot more than talk. I put the car into gear. Her phone chimed in her purse. She rooted around in the oversize bag, then checked the e-mail.

"Oh, no."

"What's wrong?"

"Professor Calder wants to meet with me tomorrow morning."

"What time?"

"Ten."

"I'm coming with you."

"If you want."

I expected more of a fight. Usually she wanted to deal with things on her own.

"I think he's sleeping with one of his students."

I pretended to be surprised, even though I wasn't. "Why do you think that?"

"Because I saw a girl go into his office and there were . . . unprofessional noises."

I'd already seen the same thing. I had to wonder how stealthy this jerk-off thought he was being. Or how above the rules he believed himself to be. "I won't be waiting in the car."

"I didn't expect you to."

I did not get to spend the night with Tenley. Lisa and Sarah, hijackers that they were, stole her from me. Which meant I had to hang out with the guys instead. Normally that would be fine, but the day had been a roller coaster and the only thing that got me through was the plan to spend the night with Tenley.

So the change in plans was a little hard to take. I would have used guilt to get my way, but I could tell she already felt bad. She said they had a little project they needed to finish before the end of the week. She wouldn't tell me what it was, but promised to make it up to me tomorrow night. When she offered to describe the ways she planned to do that, I declined, figuring it would make it worse. Now I wished I'd taken her up on it.

We ended up at Chris's place, since he had the most beer in his fridge. I planned to bail after a few, on the chance that the girls' night ended early enough for Tenley to come over.

His place was in a dodgy neighborhood in a sketchy low-rise building. Everything from the linoleum on the floors to the avocado-colored stove in his kitchen was outdated and ugly. The only new things in the place were his couch, the massive flat-screen fixed to the wall, and the gaming system set up on the coffee table. Chris was all about comfort and electronics.

Chris should have been able to afford a better place with the money he made working at Inked Armor. But a good chunk of his paycheck went to help out his family. Chris was loyal to a fault. His father practically disowned him by the time we opened Inked

Armor, but Chris refused to let his mom and sister suffer as a result. From what I knew, his dad was a real loser. Because of that I didn't get on him about his crappy apartment.

After using his germ-infested bachelor-pad bathroom, I returned to the living room to find him and Jamie watching porn. I dropped down on the couch and waited for the good parts: the blow-job scene or the nipple sucking, or the penetration from behind. That didn't happen, though, because it actually wasn't porn—it was some period drama with a lot of nudity.

"What the shit is this?" I asked.

"I don't know, but Jamie said he wanted to watch it, and there's tits, so I said fine," Chris replied.

Jamie's phone went off and he fumbled with it, his eyes half on the screen and half on the message coming though. "Holy fu—" He shoved the phone back in his pants, a massive grin on his face.

"What's going on?"

"The girls went lingerie shopping, and Lisa just sent me a picture of one of her purchases. They're all at Tenley's place now." Jamie shifted and tried to rearrange himself inconspicuously.

"I don't want to know," I said into my beer.

"Don't worry, man, you'll get to see whatever Tee picked up later tonight. Unless they all decide to have a sleepover." Chris clapped me on the shoulder. "But one night without getting any won't kill you."

I choked on a mouthful of beer. He and Jamie stared at me, waiting.

"We're, uh, easing back into things," I mumbled. I took another large swig, focusing intently on the bare ass on the TV.

"What does that mean, exactly?" Jamie asked.

I shot him an irritated glare. He and Lisa talked about everything, and I was sure she'd told him all about the "take things slow" conversation.

"It means what it means."

"Christ almighty! You haven't fucked since she came back? But it's been more than a week!" Chris looked as if his head might explode from the concept.

"Shut up, man. I never said that." I wasn't about to share that we'd only had sex once, right after she came back. That would soon change.

Chris gave me an incredulous look, but Jamie just smiled and patted my back all dadlike.

"We've had a lot of shit to work out," I said defensively.

"It's cool, H," Chris said, trying to be supportive. "I didn't push it with Sarah in the beginning, 'cause it took me almost two months to get her to go out with me. I didn't want her to think all I wanted was to get into her pants. We didn't get naked until the fourth date."

For Chris, dating usually meant sex, and then possibly pizza or fast food. That he'd taken Sarah on real dates to restaurants that required a reservation was unheard of.

"Can we talk about something else? All this sharing makes me want to try on dresses and get my balls waxed."

"Sure, bro." Chris went back to watching the period porn.

It dawned on me that Chris never let anything go so easily. He'd usually capitalize on the opportunity to razz the hell out of me. He also liked to impart the finer details of his sexual conquests. "How are things going with Sarah, anyway? You spend an awful lot of time with her but don't say much."

He rolled his beer bottle between his palms, pondering the question. "She's cool, and a closet hippie. All laid-back, you know?"

My experiences with Sarah had been anything but laid-back.

"I hope Lisa got more of the frilly ones," Jamie said, staring unseeingly at the TV screen.

"You thinking about wearing those?" Chris ribbed.

"They make my ass look good," Jamie quipped back.

I couldn't tell if he was serious, but the image was in my head and I couldn't get it out now.

"Okay, that's it, I'm going home." I drained the last of my beer and stood up.

"I call BS," Chris said as I headed for the door.

"Let us know how it goes," Jamie said, relaxing deeper into the couch.

"How what goes?" I asked.

"Good luck with your drive-by at Tee's. Come back when you get shut down by the girls." Chris flashed me a grin.

I flipped him off and pulled the door closed behind me.

The walk home from his place was brisk. I stood outside the back door to Tenley's apartment, debating whether I should call first. I hadn't been to her place since she'd come back, and I was a little nervous about going up there. I gave myself a mental kick in the ass and decided surprise might work in my favor.

Lisa came to the door when I knocked, opening it the three inches the chain lock allowed. "Well, look who it is. This is a sausage-free party, no boys allowed."

"Hi. Nice to see you, too. Sure, I'd love it if you'd get Tenley for me." Lisa was wearing pj pants with cartoon snowmen on them and a T-shirt.

"You're not coming in."

"Is it Hayden?" Tenley asked from the other side of the door.

"Hi, kitten, Lisa won't let me in."

There were some giggles, followed by the rustle of paper. The door closed in my face, and when it reopened, Lisa threw it wide. Tenley and Sarah were sitting on the floor of Tenley's living room, surrounded by rolls of wrapping paper, ribbon, bows, and tape. Sarah was also dressed in festive pj pants and a T-shirt. One of Chris's, actually. I could tell because it was more of a muumuu than a shirt on her.

A box of red wine was perched at the edge of the coffee table. Half-full wineglasses sat on top, without coasters underneath to prevent rings. Tenley unfolded her legs and rose from the floor, making her way across the room. Lisa said something, but I didn't hear a word. My erection was immediate and painful.

"What are you wearing?" I ran my hand through my hair, keeping in mind Lisa and Sarah were in Tenley's apartment. Ripping those pajamas off her was not on the agenda this evening.

"I bought some new jammies."

"I see that."

The tank top had thin, little straps that I could bite apart. Cupcakes were all over it, and I could see the outline of her barbells through the thin cotton. A lace band traveled along the edge of the top and at the bottom. Provocative little cupcake shorts barely covered her ass.

I pulled her into the hall, skimmed her sides, and shoved my hands down the back of her shorts. I met with bare ass and slid my thumbs along the divide, all the way down. Tenley rewarded me with a soft whimper.

"I guess you like them." She did that smile thing that made her look all cute and sweet. Except she was almost naked.

"You could say that." *Like* didn't quite cover it.

I closed the door to her apartment, giving us the privacy of the hall. Then I sank to the floor and kissed the warm flesh right under her navel.

"What are you doing?" she asked with a panicked laugh.

I nosed along the waistband of her shorts. "I'm having a conversation with my kitty."

I parted my lips over the seam of her shorts and pressed my tongue against the fabric. She gasped and grabbed my hair, leaning against the wall for support.

"I can't wait to have my mouth on you." I skimmed the seam

with my nose. I pulled the waistband of Tenley's shorts down to expose the top of her slit, then kissed the cupcake tattoo and then lower, where that tiny steel ball peeked out. I planned to drag those shorts down her creamy thighs and hitch her leg over my shoulder, so I could lick my way up her kitty. Fuck the location.

The door opened and Lisa poked her head out. "Your two minutes— Oh, for chrissake, Hayden!"

"What?" I allowed the waistband to snap back into place but I stayed on my knees.

"You're worse than a teenager! Get a handle on your hormones." Lisa raised her hand in front of her face to block us out.

Tenley bit her lip to keep from smiling.

"You think this is funny?" I asked.

"Not at all." She shook her head emphatically.

I stood up and put my mouth to her ear. "You remember what I said this morning?"

"Yes."

"I'm making good on that promise tomorrow, so you better be ready for me."

When I stepped away, her face was flushed. Perfect. By tomorrow night she was going to be a hot mess. Which was exactly how I wanted her.

I picked Tenley up for her meeting with Professor Assface at nine in the morning. She looked a little tired. The trip to Northwestern was quiet and I didn't push for conversation. I had a feeling we were both nervous for similar reasons. I'd had enough of people fucking with me, particularly where Tenley was concerned. I wasn't about to let anything happen to her.

In the lot closest to her professor's building, I parked and turned off the engine.

"I need to tell you something," Tenley blurted out.

From the look on her face, it wasn't good. I tried not to panic. "Okay."

"I recorded the sex on my phone."

"Pardon?"

"Professor Calder was having sex with a student in his office. I recorded it."

"Jesus. Does he know?"

"Not yet. I made it into an MP3 and saved it on a USB and sent it to my e-mail address."

"Smart girl." I smiled. She was always surprising me.

"Do you want to hear it?"

"Right now?"

"Mm-hm."

She had twenty minutes before the meeting; it couldn't hurt to have a listen. "I guess."

She passed her phone over to me, and a video popped up on the screen. The camera panned over the door, zeroing in on the nameplate as faint noises that could have been mistaken for talking changed into the unmistakable sounds of sex.

Some sex is hot to listen to. This was not. The high-pitched, whiny moans of the girl-woman on the other side of the door, interspersed with the male's deep grunts and groans, were erection shriveling. The clincher came when the female shrieked Calder's name, followed by a harsh admonishment from his easily recognizable voice and a loud slap. Any doubt about who was behind the door was erased by that wretched orgasm.

"Wow." I was a little worried I might hurl.

"You think it's enough?"

"Oh, yeah. I think it's more than enough."

Given the irrefutable evidence, Tenley persuaded me to let her go into the meeting without making my presence known. She had her phone with her and she'd sent me the file in an e-mail. There was also the backup USB of the video. This fucker was abusing his power, and I wanted her to report him.

I sat in the lounge for about five minutes before I got restless and walked down the hallway to his door. I listened to the low murmur of voices. I didn't like Assface's tone, or that he suddenly got louder.

The door flew open and Tenley stumbled out, her expression panicked, tears threatening to spill over. The neck of her dress was pulled to one side, exposing her bra strap and *my* ink. Professor Assface looked irate. My eyes dropped lower. He had a fucking hard-on.

All the anger and aggression I'd been holding back crashed over me in a wave of red.

"Wait for me in the lobby." I kissed Tenley's forehead and walked past her, closing the office door. I locked it behind me.

"You can't be in here." He reached for the phone on his desk with an unsteady hand.

"I wouldn't do that if I were you," I said through clenched teeth.

When he didn't remove his hand from the receiver, I crossed the room, clamping my hand over his and squeezing until he let go, then I shoved him into his chair. I hovered over him, the violent urge to beat him until he was a bleeding mess almost too strong to deny.

"Let me explain something to you." I took a deep breath and continued as calmly as possible, "You don't touch Tenley. Ever."

He sat back in his chair, a sneer pulling up the corner of his mouth. To make my point clear, I cocked my fist and punched him in the balls. A gasping wheeze shot out of him and he doubled over, coughing and sputtering.

I grabbed him by his receding hairline; the comb-over gave me perfect leverage. I jerked his head up. "Do you understand?"

His eyes bulged and his mouth moved, but no sound came out. Eventually he nodded. I let go of his hair, trapping him in the chair as I leaned over him, holding the USB stick in front of me. "Do you know what's on this?"

"Miss Page—" he rasped.

"Yes or no."

"Yes."

"Good. So you're aware of how fucked you are if this happens to get out."

"You can't prove—"

"It wasn't a question, and it wasn't rhetorical, fuckhead—so shut up and listen. This is what's going to happen. You're going to recommend that Tenley be paired with a different adviser, one who specializes in deviant behaviors. I know there's more than one female professor in the department who's willing to take on a new student; I've already checked into it. You will *not* recommend her to another male adviser, or I will come back here and beat the living fuck out of you. If Tenley tells me that you so much as *looked* at her, I will come back and beat the fuck out of you. And if you touch her again, so help me God, I will rip your dick off and feed it to you.

"Now, I'm not sure what your problem is with Tenley's thesis, but I think you will find, if you take a closer look, that she has been nothing but thorough and eloquent. Her connections to Merton, Routledge, and Thoreau are cohesive and provide an in-depth exploration of cultural norms and deviations, primarily based on, but not limited to, Strain Theory, Functional Structuralism, and Conflict Theory. I could go into greater detail, but I don't think I need to, since you won't be her adviser anymore."

Professor Assface looked at me as if I had two heads, his mouth opening and closing like an idiot.

"You look surprised. I can run circles around you, you dumb

fuck. Just because I don't choose to fit in with the general masses doesn't mean I have a subpar intellect."

When I grabbed a pen off his desk, he jumped and squeaked. I assumed he thought I was going to stab him with it, which I wanted to do. I jotted down the names of the professors I'd researched while Tenley was away, in case something like this happened. "This should help get you started. Someone other than you will call Tenley when a new adviser has been appointed."

"What about the video?" he asked.

"What about it?"

"What are you going to do with it?"

"That's a very good question, now, isn't it? If the board got wind of your behavior, you'd lose your tenure, wouldn't you? Not to mention your wife." I tapped the ashtray with the wedding band tossed carelessly inside. "Unless she's down with you fucking your students?"

His expression told me she had no clue as to what he was doing.

I smiled maliciously. "Just thought I'd ask. I suppose it would be in your best interest to get your ass in gear and start making phone calls, then. You might also want to consider keeping your dick in your pants. You'd be amazed at how quickly rumors spread—especially when they're vetted through YouTube."

I rose, towering over him in all his pathetic, sniveling assholeness. "Now, if you'll excuse me, I have a very distraught girlfriend to attend to because of you."

I let myself out and texted Tenley as soon as I made it to the end of the hall. She wasn't waiting in the lounge as I thought she might be, which meant she was sufficiently upset to follow my directions and wait for me in the lobby. I punched the button for the elevator, wanting to get to her as soon as I could.

I wasn't worried about Calder's calling security. He had too much to lose. Even after he followed through with my demands, I was going to encourage Tenley to bring that recording to the attention of his superiors. That dick needed to lose his job.

The doors of the elevator slid open and a familiar-looking blonde stepped out. I'd seen her coming out of Dr. Douche's office before. She clearly hadn't expected anyone else to be in the building. As she recovered from the shock, her eyes moved over my face and she smiled in a way that was meant to be sexy. It came off as insecure, which was exactly what Calder was looking for.

I moved aside to let her pass. She glanced over her shoulder as I stepped into the elevator. I put my hand out to stop the door from closing.

"I recognize you," I said. "Calder's your adviser?"

She seemed confused by the question. "Um, no, my prof, but hopefully next year . . . How—"

"People know you're fucking him."

Her horror was the last thing I saw before the doors closed.

16

TENLEY

Hayden burst out of the elevators and into the main lobby. "Let's get out of here."

He grabbed my hand, pulled me up out of the chair, and headed for the door. I practically had to run to keep up with him. His jaw was clenched, eyes blazing. When we reached the car, he helped me in and went around to his side without a word. He slipped the key in the ignition and turned the engine over.

"Are you okay?" he asked.

"Mostly, yes."

"He put his hands on you."

"I told him I knew he was having sex with a student, and he threatened to have me ejected from the program. He also said if I brought the information forward, he would make it impossible for me to secure another adviser. So I played the video from my phone. He tried to take it from me."

Hayden took several deep breaths, his hands flexing and

releasing on the steering wheel as he stared out the windshield. I couldn't get a gauge on anything but his anger, and my own emotions were pretty frayed.

"What happened after that?"

"I opened the door. You were there."

Finally he looked over at me. "That's everything?"

"He grabbed my arm to get the phone, but he didn't have a very good grip so he ended up just getting my sleeve instead."

"You'll have a different adviser by the beginning of the new semester."

"What? How is that possible? It takes months to arrange something like that."

"Calder will figure it out; otherwise, he believes the video will go to the board."

"It should go to the board regardless." If Calder had done this to me and that other girl, he'd probably done it before and would do it again.

"Yeah—but first I want that fucker to find you a new adviser. Then you can knock his house of cards down."

Hayden pulled out his phone and made a call. "Hey, Lisa." His tone was clipped. "What time is my first appointment? . . . And the next one? . . . Can you reschedule the one for noon and leave the block empty? I'm going to be late. . . . Uh-huh. . . . No. . . . Yeah." He hung up.

"You didn't have to reschedule your first client. I'm okay."

"I'm not."

"He didn't hurt me."

"He could have. If I hadn't been there, he might have tried to." Hayden reached out and touched my cheek. His fingers trembled, as he fought to stay in control of his emotions.

"But you were there, so it's okay," I said, hoping to soothe him.

"I'm taking you home."

"You don't need to do that. Do you want to stop somewhere first? We could get a bite to eat."

"I'm not particularly hungry."

"It might make you feel better."

"There's only one thing that's going to make me feel better." His dark gaze raked over me. "And while I'm perfectly content to fuck you in the backseat, I'd much prefer to do it in the comfort of my bed, because I don't think I have it in me to be very gentle."

"I see," I said calmly, even though I was anything but. "We should probably go home, then."

"That would be best." Hayden shifted the car into gear, his eyes moving to the road.

We were finally done with the sex hiatus.

Hayden could have broken the sound barrier on the way home. The tires squealed as we pulled into the underground parking garage and he slid neatly into his spot. I was out of the car and beelining for the elevator before he had the key out of the ignition. I had every intention of capitalizing on his primal desire.

"Someone's eager." Hayden's chest brushed against my back when he pushed the button for the elevator.

It dinged a few seconds later and the doors opened. Impatient, I catapulted inside. Hayden followed at a leisurely pace, enjoying my anticipation. Heedless of how desperate I came across, I pushed the button for the second floor and punched CLOSE DOORS until they finally responded.

Hayden leaned against the opposite wall, his fingers curled around the rail. His grip seemed to be the only thing that kept him from taking me to the floor.

"I shouldn't have waited this long." His tongue ring peeking out to slide over his bottom lip and click against the viper bite.

I must have looked as worked up as I felt because his mouth

turned up in a cocky grin and he pushed away from the rail. He stalked across the small space in two long strides and stopped in front of me, close but not touching.

With lazy fingers he undid the buttons on my coat, parting the sides to reveal my dress. It no longer conformed to my curves, having been stretched out in my altercation with Professor Calder.

The elevator chimed, signaling our arrival on the second floor. Hayden motioned for me to exit. His palm settled on my low back, guiding me down the hall. As soon as we were inside his condo, I found myself pressed against the wall. Hayden's mouth covered mine and he pushed my coat over my shoulders.

"You have no idea what I'm going to do to you."

It was a warning and a plea. We needed each other on the most basic level. It was that simple.

"Are you healed enough?" One hand slipped between my legs. "Please tell me this is okay."

"It's been long enough." I rocked against his palm, testing out the friction.

"Thank *fuck*."

Not interested in preliminaries, he pulled my dress up to my hips and broke the kiss to get it over my head. It joined my coat on the floor. His breath left him in a rush as he exposed the pale blue bra covered in a tiny-cupcake print. Hayden's calm composure broke as he traced the hot-pink lace edge with fingers that shook.

"How much more of this cupcake stuff do you have?"

"Let's just say my shopping trip with the girls was theme oriented." I pulled down the zipper on his coat.

"That's very good to hear."

He kissed me again, slow and deep, walking me backward down the hall to his bedroom. Light filtered through the half-open curtains, leaving nothing in shadow. When we reached the bed, I lifted myself onto the edge. Hayden didn't waste any time as he rid

me of my tights, tossing them on the floor. I returned the favor by
tugging his shirt over his head.

"I fucking love these." Hayden cupped my breasts and skimmed
lower to sweep over the satin and lace at my hips.

As he claimed my mouth again, his palms smoothed around my
back and found the clasp of my bra, freeing it. It joined the rest of
our clothes on the floor. Hayden's thumbs brushed over my nipples,
gently at first and then pinching roughly. My gasp broke the kiss.

"Sorry. I'm sorry," he murmured.

He sank to his knees and I parted my legs. Warm hands drifted
up the outside of my thighs as he placed a penitent kiss on the offended nipple. The tenderness was a stark contrast to the heat and
need in him. He sucked and nibbled his way across to the other
breast. Desire sparked fire in my veins. I was consumed by the
craving to feel him on me, in me, shattering me and making me
whole at that same time.

When he released my nipple, I moved back, making room for him
on the bed. Every tattoo, every line of ink wrapped around defined
muscles, was visible as he came after me, looking savagely dangerous.

He latched on to my ankle, preventing me from going any
farther. With a lascivious smile he kissed his way up my calf, his ascent torturously slow. When he reached his destination, his mouth
closed over the pale satin. The hot, wet press of his tongue against
the fabric was a promise of what was to come. I lifted my hips and
he hooked his fingers into my panties, dragging them down. His
hair tickled my hip as he dropped a kiss on the cupcake tattoo.

"Ah, fuuuuck," Hayden breathed. "That is so sexy."

His lips parted, transfixed as his knuckle dragged over the
curved barbell. The piercing slid along with the movement. I made
a throaty sound.

"Tell me how it feels, kitten. Is it good? Was it worth it?" he
asked in that liquid sex voice I missed so much.

I was so tightly wound, already on the brink of coming even though he'd barely touched me. He circled my entrance with a finger and pressed down on my clit. I whimpered, unable to form words. He took pity on me, watching my face as he slid two fingers inside and curled them up. There was no slow buildup, nothing gradual about the way he manipulated my body. His tongue flicked out and I closed my legs at the devastating sensitivity caused by the piercing and the gathering orgasm.

Hayden's free hand descended on my inner thigh, spreading me wider while he held the other one down with his forearm. Then his tongue flattened against my clit and he licked up; steel hitting steel. The dual sensation made me buck against his mouth. Heat coiled where Hayden's tongue and fingers moved until I fell apart, crying out his name.

He looked up at me from under dark lashes. "Fuck, you're gorgeous when you come."

On weakened arms I sat up, and Hayden rose with me. I kissed his flushed, wet lips, tasting myself, then pushed on his chest. He moved back, giving me room to climb into his lap. I took my time exploring the lines of his ink, starting with my fingers, following with my mouth.

When the need became too much to bear, I freed that straining hardness from his boxers. Gripping him tightly, I stroked once and bent to lick the tip.

"Fuck me," he hissed. "You don't need to do that."

He started to pull me up, but half a second later I engulfed the head, and the pull became a push. I took him in my mouth while he swore under his breath, muttering about porn. I popped off and licked up the shaft, spreading the wetness with my palm.

"It's been a while," I said as I straddled his thighs. "I thought it might make it easier."

He was tense as I leaned in to kiss him. When he was

sufficiently distracted, I wrapped my hand around him and rose up on my knees. The head of his cock slid over my clit and his stud made a muted clink against my barbell.

"I just want—"

He never finished the thought as I sank down, watching his eyes flutter shut and his lips part. I angled him in, taking in the studs that pierced the head one side at a time. Burying my face in his neck, I gritted my teeth against the searing burn that accompanied the invasion. It had been like this the last time, too. As though my body had forgotten how to handle him in the weeks of separation.

Hayden's breath came out in quick pants as he filled me. I couldn't stop the high-pitched moan that fell from my lips when my ass came to rest on his thighs.

"Are you okay?" He released his viselike grip on my hips.

His palms flattened against my back and moved up, curling around my shoulders, holding me still.

I waited until the hot burn subsided before I answered. "I'm better than okay." I rocked slightly, testing him and myself, desperate to move yet not wanting him to let go of me.

"Kitten." His grip tightened in warning and he exhaled slow, heavy breaths.

We sat there for a long while, bodies still. When he was ready, he pried his fingers from my shoulders and kissed where they had been. His palms came to rest on the swell of my ass. I lifted slowly, the fullness giving way to emptiness. When I felt the steel balls pass the most sensitive spot, I reversed the motion, taking him back inside.

He took over then, setting a slow, even pace. The angle, the position, the way he kept me from moving at the speed I wanted— lips brushing, but not kissing—turned my body into a wasteland of need. I looked down to the place where we were joined to watch him slide out of me. The next downward stroke came fast and hard, my moan cut short by my ragged intake of breath.

"It's too good. You feel too fucking good." He shook his head, then his body went rigid. "Shit. Sorry. I couldn't help it." When the tremors stopped, he kissed me in atonement. "Now that that's out of the way . . ."

He moved against me, igniting embers into flames. "You sure you don't need some downtime?" I asked breathlessly.

"Never with you." He laid me on the bed, staying inside me. He kissed the valley between my breasts and sat back on his knees, wrapping my thighs around his waist. Then he pulled his hips back and eased forward, gauging my response. "Okay?"

"Please."

He rose up, keeping his hold on my legs; the new angle drove him deeper. I reached behind me, searching for something to grab. The wooden slats of the headboard were the perfect anchor. I stretched my arms above me, gripping tightly. The rest of my body curved toward Hayden on his knees.

He moved hesitantly at first, but it wasn't enough for either of us. He was too needy, conflict raging as he battled for the control he didn't have.

I met his fiery gaze. "Take me."

"Fuck," he growled, and yanked me away from the headboard.

He unlocked my legs from his hips and pushed them toward my body. Leaning forward, he hooked my ankles over his shoulders, bearing down. My knees hit my chest and I gripped his forearms. The weight of his body sent another ripple of desire rushing through me. And then he started to move.

"Is this what you were looking for?" He punctuated each word with a powerful thrust, his mouth beside my ear.

I responded with a series of affirmative expletives. I was pinned beneath him as he pounded into me, unleashing sensations

I had no idea my body was capable of producing. I couldn't find leverage, unable to move. He was dominating the act entirely, making my body a slave to his.

"God, I love fucking you," he said through labored breaths, his hips slapping ceaselessly against my thighs.

It was so close to the words I wanted to hear from him, but I didn't yet deserve. I knitted my fingers in his hair and kissed my way across his jaw. His mouth opened to accept me, then he took control of that as well.

"I don't want to be without you again," I said, wishing I could tell him how I felt, afraid to.

My response elicited a deep groan from Hayden, pushing me over the edge. I was barely past the crest of my orgasm when he folded back on his knees, easing my right leg over to the other shoulder. His forearm crossed over my shins, holding my legs to his chest, my unmarked skin against the network of art that covered him. He looked down at me, all the unspoken words reflected in his eyes.

"I'll never get enough of you." His voice was rough.

He changed tempo, his hips moving inexorably slow. But the orgasm didn't wane. Instead it was wave after wave of excruciating pleasure. My body went into overdrive, so sensitive I trembled with the unending release.

"Oh, God. It's too much."

I bowed up in an arc and gripped the sheets, needing to hold on to something. He was gloriously feral as his hands moved up my shins, over my knees, and across my thighs. His fingers were tight on my hips as he continued the erotic assault.

His viselike grip relaxed and his pace slowed once again. My legs slid off Hayden's shoulders and rested limply on either side of his thighs. He splayed one hand between my shoulder blades and his other palm pressed flat against my stomach. His fingers ghosted over hypersensitive skin.

Suddenly he lifted me into his lap again and circled a nipple with his tongue, and my wilted form jerked in his arms. He chuckled darkly, trailing kisses until our mouths met.

His movements were gentle and reverent as I regained some control over my body. He pulled me close, his hands on my waist, grinding me over him. Soon, his short thrusts sped up and became more frantic.

Just like the first time we were together, he cupped my chin in his palm and whispered hoarsely, "Look at me."

His icy-blue eyes shone with vulnerability.

"I—I need—" He shook his head. "You're mine." His body stiffened.

It felt as if I had always been his. My heart belonged to him for as long as he wanted to keep it.

17

HAYDEN

I pulled into the Tiffany's parking lot. I hadn't bought Tenley a real Christmas present and I was running out of time. I'd picked up a few small things, but nothing that told her how I felt about her without actually saying it. Lisa had sent me here to rectify that. I had no idea what I was supposed to buy, but according to Lisa, I couldn't go wrong with Tiffany's, so here I was. Forty-five minutes before my next client's appointment.

I should have planned the trip out better. I was in work wear: jeans, my Inked Armor button-down, and worn-in boots. At least my jacket wasn't too bad because it was black. I hoped it was unremarkable enough that I didn't stick out like a sore thumb.

Normally I didn't care, but this was important and I didn't want to fuck up Tenley's present. It was our first Christmas together and I wanted to create new memories. Good ones that might help ease the pain of her loss. After all these years I still had a hard time around the holidays, and I was hoping now that I had Tenley, things would be better.

Locking up my car, I headed for the front entrance. Several of the cars I passed were of the luxury variety. Lots of douche mobiles, a sweet Lexus, and one very sleek Audi. I opened the door of the elegant store, prepared to be tossed out, but the place was so busy my arrival went almost unnoticed. The store was full of well-dressed businessmen on the same mission as me.

One of the girls behind the counter glanced my way, gave me a quick once-over, and smiled. Her attention was drawn away as a balding man approached. Her smile widened as he addressed her, and she unlocked a small window behind the counter to retrieve a tray of diamond bracelets. Judging by his attire, he was ready to drop a boatload of money.

I shoved my hands in my pockets, wishing I'd had the forethought to change. Even dress pants instead of jeans would have helped give me a better chance at decent service. I tried not to draw attention to myself as I browsed. All I wanted to do was buy something and get the hell out of here.

I stopped in front of a case of engagement rings. I'd seen Tenley's in pictures, and the rock was a behemoth. I couldn't imagine her picking something like that out. She was more subtle than that. Not that I should be thinking about it; her first experience with the whole engagement thing had been pretty fucking traumatic. There was no way either of us wanted that—not now. Maybe not ever.

I hadn't even told Tenley I was in love with her. I almost had yesterday morning, when I finally got inside her again. Talk about a revelation. It had been the most intense sex I'd ever had in my life, and not just because of the physical release. It went way deeper than that. Tenley and I connected on a different level and I wanted to be with her like that again.

Waiting that long had been stupid, though. Last night she was so sore afterward that I ended up soaking in the tub with her for an hour. We had a naked make-out session that got a little messy on my end. I shook my head, pushing away thoughts of Tenley naked. My dick was already responding, and I had to will it to retreat with mental threats of castration.

I checked out the next case and grinned as I spotted the perfect gift, sparkling in its plush little box. I noted movement in my peripheral vision and looked over to see the girl who'd smiled at me standing about three feet away.

"Hi, I'm Francine. Can I help you find something?"

Even her name made me feel inferior, which was absurd. I could afford to shop in a store like Tiffany's. It was others' automatic assumption that I couldn't, based on my appearance, that made me avoid places like this.

I looked around the store. All the other sales reps, most of whom were female, were waiting on suits. One man stood behind the counter, interacting with no one. He was dressed differently from those working the floor. He had to be her boss. His hands were clasped behind his back and he stared at her intently. What a douche. She must have drawn the short straw and been told to wait on me. I smiled.

"I'd like to get this for my girlfriend." I pointed at the little cupcake pendant. "I love cupcakes, and, uh . . . she makes the best cupcakes ever, so I figure it's fitting, yeah?"

I hoped if I kept talking, she'd start to look more comfortable.

Francine smiled. "That sounds perfect, and quite thoughtful. Would you like her to wear it as a necklace or a bracelet?"

"Uhhhh—"

I ran a hand through my hair, flustered. I had an affinity for Tenley's neck; I spent a lot of time with my face buried in it. Most nights my lips were pressed against it, and sometimes I liked to nibble. Would a necklace interfere with my ability to nuzzle? I was being ridiculous. I could take it off if it bothered me.

"Can we look at chains and bracelets before I make a decision?"

"Of course." She unlocked the case and lifted out the pendant. "This retails at just under eleven hundred dollars," she said softly. "We have other options if you'd like to have a look at those, as well."

She was trying to save me embarrassment in case I couldn't afford it. I was amazed something so small could cost that much money, but it wasn't going to stop me from buying it.

"That's fine."

She looked relieved that I wasn't pissed off or offended. She led me to the counter where the bracelets and chains were and pulled out two trays with a plethora of options. I shrugged and she gave me a sympathetic smile.

"May I suggest a necklace? It's typically how this pendant is worn."

"That sounds good." I nodded enthusiastically, glad she knew what she was doing.

"Would you prefer something delicate, or something more like this?" She held up a heavy linked chain.

Decisions about jewelry should be a lot simpler. Apparently I was wrong. I shed my coat and shoved my sleeves up, because I was starting to sweat. Her eyes gravitated to my wrists and up my forearms. I almost pushed my sleeves back down to cover the ink, but figured it was pointless. I shouldn't care.

"She's petite." I sized up Francine. They were about the same height, but Tenley was narrower, with more curves. "Kind of like you? And she's not into flash."

"Ah, so delicate would more appropriate?"

"That sounds good, yeah."

We settled on a platinum chain that seemed too thin to

withstand any manhandling. Francine threaded the pendant on the chain and put it into a black necklace box, which fit perfectly into one of those little, blue Tiffany & Co. boxes. Then she wrapped it in blue paper, finishing it off with a white ribbon tied into a little bow. She put it in one of those froufrou bags and tied that with more white ribbon.

I was dropping a bundle, but I didn't care. Money hadn't been an issue since my parents' deaths, and Tenley deserved something pretty. Plus I felt good about having gone out and got it for her myself, without any help apart from Lisa's advice on where to go.

Francine rang me up and I handed over my credit card. The transaction went through and I signed for it, putting the receipt in my wallet.

"If you have any problems, please don't hesitate to bring it back in," she said as she passed the dainty blue bag over.

"Right. Thanks." I nodded dumbly, not sure what could go wrong with a necklace. "I just hope she likes it."

"I'm sure she'll love it. She's a lucky girl."

"I don't know about that, but thanks for all the help."

Francine smiled warmly. "It was my pleasure."

It was a standard response, but for some reason, I believed she meant it.

I was late getting back to work and my client was there. Being late usually stressed me out, but things were laid-back at the shop this afternoon because after today, we closed for the holidays. My waiting client was my last.

"Nice of you to show up on time," Lisa snarked as I walked through the door. Her tune changed as soon as she saw the bag hanging from my finger. "Oooooh, you found something! Let me see!"

"Later. My client is waiting."

Only special clients were scheduled today, and Amy was one of the few. The shop was buzzing with excitement. Lisa had decorated the place in pale blues, silver, and black. Cookies and mulled cider were on the counter, along with cupcakes Tenley must have dropped off. They were topped with fluffy, white icing and sprinkled with little silver candies. I grabbed one on my way by and peeled the wrapper back, exposing the delicious cake.

"You want one?" I asked Amy, and motioned to the cupcakes. "My girlfriend makes them. They're awesome."

"I've already had two. I probably shouldn't have another." She picked up her mug of cider and followed me into the private room.

Once Amy and I went over the part of the tattoo we were going to shade, I left her to undress and put on the smock for cover. Lisa practically pounced on me when I came back out. If I'd been thinking, I would have left the little bag in the private room. Instead, it was still hanging off my finger. I passed it over.

I was all antsy as she opened it and pulled out the small Tiffany's box. She started untying the bow.

"Wait! What are you doing? I won't be able to rewrap that." I reached over to snatch it from her, but she put a hand up to stop me.

"Don't worry, I will." She unwrapped the paper carefully and opened the blue box, lifting the black lid. She stared at the cupcake charm resting on the black velvet.

"It's stupid, isn't it?" I asked, suddenly unsure of my choice.

"No, it's not stupid. It's perfect. She's going to love it."

I gave myself an internal pat on the back. Score one for Stryker. If only the rest of the holidays could be this easy to manage.

Tenley's irritated cursing distracted me from the task of choosing between a gray button-down and an electric-blue one.

"What's up, kitten?" I called from inside my closet.

"I need help. The zipper's stuck."

I stuck my head out. Tenley was standing in front of the mirror, neck craning as she tried to get the zipper past her waist. Her ink was mostly on display, as was the lacy bra-and-panty set she'd been parading around in for the last twenty minutes. It was the reason I'd disappeared inside the closet. We'd already had sex twice last night. Tenley had been needy and aggressive, which meant if we went another round this morning, I risked putting her out of commission or making us late for the holiday celebration at Cassie's. Or later, since we were supposed to be there in fifteen minutes and it took at least that long to get there from here.

I came up behind her and swept a few stray hairs over her shoulder so they wouldn't get caught in the zipper. Tenley let go and the dress slipped down. I could see the thick lace band of her panties and then the soft, perfect swell of her ass. My dick got excited and I mentally told it to back off.

Tenley was out of sorts this morning for obvious reasons. I remembered what the holidays without my parents had been like the first couple of years. I had coped with ink and drugs.

"We could start on the color next week if you want," I suggested as I backed the stuck zipper down.

"Really?"

"Yeah. There's no reason not to. We can work from the shoulders down."

"That sounds good. I've missed being in your chair."

I looked up at her reflection in the mirror. The chair had been the first place where we'd honestly connected with each other on more than a physical level. It was the bond that came from artist and client. Except ours went far deeper. "Me, too."

I was careful not to snag the lace overlay as I zipped her up. For all her undercurrents of rebellion, Tenley liked girlie dresses, which I liked, too. It made the ink and the steel underneath that much sexier. Her dress was so pale, the blush of pink was almost white. It was strapless, highlighting her still-too-prominent collar-bones, but she'd gained a little weight since her return, as had I. I expected the holidays would help add to the softness in her curves, thanks to the barrage of baked goods she made.

I pressed my lips to her shoulder, and because I couldn't help myself, I kept moving toward her neck. Tenley tilted her head to give me better access. Leaning against my chest, her hand came up and curled around my shoulder. I trailed kisses to the hollow under her ear.

"You look beautiful."

"Thank you," she whispered, that sultry voice making it hard to stop.

I stepped back so she didn't feel the raging hard-on that threatened to make us later than we already were.

Tenley's bottom lip jutted out in a pout. "Where are you going?"

"To get dressed."

"Oh?" Her eyes moved down my bare chest and stopped below my waist. "Maybe you need some help with that."

"I think I've got it covered."

Tenley followed me into the closet anyway, and it took a lot longer to get dressed than I'd anticipated. Tenley's version of being helpful included trying to persuade me to let her take care of the problem behind the fly of my pants. Eventually she gave up and picked a shirt and tie to go with my black dress pants.

She took her time as she buttoned the shirt, starting at the bottom and working her way up, covering the ink as she went. When she was done, she offered to tuck it in. I declined. She sighed, picked up the pinup-girl tie, and slid it under the collar around my neck.

"You know how to tie a tie?"

She nodded and bit her lip in concentration as she began a double Windsor knot. "My dad taught me when I was twelve. I was better at it than he was. He used to have me preknot all his ties so he could slip them over his head rather than fiddle with them. Connor was just as bad——" She shook her head. "Sorry."

His name was like an electric shock, she spoke of him so rarely. Her hands shook as she pulled the knot tight. Her palm smoothed down the front and I caught it, bringing it to my lips to kiss her knuckles.

"I know today is going to be hard for you. You can talk about him if you want to. It won't upset me." He couldn't come back and take her away. But his memory could incite guilt, eating away at her and making it difficult for her to be open with me.

Her eyes remained on her feet. "I can't. I'll cry."

"That's okay. I have tissues."

I pulled her into my arms and she snuggled in tight. Her slender body shook as she fought against the tide of emotion threatening to sweep her away. It had been like that the last couple of days. I'd find her standing in front of the tree, fingering an ornament with tears streaming down her face. She always wiped them away and brushed it off, but I knew what today would be like. So many years ago, I was in the same place.

When she pulled away, her focus stayed on the collar of my shirt. She adjusted the lapels and straightened my tie again, even though it didn't need it. Her breathing was deep and even. When she finally looked up, her eyes were shiny with unshed tears and her smile was weak. She'd crack at some point today. It was inevitable.

"You look so"—she cocked her head to the side—"normal."

"Is that bad?"

"Not at all. I like you dressed up. It's sexy." Her fingers skimmed the rings in my bottom lip and trailed down my throat, tracing the perimeter of the collar. "I know what's under there. I know what you're hiding, when other people don't." She stretched up on her tiptoes to kiss the corner of my mouth.

I totally understood. I loved that Tenley had my art on her back and it wasn't on display for just anyone. It would rarely be seen in all of its intricate glory, and most of the time, only the top of the wings would show even in a strapless dress. Tenley's delicate, little nose ring was the only visible sign of her inner self, but I knew better. And I liked that.

I turned my head and deepened the kiss. My hands went to her waist, and I barely resisted the urge to go lower and squeeze her ass. Now wasn't a good time to start in on that kind of thing; her emotions were already so high. I reluctantly backed off.

"I want to give you a present before we go," I said as a distraction, tucking a loose tendril of hair behind her ear.

That got a real smile out of her. "I have one I want to give you now, too."

I followed her out to the living room. TK was rolling on the floor, batting around her catnip mouse. More gifts for her were coming tomorrow, such as the cupcake kitty bed. Tenley couldn't get over how cute it was, or that I'd bought the damn thing. There had been a lot of laughter over that.

Some of the presents were packed in a tote box to take to Cassie's, but quite a few were still under the tree. I dug around in the back, where I'd hidden the gift bag. Tenley dragged a large box out from under the tree and sat on the couch, propping the box against the coffee table.

"You go first." I handed her the bag with the white, springy ribbon.

Her eyes widened. "This is from Tiffany's."

I wasn't surprised she knew where the bag was from just by looking at it. It seemed to be a girl thing. Tenley reached inside and withdrew the small blue box. Removing the lid, she took out the black box inside. She looked at me, then opened it, inhaling with a soft gasp. "Oh, Hayden."

"Do you like it?" I asked, unable to read her reaction.

"This is really"—she hesitated—"extravagant."

"Isn't that what the holidays are supposed to be about? It reminded me of you, so I wanted you to have it."

The tears she'd been holding back since she woke up this morning slipped free, which wasn't quite the reaction I'd been going for.

"If you don't like it, I can take it back and get you something else."

"No, no. It's beautiful. Too much, but beautiful."

"You're sure you like it?"

"Absolutely." She swiped the tears away with the back of her hand. "I love it," she whispered.

With gentle fingers, she lifted the chain and cradled the tiny cupcake in her palm.

"Can I put it on for you?" I took the chain from her and unclasped it. Tenley lifted her hair and I carefully fastened it around her neck. Then I pressed a kiss against her nape.

Paired with the pale pink dress and her long, dark hair, the tiny cupcake looked perfect. I adjusted it, mostly to feel the warmth of her skin. I just wanted to be close to her.

"I don't deserve this." She touched the charm and looked up at me through wet lashes. Grabbing hold of my tie, she tugged me forward, kissing me with lips that quivered. "I don't deserve you."

"That's not true," I whispered, hating how pained she sounded. Wishing I could make it better, knowing I couldn't. Today was going to hurt for both of us.

18

TENLEY

I wanted so badly to let Hayden know how much I loved the necklace. Though Connor had given me plenty of jewelry, none of it reflected me as much as the charm hanging around my neck did. Which was exactly why I was falling apart.

The absence of my family made the holiday celebrations overwhelming. Add to that the ever-heightening awareness of my feelings for Hayden, and I was a ticking time bomb. The anxiety made it hard to think, so I just climbed into his lap and fused my mouth to his.

His phone buzzed in his pocket and he ignored it, but when mine went off a few seconds later, he sighed and pulled away. "That'll be Lisa calling to see if we've left yet."

"What happens if I don't answer it?"

"She'll call until you do."

He was right. My phone stopped ringing and Hayden's started up again. He moved me over to the cushion beside his and dug around in his pocket.

"We're leaving in five minutes," he said by way of greeting.

I couldn't hear Lisa's response, but Hayden's frown told me some admonishing might have been going on. I checked the time. We were supposed to be at Cassie's already. Hayden was rarely late for anything; I'd been the one to procrastinate.

We had fallen into old habits over the past few days, isolating ourselves, blowing off offers to get together for drinks in lieu of spending time alone. Mostly in his bed. Not sleeping. The physical connection helped keep me out of my head.

"We'll get there when we get there," Hayden said a little more forcefully. "Yeah. . . . No. . . . Fine. I won't forget the salad. . . . No, it's not from a bag. I'm offended. See you in a bit." He hung up the phone with an irritated sigh.

"We should probably get going, huh?" I felt bad that people were waiting on us.

"Cassie doesn't serve dinner until five. We have plenty of time. Lisa just wants us to get there so she can start on the cocktails."

"And she can't do that until we arrive?"

"She can. She's just being a pain in the ass." He lifted the box propped against the coffee table into his lap. "I'm opening this before we go."

Hayden was careful as he slid his finger under the taped edge. He managed to remove it without tearing the paper. I fidgeted impatiently as he lifted the lid from the box and removed the foam padding that buffered the edges. Then he turned over the canvas print.

"Holy mother of fuck."

His eyes moved over the black-and-white image that started at my neck and ended at my hip. The body was angled slightly so the swell of my breast was visible, but the focus was my unfinished tattoo. Lisa would do another shoot in full color when it was completed.

"This is you."

"Do you like it?" I asked, worried about his dark expression.

"I'm going to ask you something, and I don't want you to get upset with me." When I didn't say anything, he continued. "Who took this?"

"Lisa took all of them."

"Them?"

"There are three."

"Are you naked in all of them?"

"In two, yes."

He wet his bottom lip. "When do I get to see the rest?"

"You get one at Cassie's, and one tomorrow morning. The one at Cassie's is the least revealing."

"Will I want to gouge out someone's eyes if they see it?"

"No."

"Maybe we should leave it here. Just in case," Hayden suggested.

"It's sensual, not pornographic. Like the ones in your bedroom."

He pried his eyes away from the image. "Hm. It looks like those will have to come down, won't they?"

"Looks like." I dropped my head, hiding my smile of triumph.

It was almost three in the afternoon by the time we arrived at Cassie's. I was jittery, despite taking meds before we left. Hayden suggested I bring extra, just in case.

The meds made me loopy, and I'd been quiet on the trip to Cassie and Nate's, fiddling constantly with the charm around my neck. Hayden pulled into the driveway, parking beside Lisa's Beetle. I took a deep breath as I unlatched my seat belt.

Before I could reach for the door handle Hayden put his hand on my arm. "If it gets to be too much, say the word and we can go home."

"I'm not going to take you away from your family on the holidays, Hayden. I'll be fine."

"They're your family, too." When I shook my head, he said, "Maybe not in the usual sense, but all of them understand this is hard on you. No one expects you to power through, okay?"

I nodded, unable to speak through the sudden flood of emotion. They *were* like a family. Lisa and Chris and Jamie were just as much a part of Cassie's life as Hayden was. They were like surrogate adult children to her.

"I don't know what I'd do without you," I said, leaning across the console to kiss him.

"You don't have to. You have me and I'm not going anywhere."

He spoke with such conviction, as if any other option weren't possible. Truly, there was no other way to get through this, not for me. That I had walked away from him in the first place to sort through a past full of ghosts seemed untenable now. Rogue tears leaked out and I brushed them away, but more followed.

"I'm so sorry I left you."

"What?" Hayden asked, confused.

"I shouldn't have gone back to Arden Hills without explaining. I shouldn't have done that to you, and I'm so, so sorry. I wanted to stay here. I wanted to be with you but I didn't think I could, and I wish it had been different." I could feel my hysteria rising.

"Hey." Hayden held my face between his hands, forcing me to look at him. "Calm down, kitten. It's all right. Everything is okay now. You're back with me where you belong, and that's all that matters." His thumbs swept away the tears beneath my eyes. "We'll get through this together. You and me. Just remember, you've survived worse things than this. Whatever's going on in your head right now, you've made it through worse."

"Sometimes I feel guilty for having you," I whispered.

"I get that. And I wish I could make that feeling go away for you. You know your family wouldn't want you to be alone, right? They'd want you to have people in your life to love you and take care of you. I don't know that they would have chosen me to be that person, but I want to be if you'll let me."

I would never understand why I had to lose so much to find him. "I don't know what would have happened to me if I hadn't met you."

"Well, you'll never have to know."

He kissed me, his lips soft and lingering. In that moment I knew there was never going to be another person like him in my life. No one who would make me feel the way he did.

Hayden pulled away and looked at me with determined intent. "I want to tell you something important."

In my peripheral vision, the front door swung open. I tried to ignore it, but Chris's loud voice boomed out across the driveway, his crass comment barely muffled by the rumble of the engine.

Hayden sighed. "Ruin my fucking moment, why don't you."

"If you close your eyes, you can pretend he's not there."

"I can hear him though, so it's pointless."

"I thought you had something important to tell me."

"It can wait until later. We should go in." He planted a chaste kiss on the corner of my mouth and turned off the car.

My stomach knotted as we approached the entourage waiting for us at the door. Cassie pushed her way to the front, her arm came around my shoulder, and she ushered me into the foyer. "I'm so glad you came."

"Me, too."

There was a burst of chatter as Hayden helped me out of my coat, then he went back to the car to retrieve the presents and the food. The foyer was a large, open space with hardwood floors and modern décor. In front of me a staircase led to the second floor, and to the right was a living room with a wood-burning fireplace.

The air of excitement overwhelmed me, and I excused myself

to the bathroom. I locked the door and turned on the tap, rooting around in my bag for my bottle of meds. I rolled it between my palms, reluctant to take more, even though the artificial calm would help.

I closed my eyes and focused on breathing. Eventually the rapid beat of my heart slowed. Although that anxiety attack had been thwarted, I didn't want to risk being unprepared for another. I shook a couple of pills out of the bottle and stuffed them in the hidden pocket in my dress, in case I couldn't get to my purse later.

Hayden was waiting in the hall when I came out, his arms crossed over his chest. He pushed away from the wall and ran his hands down my bare arms. I didn't want him to know how much I was already struggling. He'd internalize it as a failure on his part, as unreasonable as that might be.

"Everything all right?" he asked, his hands sifting through my hair, fanning it out over my shoulders.

"I just needed a minute to collect myself."

He put a finger under my chin and tilted my head up to kiss me tenderly. "I could show you around the house before they bombard you again, if you'd like."

"That would be good."

He took my hand and led me away from the laughter filtering down the hall. Nate's office had a therapist's vibe. A massive cherry desk was at the back of the room, and the shelves against the wall matched. In the middle of the room were two comfy-looking chairs with footstools set on a lush carpet. Each chair had a side table with a coaster perched on it.

"Does Nate work from home?"

"Occasionally. His patients come through that side entrance." Hayden pointed across the room to a door nestled between two bookshelves. "He does some work for the hospital's inpatient unit, too. He's got some big title."

"He's a busy man."

"Yeah. He's a lot like my dad in that respect." A hint of disapproval was in Hayden's tone. "Nate's a bit of a workaholic. It's why Cassie opened up Serendipity. She wanted something meaningful to do with her time."

I'd wondered about that. Cassie drove a Mercedes and was always impeccably dressed. She almost looked out of place in Serendipity, like polished silver among tarnished brass.

"She doesn't have to work?"

Hayden shook his head. "Nope. Nate's got more than enough assets and equity. It probably costs them money to run that store, but she loves it and that's all Nate cares about. Cassie hates being idle as much as I do. If she had to sit around this house all day, she'd go nuts."

"How old is she?"

"Midthirties. There was a big age gap between her and my mom, like fifteen years. They were tight, though. Cassie was always around when I was a kid. It was almost like having an older sister, but she didn't annoy me, which I thought was cool back then. She even lived with us for a bit before my teens."

"She did?" Hayden's life hadn't been much different from mine. He'd had loving parents, a solid family, although from the sound of it, Hayden's father hadn't been around much.

"Yeah, I was like her shadow. I think it's part of the reason she took me in when my parents died. She wanted to return the favor or whatever." He tugged on my hand. "Come on, let me show you the rest of the house."

I didn't press for more information, aware he was sharing these pieces of himself to distract me. We stopped in several more rooms on the main floor. The equipment in the home gym looked as if it was frequently used, and the game room was complete with a pool table and a dartboard.

We took a set of stairs at the back of the house to the second floor. The five bedrooms were decorated in various modern themes. One was being refurbished. Drop cloths covered the furniture and cans of paint were stacked in the center of the room.

"This was my room." Hayden opened the door closest to the stairs. "It's been redecorated, though."

I went in, taking in the elegant lines of the space. The cream and black and raspberry color scheme was a fusion of masculine and feminine energies.

"Cassie painted it dark blue for me. It was a waste, though, since I didn't stay very long."

"How long were you here?" I asked, running my hand over the raspberry comforter, gorgeous against the black bed frame. Though the room looked different, I imagined the memories would still be difficult. The love and care from Cassie and Nate would have been overshadowed by the trauma he'd been through.

"Only a couple of months. I was too self-destructive. Nate had this savior-complex thing going on. He wanted me to talk to someone. I refused. Cassie didn't think he should push it right away, and I was a hard kid to handle. I would have fucked up their marriage if I'd stayed."

"Why do you say that?"

Hayden shrugged. "Cassie and Nate hadn't been married long when my parents died. It shook her up, and I was just too much to deal with. I didn't follow rules. I snuck out at night all the time; came home all fucked up on drugs because I couldn't cope. Cassie didn't know what to do with me; she was just as lost as I was. I could see the strain I was putting on them. I'd seen what the crap I pulled did to my parents. I figured it would be better for everyone if I lost my shit without Cassie watching it happen."

"That's pretty selfless, for someone so young and in such a bad place."

He shook his head. "I left because dealing was too hard."

"We can agree to disagree, then. You were just a boy."

It was at the core of his makeup to save people from pain, even if it meant distancing himself from them. So it made sense that he'd want to be with me, because as close as we'd become, walls were still between us. Thinner than before, but still there.

He said, "I used to wonder what my life would've been like if my parents weren't dead, how it would've been different. But I don't do that as much anymore."

"What changed?"

"I met you. I figured all the shit had to be for a reason, right? If I hadn't gone through it, I'd never get where you're coming from, and this thing we have." He traced the line of my jaw with a fingertip. "It wouldn't be the same."

Hayden was right. Without our pasts, our connection might have been very different.

19

TENLEY

Everyone was in the kitchen when we came back downstairs. A glass of wine was put in my hand. Hayden grabbed a beer and Nate tossed an apron at him. Hayden grumbled as he pulled it over his head.

"That's what you get for being late, bro," Chris said, running his hand over the front of his apron, which showcased the ripped abs of a tattooed male body.

Nate's was a tuxedo print, Jamie's a cowboy. Hayden wasn't so lucky; his had pink and white flowers with ruffles around the edges. I giggled as he fumbled with the strings. He was too broad to be able to tie a bow.

He grabbed a whisk and pointed it at me. "What are you laughing at? I can totally pull off this look."

I raised my hands. "I'm not arguing with you. I think you look pretty."

He smacked his palm with the whisk. "Don't think for a second I'll forget you said that."

I played with the chain around my neck and grinned. If the rest of the day could be like this, maybe it wouldn't be so bad.

Holiday dinners at Cassie's weren't like they'd been in Arden Hills. My home experience was of women rushing around the kitchen while the men sat and drank. At Connor's, someone was hired to cook while the family congregated in the formal sitting room to sip expensive wine and liquor.

Here, the men took over the kitchen. Well, most of them. According to Sarah, Chris couldn't even manage a Kraft dinner without making it inedible. He was allowed to mash the potatoes, but Hayden hovered and gave directions on how much of what went into the bowl.

I was fascinated by how natural the domestic routine seemed to be for Hayden. He'd been on his own for the past seven years and wasn't a huge fan of takeout, so he'd learned to cook. Aside from his fixation with cupcakes and his love of beer and scotch, he had healthy eating habits. Sometimes it made him a buzz kill when we went grocery shopping.

Sarah let out a low whistle, bringing my attention back to the conversation. She motioned to my chest. "Is that new?"

I looked down at the charm I was playing with. "It's an early present from Hayden."

Ever since I'd put it on, I couldn't stop touching it. It was like a talisman, the only thing beside Hayden that kept me grounded enough to get through the day.

"Wow! Nice job, Hayden," Sarah said.

Chris punched Hayden in the shoulder. "I guess we know why you two were late. Someone was looking to get laid."

"Ow!" Hayden punched him back. "That wasn't my motive at all."

"You two, hands to yourself. We're not having an MMA match in the kitchen this year." Nate pointed the handle of his bread knife at Hayden and Chris.

"MMA match?" I asked.

"Last year Chris and Hayden got into the sauce a little too early. There was an issue with the potatoes. The cleanup was a bitch," Jamie supplied.

"Particularly since those two were so messed up, they had their heads in the toilet before dinner was even served." Lisa shot an irritated glare at them.

"That was the worst hangover I ever had." Chris went back to pulverizing potatoes.

"You let them get away with that?" I asked Cassie.

"I wasn't involved. Lisa and I were on an emergency run to get fresh cranberries. Chris brought canned ones and Hayden refused to serve them." Cassie smiled at Hayden.

"Who the hell eats canned cranberry sauce?" he asked, as if it were unheard of.

I raised my hand. "I like canned cranberry sauce."

"You would, Miss Let's Eat Popcorn and Reese's Pieces for Dinner," he shot back.

"Don't knock it. The Reese's Pieces are awesome when they're all melty."

"It's true," Sarah said. "It really is good."

Hayden rolled his eyes and went back to stirring the cranberry sauce. Which he'd made from scratch.

"So what happened when you got back?" Sarah asked.

"Hayden and Chris were engaged in a wrestling match on the floor," Cassie replied.

"And Nate and Jamie were busy placing bets on who was going to win," Lisa said with a laugh.

"I stood to make good money if Hayden won, considering he was the underdog," Jamie said.

"Hardly," Hayden scoffed. "Chris was way more hammered than I was."

"Yeah, but you're all lanky and shit, you Gumby-looking mother-fucker. I'm the one with the brawn," Chris goaded, flexing his thick biceps.

"Should I be worried?" I asked Cassie, who was watching them with an amused smile.

"No. This is pretty normal," she said.

"Fuck that Gumby shit." Hayden tossed his wooden spoon on the counter and went chest to chest with Chris. "You're a freak of nature. You were probably the size of a fucking toddler when you were born."

They looked frighteningly dangerous as they glared at each other, chins raised in defiance. Jamie gave a bark of laughter.

Chris fought back a grin and Hayden poked him in the chest. "I am not lanky. Right, kitten?"

"Of course not." All those hard-cut muscles? "I think you have the perfect body." It came out almost breathless.

Hayden smirked and leaned across the counter to plant a kiss on my lips. "It goes both ways, beautiful." Even in the ridiculous apron, he swaggered back to his post at the stove.

Everyone stared at Hayden with expressions that verged on disbelief; I got the distinct impression none of them had ever seen him like this before.

Cassie put an arm around my shoulder. "We're all very glad you're here, Tenley."

"So am I." I leaned into her embrace. "I'm very fortunate to have found him."

"As is he," she said.

While the men prepared dinner, Cassie, Lisa, Sarah, and I sat around the kitchen island and chatted. I tried my best to stay in the moment. The banter between the boys kept us entertained, and the constant flow of wine helped, too. Lisa topped up my glass so frequently, it was impossible to keep track of how much I consumed.

When dinner was ready, we transferred the food into serving bowls and carried them to the dining room. Hayden sat to my right, with his arm around the back of my chair throughout dinner. Every so often he leaned in to kiss my temple or play with a lock of my hair and tell me how glad he was that I was with him.

After the main course, the plates were cleared. New dishes were brought out in preparation for dessert. Since no one was ready for it yet, we relaxed in our chairs, blissed out in a turkey coma. Everyone was sipping drinks except for Hayden, who had switched to soda water. Conversation was easy, and while I was quiet, it wasn't because I was stuck in the past. I loved listening to this new family I'd become part of.

After a while Hayden and Jamie started asking about dessert, so I brought it out while Cassie poured coffees.

"What's going on? I thought you brought cupcakes," Hayden said as I set the dessert platter on the table.

"They are cupcakes."

"Really? All incognito, huh?" He inspected the wreath. White-chocolate leaves covered the layer of fluffy buttercream icing, and fresh-cut strawberries adorned the top for a splash of color.

"It's almost too pretty to eat," Cassie said.

"Almost," Hayden agreed, and took the first one. "But not quite."

He didn't bother to wait for everyone else before he peeled away the wrapper and shoved half of it in his mouth. Only when he was eating cupcakes did his table manners disappear. "Is this angel food cake?" he asked between bites.

"I thought it would be lighter. Did they turn out okay?"

He groaned an affirmative and helped himself to seconds. I peeled the wrapper from my own and began slowly disassembling the cake: eating the berries first, followed by the white-chocolate leaves, then finally the icing-covered cake. Hayden pulled me closer, until I was almost in his lap. He reached over and helped himself to a third.

"You don't have to make yourself sick. There are extras at my apartment."

"Good to know." He tucked my hair behind my ear and leaned in to whisper, "Watching you eat cupcakes is better than porn."

"You think so?" I batted my eyelashes at him, then sucked icing off my finger.

His hand disappeared below the tablecloth and he shifted in his chair. His nose brushed my cheek. "Much better. Infinitely better."

"It's a dinner table, not a bedroom. Put your hands where I can see them, Stryker," Jamie said.

At the round of snickering, my cheeks warmed. Hayden's hand reappeared, his middle finger directed at Jamie, but his hand stayed above the table after that.

Lisa asked, "Anyone have any ideas for New Year's? We need a plan."

Hayden had mentioned New Year's once in passing, but hadn't brought it up again. For me, it was yet another holiday I would be celebrating without my family.

"I thought we were going to chill this year." He stroked his thumb along my bare shoulder.

"That's one option," Lisa said. "Are you offering to host?"

Hayden snorted. "I only have one spare bedroom."

"That's all you need. Chris and Sarah can stumble across the street," Jamie pointed out.

"Forget Hayden's. I say we hop a plane to Vegas for the weekend," Chris cut in.

Sarah rolled her eyes. "Only you would suggest something like that."

"He's had worse ideas," Lisa said. "Maybe Jamie and I could get hitched while we're at it! It would save me from this business of planning a wedding."

Good-natured laughter followed.

I felt Hayden's arm tighten around my shoulder. His lips moved against my temple, but whatever the words were, I didn't hear them. My mind was stuck, skipping like a record. The static in my head became a screaming siren, drowning out everything else.

I couldn't feel my body as I lifted my wineglass to my lips. I tipped it back; the cool liquid tasted like vinegar as I drained the glass. The world went out of focus as panic took over. I knew it wasn't rational. People got on planes every day and made it to their destinations without so much as a blip of turbulence.

"Tenley?" Hayden's hand was on the back of my neck, fingers kneading gently. "Are you okay?" He sounded so far away, as if he were talking to me from underwater.

"Excuse me for a moment," I said, finding it hard to breathe. I pushed my chair back. "I just need to use the bathroom." I prayed he'd let me go before I cracked and wrecked the evening.

I placed my napkin on the table and headed for the closest powder room, then locked myself in before my legs gave out.

I sank to the floor, working to push through the panic. I wanted to turn back time. To have a normal reaction to an impromptu trip to Vegas. To be excited. But I couldn't be. Blinding panic radiated through me, seizing my chest.

I squeezed my eyes shut and clutched the cupcake charm, wishing it had the power to prevent me from breaking down. The memories came anyway—vivid and violent. They began and ended with Connor's shattered face and broken body. Always. Here I was, on Christmas Eve, barely a year after the crash, celebrating the holiday with someone else. Someone I loved infinitely more. I felt as if I were wronging Connor in some way.

I lurched forward, grasping the edge of the toilet as dinner reappeared. My eyes teared as I heaved again. When it was finally over, I braced myself on the edge of the vanity. I ran my hands under the cold water and pressed my palms against my neck. I needed to get it together. I didn't want Hayden to see me falling apart like this.

With my stomach no longer revolting, I reached into the pocket in my dress. I debated whether I had the strength to make it through the rest of the evening without the pills. But I couldn't risk another panic attack. The doorknob rattled, and I almost dropped them in the sink.

"Tenley? Can I come in?" Hayden asked from the other side, concerned.

"I need a second." I popped the pills, then cupped my hand under the tap and washed down the chemical taste.

As soon as I unlocked the door, Hayden came in and closed it behind him. He pulled me into his arms. "I'm so sorry. Lisa wasn't thinking."

"It's fine. I just needed a minute." I sighed into his chest, letting the salve of his touch ease the ache.

"A minute?" He rubbed slow circles on my back, lulling me to semi-calm. "You've been in here for almost twenty. I knocked a couple of times but you didn't answer, so I figured you needed space. Then I got worried."

I thought I'd only been in the bathroom a short time. "I'm so sorry. I didn't expect that. Just the idea of getting on a plane—"

"It's okay. Don't think about it. You're all right." His hands settled on my waist and he lifted me easily onto the vanity.

Once I was sitting, I realized how much I had been relying on him to keep me upright. I was still shaking. "I'll never be able to fly again."

"It's only been a year. You can't know that for sure." His palms moved down my arms, and he clasped my hands in his.

"You don't understand." I shook my head, all the words stuck.

"Chris meant it as a joke, and Lisa doesn't want to get married next week. And even if we did go to Vegas at some point, we could make a road trip out of it. Take as long as we want to get there."

The warm buffer of medication had yet to set in, allowing fear to spill over. Joke or not, so much about the situation was too hard to manage.

"Tenley?"

Lost in my fears, I wrapped his tie around my hand, staring at the pinup girl as she slipped over my fist. "What if Lisa's serious?"

"She's not. At least not for New Year's. A Vegas wedding is right up Lisa's alley, but it's not going to happen right away."

Driving might seem like a good solution, but everyone else would still get on a plane. What if we arrived in Vegas only to find they hadn't made it?

"Talk to me, Tenley."

I looked up, pleading with him to understand. "I can't go through that again. Losing all these people? It would kill me."

"I know. That's why we'd drive."

"But everyone else would fly!" I gripped Hayden's hand tighter to keep my shaking under control. "I can't ask them to put their lives on hold just because I can't get on a plane. I don't know if I'll ever get past this fear." I shuddered. "I only lost consciousness briefly after the plane went down."

"You—What? I don't understand."

"When I came to, the plane had crashed and it was on fire. I found Connor when I was trying to escape. He was dead. Half of his face was crushed. It's the last memory I have of him—and it still haunts my nightmares. You're asking me to entertain the same scenario. Tell me how I'm supposed to deal with that."

The color drained from Hayden's face. I still hadn't told him some things because talking about it hurt too much. "Shit. I'm so sorry. I wish I could take those memories away for you."

Enveloped in his protective embrace, I sagged against him, drained of energy. I locked my arms around his neck and my legs around his waist, desperate for the closeness, the connection. He held me for the longest time and I absorbed the comfort like a sponge.

His chin rested on top of my head. I felt the periodic bob of his throat as he swallowed, the rise and fall of his chest, the constant, rhythmic beat of his heart. I pressed my lips to his neck. Hayden dropped his head and kissed me. Fear had a way of inspiring need. My lips parted, welcoming him in.

A quiet knock at the door broke the spell. Lisa's apprehensive voice came from the other side: "Tenley? Hayden?"

Hayden pressed his forehead against mine. "Give us a minute," he called out, and then dropped to a whisper. "I'm taking you home soon."

"Please? I need you tonight."

He pressed one final kiss to my lips and helped me down from the vanity. When I had my bearings, he opened the door.

Lisa threw her arms around me. "I'm so sorry. I was caught up in the excitement. I didn't think."

I held on to her, feeling the burden of her sadness, hating that I couldn't enjoy her spontaneity. "You don't have to apologize. I overreacted."

Hayden took my hand and we walked through the dining room. The table had been cleared and everything returned to order. We went into the living room, where everyone had congregated. No one made a fuss, and Hayden pulled me into his lap in an oversize reading chair.

20

TENLEY

"Ready to go?" Hayden whispered after gifts had been exchanged.

"Please," I said, draining what was left of the tea I'd been drinking.

Everything was an uncomplicated haze, now that the medication had set in. When we got home, I could lose myself in him. He dropped a lingering kiss on my shoulder, following with his teeth, the promise of intimacy an undeniable lure.

"Tenley and I are gonna roll out."

"You're not staying the night?" Cassie asked, clearly disappointed.

"TK's by herself," Hayden said, his hands on my waist as I stood. The room shifted with the movement, the medication making me feel weightless.

Hayden packed all the gifts into the box we'd brought. He helped me into my coat, and I used the bench as a seat to put on my shoes, since I was too unsteady to stand. I didn't track the hugs and good-byes because my mind was elsewhere.

Hayden led me to the car and unlocked the door. "I'm sorry today wasn't easier." The words spiraled out in ghostly tendrils, disappearing in the cold air.

"You were with me. That made it better." I grabbed the lapels of his jacket and pulled him close.

His body came flush against mine as his lips parted, and we took up where we'd left off in the bathroom. His hands went to my hips, his erection insistent against my stomach. "I need to get you home."

"I want to be home," I said, feeling for the door handle.

Hayden helped me in and shut me inside the frigid car. He adjusted himself as he strode around the front, his intentions as clear as mine. The presents were unceremoniously tossed in the backseat.

"I should have warmed up the car first," he said as he turned the engine over.

"It gets warm fast enough." I pulled my legs up and rubbed them through the thin nylon.

He shifted the car into gear, gunning it as soon as he was on the street. Unable to keep my hands off him, I put my palm on his knee. He glanced down but didn't say anything. I moved higher, up along his thigh. The muscles in his leg tensed.

Hayden sucked in a breath as I grazed his erection. "What are you doing?"

"Touching you." I reached for his belt, sliding the leather through the buckle, unclasping it, and flicking the button open.

"I'm not sure that's a good idea."

"Can't you multitask?"

"That depends on the tasks involved."

I slipped my hand into his pants, fingering the warm steel ball at the head. Hayden gripped the steering wheel tightly.

He whispered a low "Fuck." His eyes flicked to me. "We should have left earlier."

The blinker came on and he made several turns, taking us deeper into a subdivision while I freed him from his pants and continued stroking.

"Hold on," Hayden gritted through clenched teeth as he wrenched the wheel and the car turned sharply. He eased off the gas and pulled into a short driveway before hitting the brakes with a jolt. His labored breathing was drowned out by the loud whir of a garage door opening.

"Where are we?"

"This is the place I'm working on with Nate."

"No one lives here?"

"Not at the moment, no."

He pulled into the garage. Once the car was inside, the door closed.

Hayden cut the engine and the headlights died, submerging us in darkness. We groped blindly in the inky black, hands searching each other out, mouths connecting. His tongue pushed past my lips, and I hastily unfastened my seat belt so I could get closer. We were a mass of tangled limbs, pulling and pushing as we tried to bridge the space between us.

I was pressed against the passenger door, legs spread out, one hand on the dash, the other gripping the headrest. Hayden hovered over me, halfway across the center console, contorted in an uncomfortable position he didn't seem to mind. He sought the edge of my dress, his hand snaking up my thigh, reaching the lace edge of my thigh highs.

Then he stopped. His hand slapped at the ceiling and the interior light came on. I blinked, adjusting to the sudden brightness.

"How the fuck did I miss these?"

"I put them on just before we left, while you were getting the presents together."

"Sneaky, sexy woman."

He ran his finger under the pink strap of the garter, all the way up to the satin between my legs. His knuckle grazed my clit. I arched into the touch and threw my head back, slamming it against the window.

"Shit. Are you okay?" His hand stayed between my legs, but he looked conflicted as he scanned my body and his eyes rose to mine. "Maybe we shouldn't do this here. I don't have my key to get in the house. I should take you home."

The day had been too heavy and I wanted Hayden to erase it. "I don't want to wait until we get home. I want you to fuck me now."

After a moment's hesitation he fumbled with the lever on my seat and I went crashing back. The box of presents behind me toppled over, spilling its contents onto the floor.

"Dammit." He reached out to try to stop them.

"Leave it." I gripped his chin in my hand, my need gaining urgency.

He sucked on my bottom lip and tried to straddle me, but he couldn't fit his legs in the space between the seat and the dash. He grunted when he smacked his head on the ceiling.

"There's not enough room," he lamented, shoving the skirt of my dress up to my waist.

"Maybe we should use the hood."

He froze. "Excuse me?"

"There's plenty of space there." I gestured toward the broad expanse of black metal, remembering the time he mentioned using the location, before I'd gone back to Arden Hills.

"I was kind of joking about that," he rasped.

"No, you weren't."

He was out of the car before I could react and wrenched opened my door. The interior light cast his face in shadow, making his smile almost sinister as he leaned on the frame.

"Get out of the car, kitten."

21

HAYDEN

Tenley smiled with satisfaction as her glassy eyes met mine. For a second I reevaluated the whole idea, then Tenley pushed my boxers out of the way and leaned in. My dick was conveniently located at the same level as her face.

She ran her tongue over the slit.

"Mother of— You really have no fucking idea—"

"No fucking idea about what?" She did it again.

"What you do to me. All day you've been in this dress, looking so sweet and innocent. Then you start with the hand job, and the garters, and now this. How am I supposed to say no to you?"

"Why would you want to do that?"

She wrapped her lips around me. The wet warmth of her mouth was a welcome contrast to the cool air in the garage. It wasn't as frigid in here as it was outside, but it was cold enough that my balls wanted to climb up inside my body.

She let out a needy sigh as her tongue swirled around the head, and I gripped the doorframe. As her mouth moved over me, I was aware this was a colossally bad idea. She might've been the one to suggest it, but today had been emotional and it made her unstable. Plus she was medicated.

A better boyfriend would have put a stop to this and taken her home. I was not that boyfriend. Instead, I planned to do the one thing I could to alleviate her pain, even if the location lacked romance.

I pressed my fingers into the hinge of her jaw, easing her off. "I want that mouth up here."

She came willingly, her arms winding around my neck. I bent to kiss her, tongues twining as I pulled her away from the car and closed the door. The interior light cast a pale glow over the hood.

Small, high-pitched noises came from Tenley as she tried to wrap herself around me. I gripped her thighs and hoisted her up, depositing her on the hood of the car. Her dress bunched around her waist, the flowing fabric creating a barrier. I sifted through the layers until the sexy garters came into view.

Tenley's sigh of relief echoed my own, the thin satin of her panties the only thing impeding immediate entrance. I wanted to touch all of her. I wanted her naked and spread out, but it was too cold. The dress would have to stay on, until we got home.

I rocked my hips, achieving the friction we were both looking for. She loosened my tie and popped the first few buttons on my shirt. But she was too frantic, and her hands too unsteady, to get through them all. She gave up and found the hem instead, her palm going under and up to rest over my heart.

"I can't lose you. I need you so much, it hurts." Her voice was high, reedy.

"It's the same for me."

Countless times since her return I'd woken in the night after one of the dreams, searching the bed for her warm body. Each time I found her, the promise of her constancy eased the fear.

Tonight was no different. We were both looking for a way to ground ourselves in the present.

My hand traveled up her leg, over the thigh highs and lace trim, past the sexy expanse of bare skin. I slipped a finger under the garter strap and followed it to her panties, going under the elastic.

"Please, Hayden," she whispered.

In one smooth stroke I pushed two fingers inside. Tenley's head fell back, legs sliding off my hips. She propped herself on her arms, the pale light spilling over the contours of her delicate face. Desperation was behind her desire, and I understood the feeling only too well. I twisted my fingers, adding another. Tenley lifted her hips, her body arching. She drew one leg up, her heel coming to rest on my thigh. It slid down.

"Just put it on the car."

Her leg quivered and goose bumps flashed across her skin. She was closer than I thought.

"But the paint . . . ," she panted as I thrust harder and faster, rubbing her clit with my palm.

"Screw the paint."

She grabbed on to my tie with one hand, reaching for her heel with the other. It dropped to the floor with a low thud. The other followed immediately after.

Tenley put one foot on the hood, but her nylons provided no traction. She stretched her leg up, her heel coming to rest on my shoulder. I leaned against the car as her other shin hit my forearm. She was sex and innocence, a vision in cream and pale pink, spread out on black steel.

Her teeth were clenched, the muscles in her jaw tight. I curled my fingers, and her eyes fluttered shut as she gripped my tie tighter. It bit into my neck painfully so I leaned in closer.

"Come, goddamnit," I demanded, wanting her release so I could get mine.

She shook her head and moaned. "I can't. I'm so close, *oh, God . . .*"

"I'm not fucking you until you do," I threatened, not sure if I could follow through with the asinine declaration.

Tenley's eyes flipped open, her lips a hair's breadth away from mine. The emotions that clouded her half-glazed eyes were brutally intense.

I brought my lips to her ear. "Please, kitten, I need to see you come."

She released my tie and almost set me off-balance. Her cold palm came to rest against my nape. She tilted her head giving me access to her throat. I dropped my head and kissed her neck, grazing with my teeth.

"Do that again—please." Her voice was pained. "Harder," she said, when my teeth pressed against the silken skin, and she bucked against my fingers.

I complied, because she was *right there*. She cried out, her voice echoing in the garage as her body trembled with the force of her orgasm. Then she went limp; the leg propped against my shoulder slid down into the crook of my arm.

"Are you okay?" I asked, bringing my mouth to hers.

The kiss started off slow, but as Tenley regained control of herself, the intensity increased.

With shaky anticipation I grabbed my cock, pushed her panties out of the way, and dragged the head down her slit. My body was being lit up from the inside, a meteor shooting through space, heading for impact. I should have been making love to her tonight, sweet and slow. But I couldn't control the need to own her body if I couldn't have the most important part of her yet.

"I need—" I thrust with more force than I meant to, and Tenley let out a shocked gasp. I kissed her penitently. "I'm sorry."

"It's okay," she whispered, her nose brushing mine. "I love you in me."

I wanted to tell her I loved her. I wanted to hear the same from her. All the things I couldn't say kept me bound and gagged, breaking me in ways I hadn't expected.

I cradled the back of her head in my hand as I moved, gaining momentum with each thrust. I braced one knee on the hood, my other thigh pressed against the wheel well. The metal protested and the steel caved beneath my knee, but I kept going. I could feel it coming; the tightness in the pit of my stomach became an ache as I finally surrendered and the orgasm slammed through me.

"Fuck," I groaned. "I love the way you feel."

Her mouth fell open as she came, too, quaking and shuddering. Two tears slipped over her temples and disappeared into her hairline. I stilled as more pooled in the corners of her eyes.

"Shit." I brushed them away, but new ones followed. "Kitten? Did I hurt you?"

I started to pull out, but her leg tightened around my waist. Her hands clasped behind my back to draw me in. "Stay in me, please. Don't go."

We remained that way until the cold began to register. When Tenley shivered and her skin pebbled, I eased out of her, pulling her dress down. My now-limp dick went back in my pants before I helped her off the hood.

Her makeup was smudged under her eyes, her cheeks blotchy, her hair a wild mess. After I fixed her up as best as I could, which wasn't very good, I opened the passenger door. The interior light flashed brighter, highlighting the damage I'd inflicted on my car. Besides the dent from my knee, several scratches in the paint were obvious.

"Oh my God, Hayden, the hood!" Tenley exclaimed in wide-eyed horror.

I helped her into her seat and buckled her in. "No big deal. Easy enough to fix."

I closed her door and hit the code on the garage before getting into the car and backing out into the driveway. I checked to make sure the alarm was armed before we left. Tenley's legs were tucked under her when I got back in; she was rolling the cupcake charm over her lips.

"What's up, kitten? You okay? Anything sore?"

She reached over and ran her fingers through my hair. "I don't know if I would have survived today without you," she said quietly.

"You would have found a way to get through it."

"I'm not so sure. Maybe."

What I'd just done came crashing down around me. I should have stopped her in the car. Or pulled over, gotten her off, and then taken her back to my place to finish the job. She meant more than a hard fuck in a cold garage.

"Hayden?"

"I should get you home. You look tired." I started to put the car in gear.

Tenley put her hand over mine to stop me. "Are you upset with me? Did I say something wrong?"

I didn't know what to tell her without making her feel shittier. Admitting I felt guilty for being an asshole boyfriend wouldn't go over well.

"You haven't said or done anything wrong. I shouldn't have stopped here."

"Is it about the car?"

"What? No. Fuck the car. It's just metal and an engine."

"It was your dad's—"

"It's not the car, Tenley." I kissed the tips of her fingers. They were cold. I noted the smudges of dirt on the sleeves of her ivory coat. She'd kept it on the entire time.

"Then what?"

Tenley disengaged her seat belt and leaned across the console as if she wanted to climb into my lap. I wouldn't have stopped her if she had. That's when I realized what the real issue was. It had little to do with the location, or the car, or how unstable Tenley was. The sex had done nothing to ease the ache in her, or me. If anything, we were both needier now than before. Which made sense. The gratification had only been physical; it hadn't been the connection both of us craved. The emotional piece had been missing.

"Let's go home." I tucked her hair behind her ear.

"Hayden, I——"

A new tension was in the car, the weight of unspoken words heavy in the air. I waited for her to continue, but she seemed to deflate. She kissed me and dropped back into her seat. The click of her seat belt sounded like a shotgun blast in the silence.

"Okay. Let's go home."

22

HAYDEN

We were four blocks from home when we hit a sobriety checkpoint. Normally this wouldn't have posed a problem. The two drinks I'd had this afternoon were long out of my system. There'd been plenty of time, food, and activity to dilute their effects. However, my frame of mind was shit. Getting it on in semipublic locations had never before been an issue, but pushing it on Tenley in her emotional state left me feeling hollow. Not to mention that Tenley looked a right mess.

She was curled up in the passenger seat, legs pulled up under her, her dress fanning out to cover her calves and feet. She had reclined the seat so she was almost prone, lying on her side, facing me. Her eyes were closed, her mouth lax, her breathing slow and deep. She'd fallen asleep. Which should have made me feel better, but meant that I'd worn her out.

When the car came to a stop, Tenley sat up, blinking blearily. She glanced out the windshield at the flashing lights of the cop cars lining the street.

"What's going on? Was there an accident?"

"They're just doing a drunk check."

"Oh."

She adjusted her seat back into a sitting position but she didn't relax. She rubbed at her eyes with the sleeve of her coat, leaving a mascara smear on the pale fabric. Unable to keep still, she wiped at the mark on her sleeve. Eventually she gave up and stared out the window as the line of cars moved forward. As the flashing lights got closer, Tenley became edgier.

I stretched my arm across her seat and burrowed through her hair, resting my palm on the back of her neck. "You might want to grab a tissue from the glove box. Your mascara ran a little."

I was seriously downplaying it. She looked like a Tim Burton movie character. Not ideal, considering we were about to chat with the cops, but I didn't want to stress her out more. She did as I suggested, rooting around in the glove compartment for the small packet of travel tissues I kept there. She withdrew a row of condoms. Fuckity-Fuckerson.

We'd only used condoms the first couple of times, before we had the awkward discussion about safety and previous partners and all that shit. Awkward for me, anyway, because of my dodgy past. I'd evaded providing any details at the time, and she'd trusted me enough to take my word. That conversation alone told me a lot about the limitations of her experience.

"They're probably expired," I said.

I fought the urge to throw them out the window—they weren't something I wanted to explain on an already shitty night.

Tenley squinted at the tiny date pressed into the foil square. "They're good for another six months." She tossed them at me and they hit me in the shoulder, falling between my seat and the center console.

"I forgot I even had them."

"Is there anything else in here you may have forgotten about?" she asked sharply.

"Like what?" I glanced at her as she rifled through the glove box, surprised by her tone.

Her lips were pursed in a tight line. "Oh, I don't know. A stack of random girls' numbers? A little black book? Maybe a pair of trophy panties."

"That's a joke, right?"

"No black book, then? Oh, of course not, you didn't do repeat offenses. Aside from Sienna, right? Silly me. I forgot."

She was snippy, which was totally unlike her. Tenley wasn't petty, and she never used my past against me.

"Are you mad at me?"

"Why would I be mad?" She found the tissues and pulled one out with too much force, tearing it in half.

"I don't know," I said, honestly flummoxed. "But you sound like you're pissed and I'm not sure what I did. Those condoms have been there since before I met you. I'm serious when I say I forgot about them. And I'm not so fucked up that I'd keep trophies of a previous partner's underwear."

"That's reassuring." She swiped under her eyes, black smudges appearing on the white tissue.

"What's the deal? Where is this coming from?"

"It's nothing. It's been a long day. I'm tired."

Her shoulders sagged and she dabbed at her eyes. She was hiding that she was crying. There was way more to this than she was letting on.

"What aren't you telling me?" I asked, pulling up another car length.

Only a few cars were in front of me now, and I worried we were gearing up for a fight. I wasn't all that keen on getting into a verbal battle, especially with her so fragile and me already feeling like a huge dick. Add some police officers into the mix, and I was looking at a veritable shit show. I was fully aware of the stereotype I perpetuated, especially if Tenley ended up in tears. With the way she looked right now they'd think she was a victim of abuse, emotional or otherwise.

"I'm sorry. I shouldn't have snapped at you. Today's been hard."

"You don't need to apologize. I know today's been difficult. I just want to know why you're so upset so I can do something to help."

I kneaded the back of her neck. Her shoulders tensed so I backed off. She was silent for so long I thought she wasn't going to answer.

Then in a tiny, shamed voice she whispered, "I found a box of condoms in Connor's car when I was cleaning it out last week."

Hearing his name in this context inspired the sensation of spiders crawling all over me. "In the douche mobile?"

Another car passed through the police barricade.

She nodded.

Talking about Connor like this made me uncomfortable for a number of reasons, but I'd set aside my self-doubt if she'd confide in me. I was desperate to understand where she was at right now.

"I'm sorry. I'm not seeing how that would be a problem," I replied, confused.

From the pictures I'd seen of him, he was a jockish, polo-wearing Boy Scout, so it made sense he'd want to be prepared. If she and I still needed to use condoms, I'd be wearing them as a belt.

"There were four missing."

"Maybe he kept them in his wallet?"

It was a reasonable thing to do, though four seemed like overkill. Yet the first night I went over to Tenley's, I brought three. And back then, I'd been avoiding that scenario.

"I've been getting the shot for years," she said. "I went on it pretty much right after we started dating because Connor hated condoms and I didn't want to take any chances. There was never a reason for him to need them."

My stomach bottomed out as what she was telling me hit. I thought back to those photo albums I'd gone through, and that period of time when Connor was absent from the pictures. There had to be a story there I didn't know. Had her insecurities and second thoughts originated there?

"There has to be a reasonable explanation."

"I'll never know what it was, though, will I?" She wrapped her arms around her waist, folding in on herself.

From the way she was shutting down, she had already formulated her own hypothesis—the worst one possible. To discover this after he was gone was fucked up. Since she couldn't know for sure, those doubts would linger forever, tainting his memory. While I felt threatened by him, I didn't want him demonized.

It was better for him to be enshrined in her past. Because finding out that he might have been fucking someone else led to one truth: all that death might have been avoidable if she'd known.

"Maybe they belonged to a buddy? Chris used to leave his all over the place. He got Jamie in a world of shit once when Lisa found a box stashed under the passenger seat of the Beetle."

"Maybe," Tenley replied, but obviously she didn't believe it.

We moved forward again. Only one more car was in front of us.

"There was never anyone else when you were gone," I said, seeking to reassure her that I would never do that to her. This information explained so much about her past reactions, particularly to Sienna.

"I know that." She wiped at her eyes with a fresh tissue, leaving new mascara smudges behind.

"The thought of being with someone other than you made me feel sick." I smoothed my palm down her back, along the ridges of her spine. "It still does."

The car in front of us pulled through the barricade. I moved forward, annoyed at the interruption to our heavy conversation. My headlights washed over the officer inspecting the cars, and I gripped the steering wheel so hard my knuckles went white.

"Son of a bitch."

Just when I thought my night couldn't get any worse.

23

HAYDEN

I rolled down the window and waited. Cross would push my buttons. It was a skill he excelled at.

"Mr. Stryker. What a pleasant surprise. License and registration, please," Cross said icily.

I reached across to the glove box and flipped it open. Tenley had moved the contents around in her search for tissues, so it wasn't where I normally kept it. She leaned forward to help, and the light inside illuminated her face. Her skin was blotchy from crying, her eyes bloodshot and pupils dilated. Her mascara had run down her cheeks, leaving dark streaks. On the side of her neck was a faint red mark from my teeth.

Cross rested his forearm against the doorframe and peered inside as I plucked the registration from the glove box. I flipped the compartment shut, extinguishing the light.

"Miss Page?"

"Hi, Officer Cross." Tenley lifted her hand in a small wave.

He flicked on his flashlight and surveyed my registration while I dug into my back pocket for my wallet. I was wearing dress pants, so of course it wasn't there. I had to rummage around in the back-seat, where all the presents were strewn, for my jacket. Cross shone his flashlight over the seat and I snatched up my coat. Retrieving my license, I passed it over. Cross was too busy looking at Tenley to notice.

"How are you this evening?" he asked, inspecting her in a way I didn't like.

"I'm fine." She gave him a weak smile.

"Are you sure about that? You don't look well."

His flashlight moved over her rumpled dress to her legs. Her nylons had a run and she didn't have shoes on. Fuck. They were still in the garage.

"My license." I held it up in front of his face.

He gave it a cursory glance before his cold stare rested on me. "Where are you coming from and where are you headed?"

"We were at my aunt's for dinner and we're heading home," I replied, determined to get this over with as quickly as possible. I didn't want him to get a good look at Tenley.

"Have you consumed any alcohol this evening?" He continued to shine the flashlight into the car. Tenley cringed away from the brightness when it got too close to her face.

"I had two scotch on the rocks between three and five this afternoon." There was no point in lying. The alcohol was long out of my system.

The flashlight panned over the hood, stopping at the small dent and the fresh scratches. He leaned over to have a better look and returned his calculating glare to me.

"Were you in an accident?"

"No."

"You are aware that you have a pretty good dent in your hood and some scratches?"

"Yes."

"Had to be something heavy considering the car. Would you happen to know where it came from?"

"Yes."

I didn't elaborate, although I could see he expected me to.

"Pull over and turn off the car, Mr. Stryker."

"What for?"

"Because I told you to."

I sighed but followed his directions. I'd already caused a scene with him once; if I did it again, cuffs could be involved. I'd never had a criminal record and starting now by ignoring a command from an officer or punching out the douche fuck wasn't something I was keen to do.

I pulled off to the shoulder and cut the engine. Cross circled the car until he reached the hood, shining his light over the damage. Tenley's jacket had a buckle on the back, and the repetitive hard thrusting had scratched the paint down to the steel. Cross went around to Tenley's side, leaning in close with the flashlight. He rubbed a finger over one of the scratches and it came away black.

"Miller," he called out as he crossed back over to the driver's side. "Can you come here, please?"

The female cop who'd been at the station when we were last there strode over. They had a conversation out of earshot with a lot of gesturing and frowning on both their parts.

"What are they doing?" Tenley asked in a whisper.

"Cross is probably trying to find a way to arrest me for having a dent in my hood."

"He can't do that, can he?" She crushed the package of tissues in her hand.

I took them from her and pulled another free, wiping under her eyes in a useless attempt to get rid of the smudges.

"No, kitten. There's no law against having dents in your car."

"I just want to go home."

"I know. Me, too. This shouldn't take long."

In my peripheral vision, Cross hiked up his pants and head toward my door while Miller approached the passenger side.

"Step out of the car, Mr. Stryker."

"I haven't had a drink in hours."

"Out of the car. Now." Cross's hard tone left no room for argument.

"Hayden?" Tenley gripped my forearm. "What's going on?"

I squeezed her hand as I leaned in and dropped a kiss on her trembling lips. "It's okay, kitten. This'll just take a minute. They probably want to check my blood alcohol level."

I doubted that was Cross's motivation.

"I'm not asking again, Stryker," Cross snapped.

I unbuckled my seat belt and climbed out into the cold night air. The temperature had dropped again and white flakes had begun to fall.

Tenley started to open her door, but Cross stopped her. "Stay in the car, Miss Page." He turned to me. "Put your hands on the car and spread your legs."

"You've got to be kidding me."

Officer Miller stared at me from across the roof of the car, her expression grim.

"You question one more direct order and I'm going to charge you."

"This is bullshit," I said, but I did as I was told. I was already drawing too much attention; a few of the other officers checking cars had stopped to observe the interaction with Cross.

Officer Milled rapped on Tenley's window and she rolled it down. Miller looked concerned as she leaned in, her hand on the doorframe. I could only hear Tenley's nervous tone, not her actual replies to the questions asked.

I imagined how it looked from Officer Miller's perspective. Aside from the tiny diamond stud in her nose, Tenley projected a girl-next-door vibe. With her outfit tonight, that was magnified. Someone like her hanging out with someone like me would be an immediate red flag for a lot of people.

Cross frisked me, searching for weapons or contraband I didn't have.

"Come with me, please."

"What about Tenley?"

"Officer Miller will stay with her."

I didn't ask any more questions because I wasn't going to get answers. Cross went through the standard tests to check for drunkenness, making me repeat them twice because he wanted to piss me off.

Cross led me to a cruiser and opened the rear door. "Get in."

"What for?"

"I want you to take a Breathalyzer test."

"Why do I need to get in a cruiser for that?"

"You're trying my patience, boy. Get. In. I won't ask again."

I dropped into the seat and folded my legs in the cramped space. Cross closed the door and claustrophobia set in immediately. Panic hit me like a sledgehammer, taking me back seven years to the night my parents were murdered. It was the only other time I ended up in the back of a police car. The interrogation followed.

I couldn't separate that situation from this one, and the bad place in my head got worse, dragging me down into the past I kept buried. There was no way out of the backseat unless Cross let me out. Logically, I knew nothing could happen to me, but it didn't stop my throat from closing up.

Behind the driver's seat was a panel of bulletproof glass, with a thick, black mesh barrier of metal on the passenger side. Cross sat in front of the bulletproof panel and took his time setting up the Breathalyzer machine. He fed the tube through a gap in the mesh, forcing me to lean forward until my nose hit the divider. I exhaled into the little mouthpiece.

It registered a zero blood-alcohol level.

"Do it again."

"I blew under."

"Do. It. Again."

I shook my head but complied. Again, it came back clean. "Satisfied? Can I take my girlfriend home now?"

She was standing beside the Camaro; shoeless with her arms wrapped around herself as the wind blew her hair around her face. She glanced over her shoulder ever few seconds, her eyes on the car that formed my prison. Miller put a hand on her shoulder and Tenley jumped, her attention moving back to the officer. There were questions and some gesturing aimed at Tenley's feet. Miller was frowning; whatever excuse Tenley had come up with probably wasn't very good.

She was helped back into the Camaro. The door stayed open, though, and Miller crouched down in front of her, her expression somber. A Breathalyzer test was administered once, a second time.

Cross relaxed in his seat and stared at me through the rearview mirror. "Would you like to tell me what happened to your car?"

"Last I heard, you can't detain someone for a dent."

"I can if you fled the scene of an accident."

"I already told you, we weren't in an accident."

He sneered. "It's obvious something happened to your car recently, though. Would I be right?"

I stayed silent.

"What time did you leave your aunt's tonight?"

"Around nine thirty."

"That's more than an hour and a half ago."

"We made a stop on the way home." I shifted on the hard plastic seat.

"You don't say. Is that when the damage to your car happened?"

I sighed. "Is there a point to this?"

Cross inspected his stubby fingers. "Most people would take good care of a ride like that. The last time I saw it, it was in pristine condition. Now, it kind of looks like someone had a throwdown on the hood."

When I didn't respond, he took a different approach. "You know, Tenley's not looking so good these days."

"The past few weeks have been hard for her. You know, what with her entire family being dead and it being the holidays and all." I shot him a condescending look.

He returned the glare with a hateful one of his own. "Maybe she should find someone who can take better care of her."

"I can take care of Tenley just fine."

"Judging by her condition tonight, I'm going to disagree."

"You need to back off."

"Or what?"

"Fuck you," I spat.

He turned around, sneer firmly in place. "Go ahead, Stryker. Threaten me. It would be my pleasure to take you down to the precinct so you can get what's coming to you."

"What's coming to me? I'm taking my girlfriend home from a family dinner. I don't see that as a criminal offense."

"What the hell do you do at family dinners that would make her look the way she does?"

"She's had an emotional day."

"And you thought you'd make it better for her by using her as a hood ornament?"

"That's not—"

Cross slammed his palm against the divider, making it rattle.

"Shut your fucking mouth, you little prick. You think I don't know what happened? You think I can't see what's right in front of me? She's a fucking disaster. You won't be happy until you've dragged that girl down into your bottomless pit of shit."

"You don't know a damn thing about my relationship with Tenley."

"Relationship? Is that what lowlifes like you call what you're doing with her?"

His words were like an acid bomb going off in my brain; corrosive, destructive. "You're a cocksucker, you know that."

He made a tsking sound. "Do you kiss your mother with that mouth? Oh, wait, that's not possible."

I exploded, a string of vile profanities spewing forth. I shut down the reaction quickly, realizing that he was riling me up on purpose.

When I was under control again, Cross smiled. "You done? 'Cause if you keep it up, I might just have to take you in. You and me, we've been there before, haven't we? I'm not so sure you'll like that option the second time around, any better than you did the first."

"Fuck that. You can't hold me."

"I think this time I'll put you in a holding cell with all the other losers until someone can come pick up your sorry ass. Then I'll be a Good Samaritan and drive Tenley home. How does that sound?"

I nearly bit off my tongue to keep from telling him what I thought. He was goading me, looking for a reaction that would give him the reason he wanted to put me in a cell. At least for the rest of the night. There was no way I wanted Tenley in a car with him. Especially when he seemed to have it out for me.

"Decided to keep your mouth shut for once, huh?" He opened the door and got out, leaving me locked inside.

I knocked on the window, shouting after him. The threats to

take me in had to be empty; he had nothing on me. He wanted to make me sweat, and he'd succeeded. My inability to protect Tenley made me feel powerless as he crossed the pavement to where she sat inside my car. The door was still open; she had to be freezing.

He leaned against the side of the car when he reached her, blocking my view.

Tenley shot up out of the seat and peered around him, her hands flailing wildly as she gestured toward the cruiser I was locked inside. Officer Miller put a hand on her shoulder and leaned in close; whatever she said calmed Tenley down. She glared at Cross and swiped at her cheeks while Miller helped settle her back in the car. Cross braced himself on the doorframe, looking the part of the concerned police officer as Miller headed for me.

It was the divide and conquer. Cross had done the same thing in the interrogation room after the murders. One of them would leave on the premise of getting coffee or taking a break. While the other was gone, they'd change tactics to see if the story would change.

Miller got into the driver's seat and turned so she could see me head-on. "We don't seem to run into each other on your good days."

"Looks that way." I sagged against the seat. Letting my head fall back, I closed my eyes. If I had to justify myself one more goddamn time, I was going lose it.

"First impressions tell you a lot about a person."

I cracked a lid. "Guess I'm screwed on that front, huh?"

Her mouth twitched, but she remained serious. "Take your girlfriend, for instance. The first time I met her, she seemed like she had it together. This time? Not so much."

"She's had a rough day."

"You want to tell me why that is?"

"You spent the last fifteen minutes with her. Are you saying she didn't offer any details?"

"She did. But I'm asking you."

I sighed and rubbed my forehead, sharp pain slicing between my eyes. I'd be lucky if I didn't end up with a migraine. "She was in an accident around this time last year. Her whole family died. Everyone she loved is gone. Holidays are difficult."

"That must be hard."

"Like I said, today's been very emotional for her."

"I meant for you."

I frowned. "It sucks. I can't do anything to make her pain go away."

"You could start by getting a handle on that temper of yours. That's the second time you've gone off on a police officer in a very public place. Gotta tell ya, it doesn't reflect well on you."

"I don't get heated often, and never with Tenley."

"And how do I know that? Because you told me? Because your girlfriend will tell me the same thing to protect you? Have you ever considered where the collateral damage lies when you pull something like that?"

I looked out the windshield. Tenley was still huddled inside the car, her stocking feet curled around the edge of the doorframe. Cross was kneeling down in front of her, looking up. She leaned forward, chin jutting out in defiance. Any other time, she'd back down in the face of authority. I was the only reason she would do otherwise. It unnerved me.

"You know, I ran your background after that first meeting, and I checked your girlfriend, too."

Which meant she knew about the crash before she asked. Running my background wouldn't turn up much besides a couple of the interviews I was subjected to after my parents' murder. The initial ones had likely been erased, as I'd been a juvenile.

"Other than a speeding ticket about a month back, your record is clean as a whistle."

"Surprised?"

She got out of the cruiser and opened my door. The pounding in my head and the tightness in my throat let up a little once I was free of the cruiser.

"With your attitude? Damn right. But then I went deeper because I was sure there had to be something else. The way you acted when you came into the precinct didn't add up. You know what I found?"

"I have no clue."

"Nothing. You have a perfect credit rating. You have financing pending on a joint property investment in a very good neighborhood. You own both your condo and your tattoo shop. You've never missed a payment of any kind, and you make several charitable donations a year. Interesting for someone who presents like you, don't you think?"

"And how do I present?"

"Like you're giving society the perpetual bird and you've got an ax to grind."

"My only problem is Cross."

"Yeah, I figured that out. Made me wonder what the problem was, until he told me he was the lead investigator on your parents' murder case."

"He and his partner were first on the scene. They thought I'd done it, so they arrested me. Cross interrogated me."

"I'm going to guess that didn't go well."

"You could say that." I shoved my hands in my pockets, rocking back on my heels.

"Wanna tell me more about it?"

"There's not much to tell. I found my parents' bodies, called the police, and ended up in an interrogation room. I was there for a long time before I was allowed my phone call." I wasn't sure how much detail she wanted, or how much I felt inclined to provide. I didn't know how closely she worked with him. "All I know is that the evidence in the case was deemed inadmissible because it was compromised. I don't have all the details, which is why I went to the precinct that day."

"Why'd they target you as a suspect?"

"Convenience? How should I know? I was seventeen. I came home and found my parents murdered. I called nine-one-one and freaked out because they were dead."

If she'd read the file, she knew I'd torn apart the living room, so mentioning it was redundant.

She regarded me with a speculation that was not uncommon. "I've been through what's left of the evidence. There's not much there. I have some questions, too, but without something new it would be hard to make a case to have it reopened."

I thought about the constant, unyielding dreams I had lately. "What if I had something? Who would I go to?"

"You think you do?"

"It's possible."

"Normally you'd go to the person who initially worked the case, if they're still around. But I don't see that going over well on either side. You can contact me, provided you keep yourself in check. I won't deal with a loose cannon."

"As long as I don't have to deal with Cross, I can manage myself."

She put her hands on her hips. "Not good enough. We work in the same precinct. Sometimes we work together. I can't have you going off on Cross every time you run into him."

"He screwed up my parents' case."

"So you say, but you were a kid. You said yourself that you don't have the details, and from what I read, you were under the influence that night, so maybe your memory is a little spotty."

"But that doesn't have anything to do with the evidence. If

Cross was responsible for collecting and filing it, doesn't the blame lie with him?"

"Careful with the finger-pointing. I get that it was a traumatic experience for you. I've seen the crime scene photos, but I can't help you if can't handle yourself."

"I'll rein it in."

"You'd better." She took a step toward Tenley and Cross, then turned back. "Can I make a suggestion?"

"Sure."

"All that metal in your face? It makes you a target."

"Are you telling me I need to get rid of it?"

"Nope. I'm not telling you anything. But if you came into the precinct dressed like you are tonight and all that metal did a disappearing act? You might find people react a little differently."

"I'll take that under advisement."

24

TENLEY

The conversation with Hayden, followed by being pulled over, sobered me quickly. Hayden wasn't intoxicated. Officer Cross refused to let it go, though, particularly considering the state of the car and me.

Even though the effects of the meds were still present, I hadn't missed his contrived worry over my well-being. Today had been long and difficult and he wasn't helping. His unconcealed antagonism toward Hayden made my anxiety spike.

For the past ten minutes Cross had been grilling me about the dent in the hood, my missing shoes, and the state of my jacket. At least Officer Miller had asked about other things, even if the questions were leading.

The details she gleaned from me had less to do with me and more with Hayden. She'd asked about his parents, his job, his coworkers, and where Hayden spent his spare time. Those questions were easy to answer because I could be truthful. The details painted Hayden in a positive light. He spent all his time outside of work with me, and if he wasn't with me, he was with a select group of people.

I looked over at the police car parked about thirty feet away. At least Hayden wasn't locked inside anymore. Officer Miller had let him out almost immediately. Hayden was standing with his arms crossed over his chest, but not nearly as upset as he'd been when she first let him out.

I huddled deeper into my coat, wishing we had stayed at Cassie's. TK would have been fine on her own for one night. If it hadn't been for my breakdown, we could still be cozied up in that oversize chair; rather than dealing with police. Officer Cross was still lecturing me, and my face was red with anger and humiliation. Although he couldn't be much past thirty, his permanent frown reeked of parental disapproval.

"I've told you already, we didn't hit anything on the way home," I said, done with the questions. "You've asked me the same thing twenty different ways. The answer isn't going to change."

Cross dropped down into a crouch; his wide body filled the doorframe. He reached up and held on to headrest, blocking me in and cutting off my view of Hayden. His voice dropped. "Do you think your parents would approve of your boyfriend if they were still alive?"

I recoiled. "That's irrelevant and none of your business."

"I'll tell you what I think. I think they'd be disappointed. Particularly if they knew what you let him do to you. And on the hood of his car, no less. Doesn't say much about your self-respect, now does it?"

"You have no idea what you're talking about," I said, failing to keep the tremor out of my voice.

"Oh, no? Based on the way you can't make eye contact, I'm going to go ahead and call you on that lie, sweetheart. You might want to think a little more carefully about what you do and who you do it with. It could make people think less of you."

"I think this conversation is over."

"If you say so." He rose up, his smile far from friendly. "One more thing, though. You wouldn't be encouraging Stryker to pursue his parents' case, would you?"

"Why wouldn't I, if it could get him some closure?"

"It's not always what people need. Think about it. That kid hung out with some bad people. If you want to help him, you might persuade him to let things go. You never know what kind of skeletons he might dig up."

"What's that supposed to mean?"

"You think it's any coincidence that you come along and all of a sudden Stryker's looking to clean up his act? He was with a suspected drug dealer the night his parents were killed. Draw your own conclusions."

I stared at him in open incredulity. This was new information and I wasn't sure I should trust it.

"You look awfully shocked, Miss Page. Do you even know who you're spending all your time with? The kinds of things Stryker has done?"

I didn't have a chance to ask any further questions. Officer Cross stepped away from the door just as Hayden approached. "One last word before you head home, Mr. Stryker."

Hayden didn't acknowledge that Cross had spoken. Instead, he knelt down in front of me and ran his hands down my arms. He dropped the key in my palm and folded my fingers around it.

"Christ, you're freezing." He shot Officer Cross an irritated glare, then dropped a soft kiss on my lips. "Turn on the car, kitten."

While I tucked my legs inside, Hayden rolled up the window and closed the door. I slid the key into the ignition, and the engine started with a deep rumble. I pulled my legs up to my chest, conserving body heat. I'd been so distressed when Officer Cross put Hayden in his cruiser, the cold hadn't registered. It did now. I flexed my frozen toes.

After a brief, tight exchange between Hayden and Officer Cross, Hayden rounded the car and got in. He was silent in his fury as he shifted into gear and pulled onto the street.

"Please tell me you're okay," he asked in a pained voice.

"I'm okay," I replied, though I wasn't entirely sure it was true.

He glanced at me as if maybe he didn't believe me, either. "What did he say to you?"

"He kept asking what happened to the hood."

"Did you tell him?" Hayden's hands tightened on the steering wheel.

"I didn't have to. He already seemed to know," I said, keeping my tone neutral. I didn't trust how calm he was. "It's okay, Hayden. It's fine. We're fine."

"No. It's not."

We stopped at a light and I could feel his eyes on me. He could always see right through my half-truths.

"What else did he say?"

I didn't answer right away, concerned honesty would cause more harm.

"What did he say, Tenley? He must have said something; that cocksucker can't resist stringing me up whenever he has the chance."

"That you might have been with a drug dealer the night your parents died."

"Why the fuck would he tell you that?"

Tonight had gone wrong on so many levels for both of us. "I don't know, but I would never believe anything he said."

"It's true," Hayden said flatly.

I sat there, stunned.

"I was with this guy named Damen, who ran a tattoo shop and dealt on the side. I didn't know how extensive his side business was until later, after I went to work for him. He was the one who introduced me to coke, and to Sienna."

"Oh, Hayden. I'm so sorry." No wonder he was so reluctant to talk about his past, when there were so many painful pieces.

"You shouldn't be. I'm the one who fucked up my own life."

"It wasn't your fault," I said, but I knew he still blamed himself for what happened all those years ago.

The rest of the drive home was tense. I asked him if he was okay a couple of times, but he didn't respond.

When we pulled into his spot in the parking garage, he shut off the car, then just stared straight ahead with his hands on the wheel.

I put a hand on his forearm. "Should we go up?"

He nodded and scrubbed his face with his palms. His shoulders curved in and he folded forward, his forehead coming to rest on the steering wheel. I put my hand on his back, feeling the muscles expand as he took long, slow breaths, his control slipping. A choked noise escaped, sounding like a stifled sob.

"Hayden? It's okay. We're home now."

I unfastened my seat belt, reaching over to do the same for him. Whatever had happened in that police car had rattled him.

His seat belt undone, I removed the keys from the ignition and got out of the car, then went around to open his door. I stroked his hair, but he didn't move. He just murmured something I didn't catch. I dropped down beside him, ignoring the cold cement against my stocking feet. He spoke again, repeating a phrase over and over.

"Oh, Hayden. No." My nose grazed his cheek.

He lifted his head from the steering wheel. His eyes were bloodshot and red-rimmed, but there were no tears. "I'm so fucked up," he whispered. "I'm such a fuckup."

"No, baby, that's not true." I placed my palm against his cheek.

"Yes, it is. Look what I did to you tonight. Look at you." He skimmed a thumb under the hollow of my eye, then over my lip, brushing over the tender spot where his viper bites had cut in. "You're so beautiful, and I'm ruining you."

"You're not ruining me. Why would you think that?"

"I wish I wasn't so fucked up," he said, as if I hadn't spoken.

His vacant stare unnerved me. I'd never seen him like this. Hayden could get upset, he could get angry, but I didn't know how to handle his falling apart like this. He'd always been the one to keep me together.

"Why don't we go up and feed TK? She'll have missed us today." I wanted to get him out of the car. Also, it was the only thing I could think of that might pull him out of his downward spiral. He was like a parent when it came to her.

"Yeah. Okay." He nodded robotically and let me help him out of the car.

The presents in the backseat could stay there until morning. I locked the car and led him to the elevator. He folded himself around me while we waited, burying his face in my hair. When the doors opened, I pulled him in and hit the button for the second floor. I felt no anxiety as we ascended, my concern fixed on Hayden. I unlocked the door to his place and led him inside. When I turned to lock the door behind us, he seemed to snap out of it a little.

"I ruined your coat," he said hoarsely.

"What?" I looked over my shoulder, taking in the forlorn expression on his pale face.

"Your coat. I ruined it too."

He helped me out of it and draped it over his arm. The soft cream fabric was smeared with dirt. The buckle in the middle of the back had black powder on it, which explained the scratches in the hood. I took it from him and hung it in the closet.

"Once it's dry-cleaned it'll be good as new."

TK came bounding down the hall, her excited mews stopping only when she skidded into Hayden's ankle and he scooped her up. She rubbed her nose on his chin. Then he walked down the hall with his shoes still on. On autopilot he fed TK, then stood in the kitchen staring at his feet in confusion. I guided him back to the front hall and knelt in front of him. With a little prompting he lifted one foot, then the other, as I removed his shoes and put them away.

"Why don't I run a bath?" I suggested.

It took him a few seconds to answer. "For me?"

"For both of us."

"Okay. I don't want to be alone right now."

"Then it's good that I'm not going anywhere."

I took his hand and he shuffled down the hall beside me, fingers wrapped tightly around mine. Hayden sat on the edge of the tub while I ran the water. I searched his cupboards for bath salts but came up empty-handed. His eyes stayed on my face as I loosened his tie and slipped it over his head. Next I unbuttoned his shirt, saving the cuff links until last. They were little sliver skulls.

"Cassie gave them to me a couple of years ago for my birthday," he said, taking them from me to roll between his fingers.

My heart stuttered. "I don't even know when that is."

"You didn't miss it while you were gone. It's not until the end of May."

"That's good," I said softly, pushing his shirt over his shoulders.

How we could be so close to each other but not know something so essential was beyond me. That was a question one usually asked on a first date. When he was fully undressed, I reached behind me and tugged down the zipper of my dress. Letting it fall to the floor, I stepped out of the puddle of fabric.

He exhaled and wrapped his arms around my waist, pulling me

between his legs. He turned his face to the side, resting his cheek against my stomach, and hugged me tightly. "I wish we'd waited until I got you home."

"We're home now. You can have me if you want me."

I could feel his hardness against my thigh but Hayden shook his head. "I just need to be close to you right now."

"I need that, too, Hayden."

I ran my hands across his shoulders in soothing, rhythmic circles. He looked up at me, his longing no longer reflective of desire but something deeper.

"This is so pretty," he said, undoing my garter and rolling down the stocking. He kissed my hip and moved to the opposite side, repeating the action.

Undressing each other was inherently sensual. I wanted so much to lose myself in him after this long, difficult day. But Hayden needed more than that from me right now. I sensed it in the reverent way he touched me, in the unhurried way he removed each article of clothing.

"I like you in this. Better than I like you in black."

"Why is that?"

He pulled at the loose garter, a half smile pulling at the corner of his mouth. "Because it reflects how I see you—feminine and delicate and pretty."

I wanted to ask what else he saw in me, but became distracted when he reached behind me and freed the clasp of my bra. His eyes moved over my body in a way that felt more like worship than sex, and his fingers trailed between my breasts. His hand came to rest on my hips, his eyes shifting down from my face. His Adam's apple bobbed with a heavy swallow and his tongue swept out, wetting his lip.

"You prefer me like this?" I glanced at the pile of pale discarded lace and satin, so different from some of the other lingerie I had.

"Naked? Always."

He flashed a mischievous grin and threw one leg over the side of the tub, reaching over to turn off the tap. He lowered himself into the water and made room for me between his legs. I sat on the edge and dipped a toe in, testing the temperature. My feet were still half-frozen from having been shoeless for the past hour, and the heat was a relief.

Hayden's arms came around my waist and he leaned back, taking me with him. I settled against his chest, submerged to my shoulders. The water level rose until it was perilously close to the rim of the tub, but Hayden didn't seem to care.

My hair fanned out on the surface, darkening as it sank. Hayden gathered it up and pulled it over my shoulder. His lips met my skin, moving from my collarbone to my neck, pausing when he reached the spot just under my ear.

"I left a mark," he whispered, his lips brushing over the sensitive skin.

"It's okay. It'll fade in a few days," I said, worried about the remorse in his tone.

"I left a lot of them." His chin came to rest on my shoulder.

"I don't mind. None of them are permanent."

"Not on the outside, anyway." His hand drifted down my arm. "I wish things had gone differently tonight."

"I'm sorry I lost it at Cassie's."

"You don't have to be sorry, kitten. And I'm not talking about that. I just don't want you to feel like you have to do things you're not comfortable with."

"Are you talking about the sex tonight?" I turned my head so I could see his face. "I made the suggestion."

"Only because I've mentioned it before."

"I wouldn't have said anything if I hadn't wanted it. I needed to be with you. I was the one who started it."

"I don't know if I agree with that. You have a history of caving, especially for me."

"You think so? Who let who into their apartment that first time?"

"I kissed you, though. I made the first move," he argued.

The flirting had driven me almost insane during the tattoo session. The buzz of attraction had been an aphrodisiac. "I couldn't have given you any more of an invitation if I tried. Shall I remind you that I'm the one who provided a loophole for your ridiculous rule? I knew exactly what I was doing when I lured you into my bedroom. I wanted you. It's *always* been me pushing you, not the other way around."

He smiled slightly, maybe caught up in the memories, then his expression grew serious as he traced the outline of the wing curling around my shoulder. "I'm not just talking about sex, Tenley. I'm speaking in general terms."

Water splashed and trickled over the side of the tub as I turned to see him better. "You're not referring to the tattoo, are you? Because I specifically recall coming to you with it. Not the other way around."

"No. That's not what I meant. Although, I'd like to remind *you*, I asked you to come by the shop more than once, and I'm the one who convinced you to get the cupcake first." His hand smoothed over my hip, close to the tattoo in question.

"I would have brought the design to you eventually, even without the persuasion. And the cupcake tattoo was a means to an end. The payoff was worth it."

Hayden laced his fingers through mine. "Can I ask you something?"

"Sure," I said, concerned by the serious slant of his brow.

"What would happen if Trey came back again?"

The odd question threw me. "He won't."

"How do you know that?"

"I don't have anything he wants anymore."

"What if he did, though? How do I know you won't leave again? That wasn't something you wanted to do, but you went anyway."

So this was the topic he'd been circling. I thought we'd already dealt with these fears, but in the wake of so much stress, they'd been unearthed again. What he didn't understand was that Connor had been the expectation for my future. Being with Hayden was a choice.

"I wouldn't make the same decision this time. I was in a different headspace then. I didn't know how to deal with how I felt about you. There was so much guilt, and I didn't know what to do with it."

Hayden's arms tightened around me. "I just don't want you to leave me again. I can't do this without you anymore."

His expression made my heart hurt. "Hayden, you are everything I could ever want. You are the place I want to be."

25

HAYDEN

It was noon before I opened my eyes the next day. Tenley was slow to wake up and even slower to get moving. As she tried to sit up, she cringed and moaned, then flopped back down. She rolled over on her stomach, her face mashed into the pillow.

"What hurts?" The hood of my car was no soft place to get it on.

"My lower back," she mumbled from under her veil of hair.

I threw the covers off and leaned over. I checked for bruising, then ran my thumbs down her spine. When I reached her tailbone, Tenley made a sound of displeasure.

"Right here?" I asked, putting a little pressure on the spot.

"Mm, and my hips are stiff." She blew her hair out of her face.

"Let me make it better." I started rubbing, and little sounds of approval escaped her when I hit a particularly sore spot. TK jumped up on the bed and started sniffing around, her nose bumping up against my leg. Sometimes we had to lock her out of the room when we were having sex because TK sat at the end of the bed and meowed at us otherwise. It was creepy and distracting as hell. Especially when Tenley started laughing.

Now, TK climbed right up on Tenley's back and started to knead, getting in on the action. Then she head-butted my hand and plunked herself down right where I was massaging.

Tenley peeked over her shoulder. "It looks like your other kitty is jealous."

"It's not like she doesn't get enough attention."

I picked TK up before she started in with the claws and lay back down beside Tenley, settling TK on my chest. She nuzzled right in, rubbing the top of her head under my chin, purring up a storm. "How's your back feeling now?"

"Okay. A couple painkillers should take care of it if it's still bothering me later." Tenley closed her eyes again.

I had other questions—about her use of medication, about what Cross and Miller had said to her last night, about Chris's asinine yet brilliant idea for a New Year's getaway—but all of those could wait.

"Tenley?"

"Hmm?"

I kissed the tip of her nose. "Do you want to open the rest of our presents?"

Her eyes popped open. "Oh my God! Of course!"

She rolled out of bed and sprang to her feet. In the next heartbeat she disappeared, dropping to the floor. I leaned over, not quite sure what had happened. Her hands appeared at the edge of the mattress as she hoisted herself up, coming nose to nose with me.

"Soooo," she said, "I guess I haven't fully recovered from that workout last night."

I swung my legs around and slipped my hands under her arms. She muttered something about being okay, which was a load of crap because she wobbled like a foal, using my shoulders for support.

"We need to try out different positions," I said to her boobs, which were right in my face.

"Right now?" Tenley's voice became a sultry whisper.

I looked up. Her eyes were focused on my stupid dick, which couldn't get with the program and deflate.

"Uh, no, kitten. We should put a hold on that until the staying-upright thing is less of a problem."

She pouted, but I wasn't about to cave. It was already after noon on our first Christmas together. I wanted to open presents while drinking coffee and eating the cupcakes I'd found hidden in the fridge last night.

When she no longer needed me for support, I rolled off the bed and rooted around in my dresser, yanking on a pair of festive pajama pants.

Tenley was still living out of an overnight bag when she came over, which needed to change. I'd cleared a section in my closet for her and she had a few things hanging in there, but no comfy lounging gear. I grabbed a pair of boxers for her and my STRYKER hoodie. She covered up all that sexy, bare skin, which made it easier to focus, and we left the bedroom.

After coffee was brewed and poured—Tenley making hers undrinkable with a shitload of sugar and cream—we sat down and exchanged the gifts under the tree. It was the first time in the past seven years that I'd actually looked forward to the holiday.

I passed the first gift to Tenley. She pulled the red-and-white-striped bow off the top and stuck it to her head with a cheeky grin. TK batted at the springy tendrils of ribbon as Tenley removed them from the box as well. Eyes bright with anticipation, with her fingernail she cut through the tape sealing the box. "Did you wrap this?"

"Yeah."

She paused to kiss me. "You're pretty incredible, you know that? This is a professional wrap job. You could start a side business."

"I'll get right on that." I smiled as she attempted to unwrap the box without ripping the paper. She gave up halfway through and tore into it. I'd put forth some serious effort to make the presents look good. Every single gift had bows and ribbon and all that frilly crap on it. Even the tiny ones. Her excitement made it worth it.

Tenley tossed the torn wrapping into the wastebasket I'd set up beside the coffee table. She opened the box, folding back the tissue paper. A black hoodie sat inside. Tenley traced the skull-and-crossbones cupcake emblazoned in white over the left side of the chest. She read the lettering that arched above and below in a tattoo-inspired font.

"Does that say . . ." She lift the hoodie out of the box to get a better look.

"It's supposed to be a joke." Sort of. Not really. "I like the way mine looks on you and you're always hijacking it, so I thought I'd get you your own. This one is your size." I was doing that rambling shit again.

"Oh. So the PROPERTY OF HAYDEN STRYKER inscription is the joke part?"

"You should check out the back," I replied, avoiding the question because it was not, in fact, the joke part.

She turned it over to find STRYKER in red lettering with gold piping across the back. It was about more than just liking the way my hoodie looked on her. I also liked the way my name looked across her back and chest. I would never admit, not in a million years, that I'd fantasized about inking my name on her somewhere. The crease at the inside of her thigh was definitely a favored option in my imagination. That way I'd see it every time I went down on her.

Until now, I'd never understood why people put someone else's name on their body. It wasn't erasable. Even laser was a painful and not-always-effective method of removing such mistakes. Memorial tattoos made sense, though. I'd even put one on Cassie, though we'd argued over the placement for weeks before I folded.

I could respect those guys who came in and had their kid enshrined on their back or chest or biceps. I figured it was a way for them to cement their role as a parent. But tattooing the name of a significant other on my body had always seemed ludicrous. Jamie's LISA tattoo—across his lower abdomen no less—had baffled the shit out of me. Not so much anymore.

Other than Tenley, I hadn't been inside anyone whom I wanted to refer to as significant. She'd changed that. After she left, I'd been ready to put a pinup version of her on my ribs. I still wanted to, but for less desperate reasons. I also wanted it in a much more visible location. It wasn't much different from putting her name on me.

She traced the perimeter of the S in STRYKER.

"I thought you might like wearing it at school. You know, when you have class and stuff." That way, those guys she worked with wouldn't have to question whether we were still together.

"Stuff, as in group meetings?"

"Sure." I tried to come off as nonchalant.

"So the inscription on the front, would you say it's more of warning than a joke?"

I gave her a sheepish smile. "I thought you'd prefer it to hickeys."

I smoothed my thumb across her neck where only a faint pink mark remained from last night. A couple of tiny, almost unnoticeable lines on her bottom lip were the only other reminders of the damage I'd inflicted.

"Aren't you sweet," she drawled.

"You don't like it?" My stomach did a weird flip thing.

"No. I love it. It's perfect—much better than a hickey." She leaned in and kissed me. "But there are less conspicuous, more sensitive places for you to suck on than my neck."

"Is that right?" I nibbled her bottom lip.

"Mm."

"Maybe later we could perform a thorough exploration of those locations," I suggested.

"Maybe."

She extricated herself from my arms and sashayed over to the tree. She got down on her hands and knees, ass in the air, and rooted around until she came up with a handful of presents. We spent the next hour opening gifts and tossing TK's new catnip mice around. The last present I opened was the third of the three pictures Lisa had taken of Tenley.

This one wasn't as revealing as the first one I'd opened, but it was the most provocative. Tenley was in profile, her features obscured by shadow, her fingers at her lips. She was wearing a camisole covered in cupcakes, and her pert nipple showed through the tight, sheer fabric. The clincher was the lack of panties, made even sexier by the garterless, lace-edged thigh highs. A slight twist in her torso caused the light to hit the cupcake tattoo but blacked out that perfect slit between her thighs.

My intention had been to thank her by kissing her. That didn't quite happen, and we didn't make it to the bedroom. However, I did manage to find a new position that didn't put as much strain on her hips.

By four in the afternoon we'd finished with presents, a shower, and a meal and were vegging on the couch. My phone had rung half a dozen times already, as had Tenley's, but we were both avoiding the calls. Until Tenley and I talked about New Year's options, I wasn't having the conversation with Lisa.

We were in the middle of watching an action flick when Tenley sighed and shifted around, rubbing her legs together. "I need to do something."

"Why don't we go out? We could go for a walk, get some fresh air."

She hopped off the couch and headed for the bedroom, taking the hoodie with her. I stayed put because seeing her naked would be a deterrent to going out. We needed to do something other than have sex, even though it was a way to keep our minds off the difficult stuff. While I waited, I busied myself with organizing the presents under the tree.

She came back out a few minutes later with her hair pulled back in a loose ponytail. She was wearing purple jeans that were so fitted they looked painted on and the STRYKER hoodie.

"You like?" She did a little twirl.

"Yeah. I like." I nodded dumbly, completely rethinking my previous rationale for leaving the condo.

"Are you planning to go out like that?"

I ran a hand over my chest. "You don't think I should?" The white T-shirt was so thin, she could see my body art and my nipple rings through it.

"Feel free, but I'm thinking if you get a hard-on, it might be difficult to hide." Tenley gestured at my pajama pants.

I looked down. I already had an obvious semi. "Point taken."

I changed quickly. When I came back out, Tenley was sprawled on the floor, and TK was perched on her knees batting at a string with a bell tied to the end.

"I have an idea," Tenley said.

"What's that?"

"You said you wanted to work on shading this week, right? What if we started now?" She looked hopeful and a little nervous.

"Are you sure you're up for something like that today?"

"I think so." She set TK on the floor and used the coffee table to pull herself up. "Yesterday was difficult for both of us, and I need some kind of . . . release? And I think this might help."

I weighed the options. If I worked on her shoulders it would be less painful, and we could stop anytime. There'd be no pressure to get through a certain amount of color, and we'd have no interruptions since the shop would be empty. It could be cathartic. But it could go the other way, too. It was hard to tell which was more likely. "I don't know . . ."

"Please? I promise I'll tell you if I think it's too much. We could go down to the shop for a bit. If I feel at all like it's not going to be okay, we can just go for a walk."

With no pressure in the request, I gave in. There was no way to know unless I gave it a shot. "We could try."

"Really?" She threw her arms around my neck, her excitement contagious. I hadn't worked on her since before she'd left for Arden Hills. Getting her back in my chair might be good for both of us.

"But I say when I think you've had enough."

"Of course. And if I don't think I can handle it before that, I'll ask you to stop."

She kissed me, her tongue pressing forward to tangle with mine, and I wondered if we would ever lose this unquenchable need for each other. I hoped not.

26

HAYDEN

At Inked Armor, Tenley wandered around the private room, inspecting the bottles of ink and plastic-labeled bins of supplies as she waited for me to set up. I drew it out to allow both of us to adjust to the environment and what we were about to do.

When I was done, I pulled her file. I kept it in there after she'd left, rendering and rerendering the color scheme when I got frustrated with my design. I pulled out the newest versions and spread them over the worktable. The tone of the piece had changed over time and revisions. The original design, which had initially drawn me to Tenley's art, and to her, had been altered considerably.

The blacks and deep blues and purples, along with the bursts of flame, had all been tempered, subdued by an overarching golden glow. The change in color was most concentrated at the shoulders. It gave the allusion that the sun was shining down on the wings, bringing them back to life, the blackened, damaged feathers falling away, newer growth replacing the destruction.

"I've made some alterations." I spun around on my chair, expecting her to be across the room.

She was standing right behind me. "I see that."

"We can go with the original if you prefer, but I thought I'd give you choices."

Tenley put her hands on my shoulders and leaned in, looking over the various designs spread out over the table. She moved from left to right, from original to most recently revised. "You've made a lot of changes."

"A lot has changed since we started the tattoo."

"Mm." Her fingernails slipped under the hair at the back of my neck and dragged down. "That's very true. I like these. They're beautiful." She skimmed across the last few.

"You want to go with one of them?"

At her nod, I put the others aside, except for the original design we'd started from and the ones she liked the most. Then I pulled her into my lap. We spent another good twenty minutes going over the finer points before she made the final decision. She went with the second-to-last revision, which was my favorite. I loved that we seemed to be on the same page on so many things.

I cranked the heat in the private room. As I picked out the ink and set up the tattoo machine, Tenley stripped from the waist up. When she was half-naked and everything was laid out, she dropped down in the chair, making no attempt at modesty.

"You're a hundred percent sure you can handle this today?" I asked, keeping my eyes on hers.

"Yes. If it's too much, I promise to tell you."

"I'm holding you to that."

Her broad grin eased some of my anxiety over doing this on such a critical day for her. This was exactly what I had wanted to do during my first holiday without my family. Instead, I went on a bender that nearly killed me. By that time I'd already been introduced to Chris, who'd tried to get in touch with me afterward without any luck. He kicked my ass when I finally showed up at work three days later. The black eye and bruised ribs that resulted marked the official beginning of our friendship. It was the last time I was allowed to be alone during a holiday. Aside from the Thanksgiving that had just passed.

Tenley stretched out in my chair and her hair slipped over the side. It was so long, it almost brushed the floor.

"I'm starting at your shoulders. I'm thinking a couple hours max, but it depends on you."

"That sounds fair."

I hit the music, washed my hands, and snapped on a pair of gloves. Next I prepped Tenley's back, wiping it down with antiseptic spray. The hum of the tattoo machine filtered through the room. As soon as it touched her skin, she relaxed. Her eyes closed and she melted into the chair, a tiny smile playing at the corner of her mouth. I worked in silence for the first few minutes, aware Tenley needed time to acclimate to the sensation.

"How does it feel so far?"

"It's not bad."

"It'll be more irritating because I'm shading instead of outlining, so if you need a break, say the word."

I started on the scarred side on purpose. Although the ones at her shoulders weren't bad in comparison to the ones by her hips, they were still sensitive. If I could get the most uncomfortable part out of the way at the beginning of the session, it would make the rest easier to tolerate.

After a few more minutes of quiet, Tenley asked the question I'd been waiting for.

"Will you tell me what happened last night?"

"With Cross?" I dipped the needle in the yellow and brought it back to her skin.

"And Officer Miller."

"Cross was his usual dick self. I don't know what his deal is, but he seems to have a penchant for pissing me off." I made a pass with a fresh, damp cloth. "I know I was an asshole kid, but he's got one hell of a hate-on for me."

"I wonder why," Tenley mused, echoing my thoughts.

I was quiet for a minute, but I couldn't think of anything beyond my attitude. "I have no idea."

"What about Officer Miller? The conversation with her seemed okay."

"She looked into my parents' case. Like she said before, they need new evidence to have it reopened."

"What about that painting you mentioned from your parents' bedroom?"

"Maybe. *If* it made it to the storage unit." I stayed focused on her tattoo, switching from yellow to gray ink to add depth.

"We could go this week and have a look while you have time off."

"It might not even be there," I said, voicing my predominant fear.

"It wouldn't hurt to check, though. Unless you don't want to."

She was giving me an out. "It's not that. I mean, I've been there before." I tried to go a bunch of times, but always ended up sitting in the front of the door. The one time I made it past the threshold I ended up on a drug binge that lasted a month and almost cost me more than just my job at Art Addicts.

Tenley glanced at me, her unasked question on her beautiful face.

"It's just—" I turned off the tattoo machine and put it down. I wanted to find a way to say it without sounding like a huge pussy. "I always believed whoever killed my parents would eventually be caught. Even when they closed the case, I still held on to that hope. If that painting isn't there, or I'm remembering things wrong, then

I've got nothing. I'll be back where I started. I don't know if I can face the possibility of never having an answer."

Tenley sat up and crossed her arms over her chest, coming knee to knee with me. "But if you could know either way, wouldn't that be better? Even if the answer isn't the one you want?"

I got where she was coming from. Tenley would never have the answers to some of her questions. At least I had the option. I needed to take it so I could move on, regardless of the outcome.

"Okay. We can go sometime this week."

"Whenever you're ready."

If it had been anyone other than Tenley looking at me that way, it would have been emasculating. But she got it in a way no one else ever could.

"Why don't we take a break?" I suggested.

I had reached her shoulder blades and wanted to switch sides. That way she wouldn't feel compelled to go for hours, and the color would be balanced.

"Okay."

I stripped off my gloves and hit the back room for bottled water. When I returned, Tenley was standing in front of the three-way mirror with her hands on her hips, admiring the fresh ink. It was flushed pink around the edges, irritated from the shading, but it looked amazing. The shades of bright and pale yellow, along with white and light gray, gave the illusion that the wings were shimmering.

Seeing my ink on her back along with those damned barbells pierced through her pert nipples made my physical reaction impossible to control.

"Ready for me?" she asked.

"We should probably finish the session first." My brain had clearly taken a vacation; what was in my head came out of my mouth unfiltered.

"What—" She appeared confused at first, until her eyes drifted from my face to my fly. She smiled coyly as she sauntered back to the chair. "When aren't you ready for that?"

She settled in, shifting around. I could tell her hip was bothering her by the way she moved, but she wasn't limping. I waited until she was comfortable before I snapped on a new pair of gloves.

"Can I ask you something?" I wheeled around to her left side and turned on the tattoo machine.

"Sure," she said with a hint of apprehension.

"How often do you have to take painkillers?"

"You mean because of my hip?"

"Is there other pain?" It hadn't occurred to me there might be additional issues, although it should have.

"Sometimes I get headaches. At first I had them almost every day, but they're fairly infrequent now."

"Are they like migraines?" The needle touched her skin, pigment pushing under the surface, giving dimension to the outline almost immediately.

"I guess that's the best way to describe them. It used to feel like someone was stabbing me in the head. They'd come on without any warning. One second I'd be in the middle of doing something, and the next I'd be on the floor. It was scary."

"Did they ever figure out the cause?"

"There was nothing concrete, just lots of hypotheticals. I think it might have had to do more with the trauma. My vision would go white and I'd have vague flashes of what happened. I was in so much pain, I couldn't hold on to the memories—not that I wanted to anyway. After a few months the headaches started to subside, and I could remember most of what happened." She closed her eyes and inhaled deeply. "Sorry, that's not what you asked about. Now it's just my hip that causes problems."

"It's cool. These are all things I want to know, if you want to tell me." I kissed her temple.

"It's easier to talk about than it used to be," she said softly.

"You mean since you came back from Arden Hills?" A few seconds passed before she replied, and I worried that I'd pushed too much.

"Before I left, I was trying so hard to keep my life here separate from what had happened. It's not like that anymore."

"I'm glad."

"Me, too." She was quiet for a minute. "Anyway, you were asking about my hip."

"So it's better now than it was?"

"Most days. The cold seems to be a problem, but fortunately I don't have to take anything too strong anymore." She took a deep breath before she continued. "The doctors had me on a morphine drip in the beginning. I was in such a haze, I didn't know what was real and what wasn't for the longest time. I couldn't figure out why Trey was the only person I saw. I'm sure it was better that way."

I put the tattoo machine down. "You mean you didn't know everyone was gone?"

She shifted to look at me, her eyes ancient. "Not at first."

"How long was it before you found out?"

"A week—maybe two at the most? My memories of that time aren't very clear. I was in and out of consciousness, so I can't be sure. Trey was the one who told me, obviously. I had a complete breakdown. It was . . . awful. Deep down, I knew the nightmares I was having weren't just dreams, but I didn't want to believe it."

I couldn't fathom waking up in traction, with broken bones and third-degree burns, only to find out everyone I cared about was dead. Just thinking about it gave me the chills.

"Anyway"—Tenley cleared her throat—"I don't know if this is the best my hip is going to get or not, but it's much better than it was."

"What do the doctors say?"

"As far as they're concerned, the surgery was a success. I was in bed for weeks before I was allowed to start walking. But I can walk fine most of the time and I have full range of motion, at least for now. There was a lot of damage; the doctors say I'll need a hip replacement eventually."

"That doesn't sound good." I didn't like the prospect of her having to endure something like that again.

"It won't be for a long time, though."

I wondered if we would still be together by then. I couldn't imagine my world without her, but I hadn't anticipated losing my parents the way I did, either. Heart attacks I understood; car accidents; even freak plane crashes. But murder . . .

That was the fear that had petrified me into distancing myself from even the most important people in my life. It was why I hadn't pursued Tenley initially. I'd had a feeling that getting close to her wouldn't stop at sex, and I'd been right. She'd found a way between the cracks in my armor and blew it apart. I wanted to have the same effect on her.

27

TENLEY

As unconventional as it was to spend Christmas Day in Inked Armor, the tattoo session was what I needed. The soothing buzz of the machine and the sting of the needle distracted me from the pain of the memories I shared with Hayden.

"Do you think we could go to the storage unit tomorrow?" he asked as he made another pass with a damp cloth.

"Of course." I hadn't expected he would want to go so soon.

"I haven't been there since I first moved into my condo. I was going to take some of my parent's furniture, but I couldn't do it. It all reminded me of what I'd lost."

"Did you go alone?"

"Yeah. But you'll be with me this time, so maybe it won't be so hard."

I hoped that would be true.

Eventually we found our way back to the topic of last night, and Hayden tentatively raised the subject of New Year's. Lisa had called him several times today. The first time, she mentioned Times Square. The second call was about keeping it local. Hayden said they could talk about it tomorrow. My vote was for local, but I could handle a road trip if everyone was driving.

"What do you usually do on Christmas Day?" I asked.

I could see him shrug in my peripheral vision. "Not much. Sometimes we stay at Cassie's and have brunch in the morning. Mostly we just sit around and get shitfaced. Usually I'm too hammered to drive my ass home and I have to stay another night."

I read between the lines. The holidays at Cassie's were a way for the people who cared about him to keep an eye on him.

"We could have gone back there today. We still can, if you want to." I didn't want to take him away from the people who cared so much about him.

"Nah. As selfish as it is, I want you to myself today. Besides, if we end up going somewhere for New Year's with everyone else, we won't get much time alone."

"We need to take your car to the body shop." I felt bad about the damage to the hood.

"I have a guy I deal with. He can fix her up no problem."

"That means we have to take my car if we go on a road trip."

Hayden made a face. "I guess. I'd rather drive your car than the douche mobile."

"I'm selling the BMW," I replied, my focus on his tapping foot.

"I can help with that," he said quickly, apparently as eager to get rid of it as I was.

"That would be good." I was done taking care of everything on my own.

"We'll get on it next week."

"The sooner the better."

Hayden lifted the needle from my skin and wiped my shoulder with a damp cloth. "Is it because of what you found in there?"

"That's part of it." Every time I looked at the car now, I recalled what Trey had said while I was in Arden Hills. Even if it was said out of spite, I'd never know the truth and I didn't want the lingering reminder.

"What are your other reasons for selling it?"

"You're not a fan of the car." Hayden loathed the BMW, and it wasn't just because he believed they belonged to pretentious jerk-offs.

"You don't have to get rid of it because I don't like it."

"Connor and I took a break during the last semester of my undergrad," I blurted.

The buzz of the tattoo machine ceased. "You broke up?"

"For a while."

This was one thing I hadn't talked about; not with my girl-friends or my mom. I'd made the decision and pretended it was no big deal. In reality, it had been painful. I'd hated the separation, mostly because I was scared of the unknown.

"Did you date other people?" His voice had an edge.

"A bit. Mostly, I just needed space. Connor backed out of a trip home because he was overloaded with work. He got shitty about it. His program was rigorous and so was mine. I couldn't afford the distraction. The added stress was affecting my marks, and the only way I could manage tuition at Northwestern was with a scholarship, so I suggested we take some time off from each other."

"And he was okay with that?" The tattoo machine started up again, thankfully. I needed Hayden's focus away from my face.

"No, not at all. It became this huge fight. He hung up on me and I didn't call him back. I figured when he calmed down, he'd understand my logic and see it made sense." That hadn't been the case.

"So you worked it out?"

"Eventually. When Connor got mad, he was stubborn and impossible to reason with. I knew he'd call when he was ready."

"How long did that take?"

"A month." It had seemed like forever then; now it was just a scene in a life I felt completely disconnected from. I'd put all my energy and focus into my studies and my friends during that time, determined not to fixate on Connor's silence. It hadn't worked all that well.

"And then you got back together?" Hayden asked.

"No. It was another month before that happened."

"I'd go fucking mental without you for that long."

I thought of those weeks without Hayden while I was in Arden Hills. It had been indescribably painful. The month without Connor had been hard, but I was used to the distance since he'd been at Cornell the entire time we were dating. His anger and my fear had been the hardest part to deal with.

"I thought we'd work things out when we were both ready. I was so naïve. It never occurred to me he was sleeping with everything with a pulse during that time."

Hayden looked appalled. "That's what he told you?"

"No. Trey did."

Hayden turned off the tattoo machine and set it down on the tray. His gloves came off next.

"You don't have to stop."

Even I could hear the waver in my voice. I didn't want to cry over this, but the uncertainties I'd been holding on to made it hard to keep back the tears.

"Tenley, you can't believe anything that asshole says."

"He could be right, though. Even when Connor finally called, it wasn't the same between us. He was so worried I was going to taint myself by sleeping around. I couldn't figure out why he was so paranoid about it, but it makes sense if he was doing exactly that."

"That's just speculation. Fears fed by the bullshit Trey spews to keep you under his thumb."

"Maybe." I could never be sure, though. "I was still on the fence about getting back together until Connor showed up at my convocation. Afterward, he took me away for the weekend and proposed. Everything happened so fast from there. We planned the wedding in less than six months."

"Which is another reason you have to question whether what Trey said happened. Why would he propose if he wanted to run around and bang skanks?"

"To stake a claim?"

Hayden sighed and pulled me into a sitting position. Despite my state of undress his eyes stayed on mine. "Don't do this to yourself. I know how easy it is to spin worst-case scenarios."

"I'll never know the truth," I whispered.

"Did it ever occur to you that Trey might have planted those condoms? It's definitely something he'd do."

"It's possible," I said hesitantly. "But what if what Trey said is true, and all that time I was living a lie? I keep thinking that if things had been different, maybe my family would be alive. I still would have come to Chicago for my master's. Maybe I would have met you anyway."

"There are a million possibilities. You could let them consume you for the rest of your life. It's what I've been doing for the past seven years, and it hasn't done me any good. You have to let it go, Tenley."

"I don't know how."

He cupped my cheek in his palm. His sad understanding touched that place inside my heart reserved for him alone. "I know it's not easy. But we can't resurrect the dead to find out the truth."

Hayden was right. Knowing wouldn't change the past. Letting go was the only way.

And I didn't need the answers because the person I loved and wanted was sitting right in front of me. Hayden was my present and my future.

The next morning I stood in front of the bathroom mirror with my robe hanging off my shoulders, peering at my freshly cleaned tattoo.

"You're going to get a neck crick if you keep that up." Hayden stepped beside me with a towel slung low around his hips. Water beaded on his chest from the shower, and his hair was slicked back from his forehead. When it wasn't hanging in his eyes, he looked like a '50s icon.

"I can't help it. It's beautiful." The addition of color to the top of the wings was incredible. Even though the tattoo was still a little red around the edges, the parts that had been shaded were vividly three-dimensional now.

He kissed my shoulder, right beside the tip of the wing. "I'm glad you like it."

"I love it. I can't wait to get back in your chair for another session."

"Me, neither." He nipped at the spot his lips had been, then stepped away.

Unlike with some of our previous sessions, I hadn't broken down after yesterday's. The tattoo was no longer about punishment for mistakes. Instead, our time in the shop had helped heal some of the wounds I'd created by going to Arden Hills. The intimacy of it made me feel closer to him. We both needed the connection, especially after the past couple of days.

Hayden was anxious today about the storage unit, and I was nervous for him. I wanted him to find what he was looking for, so he could get the answers he needed. He'd been too preoccupied to sleep well last night. I'd woken several times to find him wrapped around me, his hand splayed out on my sternum.

He opened the medicine cabinet and got out his shaving kit. First came the straight-blade razor, next the little bowl and the brush he used to work the shaving lotion into a lather. I pulled my robe over my shoulders, the lavender satin rough against the fresh ink. I knotted it at the waist and hopped up on the counter, crossing my legs. I found watching Hayden shave undeniably sexy, particularly since he used such an old-school method.

"Don't you have an electric razor? Wouldn't it be easier?" I'd seen the kit under the counter when I once went in search of cleaning supplies.

Hayden looked at me as if I had two heads. "That's for cutting my hair, not shaving my face. Your sensitive skin would be chafed to hell otherwise."

"So this is for my benefit." I gestured to the collection of items on the counter.

"I would consider it mutually beneficial." He leaned over the sink, his hair falling in his face as he splashed with water. He ran his wet hands through his hair to keep it off his forehead, but it had gotten so long it had become a constant battle he couldn't win.

"Speaking of haircuts, how handy are you with a pair of scissors?" he asked.

"Okay, I guess. I used to trim my dad's hair pretty regularly."

"Yeah?"

"He had a military cut. It wasn't like it was a challenge." Switching out a number four for the fade-out was easy.

"Usually I get Lisa to do it, but there hasn't been time lately. You want to give mine a go?"

"What if I mess it up?"

"Then I shave my head. It'll grow back."

"I don't know." I loved his hair. I would feel awful if he ended up having to sheer it off.

He leaned against the counter, twirling the scissors around his finger. "If we find something in the storage unit, I'll want to take it in to the cops." He glanced up at me, transparent in his anxiety. "I don't want to go to the precinct looking like this. I've already acted like an asshole there. I don't need any more cards stacked against me."

"Is this about Officer Cross?"

"No. Miller made the suggestion. She's right. It would be easier if I looked less . . . like me."

"I love the way you look." It made me resistant to the change, even though it was only physical.

"Yeah, but you're not a judgmental cop, are you?"

I could see his point. Hayden projected danger and menace; it kept most people out. I was among the privileged few who truly knew him.

"Let me see what I can do. I can't re-create what you had when I first met you," I said as he dropped down onto the edge of the tub.

"That's fine. I just want to look normal." He passed me the scissors.

"I'll try my best." I pushed his hair back from his face. "But just so we're clear, how you look won't change the way I feel about you."

I kissed him and got to work.

It didn't turn out too bad in the end; I left enough length at the top that Lisa could fix it at a later date. I ran my fingers through the short hair at his nape.

"This is good." He turned his head to check out the sides.

"The facial piercings are the only things that keep you from looking too refined," I joked.

"About those . . ."

I should have expected what was coming, but I didn't. Or maybe I just didn't want to. Why go to all the trouble to cut his hair and then leave in the most obvious signs of difference?

"What are you taking out?" I skimmed the rings in his lip with my fingertips.

"Those for starters, and the eyebrow piercing."

"Now?"

"I might as well."

"Will you put them back in?"

"I'm not sure there's a point. I'm going to have to lose the metal in my face eventually. I don't want to be one of those forty-year-old douche bags who's still holding on to their twenties."

"What about the industrial?" I touched the shell of his ear.

He smiled. "Everything in the ears can stay."

"And you won't take out anything below the neck?" I ran my hand down his chest.

"Definitely not."

I breathed a sigh of relief. "Okay. The facial piercings can go."

"I wasn't aware I was asking permission," he teased.

"I thought you might feel less conflicted if I gave it to you anyway."

Hayden's lip quirked up. I cupped the back of his neck and drew him down, going for the viper bites. I remembered the feel of that hard, warm steel biting into my lip the first time we kissed. It had been so alien, so alluring.

His arm wound around my waist, pulling me closer, seeking connection or maybe a distraction.

I took advantage of his neediness, which echoed my own, and parted my lips. He responded immediately, his tongue entering my mouth, his other hand tangling in my wet hair. He made a low, impatient sound as he picked me up and deposited me on the counter. His hands went to my thighs, pushing them apart so he could get between them. I had nothing on under the robe. He was still covered with a towel from the waist down.

"Fuck. I shouldn't be looking to get inside you again so soon." He gripped the edge of the counter.

Aside from our time at Cassie's and the tattoo session

yesterday, we'd spent an unprecedented amount of time naked over the past several days, christening all manner of locations in his condo. The opportunities for escapism had been endless.

"It's okay." I ran my palm down his back, feeling his muscles flex. "You can have me as often as you want."

He rested his forehead against mine, shoulders rising and falling with his labored breath. "It's not just about wanting you. It's this fucking *need*. No matter what I do, how close I get, it's like I'm consumed by it."

"I know how you feel." I wanted him with the same urgency. I never felt sated. Still starving for his affection; nothing but him would make the ache or the craving go away.

"I don't know that you do. This feeling"—he swallowed hard—"it terrifies the fuck out of me. And there's all this other shit happening and I can't deal with it, and all I want is for you to be mine."

"I am yours," I said, his distress heartbreaking.

"Not all of you." His lips brushed over mine. "Not the part that counts."

That was it. The emotion I'd been too afraid to express was the problem. The infinite desire was a product of unspoken words. I couldn't get what I needed from him when I was holding back what he needed from me. It was becoming torturous for both of us.

The towel around his waist dropped to the floor. He freed the tie on my robe, the sides parted, and Hayden pushed it over my shoulders. Then he pulled me forward until I was at the edge of the counter. I hooked a palm around his neck and wrapped my legs around his waist to keep my balance. His eyes were fixed over my shoulder. One hand smoothed up my spine, stopping just shy of the fresh ink.

"I want to be in you everywhere," he whispered.

"Hayden—"

"I'm sorry. I shouldn't be pushing. I should stop."

For so long, I had felt such vast emptiness. Until him. This was what love felt like—this unyielding, overwhelming need for someone that wiped out everything else.

"Hayden, look at me." He needed the one thing I could give him unconditionally, now more than ever. "You *have* all of me. I am only yours."

He shook his head. "No, I don't. But I'll deal with it."

I knew he was referring to my heart. But he'd had it all along.

"I love you, Hayden."

28

HAYDEN

I blinked, not sure if I imagined it or not. "I'm sorry. What?" Clearly, I was losing my mind. Considering how underslept I was and freaked out about going to the storage unit, it wasn't unrealistic to come to that conclusion.

"I'm in love with you," she said again.

"Are you sure?"

"Very sure." Her hands were on my face, her touch soft, soothing.

If there was anyone who could say anything to me that would get me through this fucked-up morning, Tenley was the person and those were the words. "Really?"

Her knuckles drifted from my temple to my chin. Then she followed the path with her lips until she reached my mouth. "I love you."

All the pent-up, festering emotion exploded out of me. "I love you so fucking much." I kissed her hard. "That night you left? That was when I knew. It wasn't until you were gone that I realized how much I needed you, and after you came back I wasn't sure if I could tell you, but it's been killing me not to say it. Shit. I'm ruining this. Why can't I shut the fuck up?"

Tenley's hands smoothed over my shoulders, down my arms, and back up. It distracted me from my ranting, which was a fucking embarrassment in the wake of such a declaration.

"I love you," she whispered, taking my bottom lip between her teeth.

Then she shifted and everything lined up, my cock sliding lower against her.

"We should do this in the bed," I said.

"Right here is perfectly fine."

She hooked her ankles around my waist, securing our position. It made arguing difficult. I tried anyway. "The bed seems more appropriate, don't you think?"

"Fuck appropriate." Her legs tightened and the piercing breeched the threshold.

"I really do love you. You know that?" It came out more groan than words.

"I know." Tenley pulled her hair over one shoulder, exposing that glorious fresh ink in the mirror. "Now show me."

The desperate need leached out of me, replaced by a different desire. I'd fantasized about this exact position, being inside her, having a perfect view of both my art on her body and her face. As much as I would have liked the soft comfort of my bed, the view was incredible.

What started out hot and frantic turned into something much better. It was a controlled glide and retreat, our lips brushing with every gentle thrust. The pad of her thumb swept over my eyebrow, then over my viper bites. She followed with her mouth.

"I can always put them back in if you want me to," I said.

"I'll love you just as much with or without them."

It was exactly what I needed to hear.

Tenley held my gaze as she came, and I could see the truth in the words she'd uttered reflected there. It was the closest I'd ever been to her. I never wanted to lose that feeling.

After my second shower, Tenley finally convinced me to get dressed. I was reluctant to wreck the fantastic start to my day by going to the storage facility; staying naked was a preferable option. But I'd postponed it long enough.

I put on a pair of dress pants while Tenley picked out a shirt and tie. She hung them in the bathroom while I shaved, since I'd gotten waylaid from the task earlier. Next came the steel removal.

"You're not taking out the one in your tongue, are you?" Tenley asked as she sat on the bathroom counter to watch.

"And miss out on the sounds you make when I go down on you? Fuck, no."

She flushed and smiled. "Good."

I removed the eyebrow ring, but I needed a pair of pliers and Tenley's help to take out the viper bites. I sat on the edge of the tub while Tenley carefully loosened the tiny, silver balls from each ring. She threaded the hoops through my lip and dropped them into my palm. I poked at the spot; the absence of steel felt odd.

She leaned down and kissed the place where the bites used to be. "You're gorgeous no matter what, Hayden."

I laughed to hide my discomfort. It was definitely one of the things I worried about. Part of the reason Tenley had been attracted to me was because of my otherness. Take away some of the steel and I looked just like everyone else, aside from the ink.

Tenley passed me my shirt and waited until my arms were through the sleeves before she started fastening the buttons. When she was done, she knotted my tie and took a step back. "Check yourself out."

I went over to the bathroom mirror, nervous I would end up looking like a douche. The haircut and the lack of facial piercings made the change pretty fucking extreme. Aside from the industrial and the antihelix rings, no one would know about my predilections. They were hidden under clothes and a guise of normalcy.

"You're still the same person," Tenley said, her arm coming around my waist, her cheek resting against my biceps. "The way you look doesn't have an impact on who you are."

Tenley drove to the storage facility because I was too antsy. It had been a couple of years since I'd been out here, and longer since I'd been inside. It was exactly as I remembered it—creepy as fuck. The location reminded me of the layout for horror-movie gore scenes: rows upon rows of garage-type bays with numbers identifying each one.

Tenley followed my directions until we reached the bay Nate had rented when he and Cassie cleaned out the house. Tenley let the engine idle while I mustered the energy necessary to get out of the car.

After a few minutes, she gave my hand a squeeze. "We don't have to do this."

"I'm good. I just need another minute."

Another minute turned out to be ten, but Tenley didn't push. She held my hand and waited for me to grow some balls. When I finally opened the car door, she turned off the engine and followed behind. I used the key Nate had given me, followed by the assigned code. The sound of the locking mechanism was reminiscent of gunshots, and I had to remind myself we were perfectly safe. No one was waiting inside to ambush us. I lifted the bay door and the automatic lights flickered on.

Even though my stomach was empty, I felt as if I were going to throw up. I immediately started to chew on the corner of my mouth, but the steel rings weren't there anymore. I flicked out my tongue ring and made the circuit back and forth over my lips, instead. It was moderately soothing. Tenley's hand moving in circles on my back helped, too.

Nothing had changed since the last time I was here. The unit was full of boxes and antique furniture wrapped carefully in plastic or protective blankets. I could recall just from the shape of each piece what it looked like underneath. The first seventeen years of my life was packed inside this place. I'd spent the better part of a decade trying to forget it all. It hadn't worked.

"Cassie did a better job organizing this place than she did in the basement of Serendipity. It was a shit-ton of work," I said, mostly just to fill the silence.

"She must have had help."

"She wouldn't let anyone touch a thing. She went to the house every day for weeks, boxed things up, and then moved them here."

"Everyone grieves differently, I suppose." Tenley snuggled into my side; the contact kept me grounded.

"Her way was better than mine."

Time gave so much in the way of clarity. I could see now how difficult it had been for Cassie when she lost her sister because in many ways she lost me, too. Not forever, but for a long while. We were close, even during the beginning of my rebellious, asshole teen phase. She'd been the one person I could go to when I screwed up and needed to find a way to fix things. But I'd been so submerged in guilt and blame afterward, I cut her off along with everyone else.

I exhaled a heavy breath and stepped across the threshold. As organized as it was, the space made me feel panicky—all the stuff just sitting there in boxes with no real place or function. Moving toward an ornate cherry desk, I ran my hand over the plastic-covered surface.

"This used to be in my mom's office. She always had a stash of twenties in the back of this drawer. I never touched them, though."

"That would be hard to resist as a teenager."

I shrugged. "She put a lot of trust in me, even though I didn't deserve it most of the time. I didn't want to mess with that. I miss her a lot."

"You were close?"

I nodded. "She let me get away with too much shit, but she understood me better than my dad. We were a lot the same, me and my mom."

It had been a long time since I'd let myself feel all the emotions that came with losing them. I'd been quick to don emotional and physical armor after their murders. It had been easier to bury it all than to face the pain.

Tenley gave me space as I moved around, running my fingers over all the things I remembered. Everything was covered in a layer of dust. I didn't like it. I stopped at a lamp made out of bent silverware.

"That's really cool," Tenley said from behind me.

"My mom and I made it when I was a kid. I thought it was cool because I got to use a blowtorch. Dad hated that she put it in our sitting room. He said it didn't match the antiques. Mom had all these cool ideas that didn't fit with convention. Dad was different; always looking to climb the social ladder. She couldn't have cared less. I loved that she didn't give a shit what people thought most of the time. I mean, she wasn't exactly thrilled when I came home with an eyebrow piercing on my seventeenth birthday, but she wasn't bothered by it. It was my dad's reaction she worried about."

"Did you get along with your dad?"

"As long as I followed the rules, which wasn't very often. We argued a lot. He was away on business most of the time, so it was just my mom and me. And Cassie, when she lived with us.

Mom was permissive and I took advantage of that. Dad would try and put the hammer down if I'd been a shit while he was gone. It wasn't very effective."

"Isn't that what all teenagers do?"

"I guess. But some of the crap I pulled was pretty awful. I started hanging out in Damen's tattoo shop during my junior year. I thought he was so cool back then. I came home wasted all the time, fucked up on drugs, with hickeys all over the place. That was when things went downhill. I shouldn't have been out with Damen and his drugged-up loser friends the night my parents died."

I stopped at a stack of long, narrow boxes, ones that would hold framed art. I went through them, reading the descriptors scrawled on the front of each one. I recalled every piece by title alone.

"You remember yesterday when I told you that you couldn't keep going over all the possibilities? That you had to let it go?"

"You were right on both counts. But it's not easy," Tenley said softly.

Her arm came around my waist. I looked down at her. No pity was in her eyes, just understanding.

"It was a hypocritical thing to say. I still think about it some-times—about what might have happened if I'd just stayed home like I was supposed to that night. If I hadn't started hanging out with Damen in the first place, I wouldn't have been grounded or pissed my dad off, or gotten all shitfaced. Things might have been different."

"The what-ifs are so hard to deal with."

I turned back to the boxes and continued flipping through, still caught up in memories and guilt I couldn't shake and maybe never would. This whole thing gave me new insight into how resilient Tenley was. Inside of a year, she'd got her life back together and found a way to move on that wasn't completely self-destructive. I'd taken seven times as long to do the same, and I was still working on it. The paths we took to reach the same end were vastly different.

"Shit. I think it's here." I stopped at one of the boxes halfway through the pile.

ELEANOR'S ANGEL was written in big block letters on the top of the box. If the contents matched the description, it was the painting I kept dreaming about. The one I remembered from my childhood, and the first thing I saw when I opened my parents' bedroom door that night.

I didn't know what I expected to get from it. I slid the box out from between the others and peeled the tape off. The flaps fell open. It was the right painting. I could tell because of the scuff mark in the corner of the mahogany-colored frame from when I'd dropped it a long time ago.

"I probably shouldn't touch it." My voice cracked. "I don't want to leave fingerprints. Just in case, right?"

"I don't know. Maybe we should call Officer Miller."

"What if it's nothing? What if I'm not remembering right?" I asked, irrationally panicked. My vision went blurry.

"Shh. It's okay." Her gloved fingers cupped my face. "If we call Officer Miller, we can ask her what we should do."

"If you leave your gloves on, you could look at it first. I don't want to call for nothing."

"I can do that. What should I be looking for?"

"I'm not sure. Maybe we should just leave it alone."

"I don't think it hurts for me to look," she said reassuringly.

Tenley carefully lifted the painting out of the box. In the garish fluorescent lights, I could make out the details of the art clearly. Seeing it brought back another flood of memories. It was such a strange painting. I'd never asked my mom what compelled her to use that particular color scheme. Seeing it now, with the perspective I had gained, I understood her a lot better. What I couldn't understand was why in the world my dad had let her keep it in their bedroom. It was as horrifying as it was ethereal, which I suppose was much of the appeal. The angel was painted in various shades of red. The part that freaked me out, though, was the way her wings appeared to be dripping down the canvas, as if they were bleeding feathers.

It was eerily familiar, I realized. In some vague way, it reminded me of the original version of the tattoo I was putting on Tenley. Except I'd changed most of the red to gold and silvers, so it was more a reflection of life, not death.

Tenley leaned in closer, inspecting the painting. Her leather-clad fingers hovered over the surface, never touching.

Even from where I was standing, I could make out the maroon dots scattered over the canvas and the frame. Ones that didn't match the brushstrokes.

"I'm right—I have to be. That painting was there when I found my parents." My legs went watery and I leaned against the wall in case they decided they weren't all that interested in supporting my weight any longer.

"We should call Officer Miller."

There were so many unanswered questions. It didn't make sense that this painting hadn't made it into evidence. Maybe if it had, the case wouldn't have been closed. I didn't want to speculate, but I had a pretty good fucking idea whom I wanted to point the finger at. The question was why.

"Do you see all those marks on it? What if it's blood?" I asked.

"It could be, but the only way you can get any answers is if we call Officer Miller."

"Right. Yeah. Okay." I rooted around in my pocket and found my phone. I couldn't manage punching in my pass code because my hands were shaking so badly.

"Can I help?" Tenley asked.

I passed her the phone and she keyed in the code. Miller's number was in my contact list already, so Tenley pulled it up and hit call. I didn't track the conversation that followed.

Tenley passed back my phone. "She's on her way. Why don't we wait in the car?" Tenley took my hand and tugged.

"What about the painting? I don't want you to touch it again." As irrational as it might be, I worried about its tainting her as it had me.

"It's fine where it is. Officer Miller will be here in a few minutes to take care of it." Tenley used the same tone she did when she talked to TK, all lilting and calm.

"Right. Yeah." I shivered. "It's fucking cold out here."

I let her lead me to the car and open the door. She came around the driver's side and started the engine. As I stared out the windshield, watching it unfog, I recognized that I was in shock. I kept replaying the night I found my parents' dead bodies: the climb up the stairs, the smell of blood and brain matter, the horrifying visual accompaniment, and the painting on the floor where it didn't belong.

My pocket buzzed but I didn't think to answer it. Tenley's phone went off almost as soon as mine stopped. It was Lisa. She probably wanted to talk about New Year's, which wasn't on my radar, considering the shit that was going down.

I watched Tenley's mouth move, forming words I didn't hear as she pushed her fingers through my hair over and over. Her attention remained fixed on me the entire time. She hung up after what could have been minutes or hours. I wasn't tracking enough to know.

"I really fucking love you." It came out sounding as if I'd been gargling with gravel.

"I love you, too," she said, her smile sad.

My vision did that blurry shit again, so I rubbed my eyes. My palms came away damp. I stared at them, not sure what was going on. My skin felt wrong, my chest tight.

"It's okay, baby. I'm right here with you. I know this is hard." Tenley climbed over the center console and into my lap.

Mindful of the new ink, I buried my face in her hair and tried to fight the rising tide of fear. She whispered soft words of reassurance until I was no longer at risk of losing it completely.

A police cruiser turned the corner and came down the narrow stretch of asphalt. Tenley slid back over to her seat as the vehicle came to a stop a few feet away. I opened my door at the same time as Officer Miller got out of the cruiser, along with another cop I didn't recognize. Tenley met me at the front of the car and linked our hands as Miller and her partner approached. Introductions were made, none of which I retained. Tenley did all the explaining as she brought them over to the painting.

Officer Miller and her partner snapped on rubber gloves as they looked it over.

"Have either of you touched this?" Miller asked.

"I took it out of the box, but I was wearing gloves," Tenley replied.

Miller nodded and turned back to the framed art. She and her partner inspected the piece. "Are you seeing this?" Miller asked.

There were nods and more murmuring, lots of gestures.

"That painting used to scare the shit out of me as a kid." When the male officer turned to look at me, I went on, as though it required further explanation, "I think it's because the color is incongruous with the subject matter."

He gave me a funny look. "Are you an art teacher or something?"

I pried my eyes away from the angel to meet his inquisitive stare. "Tattooist."

His eyes moved from my feet to my face. "Huh. I never would have guessed."

"I'm calling this in," Miller said. "We need to get it to the lab."

Tenley put me back in the car. I watched as Miller paced around, making calls, conferring with her partner. The painting went back in its box. Tenley handed over the key to the storage unit. Miller locked it up and came over to the car. I stared at her through the glass when she tapped on the window. She opened the door and crouched down.

"You all right?"

"Yeah. Fine."

"You did the right thing by calling me."

"Uh-huh."

"Tenley's going to bring you to the station. We've got a few questions for you."

"Okay."

"Hang tight, there."

Miller shut the door. She and Tenley had a conversation. Based on the number of times they looked my way, I could guess what it was about.

When we arrived at the station, Officer Miller met us at the front doors and ushered us quickly through the lobby. There weren't any suspicious stares this time. Their eyes slid over Tenley and me, pausing briefly before moving away. One of the receptionists even smiled when we passed.

I froze when we reached the hallway. I'd been down there before, and the memories associated with it were not pleasant. "Where are we going?"

"To my office." When I didn't move, Officer Miller's features softened. "This isn't an interrogation, Hayden."

I sucked in a deep breath, squeezed the shit out of Tenley's hand, and followed them down the hall. The fluorescent lights above hummed and flickered, giving it an ominous feel. In spite of Miller's reassurance, the farther we went, the greater my sense of disassociation became. No matter how hard I tried, I couldn't stop from being sucked back into the past.

We were led into a small office with an old, beat-up fake-leather chair behind an equally beat-up desk. Two plastic chairs sat on the opposite side. When I was offered one, I quickly dropped into it. I was light-headed. Tenley sat down beside me and I slid my chair across the floor to close the space between us. The metal against linoleum made a horrible screech.

"Sorry," I mumbled when everyone in the room flinched.

My knee was going a mile a minute. I shrugged out of my coat and draped it over the back of the chair. I yanked at the collar of my shirt; my tie felt like a noose around my neck. The office was cramped, with shit strewn all over the desk. The lack of order stressed me out even more than I already was. It was too hot, and I couldn't seem to drag enough oxygen into my lungs. I wanted to roll up my sleeves, but then everyone would know I was faking civilized in my dress shirt and tie.

"Can we get Hayden a glass of water?" Tenley asked.

"Of course. Duggan?" Miller looked to the male officer.

He nodded once and left. It was a little less claustrophobic with one fewer in the room, but not much. Tenley started up with the slow circles on my back, but it didn't help calm the anxiety. Duggan came back with a bottle of water. I drained it and immediately wanted to hurl.

Then the questions started, which didn't help the nausea. I recounted the events of the night my parents were murdered, from the moment my parents walked out the door, to the moment I came home. The more of the story I relayed, the clearer the details became. I told them about Damen picking me up, about the kids I remembered being with us, about the girls I later found out were dancers from The Dollhouse.

"There was a guy there, I can't remember his name." I rubbed my temple, the headache cropping up behind my eyes making it hard to think. "Brant or Brett? I'd only seen him once before. He was around the same age as me, I think? Is this even important?" I glanced over at Miller, who was recording everything I said.

"Anything you can remember, no matter how insignificant, could be helpful."

"Okay. This kid, I'm pretty sure his name was Brett. Anyway, I didn't talk to him because he was a loser. All annoying and shit. I remember him being way too loud, like he wanted to fit in. He pretty much attached himself to Damen both times I met him. I thought he was a creep because he kept watching me. I was with this girl—" I glanced at Tenley, mortified that I had to relay this in front of her.

She gave me a smile that held no judgment, so I continued.

"I was already messed up at that point because Damen had brought out a boatload of weed and I'd been pounding beers. That night, that Brett kid and Damen kept having these side conversations. Damen kept blowing him off. He got pretty pissed at one point and then the kid left. I never saw him again after that."

"What about this Damen person, did you ever see him again?" Officer Miller asked.

"Yeah. A few months after my parents died, I started apprenticing for him. I worked for him for almost three years. He runs this seedy tattoo shop, Art Addicts. I'm pretty sure he was questioned about the whole thing since he was my alibi."

"You got a last name for this Damen character?" Duggan asked.

"Martin. His last name is Martin."

Miller and Duggan exchanged a look.

"What's going on? Do you guys know him?"

"The name might be familiar," Duggan said. "Can you tell me a little more about your relationship with him?"

I stared down at my shoes. The toe of the right one had a scuff.

"He was my employer and my dealer for a number of years. He introduced me to a lifestyle I didn't want any part of, after I got my head out of my ass." I looked up at Miller. "I made some regrettable choices when I was kid, especially after my parents died."

"I've seen the crime scene photos. You witnessed some pretty horrific stuff."

"That painting you took? It wasn't in those photos. I remember being confused about that. I know I was messed up at the time and I wasn't thinking clearly, but that's one thing I couldn't forget. When I walked into my parents' room"—the images in my head were so vivid, my stomach clenched—"that painting was on the floor. I remembered thinking if my dad had seen it like that, he would have freaked out. But in the photos, it wasn't there at all."

"You're sure about this?" Miller asked, leafing through the file on her desk, searching for something.

"Positive." I kept telling Cross something was wrong when I was being interrogated, but he made it seem as if I were losing it.

Miller made a call. More people came into the office, more questions were asked, but it was nothing like the night of my parents' murder, or the last time I'd been in the precinct. Cross wasn't there to needle me, and no one treated me like a deviant loser. It was one of the most surreal experiences of my adult life.

I was wiped out by the time the questioning was through.

Miller said she'd call after the painting had been to the lab. Since we couldn't do anything else, Tenley and I headed home. She drove. My phone buzzed in my pocket, but it took me too long to get it out so I missed the call. There were fourteen of them—several from Lisa and Jamie, a few from Chris, one from Sarah. The rest were from Cassie. I didn't have the energy to call them all, so I shut off my phone instead. I let my head drop back against the seat and closed my eyes to try to relax. But all I could see was that goddamn painting and all the blood.

"What can I do for you?" Tenley asked as she pulled into her parking spot behind Serendipity.

I had no idea how to answer that. I stared blankly out the windshield. Snow was starting to fall again, little flakes sticking to the glass before they melted into tiny crystal tears.

"I should get you a spot in my underground parking. I'm allowed two."

"You don't need to do that." She didn't press for an answer to her previous question.

"You don't even stay at your place. The parking garage is heated. You wouldn't have to clean off your car when the weather gets bad."

"That would be convenient. Why don't we go up to your place? I'll make you a sandwich or something. You haven't eaten all day."

It wasn't a no, but it wasn't exactly a resounding yes. Even though I was strung out and my decision-making skills were questionable, the parking spot was my testing the waters. I wanted her permanence, and this was one way to achieve it. If she parked her car at my place, she might as well move her stuff in, too.

I didn't go there, though. I knew if she said anything but yes, I wouldn't be able to handle the rejection.

29

TENLEY

My phone rang and I snatched it up off the comforter. It was Cassie. For the twentieth time in the past four days.

"Hi," I whispered.

"Is now a good time to talk?"

I rolled off the bed. "Hold on."

The water was running, but that didn't necessarily mean Hayden was still standing under it. Before I tiptoed to the bathroom I ran a hand over the comforter, smoothing out the wrinkles. It was pointless. Hayden was likely to remake the bed once he was done with the shower. He'd be able to tell I had lain on it, waiting for him.

Hayden was far from okay. Ever since he turned over the painting to Officer Miller, things had gotten worse. She called yesterday to inform him several sets of prints had been identified, and they had a few promising leads. They also confirmed blood spatter on the painting. Hayden had been asked to provide a blood sample to check if the spatter belonged to his parents, but we hadn't heard anything about the results yet. I thought the progress would be a turning point for him. It was, but not a good one.

I hid the phone in my back pocket and peeked through the gap in the door. I didn't want him to know I was talking to Cassie again. He'd grown suspicious of the number of calls I received from her. I told him she was worried, which wasn't a lie. We all were. Lisa and Chris called almost as often, but no one could do anything to help.

Hayden's back was to the spray, hands at his sides, head hanging low. He'd stay there until the water ran cold, sometimes longer. I'd had to forcibly remove him more than once over the past few days when his lips went blue from standing under the frigid water. After he was finished, he'd clean the bathroom. Again. He'd been like that with everything since we'd come home from the police station—cleaning and reorganizing to the point of obsession.

Nothing was good enough. Not the hospital corners on the sheets, not the line of pillows on the bed, or the shoes in the front hall closet. Yesterday he sat cross-legged on the floor for a good half hour, spacing and respacing the shoes until there was an inch between every pair and the heels lined up perfectly with each other. His compulsive tendencies had ratcheted up to frightening heights. I was reluctant to admit how severe it had become, for fear of what it meant.

"Hayden?"

His head snapped up and the glass door slid open. Water sluiced down his back and over his chest. My eyes followed the path. His hand went to cover himself. He hadn't had an erection since the morning we went to the storage unit. I met his exhausted, anxious gaze. His eyes were bloodshot with dark circles under them.

"Is everything okay?" It came out a hoarse croak.

"Everything's fine. I'm going to the kitchen to get a drink. I'll only be a minute or two."

After a long pause he replied, "Okay."

I couldn't leave the room without telling him. If he got out of the shower and I wasn't there, he was liable to have a meltdown. It had happened yesterday.

"He's in the shower," I said once I was in the hall.

"Again? How many times is that today?"

"This is number three."

He'd been taking upward of four showers a day. I didn't know what to make of it.

"This isn't good," Cassie said.

"It's getting worse."

"You sound like you're on the verge of tears."

I had to put my hand over the receiver so I could clear my throat. "I'm okay. I'm just worried."

Cassie sighed. "Tenley, this reminds me of what happened when his parents first died. I'm afraid it isn't going to get better if we don't intervene."

It wasn't what I wanted to hear, though I suspected she was right. I dropped onto the couch. "I don't know what to do."

"Nate and I have been talking. He's called in a favor and set up an appointment for Hayden this afternoon. It's a little short notice, but we can come over and persuade him to go."

"When's the appointment?"

"Four."

"That soon?" That was less than three hours from now. It didn't give us much time for acts of persuasion.

"Do you think you can keep this up much longer?" Her tone was gentle but prompting.

I surveyed the living room. It was spotless. I was terrified to touch anything because Hayden knew immediately when I had. His quest for order was draining. I understood the reason behind it. His world and his mind were in utter chaos; he could control his environment.

"Let me see if I can convince him first. I don't want him to feel ambushed."

"Okay. But if you haven't called back within the hour, Nate and I will come."

I took down the details and hung up, shoving the paper in my back pocket. I wasn't sure how I was going to broach the subject with Hayden, but he needed more help than I could give him.

TK jumped up on the couch and head-butted my hand. She'd been as jumpy as me over the past few days, unsure of Hayden's unpredictable moods. One minute he was fixated on a task; the next he exploded out of frustration because he couldn't get it right. I picked her up and pressed my nose into her fur, listening to her motor run.

"Tenley?" The high tenor reflected Hayden's anxiety, as did the heavy thud of his feet coming down the hall.

"I'm in the living room," I called out.

"I thought you were just getting something to drink—" He stopped short when he entered the room.

He had on boxer briefs and nothing else. His chest and shoulders were sprinkled with droplets of water, his wet hair standing on end. His hands sank into it and tugged hard, the concern switching to irritation.

"This place is a sty. There's shit everywhere," he barked, his accusatory glare on me.

My phone and the pen were on the coffee table. Nothing else was out of place as far as I could see. But based on Hayden's current rigid standards, those two items constituted a mess.

"I'll put it away—"

"I've got it."

He grabbed the pen and put it back in the drawer, slamming it shut. I pocketed my phone and stayed put. Waiting. His hands went to his hips as his eyes traveled the room in search of misplaced items. The tension in his shoulders didn't ease in the slightest.

"Where's your glass?"

"I got distracted by TK."

It was a partial truth. If I told him I put it in the dishwasher, he would check and know I was lying. He zoned in on TK, nuzzling my chin. His paranoia was painful to witness. Cassie was right.

"Why don't you get dressed and I'll make you something to eat," I said gently, hoping if I did something nice I could smooth the transition to a conversation I didn't want to have.

"I'm not hungry."

"But you haven't eaten today."

"Because I'm not hungry," he snapped.

His volume startled TK. She launched out of my lap and bolted down the hall, likely seeking refuge under the bed. I wished I could join her.

"Well, I am." I gave him a wide berth when I passed him on my way to the fridge.

I collected the items necessary to make a sandwich and dumped them on the counter. My method of sandwich assembly was likely going to give him an aneurysm, but I needed to stay occupied while I figured out how to approach the topic. His hand went back to his hair as he watched me. I was glad it was too short to rip out at the roots.

I took four slices of bread out of the bag. Even if he wasn't planning to eat, I was going to make him something.

"You should let me do that." Hayden moved in, prepared to take over.

"I can manage."

"It's my kitchen."

I bit back a comment about going back to my place to make food. He would freak out over the possibility of my being more than ten feet away from him.

"I think I can handle making a sandwich."

"But you'll make a mess."

"Which I'll clean up."

He snorted with derision.

I slapped the Black Forest ham down on the cutting board and turned to face him. "Hayden, I love you, and I know you're particular, but this is too much. Do you even realize what you're doing?"

"It's not my fault you can't remember where to put things when you're done with them."

"Excuse me?"

"We both know you're not very tidy." He made it sound like a felony.

My cool slipped a little. "For Christ sake, Hayden, compared to you, Martha Stewart is a slob! I can deal with your compulsive organization. Most of the time I like that about you. But I can't even make a sandwich without you crawling up my ass now!"

He blinked, taken aback that I'd raised my voice. "I'm not that bad."

I clenched my fists to keep my hands from flailing. "You've been two steps behind me fixing my so-called mistakes for the last few days. It's giving me a complex."

His rigid stance deflated. He crossed his arms over his chest and leaned against the counter, eyes on the floor. He bit down on the spot where the viper bites used to be.

"I can't keep waiting for the bomb to drop, Hayden. You're on edge all the time," I said softly.

When he stalked across the kitchen, I put my hands up to fend him off. He walked right into my palms. He brushed my hair over my shoulders, fingers skimming my collarbone. "I don't want to be up your ass like this. I'm sorry for being a dick."

"You're under a lot of stress."

"I'd like to apologize."

"Apology accepted. This week has been hard on you." I wasn't sure if I should trust his sudden shift in mood.

"I could do a better job, though." His hand came around my backside. He pulled my phone out of my pocket and dropped it on the counter so he could grab my ass and squeezed.

Gone was the dissonant hostility, replaced with something altogether needy. Apparently, Hayden responded better to frustration than coddling.

"Sex isn't going to make this go away," I said.

"But it will make me feel better."

I grabbed his forearms. His fingers were perilously close to places they shouldn't be if I was to have any hope of finishing this conversation. "We need to talk first."

"We can talk after." His hands went down the back of my jeans.

"You're evading."

"I know. And you're going to let me." His lips parted against my neck, his tongue swept out, and his teeth followed. I closed my eyes and reveled in the sensation for a fleeting moment.

"You need to talk to someone," I said, amazed my voice stayed steady considering his wandering hands and mouth.

"I'll talk to you, after I'm done using my tongue for other things."

"I mean a professional."

He retracted his hands. His lips left my skin. I'd definitely gotten his attention.

"I can handle my own shit," he bit out.

"Hayden, I love you more than anything, and I know this is bringing up a lot of things you'd rather not deal with—but I feel like a target, not an anchor. You're not acting like yourself, and it's frightening me." Pretending everything was fine wasn't an option anymore. "I can't stay here if things don't change."

"You can't— What do you mean?"

"I can't walk on eggshells all the time."

His eyes flared with panic. "So you'd fucking leave me?"

"No, Hayden—I won't leave you. But I can't stay here when you're like this. It's not good for either of us."

"You'd go back to your apartment?"

"If this continues, I'll have to." My chest ached at the possibility, but I needed him to see what this was doing to us.

With more lip biting he mulled it over. "I don't want to screw up this relationship. Not when I've just gotten you back."

"So you'll talk to someone?" I smoothed my hands over his shoulders.

"What if I don't like it?"

If he agreed, he was going to sit down with a perfect stranger and talk about his past and his perceived shortcomings. He was not going to like it. But if I could get him to go once, I wasn't above bribing him for subsequent visits.

"If you don't like it, you don't have to go back." I didn't say anything about finding a potential alternative. I'd worry about that later, if I needed to.

He sighed. "Fine."

"You'll go?"

"Yeah. I'm only committing to one session. We'll see what happens after that."

"That's all I'm asking for. I'll call Nate to confirm the appointment."

"Wait. What?" His expression hardened.

The room suddenly felt small, and he was way too close. "Nate scheduled a tentative appointment. He said he had someone he thought you might like."

"You talked to Nate about this?"

"I talked to Cassie. She talked to Nate. He suggested it and I agreed—for the reason we've just talked about."

I was fully prepared for him to lose it on me, and for a moment I worried that was exactly what would happen. He glared at me, teeth grinding as his nostrils flared. I could sense his panic. I was sure he was mentally searching for a way to get out of this. The idea of confronting his past terrified him for obvious reasons.

"Please, Hayden. I love you. I want to stay, but it can't be like this." I put my hand on his chest.

He looked down to where my palm rested over his heart. He was silent for a minute. I started to drop my hand, but his came up to cover mine. "What time's the appointment?"

"Four this afternoon."

He was silent again. His fingers wrapped around mine and squeezed. Then, finally: "Okay. I'll go."

30

HAYDEN

Therapy sucked. It was like being under a microscope for an hour. I told the therapist I wasn't coming back. She scheduled another appointment four days from now anyway. Then she said how fortunate I was to have so many people in my life that cared about me. I grudgingly pocketed the appointment card. I could call and cancel later.

I left the quaint, little house situated among kitschy shops and crossed over to the café where Tenley was having tea with Cassie. They were sitting at a table in the back corner. Neither one noticed when I walked in, too absorbed in their conversation. In front of Tenley was a half-eaten piece of cake and a pile of torn-up napkins.

A girl dressed in a pale pink shirt and black pants stepped in front of me. She was way too close. I was used to people giving me a lot more personal space.

"Hi! Table for one?" She stared up at me with a strange look on her face. "Wow. You have the bluest eyes I've ever seen! They're, like, superblue."

"Uh . . . thanks? I'm meeting my aunt—"

"That's so sweet!"

"—and my girlfriend. They're already here." I gestured to where they were sitting.

"Oh." Her smile fell but she didn't stop staring. It was fucking odd.

I maneuvered around her and headed for Tenley and Cassie. Cassie stood up as soon as she saw me. I couldn't figure out why she looked so stunned, until I remembered no one but Tenley and the police had seen me since I'd taken out the facial piercings. She gave me a warm hug and whispered "Thank you" in my ear. I wasn't sure what she was thanking me for, but I returned the embrace.

I nabbed a chair from an empty table and pulled it up next to Tenley's. She looked anxious as hell. I hoped she'd ordered a decaf, or she was going to be a jittery mess for the rest of the day. Before she could ask me anything about the appointment, a waitress bounced over and did the same weird staring thing. I ordered a black coffee and an extra fork so I could finish Tenley's cake.

"Everything go okay?" Tenley's hand fluttered close to my arm, but she didn't make contact. Instead she clasped her hands in her lap and tried to keep them still.

Had I been that bad since the trip to the police station? I decided then that I wouldn't cancel the next appointment. As shitty as it was to talk about all the fucked-up things I'd been through and done, I couldn't expect Tenley to deal with it, or me, if I refused to.

"It was fine." I leaned over and kissed her temple. "I've got another appointment in a few days."

She seemed startled by the admission. "Really?" Her eyes got all glassy.

"Hey. It's okay, kitten. We're gonna be fine." I traced her bottom lip with the pad of my thumb.

"Well, I think I'll be going," Cassie said, pushing up out of her chair.

"You don't have to do that," I said, vaguely disappointed.

"Nate's going to be home early tonight." She exchanged a look with Tenley, and Cassie's cheeks flushed. I didn't want to know what that was about. Cassie pulled on her coat and Tenley rose to hug her. Cassie whispered something I couldn't hear and smoothed her hand over Tenley's hair while stepping away. It was a maternal, affectionate gesture.

"I'll call you tomorrow and let you know," Tenley assured her.

"There's no obligation."

Cassie kissed her on the cheek and left. They were much closer than I'd realized.

"What was that about?" I asked when Tenley sat back down.

"We've been invited for dinner tomorrow."

"Do you want to go?"

"It might be nice."

I'd been pretty reclusive the past few days; it wouldn't hurt to get out for a few hours tomorrow evening. Besides, I needed to thank Nate.

My coffee came, distracting me from the conversation. I devoured the rest of Tenley's cake and drained the cup. Got a refill. Ordered another dessert even though I usually ate only Tenley's baked goods. Tenley chattered away, talking about the tentative plans she'd made with Lisa and Sarah for next week. She stayed away from the topic of therapy, but her pile of shredded napkins grew to twice its original size. She was still nervous about something; I just didn't know what.

"I think I'm done," I said after I drained my third cup of coffee and finished the chocolate layer cake. My appetite was back, and not just for food. I had one hell of a hard-on. My dick had woken up after Tenley got her back up over my being such a prick.

"You're sure you don't want anything else?"

"Nah. I'm ready to go home." I folded up my napkin, put it on the center of the plate, and flagged down the waitress.

Once the bill was taken care of we went out to the car. I still hadn't taken mine to the shop. That would have to change. Tenley and I hadn't been out much since the hood incident, but I was already tired of driving around in something with no balls.

She was fidgety on the way home, her hands running up and down her thighs, her foot bouncing on the floor.

"You all right?" I asked when we were stopped at a red light.

"Uh-huh."

"You wanna try again? Maybe with the truth this time."

I leaned over and kissed her on the cheek, so she knew I wasn't being a jerk. I just wanted to know what the issue was.

She must not have expected it because she jumped at the contact. "Sorry. Too much caffeine."

I backed off and left it alone. She'd talk when she was ready. Pushing her would make me a hypocrite, since I wasn't about to offer up any information about my session. I would never talk to Tenley about a lot of stuff. Not because I didn't trust her, but because it wasn't stuff she needed to know.

Much of it had to do with how fucking scared I was that something was going to happen to take her away from me again. Apparently it was a residual symptom of my particular brand of PTSD. At least now I could figure out how to deal with it without freaking out on her over the position of the remote control on the side table. As I'd done yesterday.

When we got home, Tenley disappeared into the bathroom. I took the opportunity to look over the spreadsheets for Inked Armor on my laptop while I waited for her to come out of hiding. It was Lisa's job to take care of them, but I always rechecked everything.

I glanced at the date at the bottom of the screen and did a double take. Tomorrow was New Year's Eve. Lisa had taken over making a plan after the fiasco at Christmas dinner, but things had gotten crazy and I'd forgotten all about it. That must have been the reason for Cassie's invitation.

Tenley was probably sick of being holed up in the condo with me. As difficult as the therapy session had been, it had been revelatory in many ways. I was a fuckwit when I was under too much stress. It was okay to act like a broody douche when I was eighteen, not so much at twenty-five.

I shut down the laptop and headed for the bedroom. The bathroom door was still closed. I knocked. "Tenley?"

"Just a minute."

I paced around the room and went through the session again. I'd talked about my parents' murder and Tenley. We focused on how I experienced those events, and how my not dealing with them was affecting my relationship with her. Now that I had perspective, I could see the hell I'd put her through over the past few days.

The bathroom door opened and I turned around, ready to issue a full apology. What came out of my mouth was, "Oh. My. Fuck."

Her hair was pulled up into a ponytail, her cheeks flushed, and she wore only nipple shields and heels. Both cupcake themed. My instant erection almost ripped through my jeans.

She looked down at her chest. "I got new jewelry."

I cleared my throat. Twice. "I can see that."

"And new shoes."

"I see that, too."

Her eyes lifted to peek up at me. She was ever the contradiction between sweetness and sexuality.

I must have stared for quite a while because her eyes dropped to the floor and she wrung her hands together. "I'm sorry. The past few days have been so tense, and earlier it seemed like you might want me—never mind." She turned around, her art and her ass on display, and took a step toward the bathroom.

"Whoa. Where are you going?"

She glanced over her shoulder. "To get changed."

"I don't think so." I grabbed her wrist and pulled her against me.

Cupping the back of her head in my palm, I kissed her—gently. There'd been too much aggression coming from me lately, and I didn't want to bring it into the bedroom. I wanted slow and easy and close because I'd been pushing her away, too caught up in my own turmoil to see what it was doing to her.

"I missed you," Tenley whispered, her hands going under my shirt, tugging it up over my head.

"Me, too." I wrapped an arm around her waist and carried her to the bed.

She sat on the edge of the mattress and unfastened the button on my pants with hands that shook. The zipper went down and my pants dropped to the floor. I stepped out of them as she brushed my cock with her fingertips.

"I wasn't sure—" When she looked up at me, such vulnerability was in her eyes. "I would do almost anything for you."

"I know." It had only been four days, yet it felt like an eternity.

"I just want to love you."

So I did.

Things were better. I wasn't under any delusion that my problems were solved. The compulsive crap wasn't going to go away, but at least I recognized it as an issue. I didn't take it as personal sabotage if Tenley didn't put something exactly where I wanted it.

At three in the afternoon on New Year's Eve, we were getting ready to go to Cassie's. The entire Inked Armor crew had been invited. So had Sarah, but she had to work. Chris had sounded pissed when we talked on the phone. Sarah hadn't been scheduled all week, except for tonight. He was catching a ride with Tenley and me.

"You need to get dressed." I zipped up the duffel bag I'd packed in case we stayed over. It had both of our stuff in it. I liked having our things mixed together, neatly. In ordered piles.

She'd been prancing around in frilly underwear and nothing else, pretending to decide what she wanted to wear to Cassie's. Only two dresses were hanging in the section of closet I'd cleared for her a while ago, so it shouldn't have been such an issue to make a choice.

"Which one?" She turned around, holding up the dresses, one black, the other a pale blue. She was still wearing the cupcake nipple shields. They were driving me fucking insane.

"You should probably stop teasing me if you don't want to keep Chris waiting. He's going to be here in ten minutes."

She ignored me. "If you pick the black one, I can wear the cupcake shoes again."

"I like the blue one." I couldn't be held responsible for my actions if she wore those shoes again.

"You're sure?"

"Positive."

She disappeared inside the closet and came out five minutes later in the black dress and the cupcake shoes. Her attempt at seduction would have worked if Chris hadn't buzzed a minute later. We took the elevator down, me carrying the duffel and her carrying a box of cupcakes she'd whipped up this morning.

Chris was waiting for us in the lobby, looking as if someone had pissed in his shoes. His eyes went wide when he saw me, his bad mood forgotten. "Holy hell, H!"

I shrugged. "Tenley cut my hair."

"I noticed. It's this I'm referring to, though." He gestured to his face. He didn't have a lot of metal above the neck, just an eyebrow ring and some spacers.

"It's no big deal."

"If you say so."

I could see him looking at me as we headed for the parking garage, but he didn't say anything else. Tenley's car was now parked in a spot across from mine. Chris called shotgun and started toward the Camaro, stopping short when he got an eyeful of the hood.

"What the fuck happened to your car?"

"It's just a couple of scratches. I'm getting it fixed." I discovered the appointment marked on the calendar this morning. Tenley had made the call earlier in the week because I hadn't been in any frame of mind to do it myself.

Chris put his hands on the hood and leaned in. "These are deep. It looks like someone tried to gouge out the paint, and there's a dent—"

When it was obvious I wasn't offering an explanation, he looked to Tenley. Her face was beet red and she was fussing with the box of cupcakes. Chris's eyes came back to me, and his eyebrow lifted in question. I shook my head, but he didn't heed the warning.

"Tee?"

"Hm?" She looked at Chris.

"What happened to H's car?"

She glanced at me, waiting for some direction. When she didn't get any, she rolled her eyes. "The scratches are from the buckle on the back of my jacket. The dent is from Hayden's knee."

It took him a couple of seconds. "Why would you—oh! No, shit! You're a little wild, aren't you, Tee?"

"We're taking my car." She spun on her heel and strode over to the Prius, flipping him the bird over her shoulder. Or maybe it was meant for me.

"Are you sure you want to do that? I mean, the Camaro's already messed-up," Chris goaded. "I can always get a ride back with Jamie and Lisa."

I punched him in the side.

"Fuck! Ow! Sorry!"

She got into the driver's seat and slammed her door. The engine turned over with a wussy little whine.

"Thanks, asshole."

"I can't believe you didn't say anything about it. When did that happen?"

"I'm not telling you anything."

"I can always ask Tee."

"Do it and I'll punch you in the balls," I threatened.

He followed me to the car. Chris grunted as I shoved him out of the way when he went for the front seat. "No shotgun for you." I slipped in beside Tenley and locked the door before he dragged me back out. He reluctantly got in the backseat, taking up most of it. Tenley didn't say a word as she put the car in gear.

"What's your car doing down here? Can't you get a ticket for that?" Chris asked.

"I get two spots. I registered her car," I said.

"Huh. Next thing you know you'll be moving in with this anal-retentive fucker, hey, Tee?"

She choked back a cough.

Sometimes Chris didn't know when to shut his damn mouth.

The trip to Cassie's took twice as long as normal because Tenley was a cautious driver.

Lisa answered the door, and once we were inside, her hands went to my face and then my hair. "Cassie said you looked different, but, wow! Nice work, Tenley."

"I couldn't let him shave his pretty head."

"Pretty?" I gaped at her. It was bad enough for her to say things like that when we were alone, but this was twice that she'd done it in front of other people.

She smirked.

"You lose any other steel?" Lisa asked, turning my chin to the side to check out my ears.

"No!" Tenley practically shouted.

Jamie laughed. "You put your foot down on that?"

"Damn right. No way was he losing any of the important stuff," Tenley replied.

The banter was light as we moved to the kitchen to help prepare dinner. Cassie was in charge tonight, and Nate wasn't allowed past the island when she was working her magic.

Tenley donned the flowery apron, shooting me a wink as she went to work on a side dish. I was prepared to step in if necessary, but she didn't need any help. Though her baked goods were amazing, based on the contents of her kitchen, I'd assumed she couldn't cook. I was wrong.

While the girls were doing their thing, Nate pulled me aside under the guise of discussing the property we were renovating come spring. The one I'd taken Tenley to on Christmas Eve. I followed him to his office and took a seat in the chair across from his. I waited for him to ask me about the session, but he pulled out the folder that contained paperwork and spreadsheets of costs and labor instead.

"Aren't you going to ask me about yesterday?"

He settled back into his chair. "I wasn't planning to. You went. You're here today and so is Tenley, which is a good sign. I'm not going to ask for information you aren't ready to give."

Well, shit. That wasn't what I expected at all. "I have another appointment set up."

"I'm glad. You liked Beatrice, then?"

At the old-fashioned name, I'd almost turned around and

walked out before I met her, picturing an old lady in her seventies who'd take one look at my arms and make all sorts of judgments. Turned out she was a tall, thin woman in her early forties with an eclectic fashion sense. She didn't give a rat's ass about the ink.

"Yeah, she's all right." I ran my palms over my thighs. They were sweaty. "Thanks for doing that for me. I know you've wanted me to go for a long time."

"I only scheduled the appointment. You're the one who had to do the hard part."

"I don't think I would have gone if it wasn't for Tenley."

"She has quite an impact on you."

"I'm in love with her." Seriously. I should have stopped at thanking him.

Nate smiled. "It's obvious she feels the same way for you."

"Yeah. For now, anyway."

"I'm not sure I understand what you mean."

The one thing I couldn't bring myself to talk about yesterday kept plaguing me today. It was the fear that had kept me paralyzed for so long. I grabbed the stress ball from his desk so I had something to do with my hands. "Officer Miller called the other day. She said they might have a lead on my parents' case."

He rolled with the change in subject. "That's a good thing?"

"I guess. It could end up being nothing." I didn't want to get my hopes up.

"The waiting must be difficult."

"Part of me doesn't want to know anymore."

Nate nodded. "You've been a long time without closure. I'm sure the possibility of having justice is just as uncomfortable as going without it."

"It's not that. Well, I guess that's part of it." I looked at him and the thing I hadn't wanted to tell anyone came out. "What if I find out it's my fault? What if I'm the reason they're dead?" That's what I feared the most.

Nate leaned back in his chair and steepled his fingers, swiveling from side to side. "Hayden, I'm going to say something, and I hope it doesn't offend you—but your parents made some unfortunate decisions when it came to you. They weren't blind to what was going on. They knew what you were doing when you were out with your friends. You didn't even try to hide it—"

"Which says what about me?"

"That you were a teenager asking his parents to notice him. They loved you; don't ever think otherwise. But they made the choice to go out on a night you were grounded, fully aware you'd take off the second they left. They did nothing to prevent you from making those decisions. You were a kid, doing what kids do when there aren't enough restrictions placed on them. You aren't responsible for their deaths, no matter what you find out."

"But I—" I dropped my gaze, squeezing the ball in my hand until it was at risk of bursting. It took me a minute to accept what Nate was saying. "I hadn't looked at it that way."

"Of course not. You're viewing the situation from the perspective of a twenty-five-year-old who's never gotten past what happened. Not that of the kid you were when it happened."

"Which is where all the therapy bullshit comes in."

What he said was true. Beatrice had said something similar, but I'd known her for all of an hour. Coming from Nate, it finally hit home.

"Can I ask you something?" Nate rested his elbows on his desk.

"Sure."

"It's about your thinking that Tenley's feelings for you are transient. I'm going to offer you my unsolicited opinion, and you can feel free to tell me to piss off or shut up at any point."

"Okay."

"Tenley has been through an unprecedented trauma and not only survived, but thrived in spite of it. Correct?"

"Yeah."

"Has what she's been through ever deterred you from loving her?"

"Absolutely not."

"So if anyone can relate to what you're feeling, it's her. She's the best kind of anomaly. You've found an incredibly strong, resilient young woman who sees exactly who you are, and she has the same in you. There is no way to predict the future. But as an outsider looking in, what you two have isn't something most people would walk away from easily."

"So I should stop worrying about things I can't control?"

"You can try. It's not always that simple."

"I'm learning that."

Nate always seemed to know when I'd reached my limit on the sharing emotional crap. He flipped open the folder with the projected costs for renovating the house and slid it toward me.

"What would you say if I wanted to fund the project on my own?" I asked.

"I'd ask why."

"Tenley stays at my place. It's not big enough to move all her stuff in." Not that I wanted her furniture in my condo. Maybe her bed. It was nice, as long as it went in the spare room. Mine was a king; it had lots of places to hold for leverage when we got down to business.

"Can you access enough equity to cover the costs?"

"I think so. I've already started looking into it."

"Have you talked to Tenley about this?"

"Not yet."

He gave me a speculative look. "Why don't you find out about the financing first? We can take it from there."

When we were finished reviewing how much money I'd need

to free up, Nate shuffled the paperwork into a folder. "Oh, one more thing."

He dropped a paper bag on the desk.

"What's this?"

"I found them in the garage."

One glance inside confirmed what I already knew: it was Tenley's shoes. "I—uh—"

"Cassie thought it would be best for me to give them to you."

"Thanks. If Tenley knew someone else found them, she'd be—"
Embarrassed as fuck. I could feel the heat in my face.

"I'm glad you want to show Tenley what you're working on." His grin told me he knew exactly what had gone down in that garage. "For future reference, there's a switch beside the door that heats the garage floor. Or next time, you could go inside and show her the whole house."

Cheeky fucking bastard.

31

TENLEY

We were just about to round up the boys for dinner when the doorbell rang.

"That's odd. I'm not expecting anyone else," Cassie said, frowning as she looked at the time. It was almost seven.

"I'll see who it is." I tossed the pot holders on the counter.

Sarah was standing on the front porch, dressed in leggings and a sweatshirt that was so big it had to belong to Chris.

"I thought you had to work!" I stepped aside to let her in out of the cold. That was when I noticed she was wearing stilettos and fake eyelashes. She didn't have a coat, either.

"I did."

"Who is it?" Cassie called from the kitchen.

"It's me!" Sarah called back.

At the sound of her voice Chris came out of the game room. "I thought I heard your voice! Come 'ere and gimme some sugar, sweetlips."

He almost knocked me over in his quest to get to Sarah. He wrapped her up in a beefy hug. With her in heels they were almost the same height, and Chris wasn't short. I averted my eyes when they started kissing in earnest. Hayden and I were probably just as bad. I guess I understood the "sweetlips" nickname better, though.

"How'd you get out of your shift?" Chris asked when he finally came up for air.

Cassie and Lisa had come from the kitchen to greet her, and Jamie appeared from the game room, pool cue still in hand.

"Sorry I'm not dressed appropriately," Sarah said, smoothing her hands over her sweatshirt.

"No one cares how you're dressed. Did you get the night off?"

"Um. Not quite," she said hesitantly. She used his shoulder as a brace so she could take her shoes off.

"Did you quit? Please tell me you quit."

Chris took her hands in his and peppered them with kisses, pulling her in the direction of the living room. He moved the cushions around when she sat down, ensuring she was comfortable.

"Sort of."

"You sort of quit?" Chris asked, brushing her hair back off her face.

"Not officially. I went in with the intention of quitting because you were right: Sienna started to offer opportunities for . . . better tips."

"Are you fucking serious?" Chris's face turned a disturbing shade of red.

"Don't worry. I said no way, which is why they cut my shifts. Anyhow, you know that creepy guy, Damien? The one you used to work for?"

"Damen?" The red in his face became more of a puce.

"Yeah. All the girls call him the Vulture." She shuddered.

"Did he give you samples?" Chris interrupted.

Sarah nodded. "He offered a bunch of times. I only took them once, and that was a long time ago. I figured out pretty fast how he and Sienna worked the other girls."

Sarah looked around, as if unsure how much she should share. Hayden and Nate had come out of the office. Hayden was standing behind my chair, and I wondered how much he'd heard. He leaned over and kissed the top of my head. Sarah's eyes stopped on Cassie and then me.

"No one here is judging you," Chris said softly.

"Okay." Sarah leaned in and kissed him quickly. "So, things got weird when I went into the club. Max wasn't on the door, and Jay, who's like Sienna's personal bodyguard, wasn't at his post, either. In fact, no one was even manning that door to her office, which never happens. God. I'm rambling like crazy, aren't I?"

She paused to suck in a breath before she barreled on. "I went in, thinking I was going to tell Sienna I was done and get my stuff from my locker, except she and that Damen guy were having it out. He was all up in her face. At first I thought maybe they were . . . well, you know . . ."

There were some coughs, and a gagging sound came from over my shoulder. Sarah made a face and shook her head. I didn't want to think about what she'd walked in on in the past.

"But they weren't. I've never seen Sienna so freaked out. I mean, she's always freaking out about something or other, but this was different. She was way worse than usual. I heard Damen say something about the police, and I figured maybe they were getting busted, and I didn't want to get stuck there—so I came straight here instead. That's why I'm dressed like this."

"You could wear a burlap sack and you'd still be gorgeous."

While they cooed at each other, I turned to Hayden. "Do you think Officer Miller might have questioned him?" I'd recognized the name immediately.

Hayden looked pensive. "She said she was following up on leads. It's possible. Probable, even." He sat on the arm of the chair. I moved over and he dropped down beside me.

That got Chris to stop manhandling Sarah. "You think Damen might have been involved in what happened to your parents?"

"I don't know." Hayden rubbed his forehead. "I was with him the night they were murdered. The police questioned him back then."

"Maybe they wanted another statement, because of the leads," I suggested.

"Yeah. That sounds logical," Hayden agreed. "Maybe I should call . . ."

"I think you should. That way you'll know if it's related either way." I didn't want this to ruin his night, but if he didn't call, he'd probably fixate on it.

Hayden pulled out his phone and dialed Miller. She didn't answer, so he left a message.

"She'll call if anything happens," I assured him.

"I know." He kissed my shoulder.

Cassie broke the tense silence when she announced dinner was ready. It was a welcome diversion from the questions Sarah's arrival had brought up. Conversation turned to lighter subjects as we made our way through the meal. After the main course, we cleaned up and returned to the comfort of the living room. Dessert would wait until later.

Hayden stayed mostly quiet, one arm draped around my shoulder, sipping scotch as I listened to accounts of previous New Year's celebrations. I could tell a lot was being censored, whether for my benefit or Cassie and Nate's, I didn't know.

"So, Tenley, I hear you went to the house Hayden and Nate are renovating. What did you think?" Cassie asked conversationally.

I nearly choked on my wine. "I, uh—the garage is very spacious."

"Mm. It is nice, especially the heated floors. What about the master bedroom? Once it's remodeled, it's going to be amazing."

"We didn't get that far," Hayden interjected.

I could see him giving her a look in my peripheral vision. Everyone else was watching the exchange with interest. Cassie might be Hayden's aunt, but they acted more like siblings. She wasn't above embarrassing him when she had the chance, and me by proxy.

"Oh? That's too bad. Well, it's lovely. Very roomy. Almost the same size as ours, isn't it, Nate? Definitely big enough for a king bed. I think that was one of the reasons Hayden was so interested in the property—that and the backyard. There's a pool and a hot tub! How much did you get to see?"

"Cassie." Nate elbowed her in the side.

"Yes, dear?"

Hayden was staring into his glass, his cheeks were pink, and he was fighting a smile.

Nate whispered something I couldn't hear, but Chris was beside him, so he caught whatever was said. "Oh, man! That's when your car got damaged? Tee, you are awesome!"

I was so mortified, I tried to use my hair as a shield.

"What happened to your car, Hayden? Is that why you're driving that hybrid thing?" Jamie asked.

"It's not a big deal. Chris is being overdramatic. It's a scratch."

"A huge scratch, and a dent," Chris corrected.

Hayden pointed a finger at him. "What happened to keeping your mouth shut?"

"What's this about?" Lisa asked me.

Sarah leaned over and Chris whispered in her ear. Her eyes went wide. "No way!"

"What?" came in a chorus from around the room, everyone looking at Chris.

"Don't even think about it," Hayden warned.

"Oh, I was meaning to ask, did you get your shoes back?" Cassie asked, smiling innocently at me.

"What do shoes have to do with anything?" Jamie asked.

I curled into Hayden's side and gulped my wine.

"Christ," Hayden muttered. "You suck, Cassie. Seriously."

"They're nice shoes. I wouldn't want Tenley to think they disappeared."

"I'm getting you back for this," Hayden said to Cassie.

"You just try, little man. Watch what happens," she teased.

"You wait for it."

"Who's ready for dessert?" I asked, but everyone ignored me. I drained my glass.

"You know, there's an extra spot in our garage. Since you're planning to stay the night, you could always park your car in there, Tenley," Cassie said, her mischievous smile still in place.

Chris snickered.

Hayden shook his head. "You asked for it." He looked at Nate, who was wore a horrified expression. He shook his head minutely at Hayden, eyes darting to Cassie and then back. "Nate, do you still want help installing that swing in your bedroom? I think we've got the right bolts this time." Hayden grinned with satisfaction as Cassie's mouth dropped open.

"Why would Nate want a swing— Oh." I watched the color rise in Cassie's cheeks and drain from Nate's face.

Cassie smacked Nate's arm. "You had *Hayden* help you?"

"He was supposed to keep his trap shut. Besides, he's the only person I know who'd have a clue how to install something like that."

I gawked at Hayden.

"It's the same principle as rock-climbing gear, kitten," he explained.

I shot up out of the chair, empty glass in hand. I had no interest in hearing any more. "I need a refill."

"Me, too!" Lisa was right on my heels.

Everyone slept in the following day. Even then, we were slow to get moving. Hayden would have kept me in bed all day, testing how quietly I could come, if Chris hadn't banged on the door around noon.

"Brunch'll be ready in ten," he shouted.

"Shit." Hayden had been in the middle of persuading me I needed another round. "We'll be down in five," he called back.

The knob rattled. "Why's the door locked?" Chris yelled, as if we couldn't hear him through a wooden panel.

"I said we'd be down in five," Hayden growled.

Laughter filtered through the door, growing fainter as Chris moved down the hall and did the same thing to Lisa and Jamie.

"I guess we'll have to pick up where we left off when we get home," Hayden said irritably, rolling off me.

A year ago, I would never have imagined my life being so completely altered again. Nor would I have entertained the possibility of finding someone like Hayden. We spent the afternoon watching mindless TV in Cassie's living room, nursing mild hangovers. Only after dusk fell did we head for home.

We were about two blocks away when I saw the flash of blue and red lights in the distance. It looked like several sets; must have been an accident. Hayden went down the next side street, to my relief. I had no desire to put a damper on what had been a good day for both of us.

"I don't know what's going on up there," Hayden said, "so I'm going to hit the rear entrance of the parking garage."

He made a right, but then slowed down and came to a stop.

The street ahead was barricaded by a police car, the lights flashing their silent warning.

"What the hell is going on?" he grumbled, and backed up.

He circled the block; every road leading to his condo was blocked off. When he tried to go to the back of Serendipity, it was the same thing.

We were two blocks away from Inked Armor when Hayden pulled over, about fifty feet back from the wall of police cars. He palmed his phone.

"Shit. I missed a bunch of calls."

To avoid distraction he'd put his phone away last night not long after he'd called Officer Miller. He hadn't looked at it since. Putting it on speakerphone, he listened to the messages.

The voice mails were from Officer Miller, except for the last one. Her first message was a calm reassurance that they were checking into leads and she would call with any news. The second requested Hayden's location. The third was much less composed, asking for a return call ASAP. That was several hours ago. The last message was from Sienna. Hayden's finger hovered over the delete button until her frantic, high-pitched voice came through.

"Hayden? Goddamnit. Fucking voice mail. Listen, honey, I didn't know. Whatever Damen tells you, whatever he says, *I didn't know*. This is so fucked up. I'm sorry and I never meant to screw with you. That cocksucker is going to take me down with him. I know I've been a real bitch to you over the years, but I promise if I'd known, I would have done . . . shit . . . I don't know. Something. I'm sorry." By the end of the message, Sienna was crying.

Hayden played the message again. "Does that sound like I think it does?" He was frighteningly quiet.

"You need to call Miller back."

"Does it?"

"I don't know—"

"Because if I'm hearing this right, Damen has something to do with my parents being dead." Hayden looked at me with such betrayal in his eyes.

"This isn't your fault."

"I know. I was seventeen. I was just a kid." The words came out, but with no inflection or feeling behind them.

He turned off the car and unbuckled his seat belt. The cold air rushed in when he opened the door and stepped out in the dark winter night.

"I don't think this is a good idea," I said.

He ignored me and strode down the street toward the barricade, his phone to his ear. I had to run to keep up with him.

"I'm down the street from my condo. Everything's blocked off by police." After a short pause he continued, "I can almost see it from here."

Police lined the sidewalk, keeping the crowd that had gathered at bay. I looked beyond them, in the direction Hayden's gaze had gone. Squinting past the flash of lights, I saw that something sparkled on the sidewalk.

Where the windows in Inked Armor used to be were black, gaping holes. A figure was hoisted up off the asphalt by a uniformed officer. The light from the streetlamp above illuminated his features as he was hauled off to an unmarked police car.

"Motherfucker," Hayden breathed. "I know that guy."

32

HAYDEN

For the fourth time in less than two weeks, I found myself back at the police station. Miller had taken us there in her cruiser because I wasn't in any state to drive. This night was turning out to be the mindfuck of a lifetime.

Tenley was with me when I identified Damen and Brett in two separate lineups. Brett was just as I remembered him, only older and haggard. He was short and already on the road to balding. His face was pockmarked. His teeth were fucked. But that's what happened with an unchecked meth habit. It also made a person psychotic enough to rob a house with a stolen loaded weapon without checking to make sure the inhabitants weren't home.

Damen didn't look much better and it was impossible to feel bad for him. Though Brett had pulled the trigger, Damen had been the spoke in the wheel. He'd provided the drugs, he'd planted the idea, and he'd unwittingly supplied the weapon. But the part that was messing with me most was that I'd worked for him for years and never known. It was the ultimate duplicity.

As I sat in Miller's office, I briefly wondered what had happened to Sienna. It would be karmic if Damen ratted her out. All her years of pushing drugs on her dancers until they were forced to solicit was criminal. What made it unconscionable was that she'd been through it. She knew what it was like to have no choices, yet still she screwed over the people who trusted her.

Miller's partner, Duggan, was perched on the edge of her desk. He was calm and collected, but Miller looked just as antsy as I felt.

"Can I get you some coffee?" Duggan took a sip from his grungy mug.

"Water would be good, please."

My throat was so dry, I was having a hard time swallowing. I was on the verge of panic; Tenley was the only thing keeping me together. She wanted to call Cassie and Nate on the way to the station, but I'd asked her to wait. It would have been too much like the first time I was here. I kept looking over my shoulder, waiting for Cross to show up and interrogate me again. It turned out I didn't have anything to worry about.

"Cross has been taken into custody," Miller said, rearranging the pens on her desk until they formed a straight line.

I stared at her.

"I wanted to tell you earlier. I know how hard this has been on you—"

"Why?" I finally asked when the short between my brain and my mouth fixed itself. "Brett Wilson is Cross's half brother. The abridged version is that he covered up the murder to protect him."

"Sonofabitch."

"That about sums up my reaction," said Duggan.

Miller gave him a look.

I rubbed my temples, where the dull throb had instantly

become a pounding roar. The revelation explained a lot and nothing at the same time.

"What's the unabridged version?" I asked, uncertain if I could
handle any more. I'd expected to feel relief in finding out the
truth, but all it did was raise more questions.

"Brett was a troubled kid. He had some problems when he was
younger, but because Cross was on the force, it afforded him some
leeway. Brett turned eighteen two weeks before the homicide."

"You mean before he murdered my parents?"

Tenley slipped her hand under mine. I squeezed.

"Are you sure you want me to go on?" At my nod, Miller continued, "Brett alleged he made two calls that night. The first was
to Damen, the second to his brother. Around the same time, a call
came through dispatch. Cross was the first to arrive on the scene.
From what we understand, he either misfiled or tampered with
the evidence, making most of it inadmissible. Some of the reports
didn't match up. At the time it looked like Cross's partner had
been the problem, but we know now that Cross had orchestrated
it to look that way. The painting was the one thing he wasn't able
to dispose of. It was reported stolen. We believe he hid it with the
intention of going back to dispose of it later. That didn't happen,
though. Lab reports confirm both his fingerprints and Brett's were
on it."

It took me a minute to process it all as the pieces fell into
place. "Cross couldn't go after Damen, though, could he?"

"Not unless he wanted to implicate himself," Duggan said.

"Are they going to jail?" I asked.

"There will be a trial," Miller said.

"Will I have to testify?"

"Your testimony will be helpful to the case."

Reliving it all over again would suck—but I didn't want any of
them to get less time than they deserved.

*   *   *

In late February the case went to trial. Things moved a lot faster than I expected them to, which was both a relief and a challenge.

Tenley adjusted my tie and smoothed the lapels of my suit jacket. "I think we're ready."

I hugged her hard. "Whatever you hear today, please remember all of this happened a long time ago."

"And I want you to remember that whatever comes out during the trial isn't going to change anything. I'm still going to be here, trying to remember not to leave my panties on the closet floor."

I smiled into her shoulder. "I love you."

"I love you, too. Never doubt that." She took my hand and opened the door to the courtroom.

I could have sat through the whole trial and listened to Brett and Damen and Cross give their versions of events, but it wouldn't change the outcome. The only thing I wanted at this point was justice, in the form of incarceration. It was the reason I was taking the stand.

My anxiety ratcheted up as we were escorted to the front of the room. I recognized a lot of faces: girls who worked at The Dollhouse and managed to move on, others who hadn't. Some of Damen's employees were among them, as well. They all sat together, united in their stand against the people who had wronged them.

Sienna sat in the second row on the opposite side of the courtroom. She was hard to miss in the orange jumpsuit. She looked pitifully fragile and small. The scar on her face was more noticeable without makeup. It was likely orchestrated to make people feel sorry for her. She looked at me when I passed, her regret obvious. Damen had knocked her off her pedestal and then some. Beyond being subpoenaed to testify for this case, she was also up on myriad other charges. No matter how much she plea-bargained, she would do time for her offenses. I almost felt sorry for her. In her own fucked-up way, she'd cared about me once, but she'd never been what I needed.

I was the only person to take the stand. Even though I'd been given an idea as to what I might be asked, the questions were still painful to answer. I kept my focus on the front row, where my family was. Cassie, Nate, Chris, Lisa, Jamie, and Sarah were all there, a wall of solidarity and support. In the middle was Tenley. She was the reason I got through it—because once it was over, I had someone worth moving on for.

I didn't go back to the courtroom after that. There was no need. While the trial lasted weeks, the jury was quick to reach a verdict. All three of them got time behind bars.

33

TENLEY

Hayden looked up from his station when I entered the shop. "Give me a few. Nate and I are almost done."

"As in *done* done?" I leaned over the counter where Lisa was, dropped my purse on the floor, and gave her a one-armed hug.

"You need to check it out," Lisa said. "Cassie's going to freak when she sees it."

As I went to take a peek, Nate put up a hand to stop me, and Hayden batted it down. "I'm shading in her face, you stupid fuck—don't move."

"You're not even working on this arm."

"Doesn't matter. You move one appendage, the rest of your upper body shifts." Hayden's eyes stayed on the design but he pointed right at me. "You. Stay where you are until I'm finished."

I took a step back. "Sorry, cupcake."

The tattoo machine lifted from Nate's arm as Hayden raised his head to glare at me.

Chris, who had been working on a client of his own, stopped what he was doing. "Did I hear that right? Did Tee just call you 'cupcake'?"

Lisa stifled a laugh. I went behind the counter and used her as a barricade.

"I thought we agreed you'd keep that to yourself," Hayden said.

"It was a slip." Sort of.

"You'd better watch it. No one's going to be around later to save your ass." He went back to tattooing Nate's arm.

"Promises, promises."

I could see him smiling even though his head was down. His hair had grown out some since the trial ended. It was almost in his face again, as it had been when I'd first met him. I liked it a little longer, so he hadn't gotten it cut.

He took his time with the last few lines of ink. After he put the machine down, he spent longer than necessary checking it over. "All right. You're good. I'll want to have a look at it in a week or two in case it needs a touch-up, but we're done for now." Hayden's satisfaction was evident.

Nate pushed up out of the chair. He was wearing a thin wife-beater; his button-down shirt and tie hung neatly on a hook by Hayden's station. The first thing I noticed—but tried not to—was the outline of a steel ring at his left pec.

"Is that—"

"A nipple ring?" Lisa finished. "I did that for Cassie's birthday a few years back."

"Those two are kinda freaky, aren't they?"

"You don't know the half of it." Her grin said it all.

I held up a hand to stop her. I had no desire to hypothesize about any other metal Nate might have. "And I'm good with that."

Nate and Hayden had gone to the three-way mirror to check out the finished ink.

"When's your next session?" Lisa pulled at the neck of my off-the-shoulder shirt, peeking down my back at the mostly finished design.

"I have no idea."

I'd been in Hayden's chair four times in the past eight weeks; two more sessions and I'd be done. He was taking his sweet time with the shading because it needed to be perfect, and he still didn't want to work on me for longer than two hours.

I had a feeling he was prolonging it intentionally. It was the place Hayden felt most comfortable sharing what happened during his appointments with Beatrice, so I wasn't in a rush to lose the time with him. With only two sessions left, I worried how we would achieve the same connection elsewhere.

Lisa clicked the mouse and pulled up Hayden's schedule. "How's next Friday night work for you? He's got two hours blocked off at the end for no reason I can see."

"That'll be two weeks since the last session, which is perfect. He has no reason to say no." Although he was pretty damn good at coming up with one if he wanted to.

Lisa slotted me in.

"All right, girls. Hayden gives the okay to look," Nate called out.

He angled his arm to give us an unobstructed view of the art. The likeness to Cassie was remarkable. The pinup version of her was both demure and sexy.

"It's gorgeous. Cassie's going to love it," Lisa said.

Nate smirked. "I'm banking on that. It's been a pain in the ass keeping it bandaged so she can't see it. I woke up twice last week to her sneaking a look in the middle of the night."

"What a shocker," Hayden said drily. "Let's cover that up. No friction for at least a few days, Nate. I don't want to have a two-hour touch-up session."

"I'll tell Cassie to be gentle."

"Dude, really? Don't you have a censor?"

"Have you taken Tenley back to see the house yet, or are you just partial to the garage?" Nate needled him.

Hayden turned around, ready to fire off another dig. The color of my face was likely the reason he didn't.

Nate dropped back into the chair. "By the way, *if* you were thinking to take Tenley there to see it, tonight or tomorrow would probably be good."

Hayden raised a brow but didn't look at Nate. "Yeah?"

"Yeah." Nate nodded, watching Hayden smooth the cellophane over the tattoo and secure it with medical tape.

Obviously something was going on, but whatever it was, neither of them seemed inclined to talk about it while Lisa and I were hovering over them. I was glad Hayden and Nate had grown closer over the past months, but I didn't like not being in the loop.

"So," Nate said as he pushed his arm carefully through his sleeve, "when is Jamie starting your pinup?"

"Uh . . . I, uh—we haven't talked about it—" Hayden stammered.

Lisa coughed to cover an expletive.

"Pinup?" I asked.

"Oh, shit," Nate said quietly.

"Would someone care to share?" I crossed my arms over my chest and waited.

Lisa was the one who answered. "Hayden's been toying with the idea of getting another tattoo for a while. He has a design in mind, but he and Jamie are still working on placement, so nothing's come of it yet."

"Why haven't I seen it?" I asked.

This was the second time I felt that I was missing something since I'd come into the shop. Even Lisa knew about the prospective tattoo.

Hayden rocked back on his heels. "I wanted it to be perfect before I showed it to you."

"Is it perfect now?"

"Not quite, but I have a copy in my filing cabinet at home. You can have a look later."

"Sure." I backed off, aware there was more to this with the way Lisa was twirling the end of her hair and Nate was overly interested in his tie.

Nate tried to pay Hayden, but he refused to take the money. It was after nine by the time Hayden finished cleaning up his station. His first client the next day required one of the private rooms, so he took me with him to set up. I sat down in the tattoo chair and played with the recline lever while Hayden gathered ink and the various implements required for the session.

"So, I was thinking." He dropped down on the stool beside me. "Maybe you want to go look at the house tonight?"

"So I can see the inside this time?" Cassie hadn't stopped with the little barbs about that.

"That's what I had planned."

"I'd like that."

"Though if you want to spend a little extra time in the garage, I wouldn't be opposed." He rubbed at his bottom lip, trying to hide his smile.

"Of course you wouldn't." I grabbed him by the shirt, pulling him closer, and nipped at his lip. "I know you're keeping something from me."

He swung one leg over and straddled the chair, facing me. "You are far too clever for your own good. Haven't you ever heard of a surprise?"

"I don't like that everyone is in on it but me. I'm supposed to be your person."

"You are my person."

He sat down on my thighs, bracing his weight on the backrest. His head dipped down, his teeth skimmed my collarbone. I felt his erection against my stomach. I couldn't do anything but squirm since he was sitting on my legs.

"Have you ever fucked in here?" I used the profanity on purpose. I'd discovered it turned Hayden on because I used it so rarely.

"No." He shifted, nudging my legs apart with his knee.

"No?" Every time I was in his chair, I wanted to take off all my clothes and get him inside me.

He shook his head while he settled between my thighs.

"Would you fuck me here?"

He stopped with the kissing and lifted his head to look me straight in the eye. "I don't fuck you, Tenley. I have sex with you. Sometimes I even make love to you, but we don't fuck."

I stared at him in open disbelief. That was completely untrue. On many occasions sheer need had superseded either of our attempts for sweet and gentle. And that didn't bother me in the slightest.

I was about to call him out on it, but pointing out that he could love me and fuck me at the same time wouldn't help my current plan. I was horny. He'd been so tired the last couple of nights, he'd passed out on the couch as soon as he got home from work. And my courses and my thesis were demanding a lot of my attention. We hadn't had sex in days.

"Fine. Will you have sex with me here?"

"Right now?" his voice cracked.

"We could lock the door."

"No." His grip on the backrest tightened. "Not with Chris and Jamie and Lisa in the next room."

"If we were all alone, would you then?" I ran my hands down his back and slid them under the waist of his jeans. He was commando.

His forehead dropped against my shoulder. "Fuck, Tenley. Why are you pulling this shit now?" His voice was muffled by my hair.

"Because you're awake and coherent and not at risk of falling asleep on me. It's been days. I miss you."

He lifted his head and frowned. "How long?"

"Too long," I said, working to control my frustration. My nails dug into his ass and his muscles flexed under my fingers. I missed more than just the sex, though. I missed the feel of his body, the way he enveloped me, consumed me. I missed the connection we shared when he was inside me, both physically and emotionally. I craved it. Needed it.

I could see him backtracking through time in his head, trying to remember the last time we had sex. His expression changed from doubtful to penitent. "Let me show you the house first; then I'll make up for neglecting you."

With a wicked grin, he unhooked my legs from his waist and pushed out of the chair. Holding out a hand, he helped me up and pulled me close. "Just so you know, I've wanted to do you in that chair ever since I put the cupcake on you. So be prepared for me to follow through on that as soon as I have the chance."

When we arrived at the house, several sets of tire tracks were in the snow on the driveway. "It looks like someone's been here recently," I observed.

"We decided to start renovations early."

He hit a button on the windshield visor and the garage door trundled open. Hayden parked inside and we got out of the car.

"It's warm in here," I said.

"The floors are heated. I didn't know that last time."

He flashed a sheepish grin and crossed over to a set of stairs leading to a door. He grabbed my hand and led me into the house, flicking on lights as we walked down a short, recently painted hall.

More lights came on when we reached another doorway. This one opened into an expanse of open space.

I surveyed the state-of-the-art kitchen. "I thought you said this place needed to be renovated."

"It did."

"How much work did it need?" I kicked off my shoes so I wouldn't scuff the hardwood.

"Enough."

I glanced at him. He was chewing on his lip, even though the viper bites were gone. He only did that when he was anxious or interested in sex.

"Come on"—he pulled me forward—"there's more to see."

I bit my tongue against the other questions I wanted to ask; such as, why was this the first I'd heard about the "early start" to the project? The main floor was open concept with nine-foot ceilings, painted in neutral tones. A formal dining space was carved out beyond the kitchen, with an ornate chandelier. The living room was massive, with clean lines and pale walls. It reminded me of Hayden's condo, except three times the size, with architectural embellishments.

When we finished the tour of the main floor, Hayden took me upstairs. There were four bedrooms. He saved the master for last: vaulted ceilings, huge floor-to-ceiling windows, and even a reading nook.

"This is incredible." I walked around the perimeter. Like every other room, the walls were neutral. These were a soft, pale gray.

"When did you start all this?"

"Mid-January."

I spun around. "You've been keeping this from me for two months?"

"Nate suggested we get started on the interior, so all that would be left in the spring was landscaping and exterior painting.

I needed a distraction from the trial. And I wanted to surprise you."

"Why?"

"I funded all of the renovations. I want to buy Nate out."

"I thought you were going to flip it."

He was so nervous; his eyes kept darting away. "That was the original plan."

"Why did the plan change?"

"You don't like the house?" He looked almost hurt. I was getting more confused by the minute.

"Of course I like it. It's beautiful. I just don't understand when you changed your mind, and why I'm only hearing about it now."

He looked up at the beautiful ceiling medallion. "I like the layout of the house, and this room. It's a lot of space for one person, though." He pushed away from the door and took a couple of steps toward me. "It's a little closer to Northwestern, too."

My heart did a little leap. "That's true."

"The house should be ready within the next few weeks." He tucked my hair behind my ear. "It might not feel like too much space if there were two people living here. And TK, of course."

"Are you asking me to move in with you?" I was almost positive I had to be misunderstanding him.

He shoved his hands in his pockets. "Is it too soon to be asking?"

"I don't know if I can be as tidy as you."

He smiled. "I wouldn't expect you to be."

"I'd try, though," I said, unable to contain my excitement.

"This house is huge. You can have a room where you leave shit lying all over the place, if you want." He hooked a finger in my belt loop and pulled me closer.

"Don't promise something like that if you can't follow through," I teased.

"You can keep the door closed. I'll never see it."

"That might work." I laughed and looked around the bedroom, imagining it as ours. The magnitude of what he'd done started to sink in. All the late nights and the passing out on the couch had been because of this. He'd been doing this for us.

His arm wound around my waist. "So you'll move in here with me?"

"I pretty much live with you already."

"But you still have the apartment."

"I haven't slept there in months." I rose up on my toes to kiss him. "I'll give Cassie my notice tomorrow."

34

HAYDEN

I hung my keys beside Tenley's in the new house and headed for the kitchen. If I was lucky she would be pulling her domestic routine, outfitted in one of her aprons and little else. It was sexy as fuck. Much to my disappointment, she was nowhere to be found.

"Tenley?"

I dropped the bag on the counter and unloaded the groceries. I called a second time but she still didn't answer. I rearranged all the misplaced items in the fridge and the cupboards, looking over my shoulder every so often to make sure I didn't get caught. I was working on my organization problem, but I was under no illusion I'd ever be cured of it. So long as it didn't impede my ability to function or get inside Tenley, I figured it was okay.

I searched the rest of the main floor and came up empty. Halfway up the stairs, I caught the sound of her voice. She was singing. She had to be unpacking.

I found her in the spare bedroom she'd claimed as her office.

The den of disorganization. She was wearing earphones and had on '80s music-video attire: short shorts and leg warmers. Her shirt, which was virtually transparent, hung off one shoulder. She wasn't wearing a bra. The white, gauzy fabric gave me a hazy view of her entire tattoo. If I looked hard enough, I could make out the six-inch block in the middle of the right wing that hadn't been shaded yet.

Our last session was scheduled for later this evening. I'd pushed it back twice now. We'd moved into the new house. Everything but this room was organized. Tenley had a handle on her studies. I had no more valid excuses. Tenley's patience with me was running out. I was stalling for no reason other than I didn't want to be done. But I was still going to try to put it off again.

Tenley shook her ass as she shelved books, arranging them with no plan I could see. But then, she subscribed to the Dewey decimal system rather than the Hayden Stryker System of organizing books. I leaned against the doorjamb and watched. It was pretty damn entertaining, even though I wanted to get in there and move everything around. There were no straight lines, no continuity. It was mayhem. Or maybe I was being a little overdramatic. It happened occasionally.

When the box was empty, she broke it down and tossed it in the pile of discarded cardboard. The view as she bent over was stellar. I had the better part of an hour before I had to be at work; that was plenty of time to get into those shorts of hers.

Tenley turned around with a gasp, yanking out one of the earbuds. "You scared me!"

"Sorry." Not even a little bit.

Her hands went to her hips. "How long have you been standing there?"

"Long enough." I rubbed my mouth to hide my smile. "I like your rendition of that song way better than the original."

"Ha-ha. You're such a comedian." Her cheeks were pink.

"I'm serious." Her voice wasn't half-bad and she knew it. She was always singing along in the car.

She ignored the comment and turned back to the pile of boxes. "What time is it?"

"It's just after eleven."

"What? I didn't realize I'd been at this so long. I need to change." She abandoned the box and tried to get past me.

I snaked an arm around her waist to stop her. "Where do you need to be?" Nothing was on the calendar, and she didn't teach or have classes today.

"I have a meeting with my group. We scheduled it yesterday. I forgot to tell you last night."

Last night I'd been snooping around in some of her boxes. I found her porn stash. It was eye-opening; a lot of the stuff in there I hadn't expected. After she got over her unnecessary embarrassment, I kept her pretty well occupied. I could see how she might have forgotten to tell me about the meeting.

"With the Nerd Herd?"

"Don't call them that," she said, smiling.

"What time do you have to leave?"

"I don't. They're coming here."

"Here? To our place?" She tried to worm her way out of my grip, but I wouldn't let her get away.

"I thought that would be okay. It's more convenient than meeting on campus."

"But I have to go to Inked Armor." During the last group project, that Ian fucker weaseled his way back into her group. The rest of those guys were harmless nerds, but Ian thought he was slick. He was always trying to buddy up to me, telling me what a great girl Tenley was. As if I didn't already fucking know.

She frowned. "We don't need a chaperone. We're working on a project, not throwing a keg party."

"I know that."

She sighed. "They're supposed to be here in half an hour. Do I need to call Patrick and ask if we can go to his place?"

"That's not necessary. Is that dickwad Ian still in your group?"

Tenley's brow lifted. "He's not interested in me."

"Yes. He is."

"He knows I live with you."

"That just makes you more of a challenge."

"He's got a girlfriend."

"Only because you're not available."

She rolled her eyes and pushed on my chest. "He's not in our group anyway, so it doesn't matter."

"Why didn't you say that in the first place?"

"Because you're impossible. Let me go. I need to shower before they get here."

I let her go. But I caught her when she was getting out of the shower and took advantage of her nakedness. She was still getting dressed when her group arrived, so I greeted them. Just as I'd planned. There was a new girl in place of Ian. She seemed a little nervous, but I was happy to see another female in the group. I set them up in the living room and even brought them drinks like a good host. When Tenley came downstairs, she was wearing her STRYKER hoodie and a pair of jeans.

"I gotta run." I pulled her in for a kiss. She kept her lips together, even when I stroked the seam with my tongue.

She disengaged, her flush showing her embarrassment. "I'll be at the shop around seven."

Shit. I'd meant to broach the subject earlier, before I delayed Tenley with the postshower sex.

I glanced at the Nerd Herd plus New Girl. It might work to my advantage to have them here. Tenley wasn't as likely to get upset with me in front of other people. "About that—"

She gave her head a vehement shake. "Oh, no. Nope. No way."

Or maybe she wouldn't care if she had company. "But I—"

"I'll be right back, make yourselves comfortable." She flashed her group a forced smile and grabbed my hand, hauling me out of the room. She stopped once we were in the kitchen, where we'd be out of earshot and their line of view.

"You've already rescheduled me twice; you're not doing it again."

"But I have this client who needs—"

"You have lots of clients who need things from you, and I'm one of them. I've waited long enough. I want this piece finished, Hayden."

"I get that. It's just . . ." I had no justifiable reason for holding off.

"First you get all territorial about my group coming over, and now you want to cancel my session again. What's this really about?" She cocked her head and waited.

I clearly wasn't getting out of an explanation. I stared at the floor and nudged her toe with mine. "I don't want this to be the last session."

Tenley's arms went around my neck and her cheek rested against my chest. "Finishing the tattoo doesn't mean it's the last time I'll be in your chair."

"I know."

Rationally speaking, I understood that. But finishing a tattoo this extensive brought with it a whole barrage of emotions. Not just for Tenley, but for me as well. That was the part I struggled with most because I'd never felt this way about anyone else before. I'd experienced the post-ink high and the comedown many times. Sometimes the positives outweighed the negatives. Not always, though. That was part of the reason I kept postponing—unsure not only of how Tenley would handle the last session, but how I would.

"Then why keep putting me off?"

"I just want this to be good for you."

"It will be." She sounded so certain.

There was no backing out now. Before the day was over, Tenley's tattoo would be complete.

I had a full lineup of clients scheduled for the day. The guy before Tenley showed up late and needed more breaks than I'd anticipated, which meant Tenley had to wait. She didn't look happy about it, likely worried I would use it as another reason to postpone the final session.

She and Lisa went over to Serendipity to visit with Cassie and grab coffees. Tenley hadn't resumed her shifts there after she came back from Arden Hills since she didn't need the money. The job had been a way to fill her time. It had become unnecessary because she wasn't running from her pain anymore.

It was after eight by the time I finished with my client. Lisa, Jamie, and Chris were all leaving, so Tenley and I would have the shop to ourselves. The session would only last a couple of hours if I took my time and dragged it out, which I planned to do.

Even though we were alone, I locked us in the private room and busied myself with checking the tray of supplies. It was redundant. I'd prepared everything early in the afternoon to get into the right frame of mind.

Things had been so good between us recently. Aside from my display of overt possessiveness this morning, there hadn't been any drama. I wasn't losing my shit over towels that weren't perfectly lined up. She was managing school well; her new adviser was much easier to work with. Calder had lost his tenure when the video was "accidentally" leaked online and then intentionally sent to the dean. I didn't want anything to mess up the balance we'd finally established.

I'd mulled over my reaction this morning, trying to figure out what my problem was, beyond the obvious. I still hadn't come up with anything completely rational.

Tenley sat down in the chair, fully dressed. Usually she got mostly naked as soon as I locked the door.

"You're going to have to take that off if I'm going to get started." I motioned to the hoodie.

"I have a question first."

"Fire away." I started assembling the tattoo machine.

"Why are you so worried about this being the last session?"

"We talked about this earlier." I almost fumbled with the needle, giving away my nerves. Tenley was perceptive. I couldn't hide much from her.

She pulled her hoodie over her head, a well-orchestrated move to assure me that if I answered her question truthfully, more clothes would come off. She was wearing a T-shirt underneath that conformed to her curves. "Tell me again. And I already know you like having me in your chair. That's a given."

"Technically, I've never *had* you in my chair, but I suppose we could rectify that. . . ." I put down the machine and stripped off my gloves. I was in full avoidance mode.

"You've used sex as a distraction once today. You don't get to do it again."

"I thought there was a twice-a-day limit." I leaned in to kiss her, but she turned her head to the side. I bit her neck instead.

"Answer the question." She sounded just the tiniest bit breathy.

"I already did." I sucked on the skin. She tasted good, as usual.

"You can't regurgitate the same response from this morning. After what you pulled, do you think I'm going to fall for it? Give me some credit."

I hadn't expected the diversionary tactic to work, but at least I'd tried. I sat back down in my chair and rolled in close. I couldn't start the session with this tension between us. It wasn't fair to Tenley.

"I'm nervous."

"About how I'm going to react to finishing the tattoo? I'm ready for this."

She hadn't been visibly upset after a session in a long time. In fact, there'd been a peacefulness about her that I envied as we got closer to the end. I was the one who was having a hard time with it. I traced the veins in the back of her hand with my finger, needing somewhere to focus.

"It's not so much about you as it is about me." After a long pause I looked up, meeting her questioning gaze. "I don't want to lose this."

"This? Do you mean what we have when we're here?" She flipped her hand over and laced our fingers together.

"It's stupid. I'm being an idiot."

"No, you're not." She kissed the back of my hand. "We probably should have talked about this before now. The only reason I've let you postpone this session twice already is because I like how connected I feel to you when we're in here."

I shouldn't have been surprised she was on to me, or that we shared the same fears. "I'm sorry I kept putting you off."

"I figured you had your reasons." She shifted and I parted my legs so hers could fit between them. The fingers that weren't already twined with mine pushed through my hair. Her palm came to rest on the back of my neck. "This tattoo isn't a representation of loss anymore, Hayden. It started out that way, but time has changed that. You've changed that. This isn't an ending. It's like closing the circle, bringing us back where we started."

"I'm just worried that finishing the tattoo will mean you're finished with me."

She stroked my cheek with her thumb. "That's not going to happen. You're far too important for me to walk away from, Hayden."

I caught her hand and brought it to my lips. Even though they were just words, it was the reassurance I needed. "I love you."

"I know. I love you, too. Now let's finish what we started." She leaned back and waited.

I wanted to prolong every part of this process, knowing this first for her, and me, wasn't one we could re-create.

I took my time removing her shirt, skimming the delicate cage of ribs. The red bra with black polka dots and the lacy ruffle at the top came into view. I could guarantee she had on the matching panties. She was the life-size version of the outline Jamie had put on my forearm a week ago.

I didn't trust myself to undress her any further without taking things too far, so I snapped on a pair of gloves while she unclasped her bra. She was wearing the cupcake nipple shields again. She smiled innocently, waiting for me to stop staring at her breasts and get with the program.

"You need to turn around, kitten," I said to her chest. "Please."

Sessions with Tenley had become like foreplay and were almost as intimate. With the two-hour limit she wasn't put out of commission, and the connection carried over into the bedroom later. The sex was always mind-blowing. Another reason I'd wanted to postpone the final session.

She turned around and straddled the chair, allowing my brain to function again.

The area I was working on tonight was small, only about six inches high by eight inches wide. "Ready?"

"For you? Always." Tenley's coy grin alleviated some of the tension.

I started with the golds and silvers, then moved on to the reds and blues in the flames licking up the underside of the wings. I choose this section because it represented the light and dark equally. For me, she would always be the light in my darkness.

Tenley's hand rested on my knee as I shaded in the wing. She didn't complain when I went over her ribs or hit spots that were inevitably tender. She'd been like that for almost every session. Even when I went over the scarred parts, the only sound she would make was one of relief when the needle lifted from her skin and I wiped away the residual ink. The sole sign that she was in pain came from the tension in her body.

Our conversation was light, nothing like that of some of the earlier sessions, which had been full of difficult revelations.

This one was over too quickly.

When I finished, I looked over the entire piece, searching for spots that needed touching up. There weren't any. I'd been meticulous. I turned off the tattoo machine and set it down. Then I wiped the ink with a fresh cloth, admiring the completed piece for the first time.

"It's done."

Her smile was full of warm satisfaction. "I want to see."

I helped her out of the chair and led her to the three-way mirror, angling it so she didn't have to crane her neck. The reds and blues and smoky shades of purple at the base of the wings presented a striking contrast against the ethereal golds and silver at her shoulders. I doubted I would ever put anything so darkly beautiful on another person.

Her fingers trailed along the tip of the wing. She looked like an angel on fire.

"It's so gorgeous," she said softly.

"You make it that way."

Tears slid down her cheeks as she inspected the art. The emotions and anticipation that came with finishing a piece of this magnitude warranted them. I'd always looked at body art as a way to exorcise demons, but it wasn't about that at all. It was a push and pull; letting go and holding on at the same time. She wore her loss in an armor of ink, just as I did.

I covered the ink with a protective layer of cellophane, then stripped off my gloves and wiped away her tears.

Her arms came around my neck. Still in front of the three-way mirror, the reflection gave me the perfect view of her fresh ink from several viewpoints.

"Thank you for finishing this and for agreeing to be my artist in the first place."

"Like there was ever any other option?" I traced the edge of the tattoo. "As soon as this is healed, I want Lisa to take another picture."

Tenley's fingers traveled down my chest. "Do I need to remind you that I live with you? Don't you think you'll see enough of it?"

"There is no such thing as enough when it comes to you."

"I know exactly what you mean."

Her palms slid under my shirt and up my sides. I didn't stop her when she pulled the shirt over my head and discarded it on the floor. I also didn't resist when she grabbed me by the belt buckle and dragged me toward the tattoo chair. Tenley ripped my belt from the loops and popped the button on my fly.

Her leggings were next. "I love these things. No zippers or buttons to mess with," I said.

She laughed as I gave one firm tug and down they came. I dropped into the tattoo chair with my jeans pooled around my knees and took half a second to appreciate that she was, in fact, wearing the matching panties to the sexy bra she'd been sporting.

I hooked my thumbs into the waistband and pulled them down, kissing my way from her navel to the crest of her pelvis. Her hands went to my hair as they always did and guided my mouth lower. She rarely left any question as to what she wanted.

I gave her a little lick before I peeked up at her. "Maybe I should take you home."

Her eyes narrowed in a sexy, sinister way. "Like hell."

She was going to be a firecracker tonight, if I let her. She let go of my hair and pushed on my shoulders until I was reclined in the chair, then climbed up to straddle me. Hot and wet met hard and ready. I grabbed her hips and kept her from moving.

"Hayden," she groaned.

Her ponytail flared out over her shoulder, the nipple shield barely visible through the cascade. She was my ultimate temptation, gorgeous and willing and so full of fire. It would be so easy to just slip inside, but I slowed things down.

"I *need* you. Please." She kissed me, all soft and sweet.

"You think it's different for me?"

"Then take me, for fuck's sake!"

I laughed and she bit my lip, but she was smiling and she melted right into me, as if she understood.

There would never be another one of these firsts: Tenley's first finished back piece, and the first time I'd ever put something so significant on someone I loved. It was pretty damn momentous. So I was going to savor this experience. And she let me.

We were as close as we could get, fused in every way. In the years between loss and living, I'd forgotten what it was like to love. I didn't know how it felt to be whole, to be present in my own life.

Then Tenley came along and made me aware of everything I'd been missing but was too afraid to acknowledge. Just as she'd been running, so had I, but I was past that now. I had closure—but more than that, I had her. Tenley was the inception, my new beginning, the rebirth I'd been striving for. She embodied the phoenix embedded in my skin, rising from the ashes to start again.

In this, we were marked by one another. It went far beyond ink on skin. It went right down to the soul.

In this life, for as long as we had, we would be each other's armor.